ward willing

Ravaged Castle Book Three

USA TODAY BESTSELLING AUTHOR

AMANDA RICHARDSON

Ward Willing
Amanda Richardson
© Copyright 2024 Amanda Richardson
www.authoramandarichardson.com

Copy/line editing: Victoria Ellis at Cruel Ink Editing & Design
Cover Design: Moonstruck Cover Design & Photography
Cover Photography: Rafa G Catala
Cover Model: Hugo Soriano

BLURB

She was the epitome of forbidden fruit.
And I wanted a taste.

Liam

Being the oldest Ravage brother means I've always been the fixer, handling everyone else's mess.

But the one problem I can't solve?

Keeping my hands off Zoe, my best friend's daughter.

Hidden away in my remote cabin, writing is my escape until duty thrusts her into my life.

Over the years, Zoe evolves into a tempting taboo—the one person I crave but can never claim, despite what she tells me about her... inclinations.

I vowed protection at any cost—even if it's from *myself*.

Zoe

Orphaned and thrust into adulthood, I bury myself in school work and keep my eyes trained on the prize.

Now, with law school and an uncertain future looming, I'm used to doing everything myself and pushing back against Liam's stoic, overprotective resolve.

Until I learn that the vanilla, cinnamon roll of a man I've known my whole life isn't so vanilla after all.

Now, instead of infuriating me, his strict, commanding presence sends shivers down my spine.

I soon realize his resistance was never about denying desire for him—it was about fulfilling a *different* kind of hunger.

Ward Willing is a full-length, age gap, guardian/ward billionaire romance with BDSM themes. It is book three in the Ravaged Castle series. All books can be read as standalones.

Warning: This book contains an overprotective/possessive hero, explicit sexual situations, and strong language. There is a HEA.

There once was a castle, so mighty and high,
With large, gilded gates, it rivaled Versailles.
To all those below, it was splendid and lush,
But to those inside, it was ravaged and crushed.
Five Ravage boys born amongst old, rotted roots,
Their father ensured they'd all grow to be brutes.
Some said they were cursed, sworn off of desire,
But they turned into men and found what they required.
Forbidden, illicit, they had to work for that love,
They questioned that castle when push came to shove.
The curse and the rot gave way to unsavory tastes,
Dark proclivities and sick, messed up traits.
Five stories of five men with sinfully dark tales,
The Ravage brothers prove that love does prevail.

TRIGGERS

Age gap (20+ years), parental death (flashbacks, not on page, not detailed), depictions of depression/anxiety, panic attacks, violence (knives, on page, not detailed), hospitalization (minor injury), PTSD, BDSM elements (Dominant/submissive dynamics, forced orgasms, power play, edging, brat/brat tamer relationship)

*Please note that Ward Willing is *not* a dark romance. Happy reading!

*For all the girlies who are <u>*independent*</u> but sometimes need someone to spoil you, reward you, and call you a good girl.*

PROLOGUE
THE MISTAKE

LIAM

One Year Ago, Catalina Island

At a quarter to eight, I walk next door and knock on Zoe's door. When no one answers, I pull the spare room key from my pocket and open her door, but it's empty.

The scattered liquor bottles overturned on the coffee table catch my eye.

Fuck, fuck, double fuck.

Fucking teenagers.

Grumbling, I stalk over to the table and sweep the bottles into a nearby trash can, and then I pour the rest of her cheap vodka down the drain in the bathroom. When I walk back out, I notice the various items of food lying around—chips, salsa, cookies, brownies...

Without thinking, I snatch one of the brownies and

shove it into my mouth, chewing quickly. My phone buzzes, and I remove it from my pocket.

ZOE

at the bar in case youre wondering

The bar? How the fuck is she at the bar when she's underage? I swear, Zoe is going to give me a heart attack one day.

After doing one last perusal for illegally obtained alcohol, I'm satisfied enough to close the door behind me and make my way down to the bar to reprimand her for not listening to me.

My footsteps echo on the stone floor of the hallway, clicking ominously as I take the stairs. What the *hell* is Zoe playing at? I'm not sure if it's a latent rebellion or if it's a cry for help, but either way her behavior is unacceptable. Or maybe she stopped bothering to hide it from me because I don't have any say over what she does now that she's eighteen.

Give an inch, and she'll take a mile.

Like when I removed her curfew this summer and she stayed out all night.

Or when I gave her money for food last month and she spent it on a tattoo.

She's rebellious and wild at night despite conducting herself like a saint during the day—especially around other people. She has most fooled.

In fact, she will be starting at Crestwood University next week on a full scholarship.

The frustrating thing is, it's not like I don't trust her

—*I do*. She's proved herself to be more mature than any teenager I've ever known. She's easy to take care of because she hardly needs me. It's almost like she's trying to get caught doing things she know she has no business doing...and she's doing it for a reason.

If it's an attention thing, I can't fathom why she needs it from *me* of all people.

I scan the room and let my eyes flick over every face to find my ward, and I immediately see Zoe and a random guy doing a row of three tequila shots at the crowded bar.

I don't fucking think so.

Scowling, I stalk over and glare at the man until he gets the hint and leaves.

"Hey," she says casually, looking at me through her long lashes as she stands up. Her eyes are glazed as they search my face, and she has a single violet tucked behind her right ear.

"You're not old enough to drink," I mutter.

"Too late. Come on, take a shot with me," she drawls, stumbling slightly as she gestures to the three glasses of clear liquid on the bar.

The anger intensifies as I stare at her. "Are you drunk?" I yell over the noise of the bar.

Her honey brown eyes bore into mine, but she doesn't give anything away. She's composed in her obviously drunken state, yet the term *barely holding it together* runs through my mind. It usually does when it comes to her. I'm not an idiot. I know she's rebelling for a reason.

I just need to figure out what that reason is.

"Come on, Liam," she says, her voice low. "Take a shot with me."

A torrent of thoughts rush through my mind.

She has to act composed. She's had to carry her grief alone, not to mention at such a young age.

"No. You're drunk. You're out of your mind if you think I'm willing to get you more drunk, especially because you're underage. Speaking of, how *are* you purchasing alcohol without an ID?"

She rolls her eyes, and I swear to god, it's the most infuriating thing. "Don't worry about it. You only live once, Liam. You and I should know that better than anyone."

My face hardens, and I sigh heavily, trying to keep the silken thread of warning out of my voice. "Put the shots down and I'll walk you to your room. No more alcohol, Zoe."

She boldly meets my gaze, picking two of the shot glasses up. "Watch me."

Then she throws one of the shots back. My whole body tenses and my jaw tightens. I don't take my eyes off her. Warning bells go off, but I ignore them because I'm too busy seeing red. Somehow, she's the only person who is able to pierce my complacency—the only person able to find a perverse pleasure in challenging me.

It's *maddening.*

It only takes a second for my hand to grab hers, lowering my head slightly and raising the other shot glass in her hand to my lips. It triggers something warm to erupt inside of me. I keep my eyes locked on hers as I tilt the glass back and swallow the liquid easily before dropping her hand.

"Happy now?" I ask, annoyance lacing my words.

"Very."

I wipe my mouth with the back of my hand and glare down at her. Dark thoughts swirl in my mind—thoughts that have no right to be going through my mind when I look at my best friend's eighteen-year-old daughter.

But again, I'm not perfect, and I'd love nothing more than to show her who's in charge.

"Happy birthday, old guy. I don't think I've ever seen you drink tequila," Zoe says, setting the glasses down and smiling at me. Like always, her smile disarms me, and completely obliterates every dominating thought that had been running through my mind.

We're in Catalina for my thirty-ninth birthday, and we have dinner reservations. Originally I'd invited my four brothers for the weekend, but they all cancelled at the last minute, leaving Zoe and I alone at the beachfront resort.

When I don't respond, she continues. "So loquacious tonight," she mutters sarcastically.

"Loquacious? You're willing to casually drop the word *loquacious* into this conversation, but you can't bother with simple punctuation while texting me?"

She smirks and tilts her head, giving me a mischievous smile. "I only do that to piss you off."

I can't help but bark a laugh. "Good to know."

"You look like you might be sick," she adds, eyes flicking across my face. "Not a fan of tequila?"

"Not exactly. I had a bad experience once."

She grins, showcasing her dimples. "When?"

"At a show with your father. That night is a blur of loud music, mosh pits, tattoos—"

"Tattoos?" A sparkle glimmers in her eyes.

I press my lips together, but I don't answer her. I guess she knows a thing or two about tattoos now. Her lips tug into a mischievous smirk.

"So you *are* fun underneath all of that," she teases, pressing a finger into my chest.

An electric zing goes straight from her finger to my cock. *Fuck.*

I lean against the bar to move away from her, but she does the same—our bodies only inches apart. It's a trial of my restraint, and so far I'm winning.

Barely.

"I'm only fun under certain conditions," I tell her honestly. Between taking care of everyone, my job, and writing, I don't have very much *fun* these days.

"Conditions... such as?"

Don't even think about it. This is dangerous territory, Liam.

"Wouldn't you like to know?" I grumble.

"Tell me," she begs.

Maddening. She is *so fucking* maddening.

"Knowledge is earned."

She pouts for a second, which makes my lip twitch. Then she reaches out to signal to the bartender, but I grab her wrist, a charged shock passing between us again.

"You're done for tonight. It's time for dinner, anyway." Her mouth drops open as I let go of her hand.

"One more shot," she pleads, eyes widening.

"No."

"Please? Come on. It's your birthday, and we should celebrate." With one stern look from me, she holds her hands up and walks away. "Okay, fine. You win. But I'll wear you down soon," she adds. Something flashes in her expression when she says that, but I ignore it.

After making our way to the adjoining restaurant, my hand on Zoe's lower back the entire time, we settle in at our table. A tray of shots appears only moments later.

You've got to be kidding.

"Well, now you have no choice," Zoe says slowly from next to me, reaching for two shots.

My nostrils flare as I take the one offered to me, because why the fuck not? You only turn thirty-nine once.

Giving her a dark, pointed look, I quickly take another shot, and she does the same thing.

Testing me.

Every goddamn minute of this trip.

The server comes back with more tequila shots, and against my better judgement, we each do two more.

Fuck.

I manage half a taco before the tequila shots and beers have fully hit me, and I slide into a sort of euphoric, tipsy, relaxed state. Before I can protest, Zoe stands up.

"I'm going to dance."

My reflexes are more slow than normal, so it takes

me a few seconds to react. Before I know it, I see Zoe dancing on the dance floor at the front of the restaurant. And because I'm not thinking clearly, I let my eyes track every one of Zoe's movements. Tamping down my protectiveness, I stay put, but my eyes follow her. She raises her arms above her head and sways her hips to the music. Her dark red dress is a bit too tight and revealing, with a large slit that runs up her left thigh, and every time she moves, it inches up slightly.

Despite telling myself not to look, I do.

Only for a second.

She's no longer the gangly teenager hugging her knees to her chest at her parents' funeral. In place of her braces is a large smile with perfect teeth. In place of her long hair is sleek, shoulder-length, dark brown waves. Where she used to be too thin, she's filled out. Her eyes have more soul to them now. She's wiser now, and she doesn't seem eighteen. There's life and death and grief behind her amber irises. A weighted knowledge of the complexities of life that no teenager should know yet. Instead of hiding in a shell, like she used to do, she stands with confidence. She knows what she wants. She's intelligent and responsible—*usually*—and I'm in awe of her every damn day.

I frown when I see a man approach her, placing his hands on either side of her waist. I expect her to brush him off considering he's twice her age, but she doesn't. Instead, she closes her eyes and runs a hand through her hair, her bangs sticking to her forehead from exertion. Kicking off her heels she twists around, wrapping her arms around the stranger's neck, pressing her body against his as they move to the music together, abdomens seemingly glued together. His hands roam lower, gripping her ass unabashedly, and it only takes one hesitant push of her hand on his chest for me to charge forward.

I stumble over my feet, grimacing when I realize I'm *really* fucking drunk, but it's more than that; perhaps it's the combination of the beer and tequila. It takes me a few seconds to stabilize myself, but then I wrap my hand around Zoe's bare arm and tug her away from the man who won't stop leering at her.

I won't fucking tolerate it.

She's my...

She's...

The music is too loud, and my skin pebbles for no reason other than the fact that I'm touching her. It's like everything is enhanced.

"What are you doing, Liam?" she yells, trying to pull out of my grasp. I open and close my mouth to respond, but the lights from the stage are flickering around her face and combined with the bright purple flower behind her ear, she's somehow even more fucking beautiful than she usually is. "Are you *high*?" she asks, laughing hysterically. "Your pupils are dilated."

My brows furrow as I watch her. "High? Why the fuck would I be high?"

She's nearly doubled over in laughter. "Did you happen to eat some of my special brownies?"

Realization slams into me.

The brownie—the one I shoved into my mouth without thinking.

"*Edibles?* Really, Zoe?"

Her hand comes to her mouth as she laughs some more. "Please, like you never got high with my dad. Besides, they're legal in California—"

"Yes, because I'm sure that argument holds merit considering it's only legal if you're twenty-one," I snap, my eyes dragging over the pebbled flesh of her chest.

My pulse spikes when I see how heavily she's breathing, how fucking *soft* her skin looks...

Shit. It's the edible talking.

"It was fucking irresponsible of you to bring drugs with you," I snap, wavering between being impaired and wanting to scold her.

"Fine, but—"

"Listen to me," I say, emphasizing each word. I reach out and grip her shoulders, wanting her to fully grasp the reality of this situation. She could've been arrested. "I'm pretty sure it's still a misdemeanor to possess marijuana under the age of twenty-one. That's a hefty fine, or maybe jail time, or both. Is that what you want? Your entire future up in flames? This is a big deal, and I won't tolerate this behavior."

It's been drizzling on and off all day, and the rain begins to pick up, suddenly coming down harder. The man she'd been dancing with walks over to where we're standing, but I pull her away from him.

"You can fuck right off," I growl at him, my hands still on Zoe's arms.

As Zoe opens her mouth to argue, the sky opens further and people scatter. She stares up at me without flinching.

"What was that for?"

"He's twice your age," I explain.

She steps away and balls her fists, and in this moment, she looks *so* small—especially with the rain already soaking through her dress. I watch as the heavy drops cling to her golden skin and her dark lashes as she stares up at me.

Beyond the playfulness, I see the sadness behind her pupils.

The heavy weight that follows her everywhere.

The *grief.*

I know because that same weight follows me everywhere, too.

I'm an asshole for being so hard on her, because at the core of it, she *is* grieving.

"You know you can stop worrying about me now," she slurs.

"I'll always worry," I grit out.

"And I'm saying you don't have to anymore."

She looks away, and I watch her expression grow sullener by the second. She thinks she's a burden, and she resents me for looking out for her. She may fight me on things, but I know she's folding inward out of instinct.

So much like her father.

Over the years, I've tried to show her that she's not a burden, nor would she ever be. That I care about her. And not out of obligation, either. I wasn't obligated to send her care packages at her boarding school or give her an allowance. When it comes to Zoe, I've never felt *obligated* to do anything. She's my best friend's daughter, and I want her to be happy.

I also want her to be *safe* and not make bad decisions.

That translates to me being stricter than her parents, but I'm doing the best I can with the resources I have. It's not like I'm particularly *good* at being her guardian. It's not like it comes naturally to me, at least with her.

Being the oldest of my four brothers gives me a bit of experience with taking care of others, but I can't seem to get it right with her.

It doesn't stop me from trying, though.

Zoe doesn't move, breathing heavily as the rain causes her hair to stick to her face, so I don't move, either. The stage sways in front of me, and I'm acutely aware of the fact that we're suddenly alone, standing in the pouring rain.

Several moments pass as I try to regroup, try to organize my thoughts. But the tequila and beers and pot brownie have muddled my brain and cognitive thinking, so I blurt out the only thing I can think to say. The only thing that forms on the tip of my tongue. The truth that keeps me up at night, that makes me sick with the unknown.

The one thing I've been trying to tell her with my actions for three years.

"I need to take care of you. And I need you to *let me.*"

She wraps her arms around herself as she blinks. "I don't need to be taken care of. I'm an adult—"

"Barely!" I shout, startling her. Before this trip, I'd never raised my voice with her. I never yelled or scolded her. I've never had to before. The image of that man's hands on her ass, of her trying to push him away, sends a new surge of anger through me. "You seem to *need* my help," I add, flicking my gaze to the dance floor.

"God, you're so overbearing sometimes."

"Because I *have* to be. Because I promised your father that I would watch out for you."

Zoe scoffs and looks off to the side. "He's dead, Liam. That makes every promise you made dead too. And I'm telling you right now that I don't *want* to be the burden you carry."

My expression slides into a frown. "You're not a burden, Zoe. You've never been a burden. I'm not sure how many times I can say it."

"And I'm not sure I can *let* you take care of me," she replies, echoing my statement from earlier as her eyes find mine. "You can't protect me from everything, Liam."

"I *can* protect you from creepy older guys who get a little too handsy."

"I happen to like older men," she interjects with a defiant smile.

So.

Fucking.

Maddening.

I can't align my thoughts in any coherent way. Not after that confession. Instead, they tumble down and scatter into the wind, sending something potent to sink deep down into my core. Everything is hot, and I instantly know this conversation is headed down a slippery fucking slope.

"I'm eighteen now," she adds, crossing her arms and watching me with a defiant, little smile.

She must really fucking enjoy challenging me.

I involuntarily take a step closer. "Really, Zoe? You think my purview ends because you've been eighteen for a few months? You think I'm going to stop caring because of a date on your birth certificate?"

"No, I'm not saying that. I just don't need you interfering in something that's not your business."

"Everything you do is my business," I counter.

"No, it's not. I've been on my own for years."

"Yeah, at school," I say, stepping closer. "I'm going to make myself very, very clear. My culpability over you didn't end the minute you became an adult. You're living with me under *my* roof when you start college next week. I pay for your health insurance and your cell phone bill. I feed you and make sure you're provided for." Zoe opens and closes her mouth, but I'm not done. "I'm not your father, and I never wanted to replace him. But if I'm not the one looking out for you, who will?"

She physically shrivels as the hurt flashes over her expression. My words are a cruel reminder of her *aloneness*—especially my last sentence—and I know it.

I immediately regret them.

Because she's not alone.

She has me.

"I never asked you to do any of those things, Liam."

"*You* didn't. But your father did. And I will honor that wish for the rest of my life."

She swallows, and I watch the way her throat bobs. Drops of water slide down her face, and *fuck* she's so beautiful it almost hurts to look directly at her.

"I know I've made mistakes along the way. I'm learning as I go. Forgive me, please," I finish, my voice breaking slightly.

I blink away the rain from my eyes, and before I know it, she's snaking her arms around my waist and pressing herself against me.

Closing my eyes, I rest my chin on the top of her head, and everything inside of me goes molten. I want to pull away, because I know my body is not reacting with propriety right now. I'm too inebriated to think clearly. If I had any sense, I'd pull away. But I don't, and her wet body against mine fractures every ounce of self-control I have.

Pulling away from me, her eyes find mine.

And *fuck me.*

The expression on her face sends me completely off-kilter.

My heart pounds hard inside of my chest, and Zoe uses that exact moment to place her hand over it. She must feel how fucking hard it's hammering pressed against her because her eyes widen slightly.

Without thinking, I brush a hand across her cheek, under her eyes, to swipe away the black mascara running down her face. She starts to tremble—from the cold or the way I'm holding her, I'm not sure.

Somehow, the violet is still tucked neatly behind her ear, despite the pouring rain.

Any second now, she'll save me from myself and step away. She'll say thank you or offer up something about how we're soaking wet now.

But she doesn't do either of those things.

Instead, her gaze explores my face.

The suggestion of *more* written all over her features makes my breath hitch.

Her blown out pupils. The lower lip between her teeth. The *apprehension*.

I've been alive long enough to know what that look means, and it absolutely *cannot* happen with her.

Ever.

My hands shake and flutter as I drop them, and I take a step back. If I go *there* with Zoe, I won't be able to stop. I don't trust myself—and I don't trust my thoughts or actions, because right now, her small body pressed against mine has my cock so hard that I can't think straight.

There's too much between us. I can't identify it, but it's charged and scary and she's *just barely* legal.

This is *wrong*.

I clear my throat. "This can't happen. We've had a lot to drink," I say, choosing my words wisely. "We're not in our right minds."

"Are you worried you're going to corrupt me, Liam?"

she asks, pulling her lower lip between her teeth and taking a step closer. *Fuck, fuck, fuck.*

"Zoe, this is... *fuck,*" I say, resigned. Something heavy settles in my stomach at the possibility of having her. Of giving in. Of letting go, without a care in the world about who she is to me.

This is so fucking wrong.

"So you *weren't* jealous earlier when I was dancing with that guy?"

I don't answer. I don't trust myself. Instead, I focus on my pulse rushing through me, the thundering whooshing sound in my ears giving me auditory tunnel vision.

"I'm a consenting adult, Liam," she whispers, placing her hand on my chest again.

Her words and the possibilities they convey cause everything inside of me to *burn* in a way I've never experienced. But I don't move away from her. Instead, I let her touch me. My whole body shudders under her hand, and a thousand spirals of ecstasy shoot straight to my cock. Whatever strain of weed I ingested is making me want to fuck like an animal. I've been high before, but it's never felt like this.

"What the fuck was in those brownies?" I ask, my voice hoarse.

She steps closer, pressing her body against mine. "Terpene, limonene, and indica," she murmurs, snaking a hand up to my neck.

"What does that mean?" I whisper.

"It's good for the libido. Relaxation. And increased sensation," she answers.

"Zoe," I breathe, closing my eyes. My cock is so hard it hurts, and everything inside of me is throbbing. If I were in my right mind, I might be able to throttle the dizzying, electric current racing through me.

But I'm not in my right mind.

I can't move because it all feels *too fucking good.*

"You know, I see the way you watch me sometimes."

Confusion mars my features as she loops her other arm around my neck, and another shiver works down my spine, going straight from my spine to my cock. *What the hell is happening?*

Every second that passes gets more and more surreal, and between the rain, the empty stage, and Zoe's hands on me...

She continues before I can move. "At breakfast when I'm making us coffee. At night, when we're watching movies. You're not as subtle as you think you are."

It suddenly feels like someone has poured cold water over me. Despite the warm night, my skin pebbles as she runs a finger along the stubble on my neck. My stomach clenches with dread at what she's implying and... something else. Something angry and roiling and *repressed.* Something so fucking powerful it scares the fuck out of me.

I ball my fists and breathe through my nose.

She's right.

And I'm fucking *sick* over it.

I can't deny that she's beautiful and alluring. I can't

deny that I enjoy spending time with her. I also can't deny the way my eyes may have wandered, and *fuck* it makes me feel like a fucking creep.

That feeling overpowers everything—that feeling of *wrongness.*

She needs to know that something like this can *never* happen between us...no matter how much I might want it.

I huff in exasperation and take a step away from her. "This is wrong," I grit out.

In the tense seconds that tick by, the only sound I hear is the spattering of rain against the floor, and the rushing sound of my pulse in my eardrums. A few people make their way back onto the dance floor, and Zoe grabs my hands and leads me around the back of the restaurant. The rain has slowed now, and the sky is mostly dark, though I can see her face clearly.

I sigh. "Listen, Zoe. You're drunk and confused. It makes sense that you'd latch onto the only consistent thing in your life."

She laughs and covers her face with her hands. "God, you're so condescending. You're treating me like a *child*!"

"You're eighteen! And you somehow seem to think that you're enlightened enough to flirt with me? It doesn't work like that, Zoe. I made a lot of stupid decisions when I was eighteen. I didn't know what the *fuck* I was doing. And neither do you. Stop. Fucking. Tempting. Me—"

She rushes forward, and before I can react or *think,* her lips are on mine. I'm powerless to stop, powerless to resist. My hands find her waist, and I groan as my hands grip her flesh and she presses herself against me. I let her, holding onto her for dear life as my thumbs press into her, because whatever the fuck is happening is going to pull me under her spell completely. And *fuck,* her lips on mine send shockwave after shockwave to my too-hard cock. Instinctively, I pull away from her mouth as we both pant.

"I know exactly what I'm doing," she says, breathless, before pressing her lips against mine again and wrapping her arms around my neck.

Every pounding beat of my heart pulls me further and further under the blanket of intoxication, and even if I wanted to stop, I'm not sure I could. My senses are heightened, and everything else fades away as our mouths move against each other, as I curl my fingers around the fabric of her dress, as a low rumble escapes my throat. It's carnal and heady—and *wrong.* But everything is hazy now, and I can't reconcile how something that feels so good could possibly be so, so wrong.

Every brush of her fingers on my neck makes me groan.

Every tiny gasp that leaves her mouth has me grinding her against my cock to get friction.

Every movement and sound and touch is intensified, and then my rational mind drops away. It's too easy to ignore the warning bells. Too easy to listen to what my body wants.

"Inside," I command, my hands skimming to her ass and squeezing.

She pulls away and gives me a playful smirk before twisting around and opening what appears to be a spare office or storage room. I follow her inside on shaky legs, and if I were sober, it would be the point where I realize how terrible of an idea this is. If I were a better person, perhaps I'd have more control over my impulses.

"Fuck it," I mutter, pulling her into me.

I can deal with the consequences, the regret, and the implications of my decisions tomorrow. Right now, all I can think about is sinking into her and fucking her senseless.

Our teeth click together painfully due to the lack of light, and as my eyes adjust, we both pull away slightly.

"Sorry," she says quietly. "You're drunk and high, and I don't want to—"

"Shut up," I growl, pulling her to me again.

She whimpers when I lift her up and press her against the wall, hiking her dress up with one hand and running the other over the globe of her ass. Stumbling slightly, Zoe giggles as I reach underneath the hem of her dress, gripping her underwear and roughly tugging them away from her body. A ripping sound fills the small room, and her mouth drops open.

"Did you just tear my underwear off?"

"Be quiet," I murmur, something dark and unsettling washing over me. My mind is screaming to halt what we're doing, but I can't seem to stop touching her.

That *fucking* brownie.

"Liam," she whimpers. The sound of her name on my lips, doing *this*, is... unimaginable.

I go still, my thumb stopping just short of her clit. I can feel how wet she is...how much she wants this. If I were sober, I'd relish in everything. But right now, all I need is to be inside of her. My mind is both a wild mess of reasons why I shouldn't do this while simultaneously being eerily quiet.

"I need you," she adds, sounding desperate.

I don't understand why, and I can't pinpoint exactly what those words make me feel...

I just know that I want her to surrender to me.

"You drive me crazy," I whisper into her mouth. "Absolutely fucking crazy," I growl, lining her dripping cunt up with my cock. "Birth control?" I ask, the idea of consequences of my actions so fucking far off. But I know I need to ask this one thing. There's at least one responsible brain cell still left inside my head.

"Yes," she breathes.

I don't hesitate. I push into her, and she's so *goddamn* tight...

Squeezing my eyes shut, I breathe through my nose so I don't explode early. Vaguely, I register that she feels... different. It's too tight, and her face is scrunched up in pain. Through the haze, my eyes snap open as I glare down at her.

Is she...?

"Are you fucking kidding me?" I nearly scream, starting to pull out.

Zoe's hands come to my hips, stopping me. "Please. No, I'm not. I'm not," she rushes out in a heavy sigh. "I'm not a virgin."

Relief washes over me, and I take a steadying breath as her warm heat wraps around my aching cock.

"Keep going," she begs, an edge of vulnerability to her voice.

I'm too far gone to contemplate it, though I know I shouldn't be enjoying this as much as I am. Being inside of her is the best thing I've ever felt. I'm distracted and selfish, and all I can think about is watching her come undone. *Fuck the repercussions.* I pull almost all the way out slowly, and when I drive into her, she releases a deep moan that has me on the verge of exploding inside of her. My hand skims her thigh as my thumb settles over her clit, and then I groan when she clenches around me.

"Yes," she whispers, moving her hips *just enough* to draw my balls up and ready to empty.

"Fuck, Zoe," I say, my voice hoarse. "I'm not going to last."

"I thought you were drunk," she whispers, her nails digging into the back of my neck.

My whole body convulses with every one of her movements. "You feel too fucking good."

I stop moving as my thumb circles her tight bud, and I use the opportunity to bend down and use my tongue to suck against the pulse point on her neck.

"Liam," she whispers, scratching me as she throws her head back. "Fuck."

Her cunt pulses once, and I know she's close. Working my thumb quicker, I keep my cock still inside of her, not wanting this to end too early.

This is so fucked up.

"Come for me, Zoe."

"Say please, Liam."

For the second time, her vexation and downright audacity rile me up. I'm torn between stopping everything just to spite her bratty self, or to make her come so hard that she's ruined for other men forever.

I decide on the latter.

"*Please?*" I murmur, pinching her clit. "I don't think so. As a matter of fact, I think you'll be the one saying *please* after we're through."

I can make out her eyes widening in surprise at my heavy-handed tone before she explodes, panting and clenching around my cock with such force that I'm worried she's going to push me out. Her legs squeeze my hips as her eyes roll back and her mouth drops open.

Yes. Fuck yes.

I don't stop. I have a purpose now, and that's to make her come again.

Pulling out, I lower her to the ground on shaky legs.

"But you..."

"Don't worry about me," I grit out.

It's probably the least selfish thing I've done and said all night.

The room smells like sweat and sex and everything good, and when my eyes briefly wander over to the windows, I realize we've fogged them up.

Keeping her dress rucked up, I drop to my knees and pull her hips to my face. She lets out a breathy gasp.

"Liam, I'm sensitive—"

I don't listen. Instead, I hike one leg over my shoulder, use my hands as grips on the flesh of her hips, and bring her wet pussy to my mouth.

One swipe of my tongue and I know I'll never taste something this sweet ever again. She tastes like sin and bad decisions, and I love every fucking thing about it.

"Fuck," I grumble against her curls, licking and sucking, noting the metallic taste briefly before I get distracted. She shakes every time I get near her cunt. "You taste so fucking good, little rebel."

Her nickname slips out and her legs tense.

I haven't called her that since she was a kid.

Without giving her time to rethink any of this, I pull her clit between my lips and suck.

Hard.

She cries out as her hands come to my hair, gripping it tightly. I insert one finger, and even that's tight. How the fuck was my cock inside of her? How the fuck did I fit? I curl my finger and she shakes harder, her leg trembling on my shoulder.

"Oh god," she whimpers, her hands fisting my hair for purchase.

I lick and taste her until she's muttering expletives, until her pussy squeezes my finger, until she pulses around it. I keep going when she cries out again, my tunnel vision narrowing until all I want to do is ruin her with pleasure.

The trip, the defiance, the *maddening* attitude...I want to rip it all away and expose her until she's a mess on my tongue, until she knows who the fuck I am to her.

"That's my good girl," I purr. "This is where you

belong. With my mouth on your cunt and your taste on my tongue."

She comes again, this time sobbing as her body squeezes me and her toes curl. She pulls my hair so hard I think she's going to rip it from the root, but then she sags against the wall, easing up on her hold.

I remove my hand and her leg, standing in front of her as she watches me with hooded eyes.

"That was incredible..." she says, then mumbles what sounds like nonsense. Her eyes are heavy, and a similar heaviness settles over me, despite my cock begging for release.

Without thinking, I pull her dress down and take her hand, leading her out of the room. It's still raining when we get back to the restaurant, but everyone is gone and presumably back in their rooms. After we drunkenly stumble up the stairs, I pull Zoe into my room, and she walks straight to my bed before collapsing on top of it, shoes forgotten somewhere on the dance floor.

———

My head aches when I wake up, but I've had worse hangovers. There's an unfamiliar drag to my movements as I sit up, my eyes adjusting to the bright suite.

A flash of dark hair catches my eye, and next to it—a purple flower.

Regret fills me, and I jump out of bed as I stare down at my best friend's daughter. She rolls over onto her back, and when her eyes find mine, they're neutral and assessing.

Like she's waiting to see what I'm going to say.

Panic fills me. Pure, unadulterated anxiety runs through my veins, and I rub my face with my hand as bits of last night flash through my mind.

The rain.

The arguing.

The kiss.

And then...

I run my hand through my hair, nearly wincing at how sore my scalp is from her pulling my hair while she climaxed. Zoe sits up slightly, propping herself up on her elbows.

Glaring at her, I take another step back.

No.

No.

"This *never* fucking happened."

Swallowing, she nods once. "It never happened," she repeats.

CHAPTER ONE

THE PROFESSOR

ZOE

Present, One Year Later

I tap my dark red nails against the Formica desk, ignoring the tiny chips on a couple of them. I make a mental note to get them done later today. Doing my nails is low on my priority list, especially since I'm apparently psychotic enough to double up on classes this semester. I'm sure I'm the only student here *asking* for a bigger workload. Still, they're one of the things that makes me feel normal.

Like a regular college student.

"Okay, I think we can squeeze you into another class Tuesday and Thursday mornings," Lena, my academic advisor, murmurs as she clicks away on her computer. "That's really your only free period. There's only one spot left, and I'm not sure how you feel about an English major class."

"That's fine," I say quickly, perking up at the thought of taking a class that might actually be interesting. "Today's Tuesday, so I can head there after this and let the professor know."

Lena sighs and sits back in her chair, giving me a look I know all too well. *Sympathy. Pity. Worry.* She's older. Forties, I think, and she's one of those people who actually enjoys her job as a college advisor at Crestwood University. I can tell because her face lights up any time she sees a student on campus, and she seems to really *care* about her students' well-being. For me, that means a lot of good-natured advice and recommendations to rest like a normal nineteen-year-old. Which is why I know I'm about to be lectured.

"You know, it can be overwhelming to take twenty-one credits in one semester," she murmurs, arching a perfectly sculpted brow.

"Actually," I counter, leaning forward. "I'm on an accelerated track so it's perfectly normal to—"

"Are you eating? Sleeping? Having... *fun*?" she asks, as if the word is foreign to me.

I huff a laugh. "Trust me, I'm having *too much* fun," I muse, thinking of Scotty's gig and the all-nighter I pulled three nights ago because of it. "But my high school wasn't normal. I learned balance a long time ago. Work hard, play harder."

Lena laughs. "Of course. I forgot. Valedictorian of

Thatcher Prep. This is probably a piece of cake compared to that."

I grin as the printer spits out my new schedule. "Exactly."

Lena hands the single sheet to me. "No more classes this semester," she warns. "I think your schedule is full enough, Zoe. That English class is usually reserved for those who have the prerequisites, which you do, of course. You'll have to get permission from the professor since you're a sophomore and most of the students are seniors."

"Not a problem."

She stands and ushers me out. "You have twenty minutes. Go get something to eat, or you know, go sit around at The Cave and stare at a wall like a normal college student."

I take the schedule from her and blow her a kiss. "Thanks, Lena. You're the best."

"I'll see you in January when you inevitably decide to one up yourself."

Laughing, I glance down at the schedule before standing up. "Looking forward to—" I stop talking, and the smile drips off my face. "Oh, no." I hand the schedule back to her as if the paper is cursed. "I'm so sorry, but I can't take that English class."

Lena's perfect brows furrow. "Oh. How come? I've heard wonderful things about Professor Ravage."

I wince. "Yeah, well... he's sort of my..."

Lena's brows shoot up and she interrupts me before I can gather my thoughts. "*Boyfriend?*" she whispers.

"God, no. It's complicated, but he was my guardian. And I still live with him." Lena's eyes widen, and I know she's waiting for me to elaborate, so I do. "My parents died when I was fifteen, and he was my dad's best friend. He became my legal guardian until I turned eighteen last year." Lena is still stunned speechless, so I shrug casually. "Anyway, since I still live with him, it might be a conflict of interest?"

Though *living with him* was a major overstatement. I wasn't home enough to interact with him that much, instead choosing to spend time with Scotty, with friends at one of the events I organized in town, shopping, or cramming for a test. Despite that, we interacted a few times a week, both on campus and at home. We aren't *friends*, per se, but over the last year we'd settled into a comfortable routine. We're *cordial*. Which, after what happened on his birthday trip in Catalina...

When my eyes flick back to Lena, she's seated again and clicking away at her computer.

"Hmm... there's a yoga class that starts at seven in the morning? You haven't fulfilled the physical activity portion of your credits yet, so that could work?"

Yoga? At seven in the morning? I'm a night owl, so that would be like pulling teeth.

"Is there anything else?" I ask hopefully.

"You haven't fulfilled your earth sciences prerequisite. You could take astronomy, but the class meets at nine at night to observe the night sky, and since it's three hours..."

I groan and place my face in my hands. "Is there a

class at any of the normal hours that doesn't already conflict with my current schedule?"

Lena's lips flatten as her eyes scan her computer. "I'm sorry, but the English class is the only one available during your free window."

I bite the inside of my cheek as I deliberate. The problem is, I can only graduate at the end of next year if I have my degree audit completed. I'm on an accelerated program to attend UCLA's Law School in two years, and I'm scheduled to take my LSAT's next month. I know exactly how many credits I need to take each semester. I'd hoped to get away with eighteen this semester, but when I sat down and crunched some numbers last night after the first day of classes, I realized the only way to stay ahead would be to add another class.

Hence why I'd come to Lena's office in a panic.

The problem was that I'd come into college with enough prerequisites to skip most of the required classes, as well as a year's worth of units. But because Crestwood required a certain number of units taken at their university to graduate, I need as many filler units as I can get.

Lena's clicking keyboard stirs me from my stupor. "I checked the employee handbook, and as long as he doesn't grade your work, there's nothing that says living with your professor is a conflict of interest," Lena says matter-of-factly. "You wouldn't be breaking any rules by taking Professor Ravage's class."

Fuck.

The odds are stacked against me.

It makes the most sense to take Liam's class because

the hours for the two other classes available would only make my weeks harder and longer.

And again... it would be nice to take a class *for me* instead of what will get me into the best law school.

"Fine," I sigh, taking my schedule back and standing. "I better get going so I can warn him."

Lena gives me a reassuring smile. "See you in January, Ms. Arma."

I grumble out a goodbye and adjust my leather backpack as I walk through campus.

Crestwood University is a small, private university set in the suburbs of Crestwood, California—a small, beachside town smack dab in the middle of Los Angeles and Orange county. I grew up in Crestwood, but when my parents died, I'd become attached to my Northern California boarding school. Though I missed that area, Crestwood would always be home.

Lena mentioned that Liam would have to find someone else to grade my work, which is fine. It makes me think of the fact that he *insisted* I live with him for the duration of my undergrad, and as I pass the student dorms on my way to class, it makes me wonder what my life would look like if I lived on campus instead. My Aunt Carolina also offered her guest house to me, but she lives in Malibu, and it's too much of a commute.

It's definitely easier living with Liam, especially since he sometimes drives me to campus. I've come to appreciate the home-cooked meals, the messy kitchen table, and the overall comfortableness of living with my father's best friend. When I moved in last June after graduating high school, Liam had reneged on his "no internet in the house" rule.

I'm not sure how he survived without it for so long.

He still refuses to use a computer to write, preferring old-school legal pads and a typewriter.

Plus, Crestwood University has a limited number of dormitories, and winning the lottery to live in one was *almost* as hard as the actual lottery.

I walk to The Café and grab a caramel latte and a cookie on the way to Liam's class. As I head toward the building where the class is held, I realize I'm not sure what the class is called. Pulling the sheet of paper with my schedule out of the pocket of my jeans, I glance down at the information on the pertinent column.

Eco-Poetry: Nature and Environmental Themes in Verse
Prof. Liam Ravage, PhD
Tu, Thur (10:15-11:45am)
Sierra Building, Room 118

I have to contain my smirk. *Eco-Poetry?* Liam had found a knack for combining his two favorite things: being outdoors and writing.

Poetry might be fun, too, I think. I have always wanted to take a writing class.

I cross the quad and enter the Sierra building. Because Crestwood University is over a hundred years old, the building is gorgeous. It's red brick and retro-fitted, of course, to account for earthquakes. It's a quaint campus, and I've been enjoying my time here. Checking the time on my watch, I realize I only have a minute before the class starts. As I quicken my pace, my stomach flutters with nerves.

Fortunately for me, Liam never brought up that night in Catalina, and neither had I. Truth be told, I'm not sure either of us remembered what exactly happened except for bits and pieces. Certain things stand out, but...

We were drunk and high.

It was a mistake.

It never happened.

Pushing the auditorium door open, my eyes flick to the front of the class. It's empty. Which means he isn't here yet.

Which *also* means I might be able to hide out in the back of the class for today—at least.

Sneaking in quickly, I hone in on the single empty seat in the second to last row. Before I can make my way up there, a woman swoops in and claims it. Twisting around, my eyes scan the seats frantically.

The only available seat left is a seat right in the front row.

Fuck.

I quickly sit down and slouch into the chair. Maybe Liam won't notice that I'm here. There has to be nearly fifty people in this class; the chances of him seeing me are slim, right? I sip my latte and nervously eat my cookie. My stomach growls audibly, and I grimace when I think of the fact that I forgot to eat breakfast again. I'm looking down and dusting the crumbs off my white T-shirt when the class goes quiet. I snap my eyes up only to see Liam sauntering into class.

He's wearing a white oxford shirt rolled up to his elbows and dark grey, fitted slacks. Instead of dress shoes, he's wearing brown, lace-up boots, and instead of a tie, his collar is loose and unbuttoned.

"Well, hello professor Ravage," the woman next to me purrs.

When I look over at her, she's biting her pen seductively. Something possessive flashes through me at her words, and then I go back to ogling the man I've known my whole life.

Because I'm definitely ogling. There's no other word for what I'm doing.

How could I not? Especially when I know what he's like when he's turned on?

I squirm in my seat and push the thoughts away, like always. I have to push them away. It's something I've gotten good at over the last year. He drew a line that night, and I respected his boundaries enough to keep my thoughts to myself.

Though, I've never seen him in an academic setting. Never seen the confident presence he so easily exudes to the class, or the sense of purpose and guidance.

It's annoyingly hot, and I find myself thinking of anything and everything except that night.

It works.

For a minute, at least.

By the time he gets settled, my eyes are wandering over him unabashedly.

His forearms are tanned and muscled, corded with veins from chopping wood and fixing up his old cars. He's almost never clean-shaven, usually opting to have a few days' worth of scruff residing along his jaw. His hair is straight and longer on top, usually swept back slightly. It's peppered with grey, as is his beard, but they're hardly noticeable in this light. I only know because I'm around him all the time. His eyes are usually soft, making him seem approachable. But I've seen them hard and sharp with anger before. His nose is aquiline-shaped–slightly curved and sharp, giving him a regal, noble look. He's wearing his usual black, round glasses, too, which only enhances the *sexy professor* look.

"He's giving off major BDE," the girl sitting on my other side mumbles.

My cheeks burn.

Fuck, Zoe. I'm not going to last. You feel too fucking good.

I take every memory of that night and place it in the box I keep locked up unless I'm alone at night in bed. Most of the time, I wish I could lock up his entire existence.

But he was my father's best friend.

He came to my birthday parties, and I can't remember my life without him, because he's been there from day one.

It never happened.

Even so, my stomach flips when his hair falls in front of his forehead, as he looks down at his desk, his large hand splayed over what I assume is the class list.

And god, what that hand is capable of...

Crossing my legs, I watch as Liam turns around and writes his name on the whiteboard, and a murmur goes through the class.

I know *exactly* what they're thinking, too.

His ass in those pants is on perfect display. And because his shirt is fitted, his wide back muscles ripple and contract with each movement of his hand on the whiteboard.

I've always known Liam is attractive. I thought so when I was a teenager, blushing anytime he was around. I thought so as I got older and started to discover my sexuality. Growing up within the walls of a boarding school didn't exactly make me a virginal saint–I'd had my fair share of boyfriends and encounters. I know what I like and how I like it. When my parents died and Liam became my guardian, I locked my schoolgirl crush away so tight that I couldn't find the key if I wanted to.

But then, in Catalina, the cage broke, and I felt myself drawn to him like I'd never been drawn to anyone before.

Wanting him.

Needing his attention.

Maybe I still do, but I've gotten better about finding that outlet elsewhere since that night.

He's protective yet funny when he wants to be. My wellbeing was—*is*—his first priority, and he made that very clear on that trip to Catalina.

Which only enhanced my feelings.

"Welcome to Eco-Poetry: Nature and Environmental Themes in Verse," he says slowly, his low voice reverberating through the auditorium as his hand flies over the whiteboard. "In this class, we will embark on a poetic journey through the natural world and the pressing issues that surround it. My name is Liam Ravage, and I have the privilege of being your professor for the next three and a half months."

He stops writing on the board and faces us. My eyes glide over the words on the board.

Emotion, thought, action

Each word is underlined, but *action* is underlined twice.

"In a world where our connection to nature is more critical than ever, the power of poetry to evoke emotion, provoke thought, and inspire action is becoming increasingly important," he starts, pointing to the board. "This class represents a unique intersection of two profound disciplines: poetry and environmental consciousness. Over the next several weeks, we will explore how poets from different eras, cultures, and backgrounds have engaged with the natural world and addressed environmental concerns through the beauty and eloquence of verse."

He rubs his mouth with his hand as his eyes scan the room.

Don't see me, don't see me, don't see me...

His eyes slowly scan each of our faces. "We will consider the ways in which poets have celebrated the majesty of nature, grappled with the consequences of—"

My heart stops, and Liam's body jolts slightly when

his eyes land on mine. Shock, confusion, and maybe a tiny bit of amusement plays across his features.

He clears his throat and looks down, completely distracted but refusing to lose his composure.

Except he does. He shuffles through his papers, finding the one he was looking for, before clearing his throat again.

"As I was saying, we will consider the ways in which poets have celebrated the majesty of nature, grappled with the consequences of human actions, and imagined sustainable futures." His eyes flick to mine, and the hint of amusement on his lips is gone, replaced with a small frown.

And his eyes?

They're dark and stormy.

"Our journey will take us through the works of renowned poets such as Wordsworth, Whitman, Dickinson, and contemporary voices like Mary Oliver, Wendell Berry, and Joy Harjo. We'll also explore lesser-known poets whose voices have been instrumental in shaping the eco-poetry movement."

He sets the paper down and walks to the front of his desk, leaning against it with his arms crossed.

"But this class is not solely about academic analysis. It's also a platform for your creativity and your voice. You will have the opportunity to express your thoughts, observations, and emotions through your own eco-poetry, connecting with the natural world in a profound and personal way. Which is why your first lesson today is not going to be in this classroom."

Another murmur works through the room, and my eyes haven't left Liam's, despite his refusal to look in my direction.

"In a minute, I'm going to end class over an hour early, but that's not an excuse to fuck off," he warns, his voice low and threatening. A few people laugh at his use of profanity, but my spine straightens slightly, as if he's giving me the command directly.

That cage of feelings? Yeah, it's going a bit haywire right now.

"Go sit on the grass. It's a beautiful September day. Go for a walk in one of the nearby parks. Sit in nature for thirty minutes, and then write a poem. Any format, any word count. Write down whatever it makes you feel." A few hands go up, but Liam dismisses them. "There is no wrong way to do this. I'm not going to check or read them. It's for *you*. To start fostering that relationship with nature and poetry. If you still have questions, talk to me on Thursday morning. Until then, enjoy the rest of your day."

At his dismissal, everyone stands up, and I'm left grappling with mixed feelings.

For one, I didn't expect him to send everyone off within the first five minutes. Second, should I follow everyone out, or talk to him? If I don't talk to him now, he's going to—

"Ms. Arma? A word, please."

Well, that settles things.

I stand up and grab my still-hot coffee, slinging my

backpack over one shoulder as I make my way to the front of the class.

I don't think he's ever called me Ms. Arma before, but I suppose he can't exactly call me Zoe in front of other students.

The closer I get, the more my heart pounds. Liam is looking down at the paper in his hands, and I stop walking when I'm a couple of feet away so that the rest of the students have time to filter out of earshot.

When he looks up at me, the look of amusement is back on his face, and I breathe a sigh of relief as I take in the way his eyes are watching me mischievously behind his glasses.

He doesn't speak until the last student walks out, and then he cocks his head slightly, as if he's waiting for me to explain.

I open my mouth to tell him about the necessary extra units and how his class was the only one at an optimal time, but my brain shorts out.

It's usually easy for me to think up a witty remark, but Liam is the only one who's able to render me speechless.

"Hi," I say, my voice unsure.

"Hi?" he replies. His lips twitch as he watches me, rubbing his mouth with his hand and leaning back against his desk all in one motion. He must realize I'm not the one who is going to initiate this conversation, because he sighs as his eyes find mine again. "Why are you here, Zoe? Do you need something, or did you want to torture me?" I swallow back my retort. *Torture him?*

I'm about to ask him to elaborate, but he points to the piece of paper he was looking at earlier. "Your name isn't on here, so you couldn't possibly be taking my class," he adds, almost like he's reassuring himself.

"I am, actually. I'm not on the list because I only enrolled a few minutes before the class started."

When my eyes flick up to his face, I see his jaw tick slightly as he lets out a long sigh.

"And when, exactly, were you planning on doing the classwork required for this class between your *six* other classes?" he asks. "This isn't some fun elective you can take for extra credit."

"I'm planning on taking it very seriously."

"Trust me, I know you are. I'm sure you'll walk out of this class with an A, and that's with *someone else* grading you, due to the egregious conflict of interest."

"Then what's the problem?" I counter, hoisting my heavy backpack higher.

Liam notices, and his eyes track over my face before quickly scanning the rest of me. Today, I'm wearing a white tee with a plaid skirt, suspenders, and platform loafers. Despite the black lingerie underneath, I'm covered up.

But sometimes, when he looks at me, it's like he can see exactly what I'm wearing underneath my clothes.

Like he's mentally stripped me and he's enjoying the view.

"The problem is you hardly have enough time to eat, let alone tack on another class. I hardly saw you this summer because you were cooped up in your bedroom studying for your LSAT's, and when you weren't, you were off partying or out with friends."

"So?" I counter, grinding my jaw. "It's called balance, Liam. Plus, the sooner I get into law school, the sooner I can finish and become a lawyer. There's nothing wrong with working hard and having fun at the same time."

Liam's jaw tightens, and he glares at me with frustration. "You're going to burn out soon. This class alone is a lot of work."

"I can handle it." I stand up straighter. "I have to go. I'll see you at home later."

After I twist around and take a few steps, he calls out after me. "Have you at least eaten?"

I stop walking and hold up my coffee. "I had a cookie before class and now I have my coffee," I tell him over my shoulder.

He's glaring at me. *If looks could kill...*

"Stop."

I halt, his command washing over me. Turning around, I watch as he walks over to me and hands me a twenty-dollar bill. Our fingers brush for a second, but it's enough for me to remember how rough they felt *inside* of me.

I'm so fucked.

"Go buy yourself lunch and give me the receipt after."

I look down at the money with furrowed brows. Obviously, because I live with Liam, I'm not a stranger to taking his money. I'm living under his roof for free, after all. But my parents left me with some trust money, and since I'm a penny-pincher, I've managed to create a budget for myself until I'm out of law school. I'm attending Crestwood on a scholarship, so fortunately I won't have student debt from undergrad. Law school isn't cheap, though, and I want to be prepared.

Still, this is the first time he's asked for a receipt.

"If you insist." I take the cash and pocket it, rolling my eyes.

"I do. I need to know that you didn't spend it on another tattoo," he drawls, his gaze lingering on my collarbone, where I'd recently gotten a tiny rose.

Oh.

"Fine."

"I mean it, Zoe."

"I know you do. I promise to bring you proof of purchase," I tell him, not clarifying *what* the purchase will be.

"Also," he starts, eyes flicking between mine, "You don't always have to force yourself to be busy and take a million classes. Sometimes..." He shakes his head. "Never mind."

"What?"

His worried expression causes a crease to form between his brows. I want to reach out and smooth it down, to assure him that I'm fine.

To stop worrying, even though I kind of like that he worries about me.

"Sometimes I wonder if you keep busy to run away from your grief, Zoe."

His words aren't malicious. I know he means well.

Looking down at my loafers, I swallow through the bubble of emotion in my throat.

"I'm not. I have a lot of goals and aspirations."

He doesn't look convinced, but fortunately, he changes the subject.

"What time are you done today?"

"Six," I tell him, adjusting my heavy backpack again.

"Great. Meet me out front, and I'll drive us home."

I frown. "No, it's okay. Scotty is picking me up."

"You think I trust that rusty, old truck? Meet me at six," he growls, his serious expression telling me it's not up for debate.

This time, I really do roll my eyes. "His truck is fine."

Liam grunts. "It makes a noise when it comes up the hill to the house. I don't trust it. And I don't trust him," Liam adds, looking at me pointedly behind his glasses.

"Yes, you've made that very clear."

He looks like he wants to say more, but he just nods once. "See you at six," he says for what feels like the hundredth time, and a thrill goes up my spine as his expression darkens slightly.

A challenge.

"Fine," I answer, knowing full well that I will *not* be meeting him at six. Why would I, when riling him up is my favorite thing to do? He, of all people, should know that.

"Have a good day, Zoe," he drawls, not breaking eye contact for several seconds.

I turn and walk out, and I feel his eyes on my back the entire way.

My curled hand loosens as I get into the hallway, and I take a steadying breath. Despite me feeling like I have the upper hand most of the time, I sometimes wonder if Liam is really the one in control. Not that I need an upper hand. He's extremely easy to be around. It's just that sometimes it's like he's waiting for me to disobey him.

Like he *wants* me to disobey.

Even now, after living with him for over a year, I'm still not sure what to make of our relationship, and the way he still tells me what to do. It's unnerving, but it's also incredibly attractive. It's like he knows me better than I know myself sometimes.

Catalina was the only time I ever saw him break formation. The only time I really seemed to get inside of his mind and wiggle my way under his skin. And the crazy thing is, I want to push him that far again.

I want to poke the beast.

It's why I do things like save his food money and get tattoos and spend a fortune on nice lingerie.

Because a small part of me wants to see Liam Ravage *unravel* again.

CHAPTER TWO
THE LOATHING

LIAM

The slamming of a car door outside snaps me out of my writing trance. Captain Sushi's head perks up, and I see him yawn in my peripheral as I lower my gold pen that's engraved with an *R*—a nod to my last name and family history.

I figured if I could write all of my books with a pen bearing the Ravage name, maybe something good can finally come out of this family.

Well, that's *if* I can ever write something again.

Irritation trickles through me when I lean over to glance out of the window and see the familiar, rusty Chevy parked in front of the house. A quick glance at the clock tells me it's nearly midnight. I haven't seen Zoe since class yesterday, despite waiting to drive her home —to no avail because she didn't show up and didn't answer my texts. I only know she's been with Scotty this whole time because I'd turned her location services on when I became her guardian, and never bothered turning them off when she turned eighteen.

I wish she'd let me drive her home instead of relying on her pea-brained boyfriend.

She hasn't had time to get her driver's license, so she isn't allowed to drive the brand new Subaru I bought her last year, despite my nagging to get it done. And because my house is a twenty-minute drive through the woods behind Crestwood, it's a pain in the ass to get to. Hence... the boyfriend with a car.

I suppose it's better than a taxi. I'd rather not have some strange man driving her around.

But it doesn't change the fact that I *loathe* Scotty. His jeans are too tight, his hair is too shiny, and he's too fucking old for her.

I'm not a violent man, but whenever he touches her, I'm two seconds away from tearing his arm out of its socket.

I rub my eyes before flicking them back to the window. Zoe and Scotty are lit up by the motion-sensor light I had installed when she moved in. Zoe is leaning against the passenger side, her backpack in one hand. Scotty is towering over her, his long, blond hair obscuring his face. He places a hand on her cheek, and she leans into the touch.

Yeah, it's decided. I really fucking hate the guy.

Just as I'm about to tear my eyes away, Zoe tilts her

chin up as Scotty's hand slides past her ear to the back of her neck and pulls her to his lips.

The kiss is sloppy, and he hasn't offered to take the heavy backpack from her, so she's awkwardly leaning to one side.

She hasn't touched him with her free hand. In fact, when I squint and concentrate hard enough, I see her fist balling at her side uncomfortably.

Enough.

I stand up so abruptly that my chair rolls violently into the wall behind me, and I'm downstairs and opening the front door—*loudly*—in a matter of seconds.

Captain Sushi, my large Serval cat, is on my heels.

The lovebirds are done making out and walking toward the door by the time I have them in my sights. As my eyes lock on Zoe's fingers laced with Scotty's, the rage continues simmering.

No, it boils over.

Because the motherfucker is coming inside.

"Hey, Mr. R," Scotty says, giving me a lopsided grin and using the nickname I hate.

I don't smile, and I certainly don't deign him with a response. Meanwhile, Captain Sushi hisses at Scotty.

My eyes rove over to Zoe. "It's late," I growl, crossing my arms and blocking the doorway.

Scotty has been over before, but never after dark. Usually they're downstairs watching a movie on Sunday afternoons or giggling in her bedroom before one of his shifts—the latter of which causes me to leave the house and go angrily chop wood out back.

I am a walking cliché, apparently.

"I won't be long, Mr. R. Just wanted to spend some time with Zo."

Zo. Like the second syllable of her three-letter name is too cumbersome to say.

My nostrils flare as I let them inside, and Zoe gives me a chagrined glare before they walk to the kitchen.

Captain Sushi trots away, obviously irritated.

Me too, buddy. Me too.

"I made chicken if you're hungry," I tell Zoe.

"Fuck yes," Scotty mumbles, pulling the refrigerator open.

My eyes flash with outrage as he helps himself like a heathen with zero manners.

"Scotty's been working doubles," Zoe explains, grabbing two plates for them. She's seemingly unaware of the cold, flinty gaze I have aimed at Scotty. "He didn't have time to eat dinner."

I'm normally a pretty sympathetic guy. I have to be, considering I work with hormonal young adults all day long. But that empathy is nowhere to be found when it comes to Scotty. I don't give two shits if he starves to death.

I tell myself it's because Elias would hate him, too, so the hatred feels justified, at least.

Zoe was a bit too young to be dating when her parents died, so they never had to navigate these waters like I do. I'm the one who has to be strict, who has to vet her boyfriends and make sure they're not disrespecting my home in all the ways that make me rage. I'm the one who has to look out for her to make sure she's staying safe.

It's exhausting, and quite honestly, infuriating. I *fucking hate* it, but I can't tell her that. I can't admit that watching someone else touch her eats me up inside. Especially someone ten years older than her and completely lacking ambition.

To assuage my hatred, I don't interact with Scotty whenever possible.

Out of sight, out of mind.

A loud slap rings through the kitchen, and my eyes hone in on Scotty's hand connecting to Zoe's ass for a *second* time as a vein pulses in my forehead. I was about to give them some privacy but fuck that.

Instead, I grab a stool.

My eyes hover on Scotty's hand sliding into Zoe's back pocket as I sit down, and before I realize what I'm doing, I clear my throat.

Loudly.

My house, my rules.

Scotty gives me an apologetic smirk, the fucking bastard, and Zoe is completely unaware of the entire interaction, because she's too busy making her boyfriend a plate of food.

He should be making *her* a plate a food, but what the fuck do I know about chivalry? It's not like I have women lining up for me.

"I hear you've got yourself a new student," Scotty interjects, looking like a dope as he shakes his hair out of his face.

Zoe stiffens, barely, but I notice the way her spine straightens, the way her fingers curl tighter around the knife she's holding.

"Surprise of a lifetime," she grumbles, finished plating the food and popping one plate into the microwave. "But I suppose it'll be an easy A," she adds, catching my eye as she turns around and winks.

And that wink... does something to my cock.

Fuck.

Me.

I push the image of her sultry expression out of my mind and refocus.

"We'll see," I answer Scotty, crossing my arms. "I'm having a colleague grade her poems, so she won't get preferential treatment. But yes, she probably *will* get an easy A," I add, looking at Zoe now.

I swear I see a faint pink color brush over her cheeks.

Yesterday *was* the surprise of a lifetime when she informed me that she would be one of my students this semester, and I quickly realized that having her in my class was going to be the death of me.

A slow, torturous death.

Which is pretty much what had been happening to me for the last twelve months.

Everything changed between us that night in Catalina. I'd replayed everything about that night over and over in my mind so many times, but the details were always so blurry. The guilt stuck with me, though, and I'd completely obliterated any chance of it repeating by not drinking around her, and also ensuring we were never alone for too long.

The frenetic air between us was like a ticking time bomb, and every look, gesture, and touch sent me back to that night, threatening my self-control.

Most of the time, we interacted like we always did— cordial, friendly, comfortable. But every once in a while, I caught her looking at me. *Not* in a cordial way.

We never talk about that night, and she changes the subject anytime the trip comes up. I'm not about to push it. Obviously we'd had too much to drink, so who could blame us?

But something *had* shifted between us.

Alcohol makes for loose lips and loose lips sink ships.

The fucking edibles didn't help, either.

Zoe swaps the plates out as Scotty and I have a staring contest. I get the feeling he knows I don't like him. He seems to fidget a lot when I'm around, which always gives me a rush of adrenaline-fueled triumph.

He finally breaks eye contact and clears his throat.

Again.

As the second plate finishes warming, the two of them start eating at the counter.

"Oh my god," Zoe moans, taking a bite of chicken. "Your roast chicken is my favorite, Liam," she adds, smiling at me.

"What about *my* chicken?" Scotty whines, referencing the fried chicken stand where he works.

"Aw, babe. Your chicken is good, too." She stands on

her tip toes and kisses him briefly, though that's a brush off if I ever saw one.

Scotty takes a massive bite. "Damn. This chicken slaps, though. Great job, Mr. R," he mumbles between chewing.

Zero manners.

I arch a brow at the idiot eating my chicken as Zoe smirks. Our eyes meet, and it's only then that I notice the purple bags under her eyes, and the way her hair is pulled back and wrapped around one of the pens she's always stealing from me.

"How was your day?" I ask Zoe, watching her devour her meal.

"Fine," she answers after swallowing a bite. "Nearly done with my political science essay," she adds, wiping her mouth with a napkin. "But *someone* distracted me," she adds, rolling her eyes at Scotty.

I glower at him, and he looks away uncomfortably.

"I'm glad I never decided to finish college," Scotty muses, chewing loudly. "Too much work."

"What a surprise," I grumble under my breath, narrowing my eyes.

Zoe's eyes flash as they bore into mine. "Liam," she warns.

Scotty laughs good-naturedly and puts an arm around Zoe's shoulders. *Ah, there's that urge to tear his arm from his socket again.*

"I should get going. See you Saturday, Zo," Scotty says quickly, placing a kiss on the top of Zoe's head. He gives me a stupid, little wave. "Bye, Mr. R. Thanks for the chicken."

Zoe gives him a quick peck on the lips and mutters a goodbye.

I say nothing as he walks out whistling a Fall Out Boy song. *Poser.* Once the front door closes behind him, Zoe pushes off the counter and walks both empty plates to the sink.

Captain Sushi comes out from his hiding place, nuzzling Zoe's legs affectionately.

"You should stop being so mean to him," she says, her voice low.

Her back is to me, and *fuck* if I can't help the way my eyes travel south.

The way her high-waisted jeans accentuate the swell of her ass. The way her waist cuts in, and how her cropped, black tank top is *just* short enough to offer me a sliver of olive-toned skin. My fingers twitch at my side when I think of running a hand over the smooth denim and—

Fuck.

My mind wanders to yesterday, when I saw her sitting in the front row of my class, legs crossed, looking like the perfect fucking pupil. I can't deny that seeing her there—in the one place I was safe from the onslaught of *wanting* her—caused something deep and possessive to settle inside of me.

And also had me adjusting my cock in my pants.

But she's off-limits. Always and completely.

Leaning against the opposite counter, I cross my

arms. "Not possible. He makes it too easy," I grit out. "Leave the dishes. I'll do them later," I add, referring to the mugs and plates in the sink.

After shutting the water off, Zoe wipes her hands on the dish towel and turns to face me. Seeing how *tired* she looks is like a punch to the gut, and I sigh heavily as I let my eyes wander over her face.

"I can see the worry wheels spinning," she says, a sardonic lilt to her voice as she reaches down to pet Captain Sushi. "Stop worrying about me. I'm tired but I'm fine. I'm going to finish my paper and then head to bed."

And then she'll be up at six to get the reading for her literature class done, and out late again with Scotty or her friends... My hand curls against the edge of the counter. "Stay home and rest this weekend," I suggest, already knowing she's going to fight me on it.

Her lips flatten as she looks up at me. "I promised Scotty I'd go to his gig on Saturday night," she says immediately, as if there's no room for argument. Which, for her, I guess there isn't.

No matter how much I try, Zoe is going to push herself until she collapses. And there's not a damn thing I can do about it.

"I already told him I'd go," she adds, crossing her arms. Captain Sushi chirps for her to keep petting him. I swear, he's more loyal to Zoe than to me. "And I happen to like the music."

"Will it be another late night?" I ask, my voice gruff.

Her jaw hardens. "I'm not as delicate as you think, Liam. I can take care of myself."

I want to scream *bullshit,* but I don't. Instead, I run my hand over my face and sigh again. "Let me come with you, at least. I can drive you and make sure nobody roofies you in one of those sketchy venues."

"I'm fine."

"You're not fine," I growl, feeling the anger rushing into my veins. "You're out most nights either studying or with friends. You're hardly home, and I don't think you've slept longer than five hours for months. Not to mention, you're taking an entire *year's* worth of units in one semester, something Scotty doesn't seem to understand—"

"Scotty?" she asks, cocking her head. "Is that what this is about? That I spend my free time with Scotty?"

No.

Yes.

My jaw tightens. "Of course not. I'm trying to look out for you."

Zoe scoffs and looks away. "Right. You're such a martyr, Liam." Her words cut through me, and I instantly stiffen. When she looks back at me, her eyes are sharper. Sometimes I forget that she's known me her whole life. She knows my tells, my tics, and the exact buttons to push. She's always been too astute for her age. "How about you let me worry about myself and we go back to peacefully coexisting?"

"Fuck," I whisper, rubbing my jaw. "I would if I

could, but you apparently don't know *how* to take care of yourself."

"That's not true. I've been taking care of myself for almost four years."

Her remark cuts deep to my core, and I wince. Guilt, betrayal, ire... it all swirls inside of me as I push off the counter and take a step closer.

Her light brown eyes bore into mine, but I don't look at her. Instead, I look down at the floor, letting her words fill the heavy air around us. Sometimes when we argue, it can get tense. *Heated.* There's such a heavy grief between us, I swear it's about to swallow us both into the ground together. I tend to say things I shouldn't, and so does she.

The more we interact, the more we push buttons.

The more we circle the other, the more intense it gets.

It's like we're both sharks waiting for the other to bleed—*knowing* it's bound to happen and waiting for the other one to snap and spill their guts.

And I don't miss the way her eyes sometimes linger on my arms, my hands, my neck. I can't help but think back to that night in Catalina. I've buried it so far back in my psyche that I don't ever allow myself to think or ruminate on what really happened, or what we said.

Or did.

And when her eyes get that familiar argumentative heat behind them, every single wall I've erected between us threatens to crumble, because all I want to do is repeat that night.

The kiss.

Her tight, velvet heat wrapped around my cock.

Watching her plush lips part, hearing her moans and breathy pants.

Making her come and *tasting* her.

I swear to fucking god I can still remember the exact taste of her.

Salty and sweet all at once, like fucking caramel.

Just the thought of it makes me hard.

"Why do you care so much?"

She says it like I don't have a right to be concerned about her, and that pisses me the hell off.

"I'll stop caring when I'm dead," I offer up, voice thick with fury as I move to stand right in front of her. "You can't expect me to sit around and watch as you work yourself to death. I *do* care. I always will." Her expression softens a bit as her posture relaxes. I continue, thinking of how I can help her. "Let me come with you on Saturday. I can at least drive you home if you get tired."

"What about your book?"

A smile tugs at my lips. *That's what she's worried about?* "Well, staring at a blank page for years on end hasn't worked, so what's the harm in switching things up?"

She looks almost surprised at my admission. "Years? Really?"

I dip my chin and look down. "Yep. Over four years."
We both know why.

"Well, either way, it's still too much to ask of you."

She runs a hand to the back of her head, removing the pen from her hair and letting it down. I get a whiff of her shampoo.

Violets.

The action causes something to drop inside of me, my cock starting to thicken.

Fuck.

That smell. It reminds me of *her*.

It keeps me up at night, wafting through the house, reminding me of how sweet she smelled. The smell has me pulsing into my hand in the shower while I imagine slipping between her legs and making her make those sounds again.

And then I feel so guilty that I avoid her completely for days afterward.

When I open my eyes, Zoe is watching me with furrowed brows. "Why do you want to go? You've never offered to take me to a gig before."

Aside from eating dinner and breakfast together, *sometimes*, that is, Zoe and I don't really hang out. That's mostly my fault. After Catalina, she started her freshman year at Crestwood, and I took on extra classes to teach in order to avoid being home alone with her. And all of her free time was spent doing schoolwork, hanging out with friends, and keeping herself busy.

The night in Catalina was forgotten. We moved on, forming a comfortable alliance. I never tried to ask for more, never pried into her life, except when needed. We were roommates more than anything.

"I enjoyed going to shows back in my day," I tell her, lips twitching.

She gives me a small smile. "Fine. I'll allow your help just this once. And for what it's worth..." She sighs audibly. "I really appreciate everything you do. Even when you're an overbearing pain in the ass."

I huff a laugh. "I can't help it."

"Oh, before I forget, here's the receipt from yesterday," she says, pulling it out of her back pocket.

She's been carrying it around since yesterday?

My lips twitch as I take it from her, unsure if she's defying me again or if I'm actually going to find food on this receipt. My eyes narrow as I unfold it, scanning the words as they start to make sense to me.

"This is a receipt for a nail salon," I say slowly. "That's not what we agreed on."

"No, you said to bring you a receipt. So, I brought you a receipt."

I swear to god...

She leans back and places both hands on the counter behind her, elbows bent. My eyes skirt down for half a second on their own, taking in the bare slice of skin that's exposed above her belly button. *Fuck.* I snap my eyes back to hers, and she has her lower lip between her white teeth. *She caught me looking.* Clearing my throat, I take a step away and run a hand through my hair. It's not worth fighting this time, but I make a mental note to be more precise going forward.

Especially if she's going to exhaust me and push my buttons.

"You should get some sleep," I say sternly. I walk backward, deciding to do the dishes tomorrow when it's safer and I'm alone. "You have an early morning."

"Okay." Her eyes flick between mine, like she's *waiting* for something.

I don't indulge her.

"Goodnight, Zoe," I tell her, turning around and leaving the kitchen.

CHAPTER THREE
THE STORM

ZOE

It's past two in the morning by the time I finish my essay, but my brain is seemingly never tired enough for sleep, only caving when I give into pure, unadulterated exhaustion.

I don't remember what it's like to *not* be tired.

But, between school and Scotty and my friends, whom I've been seeing less of lately thanks to my school load, I hardly have time for anything.

I'm the one planning all the munches and meetups—hanging with Orion, the other life stylers, Layla, or Scotty. I'm also a part of the mock trial club at Crestwood University, and that eats up three evenings a week. Not to mention keeping up on my LSAT studying.

It's easier to keep moving—to stay busy—than to sit and *think*. Because what usually ends up happening is that I imagine a future without my parents. Weddings without a dad to walk me down the aisle. Having kids without the insight of the two people who raised *me*. Being successful and having no one here to thank or text or call...because they're gone.

It scares me so much that sometimes I think I'd rather join them than live without them.

I take a deep breath and get ready for bed, ignoring the call of my desktop computer, though I know what I *want* to be doing. Before I know it, my thoughts are running away from me, pulling me into a project I started and abandoned a million times, the one thing I look forward to whenever I have some down time. After I'm ready for bed, I walk to my desk and open the document I've been slowly adding to for years.

It started as something to work on after my parents died, but it consumed most of my free time last year. I hardly had time to work on it, but when I did...when I felt that spark of inspiration...it was one of the best feelings in the world.

In my book, Lily, the protagonist, is a poor, struggling human from a rural village who accidentally opens a portal to the underworld with her childhood best friend, Ethan. Of course, to ramp up the tension, Ethan has been in love with her for years—something he confesses pretty early on. While imprisoned, he tries to sacrifice himself to the villain in order to save her. The villain, a demon who is thousands of years old, offers her a sinister deal. Until this point, I had no idea where the story was going, or what the deal would entail.

I haven't written much of the book, but the world is built, and Lily is about to go on an adventure with Ethan. They are a *team*. And yet... there's something so *blah* about their dynamic. It's like I've suddenly had a breakthrough about where the story needs to end up.

Instead of writing, I outline the next scene between Lily and the demon.

Because all of a sudden, it becomes *so* clear to me.

The demon will let Ethan go, but Lily must agree to become his unwilling queen.

How did I ever think Ethan was a good choice?

I'm so into jotting my ideas down, fueled by pure adrenaline and excitement, that I hardly notice the pouring rain outside. It isn't until a clap of thunder sends me jumping a foot into the air that I actually look out of my window.

Every muscle in my body goes rigid as the sky lights up with lightning.

Fuck.

My heart starts to beat so fast that my throat hurts, and as another loud rumble rolls through the air, I stumble up from my chair.

I can deal with rain and a bit of wind. But if the thunder and lightning start...

Taking a few breaths, I attempt to calm my racing heart, attempt to rationalize the storm. It's fine. It's just a bit of rain, just some lightning, a bit of thunder...

Another boom has me gasping for air, nearly choking on my sobs. I *hate* this. I *hate* that something as simple as some thunder can turn me into a shivering, sputtering mess.

I *hate* that I can't ever escape it, either. No matter where I go in this house, I will still be able to hear the storm.

I'm dizzy and sick with anxiety, so I sit down on my bed and pull my knees to my chest as my fingers curl around the backs of my thighs. I rest my head on my knees, squeezing my eyes shut and rocking back and forth.

This is different.

This storm isn't the same storm.

That was a freak accident. Isn't that what the police said? That they'd never seen anything like it?

Still, I can't help but feel like I'm drowning in my panic—like the water is filling my lungs, despite being warm and dry inside.

What was it like for them?

Fear and grief prickle the back of my neck as the bedroom lights flicker as another thunderous boom pounds through the walls. I can *feel* the power of the storm shaking the house. There's nothing I can do to stop it, and it makes me... powerless.

Did my parents feel this powerless the day they died?

My breath stalls as the room goes black.

No.

I quickly jump up, stumbling blindly around my room and looking for my phone. I feel around my bed, but after checking it twice, I don't find it.

Where is it where is it where is it where is it where is it!

Two quick knocks sound at my door, and before I can respond, Liam shoves the door open, and the room is alight from the flashlight in his hand.

"You okay?" His eyes flick across my face for half a second before he comes rushing forward, pulling me into his arms. "Fuck, Zoe," he mutters, holding me against his body.

The sound of his voice breaking and the feeling of his bare chest against my body distracts me enough to quell the immediate panic. I manage to take several steadying breaths with my face against his chest, letting his warm skin and smoky, licorice scent calm me. He's so solid—like a tree. He doesn't move, doesn't waver, doesn't ask questions.

And I'm... safe.

"In for ten, out for ten," he commands. I do as he says, taking steadying, deep breaths.

Ten seconds in, ten seconds out.

We stand there for a few more minutes as time slows. "The generator should kick everything back on soon," he mutters after I'm calmer, his voice hoarse against my head.

"You have a generator?" I ask, voice thick. There have been a couple of bad storms since I moved in with him, but he wasn't usually home when they did occur... so I weathered them alone.

"Of course. I know you don't like storms."

"But—"

"I don't like them either. Not anymore."

The weight of his comforting words reverberates

through me, and I squeeze my eyes shut as I squeeze him tighter.

Fortunately, Southern California is not prone to storms, so this panic is not something I have to deal with a lot. I know it's psychosomatic. I know the fear of being caught in a storm like my parents were makes sense psychologically.

Still... when it happens, it shakes me to my core.

And though Liam hardly ever comes to my bedroom door, he sought me out tonight.

Because he knows how much they scare me.

That thought alone has me squeezing him tighter. Breathing in his familiar scent, his warm, solid body against mine... it's an instant dopamine hit.

"Can't...breathe." He gasps dramatically, a hint of humor in his voice.

I instantly pull away, feeling better now that he's here. My pulse has slowed from breakneck to rapid, and my hands have stopped shaking for the most part.

When I lift my eyes to his bare abdomen, there's not enough light to truly appreciate the view. He must've dropped the flashlight to the floor in a rush to get to me.

And that thought has me all sorts of confused and flustered.

"I was kidding," he says, crooking a smile. "You didn't have to pull away, little rebel."

Little rebel. My nickname from years ago. I can't remember why he gave me that nickname.

His voice from the night in Catalina floats through my memories.

You taste so fucking good, little rebel.

"I'm not a kid anymore. You can drop the nickname." My voice is shakier than I intend, but the adrenaline from the storm, the hug, his voice and smile, and that nickname... it makes me unsettled in the best way.

Every time I hear him use it, I remember that night and the roughness of his voice as he made me come three times in a row. It's something I've still never been able to accomplish with anyone else.

He opens his mouth to reply, but the power comes back on, bathing the room in a soft glow. I hear my computer beep behind me, and as my eyes slide to Liam, I can't help but let my eyes peruse down his bare abdomen.

He's wearing green and black checkered pajama pants with no shirt. When he bends down to grab the flashlight, I have to look away because I know I'm blushing.

"Still doing homework?" he asks, walking over to my computer before I can stop him.

"No, it's not—"

My cheeks burn as the screen flares to life, the white Word document clear as day on the large desktop. I leap over to the computer and hit the sleep button. The *last* thing I need is Liam, the *award-winning* author, to know that I'm writing a silly romance book. But when our eyes meet again, his lips are curved upward and his eyes narrow enough to let me know that he saw something incriminating.

"Are you writing something?" he asks carefully.

I shrug, trying to contain my blush. "Not really. It's nothing. Just a stupid thing I do when I'm bored or can't sleep."

He looks both highly curious and awestruck. "Fiction?" he asks, his voice a low purr.

"Yeah. It's fantasy."

Drop it, I urge him silently.

"I didn't..." He stops and rubs his mouth with his hand, and the motion causes the muscle of his bare bicep to roll. "I didn't know you liked writing."

"I don't," I say automatically.

I'm not sure why I'm lying. I suppose because my book is *mine* only. It's the one thing I have that's only for my pleasure. I want to keep it protected and hidden. I know it'll never see the light of day, and it's something that brings me joy. Something that motivates me to get through my pile of homework. If Liam knew I liked to write, he might ask more questions about it. Even worse, he might want to read it.

It's already bad enough that he knows.

He was never supposed to know.

He looks like he wants to say something else, but instead, he puts his hands in the pockets of his pajama pants.

I have to actively keep my eyes on the floor so that I don't let them peruse his bare abdomen again.

"I was making a sandwich," he says casually. "Care to join me?"

I arch a brow. "It's the middle of the night."

"You didn't eat much of the chicken earlier," he counters.

"Are you keeping tabs on my food intake?"

He steps closer. "I have to, considering you used my food money to get your nails done." His eyes turn flinty and argumentative. "Are you hungry?"

My stomach chooses *this exact moment* to grumble loudly. With a satisfied smirk, he turns and walks out of my bedroom.

"Dammit," I whisper, following him a second later.

Because I *know* he's not going to put a shirt on, and I'll have to pretend not to ogle him for at least ten more minutes.

As I take a seat at the island, Captain Sushi nuzzles my calves and jumps up, large paws on my thighs. Kissing his forehead, I hear Liam laugh.

"He only purrs like that with you. I think it's because he imprinted on you."

My brows furrow. "How is that possible? You'd had him for years before I met him."

Liam stops slicing the tomato in his hand and looks up at me, a piece of hair flopping over his forehead.

Damn. My stomach flips as his lips twitch with amusement, and I try my hardest to ignore the rampant butterflies swarming inside of me.

"You don't remember the day I brought him home?"

I tilt my head. "I was there?"

His lips curve to the side as he looks down and resumes slicing. "Yeah. You were nine. It was the week my dad..." he shrugs. "Anyway, my brothers and I spent a good chunk of that week rehoming the animals in his menagerie, and we each decided to take one with us. To my father's credit, he cared for them and hired the best help he could get, but of course, his trial meant that it was safer to rehome them before animal control came to take them away. Chase took one of the roosters, Miles took the pygmy goat, and of course I took Captain Sushi. He was young and already domesticated."

I want to ask which animals Orion and Malakai took with them, but he continues before I can.

"Captain didn't have a name when I brought him home. Your parents came over for dinner and brought you with them. Do you know what you said to me when I asked you what I should name him?"

I smile. "What?"

"You said, *he's a Captain Sushi if I ever saw one.*" Liam chuckles as he lays cheese and turkey on the bread.

I laugh out loud. "Sounds about right." Propping my chin on my hands, I watch as he works, as his muscles move and contract, as his large hands delicately cuts the sandwiches into triangles. Whenever he tells me stories about my parents, or my childhood, it makes my day. I don't have anyone to talk to about it, but Liam seems to remember everything. "I didn't realize I was the one who chose his name."

"Yeah. He took right to you. Every time you came over, he'd follow you around. And those first few weeks after your parents…" Liam slows his movement. I know it's hard to talk about it for him, too. "He didn't leave your side. He slept in your bed or with you on the couch.

And when you went back to school..." Liam swallows, setting the knife down. "He cried by the front door for days."

My heart clenches as I pet between Captain's eyes and look down at him. "Aww. I'm sorry, Cap," I say affectionately. He nuzzles my hand, and he's still purring so loudly that I can feel the vibrations against my palm.

Liam hands me a plate with a sandwich, and I thank him as I eat it quickly. The sooner I'm away from him, the better.

Sometimes I don't know where to draw the line with him. I'm comfortable around him, and every once in a while, I think I might be *too* comfortable with him and say something inappropriate. Push his buttons. *Test* him. It's not that I don't trust him. I don't trust myself around him.

Plus, he's a walking threat without a shirt on, and I can't be trusted to not gawk at his firm stomach or the way his Adonis belt cuts down into the band of his low-slung pajama pants.

I also can't help but remember how big he was and how he was almost like a different person when we were together *like that.*

That's my good girl. This is where you belong. With my mouth on your cunt and your taste on my tongue.

I think you'll be the one saying please *after we're through.*

It sends shivers down my spine whenever I remember how confident he was. How commanding and in control he was.

In fact, one taste of his dominating side was the reason I discovered what *I* liked in bed. I spent weeks agonizing over what happened. I'd never had an experience like that—in a *lot* of ways—and I prowled the internet for what it was called. I didn't know Orion was into this kind of stuff until I overheard Liam talking to Chase about it last Christmas, and when I furtively asked Orion where to find more information later that night, he invited me to my first munch. Before I knew it, I had a word for the way Liam made me feel that night.

Eventually, that led me to the BDSM lifestyle, and I started regularly hanging out with Orion and the other lifestylers. And despite *knowing* it, I still couldn't recreate that feeling—the all-encompassing, euphoric feeling. I'd tried and failed numerous times, always chasing that high.

It never seemed to work. Not really, anyway.

I learned very quickly that it had a lot to do with *who* was doing those things to me rather than *what* he was doing.

We both finish our sandwiches at the same time after several minutes of silence. Taking my plate, he loads the dishwasher, and I stand up to go back upstairs.

"Thank you," I tell him quietly. "For the sandwich, but also for making sure I was okay earlier."

"It's not a problem, Zoe."

Liam stands up and wipes his hands on the dish towel. He twirls it a few times, and I watch as his hands handle and grip the fabric with ease and sexual magnetism. He's so *giving* and capable. Always fixing things, always using his hands somehow. I mean, how could he possibly look like that and *not* know exactly what he's doing? And how are women not lining up to be with him?

Since the night in Catalina, I haven't seen a single woman leaving in the morning. He has to be sleeping with people, but wherever he goes for that, it's not here.

What is he like with other women? Is he the same with them as he was with me? Does he revel in their taste and talk dirty to them, too?

Shaking the thoughts loose from my brain, my eyes catch on the colorful book sitting on the couch across the room.

"What are you reading?"

His responding, lopsided smile sends a kick to my heart.

"Percy Jackson."

I groan as my smile widens. "You're such an elder millennial."

He barks a laugh, and I *like* that I can make him laugh like that. "Did you just call me an *elder* millennial?"

"Well, yeah." I point to the *Live, Love, Laugh* sign in the dining room. "If I didn't know how old you were, your signs would give you away."

He frowns. "What's wrong with my signs?"

I shake my head. "That's a very loaded question, Liam."

He shifts his stance a bit and crosses his arms. "I have time."

Smirking, I begin my diatribe. "Millennials love

putting themselves in neat, little boxes. You all wear your likes, dislikes, and personality quirks like badges." I hop off the stool and walk to the living room, picking up the childish-looking book and holding it up. "It just seems... *trite.*"

Liam grabs an orange pill bottle from the cabinet and throws a pill back before walking over and taking the book from me.

I've wanted to ask him about the pills for years, but it never seems like a good time. I've googled the name, but I don't know why he's taking antidepressants. It's not entirely my place to ask.

"It's not *trite,*" he retorts. "It's an escape, and the books and the signs are not meant to be taken too seriously. You forget that I'm an educator, and I know your generation all grew up with the internet, although you already know my views on that. Before we had Reddit telling us all about the horrific things in the world, we had Percy Jackson. It reminds us of simpler times."

I roll my eyes. "Right."

His eyes flash with humor and maybe a tiny bit of outrage. But then he crosses his arms, looking down at me with a stance and expression so commanding I have to bite my tongue.

"Sit down and read the first chapter. I guarantee you'll be hooked."

Before the storm started, he must've been down here reading in the middle of the night, and I can't help but think of how he's always been the brother who cares for his younger brothers.

Who cares for *me.*

Instead of finding peace in sleep at night, he chooses to spend his time reading his favorite childhood books.

It's then that it hits me: who takes care of *him?*

Does anyone allow him to... *relax?*

Between his job, his book, and me... does he ever get a chance to unwind?

I plop down on the couch and raise my brows. "Read it to me, then. Let's see if you're right."

He stiffens for a second, the book hanging at his side. Then he sighs and sits on the other end of the couch. Giving me a quick, resigned stare, he flips to the first page of the book, reaching into his pocket for his glasses.

I swallow as his voice fills the room, the gentle and velvet-y soft cadence, the low tenor... all while he's shirtless with glasses.

Pulling my legs up into my chest, I rest my face on my knees as he reads to me. Not because I want to know the story, though I have to admit, it's quite entertaining, but because he seems to need to prove a point.

And for some reason, I don't want to rile him up right now. He's extended three olive branches today; this, the storm, and offering to drive me to Scotty's show on Saturday. I like pushing the boundaries to get his attention, but sometimes it's nice to *be* with him—without arguing, without being a brat, and without pissing him off.

It's *comforting.*

As he continues reading past chapter one, I settle back into the couch. Handing me a pillow and blanket, he doesn't miss a beat as he reads on. A minute later, Captain Sushi climbs up with me, and Liam strokes his fur affectionately.

I find myself slipping into a cozy, comforting sleep shortly thereafter.

CHAPTER FOUR
THE QUIZ

LIAM

The next morning, I have a free period before my *Eco-Poetry* class. Normally, I spend my free periods in my office, fine tuning the curriculum, grading papers, or writing. But today, I woke up to a text from Orion, my youngest brother. He informed me he was going to be a guest lecturer in one of the Human Sexuality classes for upperclassmen. Professor Dimas had originally asked Juliet, my sister-in-law, but she's living up north with my brother, Chase. She's a Human Sexuality professor, so she was the natural first choice.

Orion, however, jumped at the opportunity, and I'm proud of him.

Of course, he asked me to attend the class, and how could I pass up an opportunity to see my baby brother lead a college course?

I walk to my office and drop off my bag before heading to the second story of the Maple building. The door to the classroom is buzzing with students, and I follow them into the small classroom, hoping to find a seat near the back...

Until a soft hand grips my bare forearm and tugs me into a front row seat.

My eyes snap to Zoe's as Orion clears his throat at the front of the class.

"You're taking this class?" I ask her, sitting down in the seat next to her.

"Of course I am," she hisses under her breath.

Why am I surprised she's taking a class for juniors and seniors when my class is structured exactly the same way?

I lean back and watch my younger brother lead a classroom full of people.

"Good morning," he says, voice deep. I note the light grey, long-sleeved shirt bunched up at his elbows to show off his numerous tattoos, the black jeans, and the dark hair and scruff. "I know it's a bit early to start talking about BDSM, but here we are," he jokes, cracking a grin.

The room erupts in laughter, and I glance over at Zoe, who, unlike the rest of the students, has her computer out and ready to take notes.

"Professor Dimas asked me to come in today and talk about BDSM, but before I begin, who here knows what that stands for?"

To my horror, Zoe raises her hand, and Orion's eyes

skirt from her to me, his lips pulling into a Cheshire smile.

Fuck.

He nods at Zoe, who sits up straighter and winks at him.

She fucking *winks* at my little brother. I mean, I know they're friends, but *what the fuck.*

"It stands for bondage, discipline, though sometimes domination, sadism, and masochism."

"Well done. I know you're all here to learn about human sexuality. Most of this class is spent learning about the development of sexuality, the feelings and emotions involved with sexuality/sexual feelings, and the attitudes toward others and their sexuality. But I'm here today to discuss the kink lifestyle, which is a bit of a more applicable subject," Orion begins, walking back and forth slowly in front of the white board.

"A few of you are probably wondering why I'm teaching this class instead of Professor Dimas. Well, simply put, I'm in the lifestyle, and I'm also very knowledgeable about the different facets of BDSM. I'm not a teacher or professor by any means, so you can ask me anything. I want you to feel comfortable with me today. I *want* you to spend the next hour and a half dismantling what you think you know about intimacy and kink, as well as traditional gender roles."

My comfort fades away with each second that ticks on the clock. I assumed maybe he'd be talking about his personal experience with sexuality, but the stack of papers on the desk says otherwise.

"It's rare that BDSM is brought up as a topic of discussion in a class like this, but controversial things such as sexual assault and pornography are discussed with no problem. While no less important, it is widely known that nearly a third of Americans practice some form of BDSM in the bedroom. So why aren't we talking about it?" Orion asks.

I shift in my seat and glance over at Zoe, who is watching Orion raptly.

"One explanation could be that most professors are not equipped to present the facts and facilitate learning around the subject of BDSM. Despite being a class where we talk about *sex*, kinks are still a taboo subject. But I believe it is deserving of visibility. Being that this class is for adults, and this is a course you've elected to take. The best way to grasp the nuances of kink is to self-learn. So that's exactly what we're going to do."

He walks to the desk and grabs a stack of papers.

"I'm going to be passing around an NDA as well as a basic kink quiz. The NDA is for your protection and safety. What's said in this classroom stays in this classroom. Everyone needs to understand that this is a safe space, and I won't tolerate any nonsense. The quiz is for you personally. You don't have to share your answers, and you can certainly have fun with it. I'll be asking for volunteers afterward to share their answers, and I'll answer any questions you all may have."

He starts to pass out the papers, and I shift slightly so I can stand up and leave. There's no way I'm taking this quiz with Zoe next to me, let alone chancing a glance at her answers. I have nothing to hide. Out of all of my brothers, Malakai and I are the only ones *without* a kink. I know about BDSM and kinks thanks to Chase, Miles, and Orion. I'm not a playboy like Chase used to be, but I don't abstain like Miles, either.

Orion hardly ever sleeps around, despite being in the lifestyle. For him, it's more about control than sex.

But me?

It's not like sex makes me uncomfortable. I've slept around a fair amount. Nothing crazy. Sometimes I date people for a week or two. Nothing ever lasts, and I'd mostly given up on relationships when I became Zoe's guardian. I figured having women in and out of her life wouldn't be conducive to healing from her grief. *Our* grief. Plus, it's kind of hard to date when you're suddenly thrown into the pits of depression and parenthood.

Even so, I'm on the straight and narrow. *Vanilla.* I've never been one for ropes or spanking—because that's what this entails, isn't it?

I certainly don't need a quiz to tell me that.

Just as I press my feet into the floor to stand, Orion roughly sets a piece of paper on my desk.

"Where do you think you're going?" he asks, giving me a cocky smile. "Stay. You might learn something about yourself."

"I need to prepare for my class," I explain gruffly.

Orion grins at that. "Unclench for a few minutes and take the damn quiz, Liam."

I sit back and stare at my brother, who continues passing the papers out.

"He's right," Zoe says quietly. "A healthy sexual appetite is important."

"That's enough." I turn to face her, and her eyes flash with something heady.

Well, fuck.

I quickly turn back toward my youngest brother.

"While people are looking over the instructions and NDA, can someone tell me what they think of when they think of BDSM?" He chooses a guy who's sitting a few seats away.

"Fifty Shades of Grey?" the guy asks, obviously grasping for straws.

Orion shrugs as he walks to the second row, passing the papers out. "Not quite. But I'll get into that a bit more in depth later. Can someone share where they first heard of BDSM?"

For the second time, I'm horrified when Zoe raises her hand.

"My friends," she says primly. "Once I discovered what I liked, it was easy to find like-minded people."

A few people laugh, but my mouth drops open.

She learned about BDSM from her *friends*? Which friends?

"Very good," Orion muses, finally getting to the very back row to pass the papers out.

I don't miss the way he smiles knowingly in my direction.

"Before you take the quiz, I'm curious to see what your preconceived notions of kink are. I'm going to read off a list of sexual behaviors, and I want you to tell me if you think they're kinky or not. This is going to be an open forum, so feel free to shout out your answers. Ready?"

When I look around, all of the students are watching Orion raptly.

"Reverse cowgirl."

"Not kinky!" someone shouts from the back.

Orion laughs. "Good. What about erotic asphyxiation?"

"Obviously kinky," Zoe drawls, nearly rolling her eyes.

I snap my attention to her as she shuts her computer and leans back. What the *hell* is erotic asphyxiation? And why the hell does she know about it?

"You're correct," Orion says quickly. "What about cunnilingus?"

"Not kinky," someone says.

"Foot jobs."

"It depends," Zoe answers. "Normally, no. But if it's a part of foot fetishism, then perhaps."

My mind is spinning with information, and I swallow thickly as I digest her words too slowly.

"True," Orion says slowly. "What about watching someone have sex?"

"Kinky," someone on my left calls out.

"Good. So it seems you guys have a basic understanding. I'll go into more detail after you take the quiz. Some of you might not be comfortable sharing your results, and that's fine. This class and these results are for *you*. Remember, consent is pivotal. In this lesson, we will abide by FRIES. Does anyone know what that acronym stands for?"

Zoe's hand shoots up, and she speaks before I can process what she's saying.

"Freely Given, Reversible, Informed, Enthusiastic, and Specific," she says, sitting up straight.

How the fuck does she know this stuff?

"Good. Everything in kink, unless agreed to beforehand, must be consensual. I'll be breaking you all into pairs. If you don't want to share your results, like I said, that's fine."

I glance down at the NDA as anxiety swirls in my gut. I thought Orion would be lecturing about whips and chains. I had *no idea* he'd be doing learner-led teaching. If I'd known, I might've skipped the class entirely.

"You two," Orion says, pointing to Zoe and me.

"Ri," I growl, the warning in my voice evident.

"You don't have to share your results," Orion says, smirking. "Have fun, brother."

The two of us are already sitting next to each other, but Zoe scoots a couple of inches closer. Her leg brushes against mine, but when I look up, she's concentrating on her quiz.

Her *kink* quiz.

Fuck.

My.

Life.

I glance down and sign the NDA without reading it. As I turn the page to start the quiz, my face heats.

Like I said, it's not like I don't *know* about kinks and

BDSM. I do. I've never really been into it, personally. To each their own, I suppose. But Zoe is *right* next to me. Somehow, this seems illicit, given our history.

In a way, I know what she likes, and that makes this whole experience that much more uncomfortable.

When my eyes scan the top of the quiz, I have to take a slow, steadying breath.

Apparently, we have to mark which things we're interested in and score them with the numbers one through five. Five is agree, one is disagree, and two through four are on the fence one way or another. After we total up our points, it gives us a *kink* score.

Wonderful.

I start the quiz, not letting my eyes rove over to Zoe's answers, even though I'm so fucking curious.

As my brain processes the words before me, I have to take another steadying breath when I imagine what Zoe's answers are.

You'd be open to utilizing toys in the bedroom.

That's easy. I'm definitely not opposed to the idea. I mark it as a five.

The thought of other people watching you have sex turns you on.

Nope. I mark it as a one.

The thought of giving your partner five orgasms turns you on.

I pause, my pen hovering over that line before I read it again, thinking of how Zoe's thigh shook on my shoulder that night in Catalina—like I was wringing those orgasms out of her. How *hard* her perfect cunt gripped me...

Fuck.

Now *I'm* really fucking hard.

Definitely a five.

You'd be open to blindfolding your partner.

Again, my pen hovers over the sentence. I mean... that's innocent enough, right?

Without me realizing it, an image of Zoe laid out on top of my bed with a blindfold over her eyes and her bottom lip between her teeth as her back arches forms in my mind.

This was a bad idea.

I adjust myself in my seat and mark that one as a five as well, because I can't deny that the notion of blind-folding her turns me the fuck on.

I need to get a grip.

The thought of spanking and punishing someone turns you on.

I mark that a three, which is apparently neutral terri-tory, according to the quiz. Again, I'm not wholly opposed, but in the bedroom, I'm all about pleasure.

Not pain.

Not like Orion, anyway.

However, a bit of pain mixed with pleasure, or plea-sure to follow up a bit of pain?

Perhaps.

I answer the rest of the questions, mostly staying neutral in areas I'm not familiar with, but answering with a five when it comes to pleasuring the other person.

Any and all ways I can be in control in the bedroom appeal to me, especially if it has to do with commanding pleasure out of my partner.

I've always been this way—always taking care of others. It comes naturally.

One of the questions at the end sends a bunch of ideas running through my mind, and a flash of heat works through me when I finish reading it.

The idea of your partner completely surrendering to your physical gratification (such as inducing multiple orgasms or prolonging arousal) turns you on.

Yes. Hard five. I don't even need to think about it.

I'm about to move onto the next question when I feel eyes on me. Flicking my eyes to Zoe, her gaze lands on my paper.

"Not surprising," she murmurs, setting her pen down and leaning back. "You were all about *my* pleasure that night."

I'm stunned silent.

It's the first time she's ever verbally acknowledged that night in any way. I'm too flabbergasted to say anything, instead glancing at her paper, too. The number 437 is circled twice. *Her kink score.*

"What?" I ask a moment later, covering my answers.

She laughs, but there's something dark in her expression when she leans forward. Goosebumps erupt on my skin when her lips come to my ear, and I have to hope to god she doesn't notice how my cock is pressing against the placket of my pants, begging to be let inside of her again.

"You should do research on pleasure Doms," she murmurs. "I think you might be one."

Before I can process her words, Orion claps his hands once. "Alright, time's almost up. Tally those numbers, and I'll share the results on the board," he says, turning around with a marker in his hand.

I take a few steadying breaths, willing my body to cool down. *I think you might be one.* How the hell am I supposed to react to that? Closing my eyes for a few seconds, I will my brain to calm the fuck down as I adjust my erection in my pants.

A few seconds later, I open my eyes and add the numbers up, getting 281. I have no idea what it means, so I watch as Orion finishes with the results on the board.

> 0-100: *Vanilla AKA General Public*
> 100-200: *Kinkier Than Some*
> 200-300: *Kinkier Than Most*
> 300-400: *Major League Kinkster*
> 400+: *Expert*

As the results sink in, I realize one of two things. I am apparently *kinkier than most,* even though I didn't mark higher than a three on any of the questions about sadism or masochism.

And second... Zoe had a score of 437.

Expert.

How is that possible? How does *she* know more about this than me? I mean, I wasn't born yesterday. I assume her and Scotty are... *hanging out,* as she calls it. But to be an expert on the topic of kink and BDSM?

Is she... *in* the lifestyle?

Something potent and uncomfortable snakes through me at the thought of Zoe tied up. Zoe blindfolded. Zoe being spanked. She's *nineteen.* How can she possibly know what she likes? Do these assholes know what they're doing?

I happen to like older men.

Her declaration in Catalina runs through my mind.

Scotty's twenty-nine.

And now that I think about it, most of the guys she's *hung out with* have been at least five years older than her.

My mind spins with the possibility of someone corrupting her. *How the fuck did that happen?* She's been living under my roof for over a year, and I've been none the wiser.

Orion clears his throat and starts to speak. I keep my eyes forward so I don't chance a look at Zoe.

"I hope the quiz was enlightening," he says slowly. "Whatever your results are, I hope you know that it's *normal.* There is nothing shameful about having a certain kink, and there's nothing shameful about being in the vanilla category. Remember, vanilla sex is *not* bad sex. Just as kinky sex can be terrible with the wrong person. Is anyone who scored over four hundred willing to share some of their answers?"

Zoe's hand shoots up, and I've never wished to crawl under a desk and die more than in this moment.

"Ms. Arma," Orion muses. "We are in a safe space

here, so feel free to share whatever you're comfortable with."

Zoe scoffs. "It's fine, I'm an open book."

Is she? Or am I in an alternate universe where my worst nightmare is playing out in real time?

"Why don't you share something you answered with a five?" Orion says pointedly.

"Sure. One of the questions was, 'Does the thought of being denied an orgasm turn you on?' and I answered five. Hard agree."

Fuck.

My.

Life.

"Another question was, 'Do you enjoy being praised in bed?' and again, I answered with a five."

My cock pulses as Zoe shifts in her seat, giving me a small side glance.

I am so fucking dead.

Deceased.

Completely fucking done for.

Because all I can remember is Zoe being praised by *me*. And then I imagine Zoe being denied an orgasm by *me*. Zoe being forced to come so many times, tears stream down her face.

And it's clear she's remembering the same thing.

Fuck.

"And are you comfortable sharing anything else?" Orion asks. "Perhaps something *not* from the quiz?"

I know him well enough to know that he's goading me.

"Sure." Zoe laughs. "I enjoy being dominated. I consider myself a submissive. My answers don't surprise me because they're in line with what I already enjoy in bed."

WHAT?

That's it. My brain is going to explode.

My cock might follow suit, too.

Zoe enjoys being *dominated?* Well, that's fucking news to me.

"Anyone care to share?" Orion asks, stopping right in front of my desk. "Anyone, perhaps someone who got a different score range?"

Oh, fuck him.

I'm clearing my throat before I know what I'm doing.

Maybe it's because she surprised me with her answers, so I want to surprise her with mine. Or maybe it's because I'm frustrated with the whole situation, so I want to get it over with. Whatever the case, I pick the first question and answer my eyes land on.

"I can share," I grit out. Thank god for the NDA, because the last thing I need is for any of my students to know what my personal kinks are. Or lack thereof. "'Does the idea of switching roles in BDSM, going from dominant to submissive, appeal to you?' I answered with a one because the idea of being submissive doesn't appeal to me."

Orion hums and gives me a feline smile. "So, would you consider yourself gravitating toward the dominant side of BDSM?"

My hands curl around the edge of the desk. "Yeah, I guess. But I'm not into sadism or masochism."

"So nothing like me," Orion offers, and a few people laugh.

I huff a laugh. "Sure."

"So... you enjoy dominating with pleasure, then?"

"Yes."

The answer comes so instantly that I'm sure I must be beet red. And *fuck* if I don't hear Zoe inhale a tiny, shaky breath.

Orion moves on, asking a few other people who want to share their results. I keep my eyes looking forward, but I can see Zoe looking at me in my peripheral vision.

"There's nothing to be ashamed of," she says after a minute. "Pleasure Doms are actually quite common—"

"I'm not having this conversation with you," I growl, fingers curling around my pen.

"I'm just saying, you can talk to me about this stuff."

"No." She leans closer, and my jaw ticks with frustration.

"It makes sense, considering how you acted that night."

"You're on *thin fucking ice*, Zoe."

When she doesn't respond, I glance over at her and see her watching me. Something in her expression is yielding—almost docile. So unlike the brattiness I'm used to. She looks down at her answers, and then I let my eyes wander over to her again. I don't miss the pink bloom on her cheeks, or the blush on her neck. *How far down does that blush go?*

Her hair is straight today, pulled back into a clip. She's wearing a black, long-sleeved shirt tucked into a form-fitting denim skirt and tights. Her skirt is short —*too* short—and it's riding up her thighs, exposing...

Stockings and a lace garter.

Are you fucking kidding me?

My eyes flick to her Doc Martens briefly before they find some object in the distance to focus on.

Why is Zoe wearing a garter? Is she wearing it for Scotty? Is *he* the one who dominates her? What else is she wearing underneath her clothes, and why do I want to see it so badly?

I imagine it. Just for a second.

Asking Zoe to see me after class.

Pressing her up onto my desk.

Running my hand up her thighs and finding the garter clip, running my fingers over her bare skin...

Demanding to know who dominates her if it's not *me.*

Fuck, I can't start thinking like this. I can't go *there* again.

You were all about my pleasure that night.

My pen cracks in my hand and ink spills all over my quiz results and NDA. Which is fine because I need to leave anyway.

With a quick adjustment, I hide my erection under my belt and stand up as Orion continues lecturing, ignoring the way I can feel Zoe's eyes on my back the entire time as I walk to the door.

———

A loud knock on my office door startles me, and I grunt for the person to enter.

Orion swaggers in, a rueful smile playing on his lips as he comes and sits down, legs spread wide, in my spare office chair.

I ignore him, my gold pen hovering over the yellow legal pad with one hand as the other—the one stained with ink—adjusts my glasses.

"So, are we going to talk about it?" Orion asks.

I sigh and lean back. "About what? About how I now know *way* too much information about Zoe, thanks to you?"

Orion chuckles. "Sorry, man. I thought you knew."

My mouth drops open. "How the fuck would I know she *enjoys being dominated?*"

I'd never told anyone about that night in Catalina and assumed she hadn't, either. It was *our* little pocket of indecency. I liked that no one else knew.

Liked that she's my dirty, little secret.

"She's never mentioned it?"

I scoff. "Yes, because the topic of submission and domination comes up all the time at the dinner table."

Orion laughs—truly laughs with his head thrown back.

Despite being irritated with him, I can't help but be impressed with the way he led the class today. He struggled to hold down a job for years, and at one point, I wondered if he'd drink himself to death. He was an idiot when he was younger, but he's turning out alright, I guess.

"I figured you put two and two together when we started hanging out together."

My face pales. "Have you two—"

"God, no. I mean, we go to munches together sometimes. We run in the same circles."

"What the fuck is a munch?" I ask, appalled that my youngest brother knows more about Zoe's sexual behavior than I do.

"A casual meeting for people in the alternate relationship lifestyle."

I enjoy being dominated.

I consider myself a submissive.

My answers don't surprise me because they're in line with what I already enjoy in bed.

I sigh and run a hand over my mouth. "I wish I didn't know that."

"Why?" Orion taunts.

I glare daggers at him. "Don't."

Holding his hands up, he chuckles. "What? I wasn't insinuating anything." His cocky smile tells me otherwise.

"Sure," I grumble.

"Look, she's a consenting adult. You're a consenting adult. That's all I'm going to say."

Been there, little brother. And I don't plan on ever revisiting that mentality again.

"You've already said too much."

"Fine. We can stop talking about Zoe now. What about you? Was your score enlightening?"

I shrug. "A little. I always assumed Kai and I were the vanilla ones. Between you and Chase..." I smirk.

"You think Kai is vanilla?" he asks, brows furrowed. "I'm not so sure."

I wrinkle my nose. "Alright, I'm done talking about our kinks now."

Orion laughs. "The more we can talk about it, the better. It's normal and healthy. Why did your results surprise you?"

"Because I'm not into this stuff!" I say a little too loudly. "No offense. I just... don't have time. Between my classes, taking care of you guys and then Zoe, writing, the cars, and maintaining the house, when would I have learned about it?"

I don't say it, but until I became a guardian for Zoe, I was busy making sure Orion didn't end up in a ditch somewhere. A lot of my weekends were spent being his wingman just to keep an eye on him. Miles and Chase were busy managing Ravage Consulting Firm, and Malakai was headmaster at St. Helena Academy supervising hundreds of students and being the most pious of us all.

Our fucking father certainly wasn't going to make sure Orion was okay, so that job fell on me.

Even if I wanted to explore the things on the quiz that intrigued me, I couldn't.

I had responsibilities.

First Orion, now Zoe.

"Fair enough," Orion answers, brows pinched as he taps his fingers against my desk. "Now that Zoe is mostly self-sufficient, maybe it's time to start doing something for *you*."

I scoff. "I have my writing and restoring the cars."

"No, I'm not talking about your passion and hobbies."

I look away and let his words sink in. It's the same speech I'd given him a hundred times. *Find your passion! Find something that sets your soul on fire!* It's the same speech I gave to all of my brothers. I remember giving the same speech to Stella, Miles's wife. Even Juliet at one point.

I had to be solid. I *had* to look out for them. If my father didn't, it had to be me.

Dabbling in whips and chains wasn't exactly on my radar.

"I'll think about it," I tell him to appease him.

"Good. You don't always have to live for other people."

"I don't."

"Zoe. Me. Your students. Miles. Estelle. Beatrix—"

"Bea doesn't count. She loves Uncle Liam," I counter, thinking of Miles and Stella's infant daughter.

Orion huffs a laugh. "My point is, you're like a mother hen for all of us. And if Chase and Juliet were still living in Crestwood, I'm sure you'd be hovering over them, too."

I smirk. "I said I'd think about it, okay?"

Orion hops up and pats me on the shoulder as if he's

not the youngest of the brothers.

As if *he's* the one who needs to lecture *me*.

"Fine. Have a good day, big brother," he says, smiling as he walks out of the office.

"Hey!" I yell when he's almost out the door. "I'm proud of you."

Orion's cocky expression softens for a second before slipping back into place. "Thanks. Let me know if you want to come to a munch," he adds. "They're fun. And hey, maybe you'll see a familiar face."

And he thinks I meddle?

I lean back and take my glasses off, running a hand over my tired eyes.

I pull my phone out of my pocket and stare at the blank browser page for a few seconds as Orion's words sink in.

And Zoe's.

You should do research on pleasure Doms. I think you might be one.

I must admit, the idea of domination is... kind of appealing. But only if I can utilize that control for someone else's pleasure. Like I told Orion, I don't want to hurt anyone—not really, anyway. But punishing someone with pleasure? The idea turns me the fuck on, especially if that someone is my best friend's fucking daughter.

God, why am I so fucked in the head?

After a minute, I tap out a phrase in the search bar before I can change my mind:

What is a pleasure Dom?

CHAPTER FIVE
THE MUNCH

Zoe

I adjust my tucked in T-shirt a few times before pulling it over my head and tossing it into the pile of discarded tops on my bed. When I look back at my reflection, the neon pink *You've Got This* sign taunts me from the wall behind me. *I most certainly don't have this, but okay.* In fact, nervous butterflies have been continuously dancing inside of me all day.

And all because of that quiz.

Because it confirmed what I already suspected.

And that helped *nothing*. In fact, it made my feelings for Liam that much stronger.

Huffing an exasperated breath, I grab the nearest shirt and toss it over to the opposite wall where it covers the pink sign.

Liam and his fucking signs.

I've tried getting rid of them. In fact, when I first moved in, I removed the ones in the kitchen and bathrooms. They're cheugy and basic, but Liam just replaced them with even cringier signs.

The one in my bathroom now says *#girlboss*, and don't even get me started on the ones in the kitchen.

Life happens, wine helps.

More espresso, less depresso.

Keep calm and drink on.

I get it. Millennials like their beverages and their signs.

But the worst offender of them all is the large sign in the dining room.

Live, Laugh, Love.

I pretend to gag thinking about it as I adjust the black mini skirt on my hips. I'm going to a meetup with Orion before Scotty's gig.

The same gig where Liam will be keeping me company.

That's a first for us.

I could psychoanalyze why he volunteered to drive me to Scotty's show, but right now, I need to find something to wear or I'm going to be late.

I open my bedroom door and look both ways before sneaking down the hall to Liam's bedroom. The cracking sound permeates the air, so I know he's still chopping wood outside.

He's been doing that a lot lately.

I quickly tiptoe into his closet and pull the plastic storage box out from the back. I'll never admit it, because that would be like admitting defeat, but Liam and my dad were super cool back in the day. The early 2000s pop punk music scene was their forte, and I know they got to go to a bunch of shows I'd kill to go to. I love *all* emo music. It was the best decade for music, and I will die on that hill.

Liam keeps all of his old band T-shirts in this storage box, and every few months, I steal one or two of them to wear to a gig. Since Scotty's band is a cover band, and all they usually sing is the pop punk music from the early 2000s, it's nice to have one of the original band tees. Plus, they remind me of my dad, and how I listened to that music growing up.

I always return the shirts, and Liam has no idea.

I snatch an old Blink-182 shirt from the bin before replacing the storage box to its original place. Throwing the soft, vintage tee over my head, I'm assaulted by the evocative scent of *Liam*. Musky and woodsy with a hint of licorice. I bunch the fabric up against my face and inhale, letting out a small moan.

I walk back to my full-length mirror and tuck Liam's shirt in, smiling as I admire the outfit. With a pair of fishnets, it'll be perfect.

I pull them on before grabbing socks and my high-heeled, lace up boots. Running my hand through my hair, I grab my leather jacket and pull it on. I pocket my phone, keys, and lipstick before quickly making my way downstairs. I can still hear the thwacking of wood, so I'm safe for a few more minutes. Opening the rideshare app, I request a car. Quietly, I make my way into the kitchen and fill up a glass of water while I wait. My eyes skirt over to the window, where I see Liam chopping wood in the distance.

Shirtless.

The water dribbles down my chin, and I quickly wipe it away as I watch him work. His back is to me, and with each movement, I see his muscles ripple and contract. He's wearing gloves, but they do nothing to stop his fingers from forming calluses—I know because I've felt them before.

At the funeral.

The week after.

And when his hands were on my thighs in that storage room in Catalina.

Growing up, I assumed he lifted weights or worked out every day. But nope. He spends an hour every few days chopping wood and hauling that wood to the shed out back. In the winter, it hardly gets cold enough to burn fires, but Liam loves his wood-burning fireplace, and he has enough of it now to fuel an entire small city.

After finishing my water, I check on the car I requested, noting it's a couple of minutes away. I put the glass in the dishwasher and head to the front door— which is on the other side of the house from Liam.

Just as I'm closing the door and pulling my jacket closed, I hear the crunching of boots on dirt, and before I can react, Liam comes around the corner of the house.

My brain fizzles as my eyes sweep over his bare chest, catching on a bead of sweat running down his abs. I stop walking as his gaze lifts to my face.

"Going somewhere?" he asks, his voice gritty.

"Um..."

Apparently, I've forgotten how to speak.

Because all I can think about is how Liam answered those questions two days ago.

The idea of your partner completely surrendering to your physical gratification (such as inducing multiple orgasms or prolonging arousal) turns you on.

It hadn't gone unnoticed by me that he'd circled choice five multiple times.

It's *so much* worse knowing *how* he does it—how his hands dig into your flesh, how his tongue is laid flat against your clit, how his calloused fingers curl and hook inside of you...

He answered that quiz like a Dom.

I almost wish I didn't know.

"I'm meeting with Orion before the show," I say quickly, buttoning my jacket to fend off the cool, autumn air. "I figured you and I would meet in front of the venue around nine?" A low, pleasant hum warms my body when I notice the sweat-streaked dirt covering his abdomen.

He's not muscled like a lifter, but he's not lean, either. He has wide, muscled shoulders, but they don't look like they're cut from stone. Instead, they look like they were honed over time. *Softer,* but still imposing. He carries himself with a commanding air—something he must've taught himself to do as the oldest of five.

"I'll come with you," he says gruffly, walking past me and to the door.

"It's fine. I have a car coming to get me in..." I look down at my phone. "Two minutes."

Plus, Orion and I are going to a munch, which is the last *thing I want to do with Liam.*

"Cancel it," he says, eyes finding mine. His face has a hint of dirt along his cheekbones, dusting the days-old scruff he always keeps trimmed neatly. "I'll drive us. Give me ten minutes."

"Liam, it's okay. I'll see you a bit later anyway."

He brushes his hair off his forehead with one hand, and my eyes track the movement. His square jaw tenses, and he takes an intimidating step closer.

"I'm going with you. Cancel the car, Zoe. No need to get a ride with a stranger when I can take you," he mutters. I take a step back and realize I'm pressed against the side of the house.

Liam towers over me, drops of moisture clinging to his damp forehead. I can smell the sweat mixing with the scent of licorice. I've always fought back against his protectiveness.

But now? Knowing what I know about him?

You're on thin fucking ice, Zoe. God, the way he said that. It was like a primal growl.

Why do I want to submit to him so badly?

"Besides, it's my birthday, and doesn't that mean I get to do whatever I want?"

His birthday.

Fuck.

I'd completely forgotten. It's a big birthday, too, seeing as he's turning forty.

And I forgot all about it.

Besides, it's my birthday, and doesn't that mean I get to do whatever I want?

His words roll around in my mind, and suddenly I'm transported back to his last birthday in Catalina.

"Fine," I say, my voice almost a whisper. "Happy birthday," I add, feeling guilty that I didn't remember.

His mouth curls into a small, victorious smile. "Thank you. I'll be ten minutes, tops."

I nod as he brushes past me, and my skin pebbles slightly. As I cancel the car on the rideshare app, I worry my lower lip between my teeth.

I don't bother going back inside despite the cool, cloudy weather. I sit down on the front step and scroll through Instagram while I wait for him, but I don't have to wait for long. After seven minutes, I hear the front door open and close.

"Ready?" he asks, walking past me to his parked Jeep Wrangler.

I follow him without responding, watching him as he climbs into the driver's side. He's wearing a black and grey flannel shirt and light grey jeans, his usual dark brown boots on his feet. His hair is still wet, and he runs a hand through it as I cross to the passenger side. Before I can open the door, Liam leans over the console and opens it for me.

"Come on," he orders. "Don't want to keep my brother waiting."

There's a bite to his words, and for a second, I wonder if *that's* why he's coming. Is he jealous of Orion? Or worried Orion is corrupting me? I smirk when I think about that. I'm sure Liam has no idea the meetup tonight is a munch. They're more common in LA, but once a week, I organize a munch at the local pub in Crestwood. There are larger munches in LA, and more of a variety of themes there, but this one is a free for all for anyone who is interested in the lifestyle. I try to go when I can. It's nice to hang out with Orion and other like-minded people.

"I'm sure he'll be surprised to see you," I say as I hide a little smirk.

I fiddle with the car stereo until it connects to my phone, and I play one of my favorite songs from My Chemical Romance.

Liam is quiet for most of the song. When we get to the main road, he lets out a soft laugh.

"Your taste in music is interesting," he murmurs.

"Are you insulting my taste in music or... praising it?" I ask, crossing my arms, my lips tilting up at the double entendre. As the words leave my mouth, the next song by Sum 41 comes on.

He's quiet for a minute before answering. "Because these bands were playing gigs before you were even born," he says, ignoring my bratty remark.

"So? Pretty sure the Beatles were around like eighty years ago."

"More like sixty years ago."

"My point is, I'm allowed to like music that precedes my time."

"I never said you couldn't," he acquiesces. "It's just an interesting choice."

"My dad liked it."

Liam chuckles. "I know he did. Who do you think got him into it?"

I look over at Liam. The smile that graces his lips is devastating and sensual all at once. His eyes flicker with amusement, and I see his hand twitch on the gearshift. It's almost like he wants to move it—to my hand, or my fishnet-clad thigh, maybe? His eyes rake down to my thighs as I think about it, and something intense flares through his entrancement.

It's only the honking of a horn from behind us that snaps him out of his stupor, and he clears his throat and keeps his eyes forward the rest of the drive.

I don't miss the way his fingers tap to the beat of the songs, though.

Liam parks in the small lot behind the pub, and like before, he leans over to open my door.

I inhale sharply as his shoulder presses against my chest, as I get a whiff of licorice and smoke. I ignore the heavy throb of arousal that settles between my legs from the feeling of him pressing into me. When he pushes my door open, he doesn't move away. Instead, he tenses, and it's almost as if he can feel the heady, taut chord between us.

He moves away a second later, leaving behind a cold

and empty void inside of me. I quickly climb out of the Jeep and march to the front of the pub. Liam's footsteps sound behind me, and I push the door open for us.

Orion is sitting in one of the booths in the back of the pub, and when he sees me enter, he waves me over. I recognize a few of the others he's sitting with, and I wave back. But then his gaze shifts behind me, and his eyes go wide.

I walk over quickly, hoping to explain that Liam *insisted* on coming. "Sorry, he wouldn't take no for an answer," I growl into Orion's ear when I hug him. "Plus, I forgot it was his birthday."

"It's fine. Miles and I are taking him out tomorrow to celebrate. When I talked to him yesterday, he told me he wasn't free tonight."

His words sink in. *He said he wasn't free? Yesterday?* Why did he give up spending his birthday with his brothers to come with me to the show?

"Besides, it doesn't surprise me that he's here since he knows about the munches."

"What?" I hiss, looking behind me to see an intrigued-looking Liam scanning the group of people seated in the large booth.

"He asked." Orion shrugs. "Maybe he'll find a nice, little sub to pleasure."

A twinge of unexpected jealousy flashes through me, and I smack him on the shoulder as hard as I can. "Gross."

"Or," he purrs into my ear, grey eyes twinkling. "Maybe *you* can be his nice, little sub."

"Hey."

Liam's voice cuts through the air, and Orion stands up straight. I push past him a little too roughly, then, I cough out, "Bastard!" before finding a seat at the end of the booth.

To my horror, Liam comes and sits directly next to me. I grab the drink menu to distract myself, pretending to be fully immersed.

"You're not old enough to drink," he growls, removing his flannel to showcase a tight, black T-shirt.

It's suddenly *stifling* in here.

I set the menu down and unbutton my leather jacket as I hollow my cheeks. "I probably shouldn't tell you that I have a fake ID then," I whisper, tugging the jacket off.

"You *what*?" he seethes, eyes blazing into mine. "Since when?"

I laugh as I shrug out of the jacket all the way, discarding it on the shelf above the booth. "Since I was sixteen. How else was I supposed to have fun at Thatcher?"

Liam's jaw rolls as he glares at me, but then his eyes widen as they rove downward.

Fuck.

"Are you wearing my shirt?"

I decide to play it casual. "Yeah. I discovered your box of cool band tees over a year ago. I thought you knew."

If looks could kill, I'm pretty sure Liam's icy stare could cut through glass.

"How often do you go into my bedroom?"

I shrug, looking down at the beer menu. "Not often."

When he doesn't respond right away, I look up to find his eyes on... me.

And his pupils? They're blown nearly black.

Fuck.

"Hi there."

A sensual female voice startles me. In the time between sitting down and now, a woman I don't recognize pulled a chair up right next to Liam.

He clears his throat as he turns his attention to her. "Hi."

Her eyes flick to me. She's pretty. Older—maybe mid-thirties. Straight, blonde hair. Freckles. A pretty smile and *very* full breasts she has no problem showing off in a light pink cashmere sweater. If she's at the munch—or *slosh,* as it's called when alcohol is involved—it means she's probably a sub. I can't speak for all munches in every area, but in Crestwood, new people are usually subs looking for a rich Dom. Not always, but that's been my experience.

"I'm new to this meetup," she says, looking shy and demure. "Have you been to one of these before?"

Liam looks at me uncomfortably.

Great.

"I'll go order us drinks. What do you want?" I ask, my voice a bit too sharp as I grab my wallet out of my jacket.

"A Corona for me." He reaches into his pocket and hands me his wallet. I ignore him.

He looks at the woman. "What about you?"

I'm grinding my jaw so hard my teeth start to ache.

She giggles and acts surprised. "That's sweet of you. I'll have a glass of chardonnay."

I'm walking away before she can thank me, and before Liam can try to hand me his wallet again.

I order at the bar, but the bartender doesn't ID me. I come here almost every week, and I know the staff. My foot taps angrily against the metal pole of the bar, and my blood boils. I don't look over at the booth. I *can't* watch Liam flirting with someone. I'm pretty sure it would kill me.

My nostrils flare when I think of Liam discovering his Dominant side with someone else. With *another* sub. Someone closer to his age. Someone *perfect* like her. He's a catch; I'm sure she'll tell all her friends about the nice guy she met at the bar tonight. If she's experienced, she can teach him. If not, they can discover their kinks together.

The thought makes me sick.

It's not like he'd be willing to try it with me, anyway.

This never *fucking happened.*

I think of Chase, one of Liam's younger brothers. I don't know him that well. By the time I came back to Crestwood, he and his wife, Juliet, were living in Northern California. He's a Dom, and Juliet discovered she was a sub after experimenting with him.

Is that what would happen?

One night would lead to dating, and Liam would rock her fucking world with multiple orgasms, and the next thing I knew, they'd be married, and...

Fuck.

I squeeze my eyes shut as my heart pounds in my chest.

The bartender tells me the total, but as I hold my card out, a large, warm hand tugs it down.

"It's on me," Liam says, coming to stand next to me at the bar. The bartender takes his card before I can protest. "Don't think I didn't see the way you ignored my money earlier," he murmurs, not looking at me.

God, when he talks in that voice, it makes my cunt shiver with delight.

"I'm perfectly capable of paying for drinks."

Liam's blue-grey eyes bore into mine with such intensity, it makes my toes curl inside of my boots.

"There's no reason you have to pay for a stranger's Chardonnay."

I don't say anything as I sulk, leaning against the bar. "She seems nice. You should date more."

The words taste like ash in my mouth.

"I'm not really into casual dating." My brows furrow as I study the wood grain of the bar. "Besides, I'm not sure what her ulterior motives are."

I scoff. "She's obviously sussed out that you're a Dom."

"Am I?" he asks casually.

I snap my eyes up to his. "Yeah, I mean... that's what your quiz said."

He cocks his head as he inches closer. "I thought we weren't talking about that?"

"You don't want to know?" I ask, lips curving up slightly, riling him up intentionally.

"Of course I do. You know what? Fuck it. I've been dying to ask you about it," he adds, his voice low and rough. "But that doesn't mean we *should*. Do you see the difference?"

God. When he scolds me...

"What do you want to know?" I ask, knowing my question is dangerous. Knowing he could shut me down again.

Something passes behind his eyes as he answers. A spark of curiosity mixed with something dangerous and flirtatious.

"Everything."

My stomach flips at his words, causing goosebumps to erupt on my bare skin. "Well, I'm a submissive. I don't need a quiz to tell me that because I already know. I've been with all kinds of Dominants. I can be a bit of a brat, so my flavor of submissiveness is not for everyone. I fight back. I need someone to tame me. I like to be punished," I add.

Liam looks... mesmerized. His nearness makes my senses spin, and his eyes are studying me with a mix of curiosity and something darker.

Something heated.

A delicious shudder skitters down my spine from the way he's looking at me, and he must notice, because the corners of his lips curve up slightly.

"Interesting," he murmurs. "And all this time I thought you spent your free time studying."

I laugh. "Well, I do both. It's not like being a submissive is a full-time job. It's my preference in the bedroom. And even then... not always."

Our drinks have been sitting on the bar for a full minute, but neither of us makes any effort to move.

"So is Scotty..."

I laugh again. "No. Scotty isn't in the lifestyle, but he's cool with my other relationships."

Liam's brows furrow. "Other relationships?"

"Yeah. Last month there was Komal. He's a doctor and a Dom. It was a fun fling, but that's all it was. Before that was Charlie, who *isn't* a Dom, but he was kinky—"

"Wait," Liam growls, pinching the bridge of his nose. "I thought Scotty was your boyfriend?"

I huff out a laugh. "*Boyfriend?* No. He's not my boyfriend. He's sleeping with two other people. And it's fine. It's... casual. We're hanging out."

Liam looks more perplexed as he shakes his head. "I don't get it. You'd have to kill me before I'd allow anyone else to touch what was mine."

What was mine.

Why do I want that to be *me* so badly?

"Are you at least *safe*?" he asks. "You know, sleeping around..."

I roll my eyes. "Yes. I get tested regularly and don't sleep with a new partner until they've been tested. I also use condoms."

Except with you, I think.

Liam seems to be thinking the same thing because he clears his throat. "So, did someone show you how to be..."

You, I think.

It was all you.

I almost tell him.

I almost tell him about how inexperienced I was before him. How his growly voice and mastery of my body led me into a deep dive of self-exploration. How Orion helped me identify it, and how I'd immersed myself in the lifestyle to feel a fraction of what *he* made me feel that night in Catalina.

Except, I hold my tongue. Because telling him all of that now would be the biggest slippery slope ever.

But that doesn't mean I can't tease him a little bit.

"Not really. I realized I *really* enjoyed submitting to the right man," I murmur.

I grab my drink and walk back to the booth. I head for the side closest to Orion. I can't stomach sitting near Liam as that woman flirts with him.

When I'm a few feet away, Liam tugs me backward, sloshing my beer all over the wood floor.

"We're going to talk about the fact that you're wearing my shirt later," he growls, his breath in my ear before he lets me go and walks back to the bar to retrieve the other two drinks.

My legs are like jelly, and my heart is buzzing inside of my ribcage, but somehow, I make it back to the booth. Sitting down with Orion, I don't let myself glance over to the other end of the booth. Instead, I tell Liam's brother all about my classes, and he listens intently.

Orion is a good guy. All of Liam's brothers are. And

the crazy thing is, they're good people *because* of Liam. He always put them first. Still does.

Charles Ravage, their father, is MIA, though I know Orion still talks to him sometimes. As far as I know, Orion spent most of his teenage years living a normal life with his mother, stepfather, and stepsister, Layla. She's only a couple of years older than me, and the two of us hang out a lot.

It was nice to have a default family already built into my life. They all acted like I was part of the family from day one. Even though Liam and I aren't related by blood, they all tucked me right into the family dynamic and treated me like an actual family member.

Maybe that's part of the problem. None of the other brothers ever held back affection with me. But Liam has always kept his distance—more so since Catalina. Maybe the reason I *want* him is because I'm searching for something deeper between us. I *want* him to stake his claim on me, and I enjoy it when he takes care of me. Maybe I've inadvertently blended what I like in bed with the type of person he is to me.

I *like* that he watches out for me, even when I fight back.

I *like* that he's always been there for me.

Being a submissive means I don't have to think or make decisions.

I can let go and have someone *else* take over.

And Liam? He already takes care of me. I'm sure there's a subconscious reason as to why I'm attracted to him, and why, above anyone else, I'd want to submit to him.

"He looks so fucking uncomfortable," Orion says, chuckling.

I follow his gaze to Liam, who is sipping his beer. I notice he's barely had any, whereas the woman talking to him seems to be on her second glass.

"I was uncomfortable at my first munch, too," I say quickly, hoping to change the subject.

"It's funny. Chase has been into BDSM since I was in high school. And Miles always had his voyeur kink. Kai went the complete opposite direction and chose god, but Liam..." He sips his beer. "I don't know."

I stare down at my empty pint glass. I'm going to need more alcohol to talk to Orion about Liam.

"Not everyone is kinky," I offer. "Maybe he's a vanilla guy who answered some questions the right way. Maybe we were wrong."

"Nah. I think he's kinky as fuck, but he's not like me and Chase, or even Miles. We were all content to explore our kinks with strangers. I think Liam needs to build that trust first. He's not a prude, but he needs that extra foundational layer."

Yeah, I definitely need more beer for this conversation.

"Maybe."

"Question is... where's he going to find someone to show him?"

My cheeks and chest flush with color, and when I lift my eyes to the other side of the booth, Liam is watching me intently. His blue-grey eyes bore into mine, and I suddenly can't breathe.

I never told Orion or anyone about that night, but sometimes it's like people can *tell*. Especially Orion, because he hints like this all the time, which doesn't help anything.

"I'm going to get another drink."

In half a second, I'm out of my seat and walking to the bar on shaky legs.

CHAPTER SIX
THE SHOW

Liam

An hour later, Zoe and I head back to my Jeep so we're not late for Scotty's show. I climb in first and reach over the dash to open her door, but she hesitates for a second, her hand hovering on the door frame. When she looks at me, I can't discern the look on her face. Gratitude, maybe? I'm not sure why. I've been opening her doors like this forever.

"Are you okay to drive? We can always get a cab," she says, buckling herself into her seatbelt.

"I had two sips of my beer," I tell her, placing my arm on the back of her seat as I reverse out of the parking space.

"You didn't like it?" she asks.

I'm so distracted trying to reverse out of the tiny parking space that I don't think before I answer honestly.

"I never drink when I know I'm going to have to drive you. I'd rather not chance it."

Also, the last time I got drunk around you, I lost control.

As I pull out of the parking lot and onto the main road of downtown Crestwood, the silence is stifling. I keep my eyes forward as my hands grip the steering wheel tightly. The tension is palpable as we make our way to the seedy area of the valley where the venue is located.

Zoe breaks the silence as I park in the very back of the lot. Her voice trembles slightly as she looks forward.

"Thank you," she says softly. "I know you gave up a lot when you became my legal guardian, and I'll never be able to repay you."

"It was never a problem to look out for you, Zoe. It's second nature now," I say nonchalantly.

"That's almost worse," she whispers. "You're so used to taking care of me that you can't enjoy a beer when you're talking to someone."

She stops herself and looks out of the passenger side window. I use the opportunity to drag my eyes over her face and outfit. Over her brown hair, loose and wavy around her face. How her bangs are parted in the middle. How her lips look like they're always pouting. Then I let my eyes drag over my *fucking* shirt hanging off her narrow shoulders. A dark red satin and lace strap is visible, and I so badly want to see what she has on under my shirt—the same shirt she tucked into the smallest skirt imaginable. I mean, I think I have *socks* bigger than her skirt. And her legs and that tan skin in those fishnet stockings...

I have to look away as my hands curl around the steering wheel to keep from touching her leg. "I wasn't interested in her."

When Zoe glances at me, her eyes are wide and curious. "I just assumed." She swallows, and I watch the way her delicate throat bobs. "Also, I'm sorry I forgot it was your birthday. What do you want?"

"Want?" I ask.

I *want* to trail my fingers between her legs, using her own wetness as lube.

I *want* to lick my way across her collarbone.

I *want* to watch her fall apart on my tongue again.

"What do you want for your birthday?" she clarifies.

I want you to show me how well you'd submit to me.

I almost say it. *Almost.* My mouth opens, ready to admit that I want *her.* All of her.

That nothing will top my birthday last year, because I got to spend it inside of her.

My lips snap shut, and I close my eyes briefly. "Nothing in particular."

My pulse quickens as I shift uncomfortably in my seat. Something intoxicating simmers in the air around us. How the *fuck* did I let this happen again? Whatever is going on between us feels like a delicate dance that neither of us knows the moves to. Like somehow, whatever raw and unspoken desire between us is all coming to a head right this very instant.

Again.

"We should head inside," she says quickly, opening her door before I can reach over and do it for her.

She walks a couple of feet in front of me as we weave through the parking lot to the back door of the venue. I scowl as Zoe bumps her fist with the burly security guard, and he gives me a curious look as I follow her through the double doors. I shoot him a warning glare as we make our way backstage.

"I'll go find us seats."

She laughs as she turns to face me. "Seats? It's standing room only."

Lovely. I guess I should've known that, but I'm out of practice.

"Fine. I'll go find us—"

"Zo!"

Scotty comes around the corner and jogs over to us, hugging her and picking her up before spinning her around. I don't realize I'm scowling at Scotty until he cocks his head.

"You okay, Mr. R?"

I muster every ounce of patience and goodwill that I have. "I'm fine. Come on, Zoe," I tell her, my voice a bit too gruff and irritable. My fingers wrap around her wrist, and I tug her away from him.

Her eyes widen when she looks up at me, and Scotty's bandmates stop talking as they observe the three of us.

"I can meet you in there," she suggests, a tiny wrinkle between her brows.

I lock eyes with Scotty before gazing at Zoe, not

looking away as I deliver my next line. "Come with me."

I don't mean for it to sound so domineering, but it comes off that way. Perhaps it's because of what happened in my Jeep. I'm suddenly incapable of watching her flounce around with this jackass. If I have to assert myself, I will.

"Zoe," I growl.

Scotty huffs a laugh, breaking the tension, but his eyes are hard as they bore into mine.

Fucker.

"It's fine. We need to get ready anyway. See you after our set." Leaning down, he gives Zoe a quick forehead kiss before walking away.

She waits until they're gone before spinning to face me. "What the hell was that? You're not my keeper."

"Trust me, I know," I mutter, walking past her to the front of the venue.

"What's that supposed to mean?" she asks.

I round on her. "If I were your keeper, I sure as hell wouldn't ever let that jackass *touch* you."

Before she can respond, I push through the double doors and make my way through the crowd.

Zoe's right behind me.

As much as I grumbled about the music, being in a dingy bar-like venue brings me back to going to shows with Elias. Everyone here may be wearing T-shirts showing off bands that I can guarantee broke up before they were conceived, but it still makes me want to smile when I think about the shit we used to get up to.

There's a fog machine and large, standing base

speakers in front of the stage. The overheard lights sweep over the crowd, and I'm shocked to see the place near capacity. Who would've thought that so many Gen Z'ers would be into early 2000s emo music? I have to be the oldest fucking guy here.

An electric guitar chord cuts through the noise of the crowd, and then everyone screams as Scotty's band walks onto the stage. I'm pushed forward by people behind me, and instinctively, I grab Zoe's hand. Another chord makes the crowd go wild. A guy with a mohawk behind her holds both hands up and rushes forward, and before I can think, I pull her in front of me protectively.

Immediately, I know it's a bad idea. I'm being pushed closer to the stage, which means the front of my body is pressing against Zoe's backside, and *fuck* she fits perfectly against me. My hand is still on her arm, and before she can protest, I squeeze her tighter against the front of my body.

My heart is hammering inside my chest, and I wonder if she can feel it.

Slowly nudging her closer to the stage, I keep her pressed against me as the music begins. Being so close to her makes me dizzy with desire. Every hair on my body stands to attention. Every skin cell tingles. Every neuron in my brain fires.

And then a song I haven't heard in nearly twenty-two years starts to play, and suddenly it's too much.

Being here with Elias's daughter.

With *Zoe*.

The person I was supposed to take care of.

She's here, pressed against my chest, and my best friend is dead.

He won't ever hear this song again, and all I can think about is how good his daughter feels against me?

What the fuck is wrong with me?

Except, as I take a step back, I can only move an inch or two. There are numerous bodies behind me, crowding Zoe and me to the point of her hair getting caught in my heavy breaths. I'm no longer aroused. Now all I feel is the urge to get *out.*

Zoe starts to dance, and the panic inside of me riots violently. I draw a few shallow breaths as I attempt to calm myself. The lights dance around the stage, and it smells like cheap beer and sweat already, and the desire to get out of here washes over me again. This song cuts like a knife through my chest, and all I can think of is Elias.

The last time I saw him was a few days before he and Brooke went on their fatal hike.

We'd spent a few days fixing up one of my cars because he'd had some time off from the law firm he worked at. We laughed and reminisced, but we also talked about the future. He mentioned one of his partners being recently single, and he'd wanted to set me up with her.

We'd talked about Brooke, who was the love of his life. She was in the middle of working on an extremely hard case as his partner in his law firm.

And Zoe, of course. Elias loved her so goddamn much.

The weather had been hot and unnaturally humid for California, and we'd taken turns jumping into the river, which ran through the back of my property.

The same river that eventually killed them a few miles away only four days later.

I close my eyes to ward off the torrent of emotions flowing through me.

I fucking miss him, and being here, listening to this music, with his *daughter*...

Zoe twists around so she's facing me, and it's like a vacuum sucks up all of the anxiety and grief in an instant. All I can focus on is her bright smile, her exuberant expression, her dimples, the way her eyes are shining with mirth.

It's like she's the antithesis to all of my problems.

Her energy washes over me, calming my racing heart and wrapping around the gaping hole her father used to occupy.

All the years with him by my side. Camping and going to shows and fixing up cars.

Being there when he found out Brooke was pregnant while we were sophomores in college. I didn't know her well at the time, but she soon became a close friend, too.

Watching him become the best father I knew— watching them *both* go to law school with a toddler...

Having Zoe *here* with me is healing, somehow, even though my best friend is gone.

As my pulse slows slightly and the music blends into the next one—"I Miss You" by Blink-182—a lump forms in my throat.

The music gears up, and my eyes sting with the weight of everything.

But then Zoe places both of her hands against my chest, and we sway to the music.

She doesn't have to say anything; I know we both feel her father here with us right now.

A few people sing along to the lyrics, but my eyes don't leave Zoe's.

Not when her eyes get glassy, or when a tear falls down her right cheek.

Not when my chest aches so much that I have to close my eyes.

Not when someone bumps into us, but I stand steady and reach up to grab her hands so she doesn't fall.

I don't let go, either.

Because we're not alone.

Not if we're together.

The song changes, and it snaps us out of our trance. I take a half step back from Zoe, and she does the same, until she's pressed against the stage facing me. I open my mouth, but someone shoves me forward, and the only thing I can do to keep from hurting Zoe is brace my hands on the stage behind her, so I'm caging her in with my arms.

Even over the deep bass, I hear her sharp inhale as I inadvertently press against her, and *fuck* if it doesn't feel good and so, so right. Her wide eyes bore into mine, and the emotional last song seems to have melted all of my resolve, because I could kiss her right now.

With this music and that *fucking* shirt hanging off

her shoulders…

Her perfect red lips and narrow waist, her dark hair framing her gorgeous face…

What I'm feeling has nothing to do with reason, and everything to do with being completely fucking out of control.

Again.

My eyes zero in on the base of her throat, and I watch her pulse beating and swelling rapidly, as though her heart has risen from its usual place. As my eyes trail back up to her face, a rush of pink stains her cheeks, and it takes every ounce of willpower I have to keep from reaching over and touching her.

She doesn't move away. Instead, as the bass shakes and vibrates around us, she only seems to lean into my body more, arching her back slightly.

Fuck.

The pulsing knot in my stomach drops lower until my erection presses against her stomach. I have no idea if she feels it, all I know is that I either need to do something about it or walk away from her *right fucking now.* Like before, her energy pulls me in, luring me like a siren song.

Without thinking, I knock her legs apart and let my thigh settle between hers as people around us move to the music, as the lights strobe. I don't pull away, but I also don't make another move closer.

I'm no longer toeing the point of no return.

I'm already fucking *there.*

The song ends and the next one comes on, and still, I

don't move. Heat fills my veins as "Scotty Doesn't Know" by Lustra begins to play, and the irony of Scotty singing this song while my thigh is between Zoe's legs isn't lost on me. In actuality, it only enhances the intoxicating atmosphere and how fucking *warm* she is against me. In a bold move, I angle my thigh an inch higher, and then Zoe's eyelashes flutter against her cheeks.

Fuck.

Fuck, fuck, fuck.

Her chest rises and falls as the lyrics of the song wash over us, and what happens next can only be described as being swept up in the song and people jumping up and down around us. I pin her against the stage completely, my thigh pressing between her legs until I can feel how damp she is, and that thought makes me nearly lose my mind.

The only thing I can think to do is smirk, *daring* her to stop me during this song.

But of course, she doesn't.

Zoe's pupils blow out as the song gears up, and she begins to move her hips in small circles against my thigh.

It's the most erotic thing I've ever seen in my whole life.

The music—the atmosphere—everything *overwhelms* me completely.

Even if I wanted to stop this, I couldn't.

I'm not technically touching her, at least, so I won't have to feel guilty tomorrow morning. My hands are sitting against her hips on the stage, but I don't move closer or initiate anything.

We're at a show.

That's all.

My leg happened to move between her thighs... that's all.

For all I know, she's moving her hips to the music.

Shivers of desire race through me as she squirms against the top of my thigh.

I'm not going to fucking stop her.

She's just dancing to the music.

That's what I tell myself when her mouth drops open slightly and when a low, tormented groan leaves my lips.

I'm entranced. So fucking entranced that I can barely breathe.

I want to touch her so *fucking* badly, but I refuse to let myself. I'd give anything to place my hands on her hips, to guide her up and down my thigh until she loses herself in ecstasy.

Instead, the music swells and the chorus repeats itself, and the only thing I can think is how we've already crossed the line, and how much I want to watch her as she falls apart on top of me while her *fuckboy* sings this song on stage mere feet away.

In fact, the need to make her come overpowers every single thread of rational thought.

I grind my leg into her wet center.

I can feel the way she begins to shake on top of me, and that makes me remember how wet she was for me in Catalina. How responsive she was. I can still imagine the hot, tight heat and how it felt to sink into her without abandon.

And as the crescendo of the last chorus begins, she squeezes her eyes closed. Her orgasm is so pure and explosive... if I wasn't so mesmerized, I might make her open her eyes. But I don't. Instead, I watch as she gasps in sweet agony, a low growl leaving my chest at the feeling of her pulsing heat against my thigh.

I'm fucking *hypnotized.*

I may be merely filling a moment of physical desire for her tonight, but at the same time, I'm allowing her to tear my soul apart.

Because after this, there's no going back.

There's no way I can pretend something didn't happen between us twice.

My brain completely shuts off then, arousal rising in me like the hottest fire, consuming me—consuming *us.* My thoughts are fragmented as she stops shaking and opens her eyes.

I suck in a breath as electricity swims around us for the ending of the song. Scotty is screaming *"Scotty doesn't know,"* over and over, and people are screaming with him.

And Zoe came on my thigh.

The next song starts, and my whole body goes taut as one of her hands brushes against my cock.

It's like the fact that it's *Zoe* touching my cock causes me to wake from whatever stupor I've been in.

The music is suddenly all wrong. And it's too hot.

Too crowded.

Too... *everything.*

My surroundings become clear, and the implications of what we did, what I let happen again...

"I need some water," I say quickly, turning around and pushing through the bodies like a coward. I know I shouldn't leave her alone, but I have to get away.

Bypassing the bar completely, I push the front double doors open and walk out onto the street. After running my hands through my hair, I find an alley a couple of blocks away and press my back against the cool brick, letting my head drop back with a hard smack.

I can only *wish* for a concussion right now.

What the fuck did I do?

I need to compose myself and my thoughts, as well as my raging erection.

I can't be lusting after *Zoe*; the notion is too preposterous, too precariously delicate to entertain.

Except I did.

I *do*.

Because watching her falling apart, watching those cherry red lips part as her hips jerked on top of me...

Fuck.

I am so, so, so fucked.

Because as far as we went in Catalina, I was so fucked up that it's a blur. But tonight? I'll *always* remember what her face looks like when she comes.

I sag against the wall as humiliation and shame course through me, causing my stomach to heave. My best friend trusted me, and I've now broken that vow of protection *twice*.

Nothing comes up, of course, but the self-loathing is

so potent that I physically ache with guilt.

I'm so absorbed with my own feelings that I barely notice the two men walking through the alley until they're standing right in front of me. As I lift my head, my eyes catch on the glint of metal.

A knife.

Anger courses through me unexpectedly, and my first thought is that this is *exactly* why I don't like Zoe coming to these gigs alone.

My second thought is one of self-preservation: I hold my hands up.

"Give me your wallet and no one has to get hurt," one of them says gruffly. They're both wearing hats low on their heads, so I can't see their faces.

"I'm getting my wallet right now," I repeat slowly, my voice clear. I know enough about being in this situation that I try not to overreact, because unfortunately I've been mugged at a show before.

Just give them what they want and be done with it.

I hold my wallet out, and they snatch it out of my hand quickly. My anger blooms into pure fury when I imagine them hurting or mugging Zoe.

"Hey, guys? Fuck you," I snarl.

One of them twists around and lunges for me.

I expect the sharp tip of a knife against my ribs, but instead, he rears his hand back and punches me so quickly, I don't know what happened until he does it again, and I'm on the ground.

I look up at the moon, wondering if the stars are real or fake, before everything goes black.

CHAPTER SEVEN
THE BRINK

ZOE

It takes exactly six songs for my cheeks to stop burning, and four more songs after that for the shock to wear off. I face the stage and dance to the songs absentmindedly, and at one point, Scotty bends down to kiss me, but my mind is on the man whose thigh I just came on.

The man who disappeared the instant I tried to reciprocate and ran away looking like he would rather be anywhere else.

It had all happened so organically that my mind is still reeling with ways I could have or should have stopped myself.

If I had a time machine, I'd go back in time by two hours—or rather, to the night in Catalina when things happened between us the first time.

But especially the last two hours.

Because we'd fallen into a comfortable agreement to never talk about that night, it was rarely awkward with him now. However, what happened tonight would propel us back into the *months* of silent dinners and avoidance.

Am I supposed to deny what happened? I might've been able to once, but not again. The fire between us burns too strong now.

But on top of all of that is the underlying thing that's bothering me the most: I want *more.*

As I fidget with the hem of his shirt and sway my body, I'm in such a daze that I'm shocked to see Scotty say goodbye to the audience, who erupt with shouts and screams as he sings his last song.

Where is Liam?

He's been gone for over an hour... possibly longer. I look over my shoulder and scan the crowd, searching for his tall frame and flannel shirt, but I don't see him. As I wait for the song to finish, I skirt the edge of the stage and walk through the back door to await Scotty.

I hear the venue shudder with shouts and screams when he finishes, and as I wait for him to come through the back door, I wipe my sweaty palms on my skirt and take a few pained breaths, closing my eyes.

Scotty and I aren't dating. So why do I feel guilty?

Or do I feel guilt pertaining to Liam?

Thoughts of self-loathing rush through me, and behind my closed eyes, all I can see is how Liam watched me so intensely–how his mouth dropped open slightly when I came. How his normally blue eyes had turned a deep, dark navy while he watched me—like I was the only thing he ever wanted to look at again. My whole body is hot and flustered when I hear the back door open.

I snap my eyes open.

"Zo!" Scotty shouts, grinning and sweaty as he jogs over to me. I can tell from his sweat-soaked shirt and exuberant expression that we're on totally different energy planes, but even so, I let him wrap his arms around me and pull me close. He lifts me up and kisses me, but it's all wrong.

I *should* feel like I'm cheating on Scotty, but we're not exclusive. I don't realize until his tongue sweeps between my lips that the reason it seems wrong is because of Liam.

Because it feels like I'm betraying Liam.

I push against Scotty's chest as his bandmates shout at him to join them at a nearby bar. Fortunately, he lowers me to the ground and pulls away.

"You coming?" he asks, still breathing heavily.

"I'm kind of tired. Maybe next time." It's not a lie, but all I want to do is find Liam.

"You sure?" he asks, cocking his head as he licks his lips.

I nod. "Yeah. Liam can drive me home. Have fun, okay?"

His eyes search my face. "I guess it's a good thing he drove you," he adds, a bit of a bite to his words that wasn't previously there.

"Yeah, he wanted to make sure I got home safely," I explain defensively.

Scotty looks like he wants to say something else, but instead he plasters on a fake smile. "Fine. See you later, babe."

As he turns and walks away, I know I should tell Scotty that it's fine, that Liam is overprotective. That he asked to come with me tonight to save the long taxi ride from the valley to Crestwood. That we were just dancing earlier, and nothing more—*not that he could see us.*

That I didn't mean for any of it to happen.

Instead, I watch as his friend places an arm around his shoulders and leads them to the side entrance.

I hug myself as I walk back into the venue, where the crew is taking down Scotty's equipment and getting ready for the next performer. There are less people now; Scotty and his band have amassed quite a following. I quickly check for Liam. I do two laps before I decide he must be outside, because he's certainly not in here. Slipping past a large group of women near the door, I see Bart, the security guard for the front door.

"Hey, have you seen a guy in a plaid shirt?"

"Oh hey, Zoe," he drawls, giving me a slow smile. "You're looking good. How's your night going?"

I tamp down my annoyance. I just want to find Liam.

"Yeah, it's fine. So, have you seen him?"

Bart squints as if he's trying to remember. "Tall, brown hair?"

I nod eagerly. "That's him."

He grimaces. "He went that-a-way about an hour ago," he says, pointing to the dimly lit street to the left. My heart sinks.

Did he leave?

He wouldn't drive home without me, would he?

"Thanks," I mutter, giving Bart a worried smile before I quickly walk away toward the dark end of the street.

When I get there, I look both ways before I turn left, where several small alleys break off the street. As I walk past each one, I keep an eye out for him, hoping he's getting air somewhere. I don't see him and it's cold, so I decide to try the other way, but movement on the ground catches my eye.

A leg behind a dumpster.

Liam's leg.

My blood cools as I quickly jog over to him, and my heart sinks when I see him slouched against a wall with blood coming out of his nose and a black eye forming.

"Hey," he warbles.

Short-lived relief washes over me before I take in his injuries, which don't look to be life-threatening.

He's okay. He's talking. He's okay.

He's okay.

He's okay.

He's okay.

I crouch down and run my hand over his face, brushing the hair off his forehead to assess the damage.

"What happened?" I ask, my voice shaking with adrenaline.

"Some guys mugged me. Stole my wallet. I told them to fuck off and one of them punched me. Twice."

"*What?*" I screech, looking around. "Why were you out here alone?"

His eyes find mine. "I needed a minute to think."

"You're an idiot," I grumble, reaching for his hand, which is cold. Pulling him a bit more upright, I'm able to get a better look at his face. "Should I call an ambulance? Should we go to the ER?"

He gives me a look that says *absolutely not,* but I grab his hand anyway and help him up.

"I'm fine. I've been punched before. Just needs ice and rest," he grits out, spitting blood onto the ground.

"What? When have you been punched?"

He grimaces as he feels his face. "Like I said, I was an idiot when I was your age."

I want to ask him about it. I want to know what he was like, and why he got punched. Something tells me there's a lot I don't know about Liam Ravage.

"I could call Orion?" I offer, wondering if that's a better option than him driving us home.

"No," he growls, helping me up and walking us out of the alley. "I don't want to worry him."

I grind my teeth together to keep myself from telling him that he doesn't always have to feel like such a burden. That perhaps Orion would be happy to help.

But I don't, because I know Liam well enough to know that he'll refuse to bother his brothers until his dying breath.

"Let's go home," he tells me, wiping his bloody nose on his sleeve. I wince as blood tracks against his cheek.

"We should clean you up before I drive you home."

He stops walking and glares at me with furrowed brows. "You don't have a license."

I shrug. "You're bleeding. I know *how* to drive, Liam. I used to drive my friend's cars all the time at Thatcher."

"Why the *fuck* your parents sent you to that delinquent school is beyond me."

I grin. "I probably shouldn't tell you about the magic mushrooms..."

"I'm driving," he growls. "End of discussion."

"Fine. But we're going back to the venue first to clean you up."

"Wonderful," he says under his breath.

"Scotty isn't there," I add, crossing my arms.

I don't miss the relieved look that passes over his face.

As we walk, all I want to do is reach out and make sure he's okay. My heart is still pounding, and my legs are unsteady beneath me. As we get to the front door of the venue, Bart's eyes widen.

"Whoa, dude. You okay?"

"He's fine," I say quickly. "I'm going to clean him up in the bathroom before we go."

"Take him up to the staff bathroom," Bart says, looking between us. "Upstairs and to the right."

I bump fists with him before leading Liam up the narrow staircase near the ticket booth.

"You know him?" Liam asks.

"Not really. Why?"

He doesn't answer me, but I have to wonder if he's

asking because of the fist bump. Hiding my smile, I push the door open to the very *tiny* staff bathroom.

"Inside," I tell him, holding the door open.

He brushes past my chest, and I have to tell my nipples to calm down.

The door closes, giving us another couple of feet of space, but it's still a tight fit. Liam leans against the pedestal sink, and I grab a few paper towels and wet them.

"Let me see," I say quietly.

Liam is still scowling—as if this is his worst nightmare. As if he doesn't have blood dripping down his face and onto his neck.

As if he's invincible, which he's very much not.

He doesn't move, so I reach up and brush his hair off his forehead. I have to stand on my tip toes, and even then, he's a fraction too tall.

"You're too tall. Sit on the toilet," I command, stepping back.

Something akin to amusement flashes over his features as he pushes off the sink and walks to the toilet, putting the lid down and sitting. I walk over and he opens his legs so I can step between them. Flashes of earlier penetrate the control I'm pretending to have, and after getting a heady whiff of his scent, I nearly moan out loud.

Reaching over to his face, he goes still at my touch. He's just below my line of sight, so it's a lot easier to see him this way.

I take the wet paper towels and clean his skin, starting

with his cheek. His eyes find mine, and I have to slowly inhale and exhale to calm my jumping nerves. The paper towel catches on his scruff, and I have to dab his skin there before working down to his neck. I go through a few wet paper towels. Other than the blood I've mostly cleaned off and dark red ring around his right eye, he looks okay.

I let my other hand come to his nose as gently as possible, examining it.

"Do you think it's broken?" I ask.

He swallows. "No."

As I trail my thumb over his other cheekbone, a shiver goes through him. The thought of making Liam shiver with a mere touch...

I pull my hand away. "What about the back of your head? You fell—"

"It's fine."

"Let me check," I insist, running my left hand behind his ear and feeling for blood.

"I promise you, I'm fine."

His skull feels okay to me, so I remove my hand from his soft hair.

I'd forgotten how soft it is. How easy it was to pull when his face was between my thighs...

That thought scatters in my brain, branching off into a bunch of different tangents.

How did I never know his eyes are mostly grey with blue speckles?

How did I never notice the single freckle on the bridge of his nose?

What if he'd been really *hurt tonight and he'd bled out in that alley before I found him?*

That last thought hits me, and I have to steady myself. A million other thought fragments explode in my brain, with one single train of thought practically screaming for attention.

If something happened to him, I'd have no one left.

But it's not about being alone. The thing that makes me panic is being without *him*.

My chest aches as I grab a new paper towel, wetting it in the sink before stepping between his legs again. I dab his nose, and he winces as I clean the rest of the blood slowly and diligently.

My vision blurs when I think of all the worst case scenarios that could've happened tonight, and regret claws through me. My breath catches when I look down at all of the bloodied paper towels I've used. Blinking rapidly to dispel the tears threatening to spill, I lean back and look at his face, hands on his shoulders. The blood is mostly gone, but the black eye is going to be around for a few days.

His eyes dart between mine, widening slightly when he notices my eyes are starting to tear up.

"Hey, Zoe—"

"Why did you tell them to fuck off?" I interrupt, angry on his behalf and also exasperated that he'd willingly put himself in danger.

Something shutters behind Liam's eyes. "Honestly?" I nod as he takes a deep breath. When he exhales, I get a whiff of licorice again. "I was angry. What if it had been *you* in that alley?"

My eyes sting, and my hands curl around the fabric of his flannel shirt. "Well, that was stupid," I whisper, giving him a quivery smile. "What if they'd had a knife or a gun?"

Liam's nose scrunches so imperceptibly that I wouldn't have noticed it if I weren't looking for a reaction.

Outrage sparks through me. "They did, didn't they?" I ask, my voice catching. His morose expression is an admission of guilt if I ever saw one. "You could've been *killed*," I hiss. "You're lucky you were just knocked out. And on your *birthday*," I chastise.

I almost ask him why he chose to spend his fortieth with me at my Scotty's show, but I have a feeling I'm not ready for the answer. I learned a long time ago that Liam's love language is acts of service; he's always *doing things* for other people.

"It's almost like you're worried about me," he replies, the corners of his lips curving upward.

"That must be a foreign feeling for you," I blurt. "Since you seem to worry about everyone but yourself."

He barks a laugh. "You're not wrong. I grew up worried about my father drinking too much. Worried about Orion with his new stepfather and stepsister, and then *his* drinking. Worried about the staff at the castle whenever my father would have one of his outbursts. Worried about Chase never finding someone who accepted him fully. Worried about Miles never letting anyone in. Worried about Malakai and the fact that he internalized everything growing up. Worried about you..." His eyes lock on mine.

"*I'm fine*," I urge. "You don't need to take care of me anymore."

"But I do. Because if I don't, who will?"

Warmth fills me, and I can't deny I love hearing him say that. Love hearing how much he *wants* to take care of me.

There are so many nuanced reasons why it makes me happy that I won't get into, but right now, I'm grateful to be on the receiving end of it.

"Okay, then riddle me this. If something happened to you, I wouldn't have anyone anymore."

His brows pull together, but I continue.

"You're so busy taking care of people, but who takes care of you?"

Liam's face pinches slightly, almost as if he's never truly considered this question. I want to run my hands over his face, touch the soft scruff and hair tinged with silver, feel the rough pads of his fingers and the calluses on the inside of his palms. Press my hands against the hard planes of his chest and ruminate on how well we seem to fit together.

"Let me take care of you," I say boldly. "Because if I don't, who will?" I say quietly, repeating his words back to him.

For a second, his face grows soft. His eyes roam down to my lips briefly, and my heart turns over in response. As his gaze slowly drags back up to mine, my pulse begins to race. He moves his hands to the backs of my thighs, and I release a tiny gasp. Despite laying in that alleyway for over an hour, his hands are already warm again. And when I look at Liam—*truly* look at him—he looks terrified. Unsure. *Out of control.*

And then his hands move up my thighs, his fingertips grazing the fishnet material, sending a shiver through me. I gasp again as my blood heats and my skin tingles. Emotions flit over his face, and his dark greyish-blue eyes roam over my face like they're trying to memorize every part of me. Every perusal sends my heart dropping into my stomach and causes the space between my legs to pulse.

God, it's so intense with him.

As his rough thumb rubs once against the delicate skin of the back of my thigh, my lips part slightly.

"Zoe," he says, his voice rough.

And I know—I *know*—he's about to reject me.

I take a sudden step back as someone knocks on the bathroom door, breaking the spell completely.

I don't look back at him as I open it, only to find Bart standing there.

"Just wanted to make sure you're okay," he says to me.

I see Liam stand in my peripheral vision, and I nod at Bart once. As I open my mouth to respond, Liam comes to stand next to me, hip to hip.

"We're fine," he tells Bart gruffly. And then a warm hand wraps around mine. "Let's go home."

I don't have time to respond to Bart as Liam tugs me

to the staircase. He drags me down the stairs and out the front door before I can get out of his hold.

"Hey," I snap. "He was making sure you were okay! You didn't need to be rude."

Liam puts his hands on his hips as he walks over to me, looking down. "Yeah? Are you sure about that?"

I roll my eyes. "Bart is a nice guy, and he was checking on you."

Liam laughs. "Right. Because nice guys can't take their eyes off your ass."

My mouth drops open. "He was *not* checking out my ass."

Liam steps into my space so that we're torso to torso. "Trust me, Zoe."

I'm flustered from what happened in the bathroom, and completely plagued by what happened earlier tonight, so my filter is nonexistent. I ball my fists and press my lips together, wanting to catch him in a lie, or somehow *force* him to admit that he wants me.

"So what?" I screech. "So what if he was? Scotty and I aren't exclusive. And I haven't promised myself to anyone else," I challenge. "Right?"

I see Liam's chest rise with each inhale, and his warmth is so fucking intoxicating.

He's *intoxicating.*

Admit it, I think.

Admit that tonight wasn't a fluke or a mistake.

Admit that you're jealous.

"We should get home," he says instead, taking a step away.

"Liam."

As he faces me again, his expression is closed off. "What happened tonight can and will never happen again. I'm sorry I let it go that far. Again," he explains, his stoic manner faltering for half a second before he turns and continues walking without letting me respond.

Hurt and rejection lance through me in quick succession, and I blink back tears as I follow him to his car.

He doesn't give me the option of driving. He opens the driver's side and climbs in quickly. Before I can reach my door, he's already leaning across the seats and opening the passenger door.

I don't say thank you.

I don't speak. Don't look at him. Instead, I choose to stare out of the window the entire drive home.

Because tonight, I realized that this goes *way* beyond being attracted to Liam.

Instead of admiring the gorgeous pool from afar, I've jumped right into the fucking deep end.

And I am *so, so* fucked, because he'll never admit that he wants me.

The only thing I'm going to get out of this is a broken heart.

CHAPTER EIGHT

THE ANNIVERSARY

LIAM

The weather turns cooler over the next two weeks, and it takes every ounce of spare energy to keep all thoughts of Zoe locked up in the back of my mind. I suspect she's avoiding me, which is fine because every interaction with her lately feels tenuous and delicate. The less we're around each other, the better—especially after the night of the gig.

I waffle from one end of the spectrum to the other with regards to that. When I'm twisting and turning in my sheets at night, I can't help but remember how soft her thighs were. How *warm* she was, how well she responded to me—like every one of my touches pulled some deep, untouched string inside of her. And when I stroked myself in the shower each night, the only things I could think about were her scent, the tiny, little noises she made when she came, and the way her hips circled skillfully on top of my thigh.

It was enough to get me hard whenever I allowed myself to think about it.

However, on the other end of the spectrum, I *hated* myself for letting it ever get that far again. I'd worked so hard to push past what happened in Catalina. And because of what happened to me, because of my injuries, she'd taken it upon herself to do more things for me, which only worsened whatever I was feeling.

With midterms coming up and Zoe taking double the required credits, I'd hardly seen her outside of class, but there had been plenty of clues.

Random plates of breakfast left for me in the morning with my coffee, or the leftovers sitting in the fridge with a note to eat it before it went bad. She didn't usually cook because I was home more often, but she'd started trying.

For me.

There was the time she'd folded all of the laundry, and I'd walked into my bedroom to see my bed covered in neat stacks, and sitting right next to the clothes was a stack of receipts for food.

Almost like it was her way of apologizing.

I'd never asked her to do chores around the house, and though she never asked me to do anything for her, over the last year and a half, I'd enjoyed doing it.

Having Zoe *want* to take care of me causes a messy torrent of emotions to buzz through me.

On the one hand, it's not her job, but I can't deny that

for the first time in my life, I have someone on *my* team—even though I'm supposed to be taking care of her, but that's beside the point.

It feels... good.

The new routine is so distracting that I don't realize it's early October until I'm sitting in class and going over the midterm scheduled for Friday.

"The first part will be multiple choice, which will go over the poets we've discussed, facts about them, and the themes in their poetry. This section is short and only worth ten percent of the overall grade. If you've been paying attention during class, this will be a breeze," I start, narrowing my eyes as I see Zoe enter the class—twelve minutes late.

I track her movements, watching as she takes a seat in one of the back rows–and my mind becomes a jumbled mess of words.

Again.

Despite not seeing her much at the house, I still see her a few times a week—during the two morning classes, and sometimes around campus.

I clear my throat and continue.

"The multiple choice portion will be followed by a short essay section. There will be four prompts to choose from. It's up to you which one you'd like to do, but you only need to answer one of them. I'll be looking for your ability to demonstrate your understanding of eco-poetry, its key concepts, and your ability to analyze and critically engage in the course material we've covered thus far." Pushing my glasses up, I look up at the clock. "It's Tuesday, October 4th, so you have the rest of the class to form discussion groups before the midterm on Thursday—"

My words slam back into me.

October 4th.

Fuck.

I'd completely forgotten.

I look down at my desk, trying to form the words I need to say in order to form breakout groups.

Think, Liam.

Four years.

Do something.

Four years.

A few people snicker, but I don't look up. I can't—I can't make eye contact with Zoe while I'm teaching.

Fuck, how did I forget!

Four fucking years.

I take a deep, steady breath. "Find a partner and spend the rest of class time going over anything you need clarification on. I'll be here, so raise your hand if you have any questions."

Everyone stands up and shuffles around, and the movement blocks my view of Zoe. Once people have located a partner and are seated, I notice that she's still by herself.

Fuck, fuck, fuck.

I climb the stairs to the upper seats, stopping in front of her, but she's staring forward and doesn't look up at me.

"Ms. Arma, a word please."

Slowly, she lifts her gaze to my face, and something

sharp pierces my chest when I see the purple bags, the lifeless eyes, and the tiny frown lines bracketing her full lips.

"I didn't find a partner because I don't have any questions," she says, her voice low so that no one can hear her. "Plus, everyone's paired up already."

"Zoe," I urge, emotion clawing up my throat. "Go home and take the rest of the day off."

Her expression hardens. "Absolutely not. I have classes all day."

Fuck.

She wouldn't know self-care if it hit her in the face.

Looking around, I see that everyone is grouped together and talking amongst themselves. I can't have this conversation with her here.

"Hallway. Now."

I turn around and jog down the stairs, curling my fists as I walk to the classroom door. I'd promised my students I'd be there to answer questions, but right now, I need to make sure Zoe is okay.

I hear her follow me out, and I take in the empty hallway with a relieved sigh. Before she can fight me more, I take an intimidating step closer so she's pressed against the wall of the hallway, clutching a book to her chest.

"Go home, Zoe. I'll excuse your absence."

She scoffs. "Isn't that called preferential treatment?"

My brows furrow. "No, because if it was the anniversary of their parents' death, I'd give them the day off, too," I say, my voice a little too sharp as I nod toward the door of my classroom.

She flinches, and her eyes well with tears. "How *kind* of you."

I grit my teeth together. "Go. Home."

"I don't have a home!" she yells, one of the unshed tears slipping down her cheek. "You keep telling me to go *home*, but I have no idea what you mean by that."

My chest, my throat, my eyes—everything *aches* at her words as I rear my head back. Pressing my lips together, I place one hand near her head, pinning her in place.

"You do have a home. *My* home. And it will always be your home. Today, tomorrow, or years from now. They might be gone," I add, my voice cracking, "but I'm not."

Her eyes search mine as another tear spills over. She swipes it away quickly, and I wish I could take away every ounce of pain, every single tear, and every broken thought.

"I know you're trying to make me feel better, but please stop. Not today. You can't possibly know how it feels to have your whole world swept out from underneath you. I'm... displaced," she adds, emotion clawing at her words.

I want to protect her from all the pain and be a bigger person, but her words cut deeply for me, too.

I lean closer so that our faces are inches apart. The rational side of me knows that I should take a step back so that we're not discovered in an incriminating position, but I don't give a fuck right now.

Grief clogs my throat as I try to find the words to explain. "When my mother died, I felt that tether snap, too. And I never really felt that sense of 'home' with my father, so growing up, despite my parents being around, it never felt like *home* because my father never gave anyone his affection. Not even my mother. I used to watch movies like *Home Alone* in awe because I never had that. My father never gave me a fucking ounce of love, instead choosing to toughen us up for the real world. Chase had Jackson, his best friend. Malakai had god, and Orion had his new family that wasn't so fucked up. Miles put everything he had into Ravage Consulting Firm. Guess what I had?"

Zoe is crying fully now, her shaky breaths bracketed by sniffling as she swipes at her cheeks with her free hand. A tremor of guilt passes through me, but the point I'm trying to make is sitting on my chest like a heavy, weighted blanket.

"I had Elias Arma. My best friend from the time I was seventeen. The one person I could tell anything to. The person who never judged me no matter how different our lives were." I rub my eyes to quell the tears threatening to spill out. Even now, talking about him and realizing I'll never get to talk to him again... It's like someone is squeezing my heart before tearing it to shreds. "And he's gone now, Zoe. He's gone, and I'm alone."

Zoe's anguished expression falls as she begins to sob, and I can't take it anymore. I grab her and pull her into me, wrapping my arms around her as she cries. As her sobs cleave through her. I squeeze my eyes shut and let the grief wash over me slowly. I hear her drop her book as her arms snake around me, clutching me tightly.

"You're not the only one who feels displaced and alone. *I'm* here. We're both grieving the same two people, Zoe. And we're all that's left of them."

She cries harder, and I squeeze her tighter as I rest my chin on the top of her head. *Fuck,* this is hard.

After Elias and Brooke got swept up in the flood, Zoe and I joined the search team. We didn't give up for over ninety hours—looking through the night, taking turns napping, staying positive. But when they found the bodies...

I'd never seen anyone so distraught. She was *fifteen.* The last thing she needed was to bury her parents. I was too busy grappling with their loss, getting lost in my very own darkness, to really *see* how hard this was on her. Not just imminently, but in her everyday life.

Staying at Thatcher instead of living with me.

Never coming home except for a day or two for holidays—because it wasn't her home, was it? It was mine, and despite knowing her since she was a baby, I wasn't *them.* I wasn't *family.*

The day of their funeral, Elias's estate manager gave me a copy of his and Brooke's will, listing me as Zoe's guardian should anything happen to them. I was flabbergasted; Elias had a sister, Carolina, and I assumed Zoe would go live with her.

But Elias left a note for me explaining why, and I was too much of a coward to open it.

I still haven't mustered up the courage to read it.

After she went back to school, I barely saw her shed a tear. Instead, she put on a brave face and continued with her daily routine. It made sense to me at the time, but now I realize she shoved that grief somewhere deep inside to get away from it.

I didn't see her for six months, only getting vague responses when I texted her and progress reports from school that said she was excelling in everything, as always.

Because that's what she does.

She excels at life.

But what about her emotions?

Would she ever slow down enough to properly grieve?

She never saw what I went through when I lost Elias and Brooke, so I could never model my grief for her. I'm now realizing that perhaps that was to her detriment. We never processed what happened together. Not really. Not beyond a few hugs and murmured words in the thickest of it.

I wish I could ask him, *why me?*

Why entrust the most important thing in your life to me?

I hunkered down and got through it, but she never saw the days I couldn't crawl out of bed. I did, eventually. My brothers needed me, so I was there for them. I'm the oldest, and since my father fucked off to France, I'm the one who's there when they need anything. It's how it's always been, and I don't mind it.

But Zoe? As I hug her, I realize she's been running from this for four years. The extra credit in high school, being the Valedictorian, graduating early, taking the LSATs later this month, using the fast-track lane for her life like she's trying to run away.

Because she is.

She stays busy so she doesn't have to think about her grief, or them.

"Go home," I say softly. "Sleep, order pizza, watch TV... *please*." My voice is hoarse as I let go of her small frame. "Whatever you do, don't go out."

She sniffles once and then nods. "Fine."

I pull my wallet out and hand her my credit card— one of the new ones. I'd had to replace my old ones after my wallet was stolen.

"Money for the pizza. You don't need to bring me a receipt this time."

She nods and pockets the card. My brow furrows at her lack of banter.

"On one condition," she says, looking so frail and tired. "Mark me absent, but don't excuse my absence."

"Zoe."

"Please. It's not fair."

I press my lips together, but I don't argue, knowing I'll do it anyway, whether she likes it or not. "Fine."

"I mean it," she adds, shoving her hands in the pockets of her overalls. My lips twitch as she rolls her eyes and sighs. "So overbearing," she murmurs, so low I almost think I don't hear correctly.

I kneel down and pick up the book she dropped, stunned into silence for a few beats.

"Percy Jackson? I thought it was too *trite* for you," I tease, handing the hardback to her as I stand up.

"I was hooked from the first chapter. Though I do wish Percy was a girl. Imagine a series about kickass demigod women?" Her face lights up. "That's not a terrible idea."

"And you're on the last book?"

She shrugs, beginning to walk away from me. "I read all the others in like two days."

I stand up straighter. "Wait, I want to know what you think of *The Titan's Curse*."

"Goodbye, Liam!" she shouts over her shoulder before disappearing around the corner.

Unease settles inside of me, and I debate whether or not to take the rest of the day off so I can be with her. But just then, one of the students from my class pokes his head out.

"Professor Ravage? I have a question about that Walt Whitman theory you explained in class last week?"

I glance back at the hallway once before turning to face Trevor. "Yeah. I'm coming."

Walking back into the class, I pull my phone out and quickly send a text to Carolina, Elias's sister, knowing she'll want to hear from me. I suggest the three of us get together for dinner soon.

Then, I check Zoe's location. Something tells me that she's going to do something crazy today, and I need to keep an eye on her.

Because if I don't, who will?

CHAPTER NINE

THE BAR

ZOE

Of course I don't wait for Liam to come home. Instead, I convince Scotty to take me to the swanky, newly-opened bar in Crestwood. I'm feeling way too emotionally raw to hang around his house and *wait*. I need to numb the pain the only way I know how.

When Scotty shows up just before six, I shoot a quick text to Liam.

> going out w scotty. b back late so please dont worry.

He doesn't respond right away.

Scotty leans over and kisses me before making the twenty-minute drive to Crestwood. We chat about his band and my classes, and I casually mention that I'm thinking about possibly doing a minor in English, because I'm enjoying Liam's poetry class so much. He tells me about his job working at The Stand, a fried chicken food truck. I'm holding my phone on my lap in case Liam responds, so when the phone vibrates against my bare thigh, I unlock it in record time.

> OVERLORD
>
> Jesus, Zoe. It's like you're incapable of doing what I ask you.

I smirk.

> dont wait up 4 me

> OVERLORD
>
> As long as you're living under my roof (and going out to drink illegally, I should add) I'll wait up until the moment you open the door.

My breath catches.

> promise 2b safe

> OVERLORD
>
> You know, there is such a thing as grammar and spellcheck for text messages. Maybe give it a whirl sometime.

My lips pull into a small smile.

> but its so much fun to mess w u

OVERLORD

It hurts my eyes.

does it trigger u

OVERLORD

Doesn't your phone have autocorrect?

turned it off

OVERLORD

Makes sense.

OVERLORD

Regarding tonight, I'll come pick you up
when you're done.

scotty can drive me home, but thx

OVERLORD

Absolutely not.

ill be fine. stop worrying. scotty will
drive me

OVERLORD

If he so much as looks at alcohol before
driving you, I'll murder him.

homicide is a crime

OVERLORD

And? I think you'll find I'd commit any
and all crimes to keep you safe.

Something heavy drops inside of my stomach before

exploding into a thousand, tiny butterflies. My skin heats as Scotty mumbles something about the parking situation at the club, but my mind is elsewhere.

> you cant go to prison because sushi would be sad

OVERLORD
> I don't think Captain would miss me if you were around to take care of him.

> id miss you, tho

I send it without thinking, and my cheeks burn hotter. Three dots appear, and I hold my breath until they disappear and reappear several times. *What are you trying to say, Liam?*

OVERLORD
> *I'd

OVERLORD
> *though.

OVERLORD
> Please. My soul is crying.

I laugh out loud at that, and Scotty leans over before I have a chance to hide my screen. I lock it quickly and look around, realizing that we're already parked behind the club.

"How's Liam?" Scotty asks, his dark eyes narrow as he watches me for my reaction.

I keep my expression neutral as I answer. "Fine. He was making sure I had a safe ride home."

Scotty chuckles, but it's not a kind laugh. His hands grip the steering wheel of his old truck.

"I know he doesn't trust me."

"He doesn't trust anyone," I offer, brushing it off.

"No, but he, like, really hates me," Scotty says, blowing out a frustrated breath of air as he looks forward.

"He doesn't. He's just overprotective. Hence his nickname in my phone." I say softly, reaching out for Scotty's hand on the wheel. He pulls it away from me, and I ignore the sting of rejection.

Scotty lets out a slow sigh before turning to face me again. "Overprotective? Or is he actually jealous?"

I bark a laugh. "Jealous? Of what?"

Scotty's jaw hardens. "Of us. He's always giving me back-handed compliments and insulting me under his breath. Don't get me started on the way he looks at you. It's beyond creepy."

My hackles rise on the back of my neck. "Hey, that's not fair."

"It's true. We all see it."

"We?" I ask, swallowing.

"Yeah. My band."

I try not to laugh. This whole conversation is ridiculous. The hackles from a second ago rise higher, and I suddenly feel the need to stand up for Liam. He's never crossed that line without my consent before, so there's nothing creepy about it. He'd stop the second I said no.

"Listen... Liam is the only thing I have left of my

parents. He was my dad's best friend. We're close, but it's not like *that*."

Liar, liar...

Scotty looks down at his lap, and for some reason I know what he's going to say before he says it.

"I don't want you being alone with him. He's like a predator. I mean, he's known you since you were a *baby,* Zo—"

"Stop," I snap. "You're being an asshole. And since when do you forbid me to see other guys?"

As he runs his hand over his mouth, I'm suddenly aware that his feelings for me have progressed past *hanging out.* And mine... haven't. Scotty is fun, but I'm nowhere near in love with him.

"I was thinking... we could... be exclusive," he mumbles.

I open and close my mouth. This is a far cry from a couple of months ago when we first met. I was at a munch with Orion, and Scotty was having drinks with friends. We happened to be waiting for the bathroom together, and one thing led to another...

He was supposed to be *fun.*

It was never supposed to be serious. It was never supposed to go beyond that. Scotty fit perfectly in the box I placed him in two months ago. A good time, good sex, and he was always willing to drive me where I needed to go, which was very kind of him. I never had to ask, either. He was aloof, but nice.

Still... I don't want to be exclusive.

Not with him.

There's only one person I'd ever consider being exclusive with.

The thought slams through me, but I push it so far back in my mind that I nearly give myself a headache.

"Scotty..." I trail off, working my lower lip between my teeth.

"You're not seeing anyone else, are you?" he asks quietly, almost hopefully.

I shake my head. "No, it's not that. I think that maybe we need to take some time apart. I don't know what I want, and this was only ever supposed to be casual."

Scotty's nostrils flare as he stares straight ahead. "Really, Zo? *Casual?* If that's how you see this, then maybe we should take some time apart," he growls.

I fight against the urge to apologize because I have nothing to apologize for. Instead, I grab my phone and pocket it.

"Are you still coming in?" I ask, nodding to the back door of the bar.

"No. Do you want me to drive you home or are you going inside alone?" he asks, looking at me with irritation.

Go home and face Liam? On today of all days? No, thank you.

"No. I'll grab a drink and call a cab later."

Scotty nods before I reach for the door. "Zo?"

I turn to look at him before climbing out. "Yeah?"

"Be careful. With Liam, I mean."

I press my lips together and shut the door without replying, because the truth is, Liam is the *only* person who makes me feel safe. I don't have to be careful, or whatever other narrative Scotty is trying to insinuate. *If* there's something blossoming between us, it's only because I've chipped away at his walls piece by piece over the last year.

A person can only take so much temptation before they give in.

He's not a predator. He's not pursuing me. He's *actively* fighting against it.

It makes me angry that someone else would see it in an entirely different light, and I stomp toward the door as my mind spins.

After I show the bouncer my fake ID, I walk into the bar and realize almost immediately that it was probably the wrong idea to come here alone. I feel eyes on me as I make my way through the bass-heavy electronic music, taking in the flashing lights, black velvet, gold accents, and people dressed to the nines clumsily stumbling around. I wish I could remember what this building used to be, but of course I don't spend enough time in Crestwood to know. It's large and open, almost like a warehouse, and despite the swanky atmosphere, the music is a bit too loud to be considered upscale.

As I make my way to the bar, I quickly text my aunt Carolina before scheduling a ride home on my rideshare app for three hours from now in case the alcohol hits harder than I expect it to. Because truthfully, between what just happened with Scotty, what's currently happening with Liam, and the fact that my parents have been dead for four whole years...

I start strong. Using Liam's credit card, I order two shots and throw them back on a nearly empty stomach. The alcohol does its job quickly, making my skin buzz before I've gotten to the dance floor. Tucking my phone into the waistband of my skirt, I decide that tonight, I don't give a fuck.

About *anything*.

I let go of my worries about grades and classes, LSATs and law school, being an orphan, Scotty, Liam...

This, tonight, is for *me*.

As I lift my arms, my silky red tank top rides up, exposing my stomach. My short, black skirt shifts against my thighs, and all I can think about as I dance with strangers is how it felt to have Liam's thigh between my legs.

How the last time I fully gave into music was when I was coming right in front of him.

How he *saw* me, how hard he was...

When the song ends, I walk to the bar and order two more shots, because I don't really want to think about him and how *nice* he is. How *polite* and *caring* he is.

Because it makes me want him more, and he doesn't want me, so what's the point?

This time, a slower song comes on, and the soft music hits a different chord. The events of tonight, of the last month, really, hit me all at once. My breathing gets labored as my eyes sting with tears. I'm just drunk enough to slink off to the bathroom, and the emotions of the day hit me all at once, square in the chest. I'm barely inside the stall when the hyperventilating begins. When the ache in my chest becomes too much, I almost scream for someone to call an ambulance. Tears stream down my face as the grief washes over me.

Four years.

Soon, it'll be five. Then ten. Then fifteen.

And I will have lived longer *without* them than with them.

The thought spirals until I'm crumpled on the floor, trying to mask my sobbing. A couple of people ask if I'm okay, but I don't answer. I wring my hands as I look up at the ceiling and let the tears fall into my tank top, wishing I'd joined them on that hike.

I'd been home for the weekend, which wasn't the norm. They'd planned this day hike in the woods behind Crestwood for weeks, and when the day came, I asked them if they should be hiking in the rain.

They offered to take me. My dad's face lit up when I considered it.

But I had to study for a big test on Monday; it was a social justice report for my American Politics class.

My dad had rubbed my hair before kissing the top of my head, calling me his *future little lawyer*, and my mom chuckled and pulled me in for a tight hug.

And then they left, and I never saw them again.

I cry harder as I remember it—as I think over what Liam said.

How I've been running away from the grief.

He's wrong, though. I let myself grieve on this day every year. I let myself *feel* it. Tomorrow, my life will go back to normal.

After cleaning myself up, I wash my hands and wipe the mascara tracks off of my cheeks. My eyes are bloodshot, but no one is going to know.

I order two more shots, and when I finish them, my stomach rolls in protest. Time blurs, and I have no idea how long I'm on the dance floor.

I dance.

I sing.

I jump around, forgetting that I'm an orphan for one day.

The taxi I scheduled comes and goes. I ignore the calls. The texts. They can charge Liam, I don't care.

I don't want to go back yet.

I don't want to forget them again... yet.

A man wraps his hands around my waist as we dance. My tank top is sticking to my back, but it doesn't matter. All I hear is the bass, and all I feel is a stranger's hands on my hips.

I wish they were Liam's.

When I open my eyes, I'm sure I've manifested him somehow, because he's glaring at me from across the dance floor.

It's an illusion, I think.

But then there's a firm grip on my arm pulling me away from the man I'm dancing with, and when I stumble back into a hard chest, I know it's him before I can see him, because the scent of licorice and wood permeates my senses.

He drags me away and I let him, knowing he'll only be angrier if I fight him. I stare at the back of his head as we make our way through the crowd, and his ironclad grip on my wrist doesn't loosen.

How did he know I was here?

I'm about to shout and ask him over the music, but he pushes through one of the doors in the back hallway, and suddenly I'm staring at Orion leaning against a modern, wooden desk.

Well, that explains things.

I'm drunk off my ass, but I can put two and two together.

As Liam closes the office door, the heavy, thumping music lessens considerably. I'm still breathing heavily from dancing, so my chest rises and falls as I look between the oldest and youngest Ravage brother. It's the only sound for a few seconds until Orion pushes off the desk and pats Liam on the shoulder.

"Have fun with this," he says, cracking a small smile. When he looks down at me, his brows furrow for a second until his normal playboy smirk returns. "Sorry, Zoe. I had to call him when I saw you drinking. It's one thing for you to use your fake ID at the pub for munches, but this place is on a totally different level, and the bartenders could get in a lot of trouble for serving alcohol to a minor. Figured you'd want me to call Liam," he says. "Also, you were dancing with Ben Hearst," he adds.

He gives Liam one more apologetic look before he opens the door. The loud music shocks me for a second before he closes it behind him, and when I look at Liam, the near silence somehow louder than the music. His eyes slowly drag down my body, and they flash with something that makes me want to squirm.

"I was fine."

"Bullshit," Liam growls. "Ben Hearst? Really?"

My eyes blink slowly as I try to process the name. *That's* what he's mad about? Not the underage drinking? Either I have it all wrong, or Liam Ravage is more jealous than I thought.

"Who...?" I ask, slurring the one word slightly.

Liam looks away as he rubs his mouth in frustration. "I don't know him personally, but Orion and Chase are familiar with him. He's a predator and loves to take advantage of unsuspecting women." He shifts on his feet slightly. "Orion told me he's a fake Dominant, and he wasn't supposed to be here. He must've given a fake name."

I squint up at Liam. "I didn't have to give a name."

"Orion's rules dictate that women are allowed inside the club, but men have to register. It's a safety protocol."

"I see. Can we talk about how Orion has a *club*?" I slur. It never came up in conversation with him when we hung out last week.

Liam's lips twitch. "It's another one of his ventures."

"And he called you?" I mumble.

Liam's jaw rolls as his gaze flicks down to my chest for half a second. "He did."

I start to make a joke about how ironic it is that Orion, who is sober, opened a club... but then my drunken mind skirts over to what else Liam said.

"I'm trying to understand the problem with me going out."

"It's nearly two in the morning. My mind was unraveling with worry, Zoe," he growls. "Also, where the fuck is Scotty?"

I hardly hear his question, because the first part replays in my mind over and over.

My mind was unraveling with worry.

My mind was unraveling with worry.

My mind was unraveling with worry.

I'm not surprised, but the idea of Liam pacing the house because he was *worried* about me...

The swarm of butterflies I've been pushing away the last few weeks erupt inside of me, making me inhale sharply.

"Where is Scotty?" Liam asks again, taking a tiny step closer.

Almost like he's waiting for my answer.

My mind is buzzing with something heated, and everything seems like it's moving in slow motion. I take a deep, shuddering breath, realizing too late that Liam's scent is surrounding me now, and all I can think about is how much I want him to kiss me. Fuck me. Command me. *Devour* me.

"Scotty broke things off," I tell him honestly.

Confusion and... relief pass over his expression. And then... hunger. A low, deep hunger that makes my knees weak and my heart pound against my ribs. Liam makes a low noise in the back of his throat, and my core clenches at the sound. The pulsing begins between my legs and then radiates outward so my whole body seems to be thrumming with need. It sits between us in the air, like a lion waiting to pounce.

Liam expels his breath in a steady, slow hiss as he closes his eyes. "What happened?"

His voice is soft, and I know both sides of him are fighting to the death for dominance. The guardian—my father's best friend. The one who came here and told himself it was because he was looking out for me. It's fighting with the other side—the one who looks at me for a second too long in class. The one who knocked my knees apart at Scotty's show two weeks ago and let me grind against it as he watched me, spellbound.

The one who called me *his* good girl that night in Catalina while he fucked me against a wall.

I shrug. "He wanted more, and I didn't."

I don't tell him about the texts, or how it set Scotty off. I don't relay the things Scotty said. It's not important, anyway.

"Are you okay?" he asks.

The gentle way in which he asks—it's genuine. And that thought sends a wave of emotion to crash through me.

"I'm fine," I mutter. I look around the sparsely decorated office, taking in the computer, filing cabinet, and large, oak desk. "And I was fine here by myself, too," I add, looking up at Liam again.

Liam's eyes search mine for a second before he responds. "Are you sure? Because you don't look fine."

Of course. Because no matter how much I try to hide

myself away from him, he always manages to figure me out.

"Come on. Let's go home," he says. I open my mouth to protest, but Liam presses himself against me. "If Orion weren't here—or if I couldn't see your location—what do you think would've happened to you tonight, Zoe?"

"I would've called a taxi," I offer.

"You don't think Ben would've offered you a free ride home? And because you're drunk, you would've said yes," he growls, his breath fanning my face. "And you think he would've actually taken you home?"

I grind my teeth together. "That's a lot of assumed hypotheticals, Liam. I don't need you controlling my safety at all times. I can take care of myself."

"It's not about assuming hypotheticals. I'm not trying to control you. I want to make sure you're okay." He swallows, and I'm completely hypnotized being this close to him. *Feeling* his chest pressed against my face, hearing his quick, panting breaths. "I care about you, and I can't help but be overprotective," he adds.

His eyes pierce into mine when he looks down, and white-hot heat flares through me as his thumb, which is gripping the side of the desk I'm leaning against, brushes against my thigh.

"Liam."

"You're mine to protect. Let me do that for you, Zoe."

"I'm sick of being a burden," I whisper, the alcohol burning every hesitation and second guess away until the only thing that's left is the hard truth.

He moves slightly so that his warm, large hand is on

my bare thigh. And then... it snakes up past the hem a couple of inches.

The inferno inside of me explodes, and a breathy pant escapes past my lips.

"It's not a burden to look out for you. It's a privilege," he says slowly, removing his hand.

My hand shoots out and grips his, and as his eyes flash, I try to convey that I want him to keep going, to keep touching me.

I want him to go farther, past my soaking wet underwear.

I want him to feel how drenched he makes me.

Instead of moving away, though, his lips twitch slightly as he cocks his head. "If I wanted to keep going, I would've."

I let out a whimper at his dominance, and he continues.

"You may think you're in control here, but let me make one thing clear," he says, my grip on his hand tightening. "You don't get to decide when we cross this line. I do."

The controlled way with which he speaks only fuels my desire. Is *this* the Dom side of him coming out? Is this what it would be like with him? I nearly soak through my underwear at the thought.

I need this—need *him*.

He steps away, his cocky expression giving way to something solemn. "Today is hard for both of us, and I don't want to do something stupid." His eyes search mine for a second before he shakes his head. "We can't escape the grief this way, Zoe."

"Why not?" I ask, my voice breaking. Something cracks inside of me, spilling the grief from earlier. I know the tears will come before I can feel them, and his rejection doesn't help things. "Can't you tell how much I want y—"

"Stop," he growls, eyes narrowing. "You're drunk. I don't want you to regret this tomorrow, okay?"

Like last time?

Except... I didn't regret a thing.

"I won't," I protest, releasing a sob.

Liam sighs, and he looks genuinely concerned. "I can see the pain written all over your face. I don't want to be a distraction. And as much as I want..." He scrubs his hand over his mouth. "This isn't what you need."

I want to scream and shout like a petulant child that it *is* what I need, what I want, and the perfect way to distract me from the date, but I know he's right. If I told him that, I would only be proving his entire point.

I swipe at my cheeks as I take a couple of steadying breaths. "You're such a giver, but sometimes you take so much, too. Saying those things, your thumb... and then you rip it away." I push off the desk and cross my arms. "Either leave me be or do something about whatever this is between us. I'm fine. I can take care of myself. It's getting too hard to be around y-you when—" I stammer as a single tear runs down my face.

When I'm falling for you.

When I want you this much.

When I'm not quite sure how you *feel.*

"You can't fool me, Zoe," Liam says softly. "I know that look in your eyes. The one that says you're trying to be strong when you're falling apart inside."

Fuck.

His words tear through me, unzipping the part of my soul only he recognizes.

I start to sink down onto the ground, but Liam's arms are there to catch me before I fall, pulling me into a hug as I cry.

"I can't leave you alone," he says into my hair, the anguish in his voice making me cry harder. His hand comes to my hair, and he begins to run his fingers through my strands. "I can't stand by and watch you suffer alone. You. Have. Me," he finishes, his words resolute.

My crying subsides as he holds me, and when I go to wipe my face, I realize that I feel so much lighter after crying. It still hurts—the pain of losing my parents is like a gaping wound. But right now, after a night of drinking and crying and getting everything out on the table... I feel... almost okay.

"Let's go home," Liam says, pulling away.

His hand brushes against my cheek, and when his eyes find mine, his mystified expression mirrors my own.

CHAPTER TEN

THE ADVICE

LIAM

Three Weeks Later

"To Liam's mid-life crisis," Chase says, a rueful smile on his lips.

I scowl and clink my beer with his whiskey and Orion's soda water, regretting the idea of going out to Orion's new club with my two youngest brothers. But I hardly see Chase anymore since he and his wife, Juliet, moved up to Northern California.

"Fuck off," I grumble. "And what, exactly, is this mid-life crisis you're referring to?"

"Right, about that..." Orion mumbles, looking at Chase before turning back to me with an apologetic smirk. His arm is slung casually over the back of the VIP booth, one leg crossed over the other, showing off the holes in his jeans and converse. I suppose if you *buy* an entire franchise of struggling businesses in cash, including this bar, you can wear whatever you want. "He knows everything."

I stiffen as I press my lips together. "You're going to have to be more specific."

There's no way they know about Catalina, right?

"I know about the quiz," Chase says in a low voice.

Ah.

He leans forward in his seat across the table from me. Unlike Orion, he's in a dark blue three-piece suit that I'm sure cost him more than most people make in a month.

I glare at Orion as I take a large sip of beer. "So much for the NDA, then."

"He asked how you were, and I told him you were pining over your ward and struggling with your dominant side..."

"Okay, that's enough," I bark, using my big brotherly voice.

"That's why I invited him," Chase says confidently, gesturing to Orion. "Figured you could ask us anything. You know, as the two other Dominants in the family."

Wonderful.

Just your run-of-the-mill family gathering where we discuss BDSM and sex.

"And here I was thinking my two baby brothers wanted to *see* me," I tease, smiling. I can't help that my interest is piqued, though. Despite doing my own research, a lot about the *lifestyle* still confuses me.

Maybe they have a point.

Maybe they can clarify some of the questions I have.

"So, Zoe is a submissive," Orion states factually. "How does that make you feel?"

I grunt. "All sorts of things I shouldn't be feeling."

Chase chuckles. "Sounds about right."

I eye my second youngest brother as I take another sip of beer. "How did you... and Juliet..."

Should I be asking him?

He doesn't hesitate, though. He clears his throat and sets his empty glass down.

"We were sort of opposite of you and Zoe. I knew I was a Dom, and she discovered her submissive side through me."

I take in his words, already knowing the gist of how they got together. Then, I pivot my gaze to Orion.

"And you? Is there someone...?" My question is intended to be open-ended.

Orion stares down at his nearly full glass of soda water. His finger traces the rim of the crystal glass, and his whole demeanor seems to change.

"No," he says, a small smile tugging at his lips. "It's just for me."

"One day," Chase offers.

But I don't miss the way Orion's brow furrows slightly as he continues to trace the rim of his glass. He must notice my gaze because he looks up at me and smirks.

"Don't give me that look."

I roll my tongue along the inside of my cheek before finishing my beer. "Seen any good ballets lately?" I ask, narrowing my eyes.

Orion's expression drops into a frown. "Not really."

Chase looks between us as if he's waiting for someone to fill him in, but I don't indulge him. Orion's obsession with Layla, his stepsister, well, technically *our* stepsister, but I'd only met her a few times, was not a new thing.

She just so happens to be a ballet dancer, and I know Orion likes to attend the shows when he can.

But I only know about that through sheer determination. None of the other brothers know about his little habit, but as long as it's not drinking again, I don't care how much of a stalker he appears to be.

"Are we going to acknowledge the elephant in the room?" Orion asks, eyes boring into mine.

"Right," Chase says slowly, looking back at me. "Tell us about Zoe."

Now it's my turn to look down at my empty beer glass. "What about her?"

"You have feelings for her," Orion says confidently.

I open my mouth to argue, but then I remember how *fucking* turned on I was at Scotty's concert, and in Catalina...

And it's not just physical, either.

I care about her as much, if not more, than my own brothers. Despite not seeing much of her these last few weeks, I check her location obsessively to make sure she's home safe. My eyes search for her when I walk into every Tuesday and Thursday morning class. I smile whenever I see that she has attempted to make me dinner and packaged the leftovers in the fridge, or when there's a new pile of clean laundry on my bed.

And I definitely can't deny the way my eyes linger on her whenever we're in the same room or the spike of adrenaline whenever she's close by.

"And?" I ask as a server brings Chase and me another drink.

I see Orion slip him cash before the server ducks out of our private booth.

"And she likes you, too?" Chase asks.

"Yes," Orion answers. I scowl at him, but he chuckles and sips his water. "It's so fucking obvious. It has been for months, if not years. I thought you knew."

I take two large sips of beer. "It's possible I knew she had a little crush," I admit. "But she was—she *is*—so fucking young."

"Listen," Chase starts, leaning closer. "Juliet is six years younger than me."

"And Stella is eight years younger than Miles," Orion adds.

"That's nothing," I mutter, taking another sip of beer. At this rate, the club will run out of beer before I'm done spilling my guts to my brothers. "Zoe is twenty years younger than me. I held her in the hospital right after she was born. I was already a full-fledged adult by then," I add. The usual guilt and loathing claw at my stomach as I say the words out loud.

"I thought you might say that," Chase says quickly, pulling his phone out. "I compiled a list of why this might be the best thing that's ever happened to you."

Orion snorts. "You're turning more into Juliet every day," he tells Chase.

Chase frowns as he looks down at his phone. "There's a time and a place for lists. This is one of them. First, did you know that couples with a large age gap communicate better?"

My lips twitch as I realize Orion is right. Chase is morphing into his wife with every passing day. Soon, they'll be one homogenous blob of flesh.

"Second, relationships that carry a stigma tend to have higher levels of commitment than relationships that are more traditional. Third, people with a large age gap tend to live longer than other couples—"

"Alright, I get it," I grumble. "And I might actually consider it if she weren't Elias's daughter."

Chase looks at Orion, and they share a look. I *know* that look.

Pity.

Both Zoe and I got a lot of those fucking looks four years ago. It hits me then that despite my brothers having empathy for our situation and helping out with Zoe whenever they were needed, they didn't *actually* know. They *couldn't* know. What Zoe and I went through, what *she* went through... they weren't there when she would come home for holidays and act like a zombie, or plaster on a fake smile. They weren't there when I couldn't get out of bed, even though I know they tried their best. For a while I could barely breathe from the grief and the weight of responsibility bearing down on me.

Though I have my depression and anxiety under control now, the way with which Zoe came into my life —and my home, permanently—couldn't be overlooked.

"Juliet is my best friend's sister," Chase says after a minute of having a silent conversation with Orion. "Miles and Estelle were an arranged marriage..."

"Technically I'd call it a marriage of convenience," Orion interjects, grinning.

"I get it," I tell them honestly.

"Look, you're sort of past the point of no return," Orion replies. "She's pining after you, and you're pining after her. I saw the way you two were eye fucking in the pub a few weeks ago."

"Uh, that was not eye fucking."

"Definite eye fucking," Orion grumbles, leaning back. "It's done now. You've crossed the line. From now on, it's a matter of *how* you're going to cross the finish line."

"I don't know how to start."

"First of all, safe words. Zoe is adamant about consent and limits."

My eyes widen with horror. "I'd sure hope so."

"It's something you'll want to discuss together. Most of your time is going to be spent communicating, so both of you knowing the safe words is pivotal," Chase adds. "As for aftercare, it depends. You should ask her what she prefers, because she's been active in the lifestyle for about a year, so she knows what she's doing."

I grab Chase's whiskey, much to his chagrin, and slam the rest of it down. "Okay."

"Zoe likes to brat out sometimes, so don't be afraid to punish her," Orion says.

I could've told him she was a brat. Not only has she been testing me for months by walking around in skimpy towels and making miscellaneous charges on her emergency credit card, she's also been mouthier and more argumentative as of late. Her last poetry assignment, which I hadn't graded but had looked over, was an erotic retelling of Romeo and Juliet in sonnet form.

She'd titled it *Catalina.*

My jaw tenses. "Punish her, how?"

"Light spanking—since you're all about pleasure—and maybe some teasing. Toys. Sensory play. Anything that gives her pleasure, since that's your thing," Orion explains. "Chase and I can send you our contracts so you can go through the kinds of things you both like."

I rub my eyes and heave a heavy sigh as I imagine Zoe on my bed, hands tied up as she writhes underneath me...

"Fine. What else?" I ask, suddenly overwhelmed.

This conversation, mixed with my own research, is making me want to do very bad, very unreasonably sporadic things.

Like walking up behind Zoe when she's doing dishes and sliding my hand down her pants to touch her soft, warm thighs. Remembering the night of the club, how I'd allowed myself to touch a bit *more* of her...

I'd reprimanded myself for that later—that one, single touch.

Still, my mind is spinning with how I could ask to see

her in my office after class and then pushing her up against the door, fucking her against it.

My raging hard on presses against my pants painfully, throbbing with desire.

I haven't let myself think of whatever this dominant side of me is in relation to Zoe. It's always been thought about in some sort of abstract way, always a faceless woman, always someone I don't know. It's still so new, and it's still too raw to bring Zoe into it.

But when Zoe enters the equation, it makes me want to go straight home and show her how much I want her to submit to me.

Suddenly, all I can think about is doing just that.

Watching her mouth drop open again.

Because I'm positive that watching Zoe come, four times, now, will haunt me until I can do it again.

And again.

And *again*.

"Tomorrow is the Halloween party," Chase suggests. "Maybe it's time you make your first move. Think about it."

"If she doesn't make it first," Orion mumbles, giving me a cocky grin before sliding out of the booth to get more water.

"What's up with him?" Chase asks after a few seconds.

I shrug. "Layla."

He makes a humming sound, but before he can ask the questions I've promised not to tell, I open my mouth to speak.

"When you... with Juliet... was it weird?" I ask. "To be a Dom for someone you'd known for years?"

Chase considers my question for a minute. "It wasn't weird at all. I think we'd had enough built-up tension that when it happened, it came naturally," he explains.

"Understandable," I say, thinking of Catalina.

"Listen, I don't know Zoe that well. I didn't know Elias that well, either so maybe I'm overstepping. But at the end of the day, he would want you to be happy. Both of you."

I consider his words as I play with the label of my beer. Neither of us says anything until Orion opens the velvet curtain and slides into the booth with us again.

"What did I miss?" he asks, taking a sip of his soda water.

I look at Chase and he shrugs. "Nothing. So, tell me again why you bought a bar?"

CHAPTER ELEVEN
THE TEST

ZOE

The tension with Liam has only grown over the three weeks since he drove me home from the club. It doesn't help that the LSATs are coming up, so without Scotty as a distraction, I spend all of my free time studying. I'd gone over most of the studying this summer, before classes began, but this month I decide to do a couple of mock tests every week to refresh my memory, and despite scoring highly, I still worry that I'm going to walk away with a low score.

On top of everything going on, the idea for my fantasy book continues to knock around my brain, most notably when I'm in Liam's class. He's been extremely distant, and though I see him in class, he leaves before the class ends. He's also not home at dinnertime, something that's particularly unusual. Before, even with the added tension, we seemed to settle into a routine again after a few days. But now it's like I'm living with a ghost. He's gone before I leave in the morning, and he doesn't come home until midnight most nights, just as I'm getting into bed.

I don't want to think of where *else* he could be going, or what he could be *doing*, for that matter.

No matter what time he leaves or comes home, though, one of Liam's brothers, Stella, or Layla offers to pick me up and drop me off from Crestwood University every day.

Instead of fretting over what his distance could signify, I throw myself into prepping for one of the biggest tests of my life—aside from the bar exam I'll have to take to become an actual lawyer. When my brain allows it, I also chip away at my fantasy world; I've added more words in the last three weeks than I have in months. I hardly have time to breathe, but the writing fills me in a way I can't describe. Somehow, the outpouring of creativity *helps* me with the mock tests and studying. It doesn't make sense, but I don't ask questions.

Lily, Ethan, and the villainous demon are with me before I fall asleep and when I wake up. In a weird way, it's nice having them bouncing around my head when I *should* be studying boring shit all day long.

The day of the test, I'm up at five in the morning going over my flashcards. Sushi is laying at my feet, his heavy, constant purr a comfort to my frazzled nerves.

Just as I'm about to stand up to brew another cup of coffee, Liam saunters into the kitchen.

Shirtless.

He stops when he sees me, looking almost embarrassed to see me. It hits me then that perhaps he has... company. My eyes flick behind him, but no one appears.

Instead, he walks over to the coffee machine and presses the button for a double espresso. Then he opens the cabinet and pops his pill before swallowing it dry.

I could ask him about it now...

"Morning," he says, his voice groggy. "You're up early."

"Um, yeah. I have my test at eight," I reply, shifting in my seat.

He turns around to face me while the machine makes his coffee. "Shit, of course. That's today."

"Yep." He nods, crossing his arms, and I try not to stare at his bare skin. "Late night?" I ask casually.

He rubs his eyes. "Yeah. Chase and Juliet are back this weekend for the party, so I went out with him and Orion last night."

Miles and Stella are throwing a small Halloween party at Ravage Castle tonight with all of the brothers, and though I'd agreed to go with Liam weeks ago, I'd forgotten it was tonight.

"Oh, right."

"Yeah." He nods again before turning back to the machine.

I hate how awkward it is between us now.

I haven't let myself ruminate about the night of the bar, at least not too much, because all I can think about is how rough his hand felt on my bare skin. How he *smelled* so fucking alluring. How he stood there and argued his way into my heart by telling me that he'd always look out for me.

You're mine to protect.

I can't leave you alone.

I squeeze my eyes shut as an idea forms. "Can you drive me tonight?" I ask.

He stops wiping up the machine as my words wash over him.

I don't think I've ever asked him for a ride before. To me, it's admitting defeat, like I can't take care of myself, and in fact *do* need him. I mean, I don't. I am a capable woman. But it feels like a peace offering. Something I've never done before.

He usually has to force my hand, but today, I'm holding mine out to him.

From here, with his back to me, I let my eyes linger on his bare skin—on the thick lines carved into his back, and how his waist tapers into the low-slung grey sweatpants he's wearing. I've never seen him naked, obviously, but I can imagine the way his wide back narrows and how his muscular thighs connect to his ass. I can *almost* see the outline through his sweatpants, too, and I feel like a pervert when he turns around and catches me staring.

My cheeks heat.

"Of course," he says, drinking his espresso. "As long as you won't be too tired."

I shrug. "The test ends around noon, so I can nap if I need to."

He considers this for a second before responding. "Okay. I'll drive you to the test and pick you up."

Apparently offering him one ride means he's driving me around all day.

"I already scheduled a ride."

"Cancel it," he says authoritatively. "Where's the test?"

"UCLA."

He nods. "Okay." Taking another sip of his espresso, he leans back against the counter fully. "It's a costume party tonight," he adds, his expression unreadable, like he's waiting for me to change my mind.

"I have a costume," I say quickly.

"Alright. Do you... need anything?" he asks, looking at the flashcards scattered across the island. "I could quiz you."

I shake my head. "No, I'm as prepared as I can be. But thanks."

His lips twitch. "Of course you are." He looks down at the floor, and despite my stomach being filled with nerves for the test, I can't help but feel calmer now that he's here.

Calmer because he'll be there before and after and because I have something to look forward to tonight.

He clears his throat as he looks up at me. I avert my gaze quickly. "What time do you need to leave?"

"Seven," I tell him. "The test starts at eight-thirty, but I have to be there at eight." I don't have to explain that despite UCLA only being thirty or so minutes away, I need to mentally prepare myself.

"I'll see you at seven," he says, giving me a small smile.

The tension dissipates slightly as he walks out of the kitchen, and I blow out a long, slow breath of air. I go through my flashcards twice, and as I hop up to make breakfast, Liam walks back in the kitchen, buttoning his dark blue flannel. My eyes quickly take in his dark grey jeans and wet hair as a whiff of licorice permeates my senses. The smell makes me think about him showering in his large shower, and *that* makes me think of what else he does in the shower.

I quickly push it out of my mind.

After today, I will be free to think about Liam doing all sorts of inappropriate things underneath a stream of hot water. But right now, my sole focus needs to be on reasoning and comprehension. It doesn't matter that I find all of it boring as hell—it's something I need to do before I apply to law school. These steps have been pre-programmed into me for years. Today is *the* day.

"I'll make breakfast," he says, pulling a pan from under the stove. "Eggs? French toast? What sounds good?"

"Honestly, I'm too nervous to eat."

"You need food. I'll make French toast with some fruit and yogurt for protein."

My lips twitch. "Sure. Thank you."

He begins to prep the bread and eggs, and then I see

him shaking his head. "Like I would let you take the LSATs on an empty stomach," he grumbles.

I laugh. "I meant to ask earlier, but what's your costume?"

"You'll have to wait and see," he answers, his voice gravelly.

"I'll go get dressed," I say quickly, hopping off the stool. I've been sitting for the better part of two hours. Sushi stands and stretches, sauntering off into another room.

As I stretch, I realize my mistake immediately. Liam turns around and drops the spatula when he sees me.

Instead of my normal robe and flannel bottoms, I am wearing a cropped sleep sweater and tiny bike shorts. I assumed I wouldn't be seeing him this morning—like every morning for the last three weeks—so I hadn't bothered to wear actual pants.

His mouth drops open a fraction before his hooded eyes find mine, and then he bends down to pick the spatula up.

I pass by him as I leave the kitchen, and I swear the air between us is electrically charged.

Once I'm clean and wearing black leggings and a brick-red UCLA sweatshirt, I pull my hair into a loose bun. I figured I'd better manifest my future with the UCLA sweatshirt. This test will determine if I'll be able to apply for next fall, after all. Besides, I've been so... *blah* about the whole thing. This sweatshirt reminds me of what I'm working so hard for.

I need the reminder of *why* I'm doing this.

But... to make it fair, I also grab the ring I bought a couple of weeks ago. Someone on campus was making rings out of old forks, and this one has a purple stone that reminds me of my fantasy book.

After tucking my phone into the pocket of my leggings, I head downstairs to find two massive pieces of French toast, strawberries, blueberries, and bananas on top with a sprinkle of powdered sugar. There's also a bowl of my favorite plain yogurt.

I sit as Liam brings me another coffee. "It's a plain latte. I know you like the caramel syrup, but the last thing you need is a sugar crash," he lectures, pushing the mug to me.

As I take in the food and coffee, I can't help but be grateful for him. Grateful that not only does he take such good care of me, but he's *invested* enough to know how to maximize the results of the test.

"Thank you," I say quietly.

I eat as much as I can on a nervous stomach, which is more than I expected. Liam eats silently next to me. After finishing the coffee, I use the restroom and grab my wallet for my ID. Once outside, Liam leans over the seat and opens my door for me, and we drive to Westwood listening to a playlist I created to gear myself up for the test. Liam pulls off the road and into the parking lot for the test, and because we're thirty minutes early, he turns the car off and looks at me.

"Nervous? Excited? How can I help?"

I smile. "I'm okay, actually. I want to get it over with so I can focus on other things."

Like my book.

And figuring out what the hell is going on between us.

He opens his mouth to say something, but he must change his mind because he leans over and opens my door. I go still as his shoulder presses into me, and I can't help but love the feeling of him being so close.

Pulling away quickly, he nods to my open door. "Might as well go wait outside the door. Come on. I'll walk you."

I follow him through the parking lot, following a few people onto campus. He walks beside me as we follow the signs for the testing center, and once we approach the building, he turns to face me.

"Are you sure you want to do this, Zoe?"

My brows furrow as I look up at him. "Of course. Why wouldn't I be sure?"

What I don't say is that I've been preparing for this for three years. That I've spent the last six months in a near-constant state of burnout, so giving up would be a waste of that time. That ever since I applied for college, I knew I wanted to become a lawyer like my parents.

That was years ago...

No.

This isn't about *me*. It's about my dad and honoring him.

I want to make him proud.

Liam sighs as he runs a hand through his hair. "That came out wrong. I mean... you don't have to go through with the test. If it's not something you want to do, no one here will care if you show up to that room in half an hour."

"I want to be a lawyer," I tell him defiantly. "My parents were lawyers, and I—"

"Zoe." His firm tone sends shivers down my spine, and any other conversation about this would have me aroused. Instead, I'm irritated that he's throwing me off of my game before such an important test. "Your dad was my best friend. I know for a fact that he'd be proud of you no matter what you decide to do with your life. You don't need a law degree to prove anything."

I let his words roll over me. "I've wanted to be a lawyer my entire life," I respond, digging my feet in.

"And all I'm saying is, you're allowed to change your mind. Not just today, but any day. Life's short, little rebel."

He's... wrong. He's trying to play devil's advocate. I am *going* to be a lawyer, and I'm *going* to make my parents proud.

Besides... doing this is the only way I can still feel connected to them. They were both successful lawyers. In fact, watching my mom get ready to go to the office everyday was just one reason I aspired to be one.

I wanted to be just like her.

"I'm not going to change my mind," I say, and then I turn around and walk to the line forming in front of the door.

I try to ignore the way Liam takes a seat on a nearby fountain or how he watches me as the line slowly moves forward.

As I get closer, I lock every single thought about Liam and what we talked about in a small box in the back of my mind, clearing the way for the test. By the time I put my phone and wallet into the locker and take a seat at my designated desk, I'm calmer than I have been in weeks.

If I don't sit for this test, what would I *possibly* do with my life? I'd have to change my major—and I'd probably have to take more prerequisites for any other major. Was becoming a lawyer a dream I had as a child? I saw how happy my parents were. In California, I could make good money. I'd never have to worry about it again. I could find some niche of law that interested me enough to be fulfilling. I hadn't found it yet, but I would.

The more I let go of what Liam said, the calmer I feel. And when I open the test booklet and begin, a calm sense of duty overcomes me.

I worked hard for this. I kicked ass taking mock tests and staying up late to study. I'd ace this test and prove to myself that I could do anything.

I'm about to begin the reading comprehension part when two names on the page, a hypothetical scenario, pop out at me.

Lily and Ethan.

The names of my characters.

Seeing their names here, on *this* test... it suddenly crashes down on me, and my chest tightens.

Lily and Ethan are rival jewelers, and they need help litigating...

The blood drains from my face, and the words trail

off in my brain as I stare down at the paper. I've never had an out of body experience before, but right now I'm having one. I can almost *see* my fidgeting feet, ankles crossed under the desk. I can *hear* the tapping of my pencil.

This is where I'm supposed to be. *Right?*

My skin is hot, and I remove my sweatshirt, leaving me in only a tank top. I crack my knuckles before I rub my eyes and look down at the booklet.

Lily and Ethan are rival jewelers, and they need help litigating...

I sit up straighter.

What if this is a sign? What if... Liam is right?

Fuck, I have to focus.

I finish reading the page, but I don't feel better. Not at all. Instead, sweat clings to my hairline as I squeeze my eyes closed.

My shallow breaths come quicker, and my grip on the pencil nearly snaps it in half. Goosebumps erupt along my skin as I realize I'm having a panic attack.

Right in the fucking middle of taking the LSATs.

I have to get out of here.

I have to... be *anywhere* but here, with my predetermined future looming before me.

Because if I stay, I'll never let myself consider any other alternative.

Lily and Ethan.

The names aren't a coincidence.

I stand abruptly and walk over to the administrator, explaining that I'm not feeling well and that I'm forfeiting the exam. She starts to explain how I can reschedule for another test day, but I turn and walk out of the classroom before she finishes.

My breaths are heaving now, and it's like someone is sitting on my chest. I vaguely register the fact that I've left my sweatshirt on my desk, but I don't care.

It suddenly feels wrong.

The LSATs.

UCLA Law School.

Being a lawyer.

I'm hyperventilating as I push the double doors of the building open, and before I can look for him, Liam is there, gripping my arms.

"Zoe," he says, but it sounds like he's speaking to me from the other side of a tunnel.

I slide down the side of the building and put my face in my hands as I attempt to take steadying breaths, but it doesn't work.

Suddenly, Liam is crouching in front of me, and his large, warm hands are cupping my face gently.

"In for ten, out for ten," he murmurs.

I do as he says, inhaling for ten seconds before slowly exhaling. My racing heart begins to calm as I wipe my sweaty palms on my leggings. My whole body is trembling, and as I repeat the breathing, I finally let myself open my eyes and look up at Liam.

"Sorry—th-thank you—" I stutter.

"Let's go grab something to eat."

————

I don't know how he does it, but by the time we arrive in the student social lounge–which, fortunately for us, is open on a Saturday morning, I'm almost back to normal. My heart isn't racing anymore, and I'm no longer shaking, thanks to the fact that Liam pulled my arms through his flannel shirt and buttoned it up for me.

I have to roll the sleeves five times to get them to my elbows.

He finds us a table by a large window before he walks off, stating he's going to order us some breakfast burritos from one of the food places.

I sit down as everything comes crashing back to me.

Did I seriously walk out of the LSAT?

I don't have long to consider my chaotic energy, however, because soon Liam is back with a tray containing two massive burritos.

"Thank you. For helping me. I don't know what happened in there."

Liam doesn't touch his food, and when I look up at him, his brows are pinched with worry. "Have you always had anxiety, or is it a new thing?"

I huff a laugh. "Who doesn't have anxiety?" When he doesn't smile, I sigh and lean back against the hard, plastic chair. "I started getting anxiety attacks when I was little. They didn't happen often enough for medication, but I hold things in, and sometimes they come out like...like—" I gesture wildly to myself. "So no. It's not a new thing."

He considers my words for a minute before speaking. "Is it because of what I said?" he asks.

"Not really. Sort of. I don't know." I take a bite and look out of the window. When I finish, I look down at my lap, where my hand with the ring is resting. "In my fantasy book, my two main characters are Lily and Ethan. Well, and the demon, but I'm still not sure what to do with him," I add. "Anyway, everything you said was sort of rolling around in my mind when I sat down and began the test, and you'll never guess what two names popped up in the first section. It was *literally* the first sentence of the test."

"Lily and Ethan?" Liam offers, smirking.

I nod. "And I guess I sort of... panicked."

Had an existential crisis is more like it. Semantics.

Liam leans forward and clasps his hands together. He's wearing a plain white T-shirt that's entirely too tight to be decent, and I notice a few of the college-aged girls gawking in his direction.

"I have panic attacks too," he says slowly.

"Is that why you take medicine?" I blurt.

His lips quirk to the side. "Panic disorder and depression."

"That sucks," I mumble.

"I'm used to it now. The pills keep me even. You should talk to someone about it," he adds.

"I know." Swallowing, I ask another question. Or rather, make a statement. "You haven't written anything in over four years. Because of my parents?"

He looks over my shoulder, almost grimacing as he responds. "Yeah. I think I'm still in shock, to be honest. In one day, I lost my best friend and became a guardian."

"To me." The niggling thought about being a burden suddenly bursts through my consciousness, and I visibly wince.

Liam leans forward, and as I look him in the eyes, he gives me a solemn smile. "I didn't stop writing because I became your guardian. I stopped writing and had to go on medication because I lost my best friend. Because it reminded me—just like when my mom died—that life is too fucking short. One day they're there, and the next, they're gone. And quite frankly, I stopped seeing a point in writing. In creating. Why bother, you know?"

My eyes burn as I wait for him to continue.

"But... for the first time in years, I'm starting to feel like I might be okay. I've started dreaming about my books again, at least, so that's something."

"I dream about my books, too," I tell him, smiling softly.

We watch each other for a few intense beats before Liam clears his throat. "I meant what I said earlier. You becoming a lawyer isn't something that's predestined. You're allowed to change your mind."

"That's just... scary to think about," I admit, my voice a whisper. "For as long as I can remember, it's what I've been working toward."

"I know. But those names were on that test for a reason."

I chew on my bottom lip as I consider his words. The burrito isn't as good as I imagined it to be, and the bite I took a moment ago sits uneasily inside of me, making me slightly queasy.

Or maybe it's the quarter-life crisis; can you get those at nineteen?

"If money were no object, what would you want to do for a living?" he asks, blue-grey eyes boring into mine.

I shrug. "I'd probably write."

"Then write," he says, smiling.

A barrage of excited butterflies flits through me at the thought of being a *writer*. Of staying up late to meet a deadline, of carrying my laptop everywhere so that I can write in coffee shops or cafés. I'm suddenly dreaming of querying agents and selling my book for pennies, and the thought of *having* Lily and Ethan's story in my hands in the form of a physical book.

My smile widens, and I let out a nervous laugh. "Oh my god, I can't believe I walked out of the test because of a book," I say, nearly breathless again.

"But it feels good, right?" he asks, his voice low. "That excitement? I can see it in your eyes," he murmurs.

My heart skips a beat as his eyes peruse my face. Something soft and warm washes over me, and I'm suddenly so grateful for him.

"Liam, this is crazy," I say softly, leaning forward so that we're inches apart.

"What's crazier is that you were content to live a life without that excitement."

His words hit me like a ton of bricks.

I've been running toward the goal of being a lawyer for years without thinking of what I might *actually* want. Instead of moving forward, I'm clinging to some semblance of the past.

"You're right," I say, pushing the tray away.

For the first time in my life, I have an inkling of clarity. Something *tangible* and exciting is on the horizon. I have no idea what will happen with my book, or Lily, Ethan, and the demon, but it's insanely exciting to think about.

"It doesn't hurt to regroup and really think about what *you* want, Zoe. The world is your oyster," he adds, a mischievous glint in his eyes. "Take advantage of it. Life is short."

What would he say if I told him that I wanted him?

That I wanted to be held by his strong arms and see the look in his eye when I come.

That I want to do things for him and watch his mystified expression.

That I don't care where my life takes me, as long as he's by my side...

"Do you ever take your own advice?" I ask.

"I love teaching. And writing. It's the best of both worlds."

I take another bite before grimacing and wrapping the burrito up. "Why have you been avoiding me?" I ask quietly, after a few seconds of silence. Liam's brows pull together, but he doesn't answer me. I continue. "Before today, I've only really seen you in class," I start, wincing a bit.

God, I sound like an obsessed schoolgirl who has a crush on her professor.

"It's not easy to be around you, Zoe," he answers, his voice low as his eyes bore into mine.

I'm surprised at his honesty.

Then again, Liam has never played games. He's always candid, always telling me exactly how he feels. He doesn't have time for bullshit because he's above that.

"How so?" I whisper.

Sighing, he leans back in his chair and gives me a wounded look. "Because I'm no longer in control when I'm around you," he says, assessing me boldly.

My lips quirk up as my skin heats. "And you prefer being in control," I finish.

"Yes."

"Maybe losing control isn't such a bad thing," I offer.

The expression that falls over his face after I say that is almost *sad*. "You're right. I'm not going to beat around the bush," he murmurs, eyes blazing with... *something*. "The problem is, you're everything I want, and everything I can't have. Do you understand how *fucking* exhausting that is?"

Oh.

"Who says you can't have me?"

"You're so sure you want this," he says, voice low. "And yet you have no idea what you're getting yourself into."

He's wrong. Completely and utterly wrong. I do want this—with *him*.

"I enjoyed our time together in Catalina, and I know you did, too."

"Fuck, Zoe. Are we really going to talk about this now, in broad daylight?" My face falls a bit, and I hear him mutter *fuck* before rubbing his mouth. "I'm sorry. I know you've had an eventful morning."

"What are you so scared of?" I ask, tilting my head as he watches me.

"Careful. That's a loaded question," he purrs.

I squirm in my seat, but before I can get him to elaborate, he stands up and changes the subject.

"The burritos are garbage here anyway," he jokes. "You would've been unhappy here."

I laugh as we make our way back to the locker, where I retrieve my phone and wallet. I decide to leave my sweatshirt in the classroom because he's right.

Maybe UCLA was never for me.

As we walk to the car, he hands me a small, purple flower.

A violet.

"What's this?" I ask, taking the flower from his hand.

"It reminded me of you."

I almost ask if he remembers that I was wearing a violet behind my ear the night in Catalina, but I think better of it.

The rest of the walk is quiet, and when we get into the car, Liam's finger pauses over the *start* key, and I look up to find his eyes on me.

"I'm proud of you, little rebel," he says quietly, his voice a dark purr. "Really fucking proud of you."

If I were a peacock, I'd be preening at his words. Instead, I smile and blush, looking out of the window as he pulls out of the parking lot.

It also doesn't go unnoticed that praise seems to

come easily to him, and the entire drive back, I think of the kinds of things he would say to me in bed.

Because I'm no longer in control when I'm around you.

The problem is, you're everything I want, and everything I can't have.

He needs someone to push him. He's so stubborn that he won't act of his own accord unless he's inebriated, and it's not like I can force alcohol down his throat, knowing he refuses to drink around me.

But what else can I do to get his attention?

To show him, in his own way, that I want him?

Because as his large hand shifts us into third gear, and as my eyes peruse his corded arm, I can't help but be entirely worked up over the idea of him losing control again.

I have to see it, his face, his eyes...

I *need* him.

An idea begins to form in my mind. It's absolutely crazy, and like nothing I've ever done before, but without the weight of the LSATs and law school weighing on me, I feel... free.

For the first time in a long time.

And that freedom has given way to something dark and dangerous when it comes to Liam.

What I'm doing isn't working.

I have to make a *bigger* statement. I have to show him that I won't stop trying to pursue this thing between us. I can't. Not anymore. It went from a crush to something so massive that it scares the hell out of me, but his words from earlier ricochet inside of me.

Life is short.

I want him, and I know he wants me.

Plus, there's something about him that makes me want to keep pushing—keep beating against this barrier he's erected between us. We know each other well, and I've never done anything this big to provoke any of my past Doms. I don't have to pretend to be polite because he *knows* me better than anyone.

In a way, being around him is freeing.

He'll never make the first move, never find his way to me through the fog of the guilt and shame he carries inside of him.

So maybe I'm going to have to show him the way.

Maybe I'm going to have to do something so crazy, and it might backfire completely.

But... I have to try.

CHAPTER TWELVE

THE PROVOCATEUR

LIAM

I spend the rest of the day in the garage, working on a green 1966 Lamborghini Miura for Chase. Zoe asked me to drop her off in town, and didn't specify why, though I figured after the day she had, she could use a little time to herself. Besides, I promised my younger brother that I'd finish this car weeks ago.

I'd been too distracted by Zoe to actually work on it.

The hours of manual labor do nothing for my wandering mind, though. As I'm bent over the hood checking things over for the hundredth time, my mind still wanders to our conversation earlier.

It's getting harder and harder to resist, and with every interaction, my resolve crumples a little bit more. After Catalina, I'd built my walls up extra high—higher than before, to account for the mishap.

But I'd forgotten that Zoe wasn't the kind of woman to be deterred by a wall.

She would eventually figure out a way to climb over.

And truthfully, I'm not sure how much longer I can fortify my determination to stay away—not sure how much longer I'm going to *want* to stay away.

I'm starting to forget why I decided we'd be better apart when all it seems to do is cause problems.

Around five, she texts me that Layla is driving her home. And approximately two minutes later, I get a text from my bank.

> We've noticed some unusual activity on your card ending in 3117. Please confirm any recent purchases by logging into the app and contacting us if you have any questions.

Brows furrowed, I log in, only to see my balance in the mid five figures.

What the actual fuck.

Clicking over to recent transactions, my eyes go wide when I see most of them were made today.

Agent Provocateur: $12,456
Coco de Mer: $27,890
Bordelle: $15,127

My finger is on the call button before I fully process the charges. It's not like I don't have the money; thanks to my father, all four of my brothers and I have bank accounts in the billions. However, the fact that this is the card Zoe's been using...

It goes straight to voicemail.

Fuck.

Pocketing my phone, I finish up my work until Zoe gets home, my hands angrily gripping my tools. She's been using the card for a few weeks. I never bothered to ask for it back once I gave it to her, because for once she wasn't fighting me on taking my money. But $55,000? What, did she buy a fucking *boat* or something from one of these places? My mind is still reeling when I hear a car coming up the drive. I throw the wrench down on the concrete floor and walk up to the front of the garage, arms crossed. I don't care that I'm covered in grease.

My blood is *boiling.*

Just when we hit an impasse—just when I think we're on the same page—she goes and does something to drive me fucking mad.

I watch as Zoe exits Layla's car, walking to the trunk. She hoists multiple bags onto her arm, and I hear her tell Layla thank you before Layla drives away.

My jaw aches from where I'm grinding my teeth, and as my eyes scan over the shopping bags, I guess I have my answer about whether or not the purchases were legitimate.

"Care to explain?" I ask, startling Zoe.

She drops a bag onto the ground before turning to face me fully. "I went shopping," she says confidently, giving me a little smirk before picking the bag up and walking to the front door.

I don't fucking think so.

I follow her inside, shutting the door behind me a little too roughly as she makes her way to the kitchen. I watch as she offloads her bags onto the island; they take up most of the enormous slab of marble. After placing the last of them, she sighs.

"Those were heavy," she says, leaning against the counter.

She's still wearing my flannel from earlier, sleeves rolled up, and for the second time, the thought of her wearing my clothes sends a wave of possession through me.

"You didn't answer my question," I growl, pulling my phone out and unlocking it to show her the credit card balance. Stepping forward, I set it down on the island in front of her. "Is this some kind of joke?"

When she's done looking down, her eyes lift and bore into mine with a defiant gleam. "Of course not. I needed new underwear."

A low, deep rumble escapes my chest. "You mean to tell me that you spent fifty-five *thousand* dollars on... underwear?"

"Not just underwear. I got bras, corsets, toys, body-suits, harnesses—"

"Harnesses..." I rasp, my fists curling.

"Yeah. For my future Dom." When I don't respond, she tilts her head and gives me a look of what I can only describe as smug delight, as if she knows she's pushing every button I have and will ever have. "To tie me up," she adds, a sly smile spreading across her face.

My eyes flick over to the bags and then back to her, where she's still watching me.

Waiting for my reaction.

Because as much as she's pushed me, she's never gone this far before.

And she knows it.

That's the entire point, though, isn't it? She's trying to push me—trying to prove some kind of point after our conversation at UCLA earlier.

Build the wall, and she'll find a way to climb over it indeed.

Zoe taps one of the bags. "I happen to have a thing for nice lingerie. Don't worry, I asked for receipts," she adds, eyes sparkling.

No, not sparkling—*flashing* from the challenge.

Fifty-five thousand fucking dollars.

The resistance I've been maintaining since Catalina goes completely taut, and then it splinters when I think of her wearing those things. The tattered shards of my self-control go flying all around me, and I snap.

"Go ahead," I growl, gesturing to the bags. "Show me."

Her smile drops, and she looks down at the bags. "What? The lingerie?"

I cross my arms, and I see her eyes roam over my dirty white T-shirt, grease-stained hands and arms, and disheveled hair. And if I'm not mistaken, her lips part slightly from arousal, not disgust.

"Yes," I answer, my voice laced with dark venom. "Show me what my money bought, little rebel."

Her eyes flutter slightly, and her chest rises and falls. "But I'm not wearing it now," she says slowly.

I take another intimidating step closer, and she inhales so subtly that if I weren't so in tune with her reactions, I might've missed it.

"Show. Me."

My words sink in, and her nostrils flare as she reaches forward, grabbing something copper colored and lacy from one of the bags and setting it down in front of her.

My cock is so hard against the placket of my pants, and when Zoe glares at me while unbuttoning *my* flannel...

Fuck.

Slowly, she removes it, leaving her thin tank top underneath. Her hands come to the waistband of her leggings, and she slides them down to her feet, bending forward and stepping out of them.

I can't think—can't fucking concentrate—on anything other than her bare legs and tiny thong. Without breaking eye contact, she removes her tank top and bra, discarding them on the floor.

Then she steps out of her thong, and it takes every ounce of resistance to keep my feet planted on the kitchen floor.

She's completely naked in front of me, and I let my eyes rake over her body slowly. She's petite yet curvy and has an hourglass shape with round hips and muscular thighs. Her breasts are small and firm, and her taut nipples are light brown. My gaze wanders over her flat stomach to her soft, dark curls, and I swear I can smell her arousal from here.

She has a few tattoos that I didn't know about.

The tiny flower on her right collarbone is actually part of a delicate tattoo that loops around the outside of her breast and ends near her ribs. When she's wearing a shirt—even a tank top—you can only see the top.

There's also a smiling, cartoon cat face on her hip, and a smattering of hearts along her left ribcage.

Smiling slightly, she takes the copper colored set and pulls on a delicate-looking copper and black lace thong, letting the luxe material snap against her hip bone. Then she pulls on a matching bra, clasping it behind her back. The cups are made of frilly copper lace, and the silk straps form a triangle above her breasts, meeting and forming a bow. She grabs the largest piece—what looks to be a corset—and holds it out to me.

"I need your help with this one," she murmurs.

Taking a step forward, I grab the corset from her. "Turn around and put your hands on the cabinet."

Her cheeks are flushed and she's watching me with a smoldering expression. She does as I say, turning slowly and placing her small hands above her head on the wood cabinet above her.

"Stay still," I murmur, leaning down close to her ear.

"Be careful," she whispers. "It's Chantilly lace, and it's made with Swarovski crystals. You might want to wash your dirty hands," she adds.

"And how much, exactly, did this little piece cost you?" I ask, my voice low.

"Twenty-five hundred dollars."

I let out a low whistle. "It would be a shame to ruin something so luxurious."

Before she can react, I take the corset from her hands and bring it around her front, fastening it one clasp at a time. Every time I touch her, she shivers, and I chuckle as I drag a finger down her spine, marking her with black grease—and making her shudder and gasp.

My cock is a heavy, pulsing knot, and I swear when I'm around her, I'm drunk with desire.

When I finish clasping the corset, which is tight but not restrictive, she turns around and takes the hair tie out of her hair.

Fuuuuck. Me.

The copper lace is the exact shade of her eyes, and it also brings out the golden undertones in her skin. Her dark hair cascades down past her shoulders. Crossing her legs, she leans back against the counter.

"So? Are you happy with your purchases?" she asks, her voice husky.

"It depends on who they're for," I respond, watching her reaction.

"I told you. For my future Dom," she says, a snarky tone to her voice.

My jaw hardens. I take a step closer—so close I can smell her shampoo. *Violets.* Why do violets always remind me of her, of that night? Her breathing hitches when I stop an inch away from her, and as I peer down at her face, I realize that her normally light brown eyes are nearly black right now.

"Are you trying to rile me up, Zoe? Is that what this is about? You want me to be your Dom?"

"No," she argues, eyes full of mischief. "You're too polite to be my Dom, Liam."

I smile. "You're right. I am polite. Just not in bed."

Zoe goes still at my words, but before I walk away, I admire the way her eyes soften, the way she seems to lean closer into me. All signs she's comfortable with me. All signs she'd submit to me if I asked her to. And that fact alone blows my mind more than anything—that she doesn't seem to struggle with her submission at all. She *embraces* it. In real life, she's one of the smartest people I've ever met. Her mind is filled with maturity and intelligence that have taken me two decades to achieve.

She could *do* anything.

Be with anyone.

And yet...

If I asked her to kneel before me, I know she'd do it without hesitation.

That thought alone has me so hard it's painful.

I walk away and go upstairs, mumbling something about showering and changing into my costume for tonight's party. Instead, I walk into my bathroom and shut the door, unbuckling my pants, and unsheathing my cock before I can start the shower.

Images of her naked body float through my mind, and I piece it together with how it felt to be inside of her.

I think of what I would've done downstairs, how I would've made her scream, how I'd mark and claw that pretty lingerie up and be glad for it. I *wanted* to show her the consequences of her actions.

I think of all the ways I want to watch her come apart —all the fun I could have torturing her with pleasure. Of utilizing the power play to make her come over, and over, and over.

And I think of sinking my cock into her cunt again, sliding in slowly and watching her mouth pop open.

Feeling the velvety sensation of her pussy squeezing me. Remembering how tight she was that night.

Watching her eyes roll into the back of her head.

Again.

My balls tighten, and my cock throbs with my imminent release when I think of how she'd look spread out before me as I feast on her right after she comes.

Of her twitching body, of making her *scream* the way I know she's capable of.

A low groan escapes my lips when my cock curves up and in, and I squeeze my eyes shut as pleasure claws up my spine. Hot jets of cum paint the marble floor of my bathroom, and it seems like I come for over a minute straight. When I finally recover from my orgasm, I tuck myself away and clean up, washing my hands and splashing my face with cold water.

Fuck.

At this point, we've said *fuck you* to the line I drew for us in Catalina, so I might as well embrace it.

If I'm going to toe the edge of insanity, I might as well get a running start and leap off the edge with zero abandon.

When I'm done showering, I change quickly—a white oxford, tan khakis, and a tweed jacket for Miles and Stella's Halloween party tonight. I pull my glasses on and grab the ruler I'd nicked from Crestwood University before heading downstairs. The bags of lingerie are still on the island, but Zoe is nowhere to be found.

The only evidence that she was here is a note next to the ruined, stained set she was wearing earlier. The delicate lace is smudged with grease.

I hope you know that this means you're buying me a replacement.

Fucking brat.

Smirking, I pick one of the black bags and peek inside. A few boxes are stacked up underneath some tissue paper, and I pull a black velvet box open. I use my thumb to snap it open, and the lid unhinges. Using my other hand, I lift the lid and look inside. My brows furrow, but before I can process what I'm looking at, Zoe walks into the kitchen.

Wearing a witch costume.

A short, black skirt, white button-up, a black tie, and a cape. Underneath the pointy hat, her hair is pulled back into two French braids, and she's wearing dark lipstick.

My brain short circuits, and I nearly drop the box. *This* is somehow hotter than crystal lingerie. She doesn't seem to notice because she's looking down at her phone, but when her eyes find mine, she gives me a knowing smirk.

"You're not dressed up," she says, pouting as her eyes rake over my costume.

"Of course I am. I'm a professor."

Her eyes flick to the ruler in my pocket. Crossing her arms and legs, she tilts her head slightly, propping one leg out of her black skirt.

"Do you have a ruler in case you need to punish a pupil?" she asks, her voice husky as she plays with one of her braids.

Fuck.

"Perhaps," I mutter, taking the ruler and placing it in my jacket pocket. Her eyes track my movements, and when they find my eyes again, she's watching me with a gleam of interest. "But I only dole out punishment for the pupils who misbehave."

"That's too bad," she adds, smirking.

Dammit.

I let my eyes trail down to her bare legs and platform loafers... "You forgot your wand," I add, my heart racing inside of my chest the longer I look at her.

She walks over to me and lifts her skirt slightly, exposing her golden thigh, which has a holster on the outside of her left leg that's holding a wooden wand.

Kill.

Me.

Now.

She's literally trying to give me a heart attack.

"Layla is going as a vampire tonight, so I agreed to go as a witch. She doesn't know that Orion is *also* going as a vampire," she adds.

"Are you meddling?" I ask her, smiling.

She shrugs. "I may have given them both a little nudge."

"Of course you did," I mumble, thinking that perhaps she's spent too much time with Miles these last few weeks, considering he's the biggest meddler of us all.

"What are you looking at?" she asks, pointing to the black box in my hand that I'd nearly forgotten about. I hold it up, and she smiles. "It's a wearable vibrator," Zoe answers. "It comes with a remote that someone else controls."

I peer down at the box again, and my thumb grazes the black and gold remote.

"Where's the vibrator?" I ask, blood rushing south.

Zoe steps forward and takes the remote. Her eyes bloom with darkness as she holds the remote out to me, and everything clicks.

Fuck—she's already wearing it, isn't she?

My mind spins with an explosion of words and phrases. Safe word. Consent. Brat. Punish. But none of it sticks. I'm *not* Chase or Orion. I'm not about to make her sign a contract before I make her come so many times, she'll see stars.

But fuck, I want this control.

I don't say anything as she slips the remote into my jacket pocket, all while giving me a devious, little smirk.

And then she turns and walks away, leaving me with

clenched fists and an erection so hard I worry it'll never go down.

When I hear the front door open, I take a stuttering breath, willing my cock to calm down.

Zoe is going to push me to the breaking point until we both get exactly what we want—which means I'll have to show her how far I'm willing to go.

Once we cross that line, there's no going back for me.

CHAPTER THIRTEEN
THE POSSESSION

Liam

The car ride to Ravage Castle is quiet, so by the time I get onto the main road, I decide to break the tension a bit.

"How are you feeling? About the LSATs," I clarify.

"Good. Really good. I didn't realize how stressed the LSATs were making me, and now that I've removed law school from the table, it's a huge relief."

"And your book?"

"I really like where the story is going."

"Any chance you'll let me read it?"

She laughs. It's a low, deep sound that I don't hear enough. "No way in hell. You write literary fiction, and my book has some magic, but it's mostly fluff and smut."

"So? You think I've never read fluff and smut?"

"Have you?" she asks, eyes sparkling when I stop at a light and glance at her.

"Of course. I read everything."

"Name one smut book you've read," she challenges.

Fortunately for her, I'm not lying, and I'm ready to prove her wrong. "Stella roped me into her smut book club a few weeks ago. I'd asked her for recommendations for BDSM books, and somehow now we're meeting every other Monday night to talk about tropes and book boyfriends with some of her friends."

"BDSM books?" she asks.

"Yep," I answer.

I fucking *love* the way I can hear her inhale sharply at that.

"Like what?" she asks.

I grin. "I'll send you recommendations," I reply, realizing too late that we're flirting. "If you want them."

"I'll take you up on that. But no, you can't read my book. No one can. Ever."

I chuckle as I turn onto the main road, and we lapse into silence again.

A few minutes later, I valet my Jeep as Zoe and I walk into the place I called home for eighteen years. It looks nothing like it used to, all thanks to Stella. She's infused the entire building with color and personality. What used to be an imposing stone castle is now bright and cheery with daisies, tulips, and roses at every corner. Instead of the gravel I grew up with, the surrounding area around the castle is made up of drought-friendly succulents and plants, trees, and fountains. Zoe's been to the castle a few times since I became her guardian, but

Stella really went out of her way to brighten the place up recently.

As we walk in, there's a table filled with yellow and orange tulips, and piles of candy corn. The marble floors are adorned with bright, patterned rugs, and I swear there's a new pink couch somewhere every time I come over.

"Looks like we're the first people here," Zoe says, arms crossed as she takes in her surroundings.

"Miles, get your bloody arse down here before I have to come up there and style your perfect hair for you—"

Stella comes around the corner holding Beatrix, the nine-month-old daughter she and Miles share, on her hip. She's wearing a black one-piece unitard with cat ears, a black nose, and whiskers. Bea is dressed as a mouse, and it's fucking adorable.

"Oh my god!" She chuckles, walking straight toward me and handing me my favorite person in the whole world—other than Zoe, that is. I settle Bea against my chest. "Miles is taking forever up there, and I still have the slime and eyeballs to make," she says, exasperated. "Would you mind looking after her until my husband's pompous arse makes an appearance?"

Zoe snorts, and I try to hold my laugh in. "Of course. Are we the first people here?"

Stella makes a waving motion with her hand. "No. Orion, Layla, and her guest are in the kitchen." She looks at me. "Can you please go get your exasperating brother?" she asks me. "And Zoe, would you mind helping us with the meat in the kitchen?"

We share a look. *Meat* could mean anything, and Zoe's lips twitch as she follows Stella to the kitchen on the other side of the castle, the remote in my pocket forgotten temporarily.

As they're walking away, I look down at Beatrix, who is smiling at me with all four of her teeth. She has wild, blonde curls like her mom, but her large, green eyes are all Miles.

"So, what's new with you?" I ask Bea, my voice soft. When I look up, Zoe is looking over her shoulder at me as she walks away, and something heavy settles in my chest at the affectionate look on her face.

"I'm in trouble," I tell my niece, my voice low so Zoe and Estelle don't hear me. "So much fuc—*freaking* trouble."

Since Estelle, Zoe, Orion, Layla, and her mysterious guest are in the kitchen, I head upstairs with Bea to grab a CD from my old bedroom. When I went to college at eighteen, I left a lot of things here and never moved my things to my own house. Bea warbles and places her little hands on my face, making my glasses go askew as I walk to one of the large bedrooms on the top floor—the bedrooms that were used by Chase when he used to live in Crestwood, and before Estelle lived here, too.

I push my bedroom door open, and a wave of nostalgia washes over me. Suddenly, I'm sixteen again listening to my first Good Charlotte album on my CD player—which still sits on my desk. My sheets are black with white anarchy symbols all over them. There are

Vans Warped Tour posters from 2001 until I stopped going a few years after that.

There's a massive bookcase piled with CDs, too.

"Which CDs should we take back for Zoe?" I ask Bea, and Bea reaches out for a Blink-182 album.

"Good taste," I tell her, and she gives me a toothy grin.

After I pick and choose my top 5 CDs—with Bea's input—I slip out of my old bedroom with my arms full.

I nearly run into Miles, who looks a bit frantic.

"Fuck, there you are," he says, reaching for Beatrix.

I look at my brother, quirking a brow at his costume —or lack thereof. It's a dark grey suit, which looks eerily similar to his normal everyday suits.

I'd be a hypocrite to point it out, though, since I'm dressed as a professor.

"And here I was thinking you were worried about me," I mutter as he places kisses all over Beatrix's head, taking her from me since my hands are full.

Miles chuckles. "I was looking everywhere for this little angel," he drawls. I roll my eyes. "Nice costume," he adds, eyeing my tweed jacket. "Are you supposed to be Sherlock Holmes?"

I press my lips together briefly before answering. "I'm a professor."

Miles narrows his eyes. "That's cheating. But I like it," he adds, smiling.

"And you are...?

"Chase," he answers instantly.

"You... dressed as Chase for Halloween?" I deadpan. He's probably fucking with me, but I'll indulge him.

"Yes."

"So if you're Chase, is Chase dressing as you?"

"Of course not. He dresses as Wolverine every year."

I laugh. "Right. How could I forget?"

"What were you doing up here anyway?" he asks, eyeing the CDs in my hand as we walk down the hallway.

"Just grabbing some old CDs from my bedroom," I tell him. It's only half a lie, but he doesn't need to know they're for Zoe. I'd noticed she tends to gravitate toward these bands with her playlists, and I'm sure she'll enjoy seeing how we used to have to listen to music in the dark ages.

"Fuck. We really need to clean out all of the bedrooms."

"If you've neglected a bedroom for twenty years without realizing it, you might have too many bedrooms."

"Fuck you," he grumbles.

Just then, Bea laughs—a tinkling sound that makes both of us go still. Miles looks like he's in awe—it's the exact same expression that passes over his face whenever Stella is nearby.

"You guys have the cutest kid," I tell Miles, ignoring the emotion clawing up my throat.

He walks down the stairs, and I follow him. "You should have one. They're kind of cool," Miles replies.

"If I had a kid now, I'd be almost sixty when they graduated high school."

"So?" Miles furrows his brows as he looks at me. "Age is just a number. Do you want kids?"

I look at Bea, and I already know the answer. The problem is, whenever I think about kids lately, all I can picture is Zoe as the mother.

"Of course I do."

"Better get cracking then, old man," Miles teases. "You're forty now. No more time to waste."

I swat his shoulder as we get to the ground floor, and I set the CD's down and take Bea from him so he can help Stella with the food.

When I walk into the kitchen, I notice Zoe in one of the corners whispering animatedly with Layla.

Orion is sipping his water bottle, watching them. Watching *her*.

With black clothes, fangs, and a cape.

"Hey, Dracula," I say, adjusting my grip on Bea as I grab a box of Cheerios from the counter.

"Where's your costume?" he asks, brows furrowed as I put Bea into her high chair and dole out a small pile of cheerios.

I point to my jacket. "This is my costume." I look at him, but he's already looking away. "You okay?"

Orion is quiet for a minute, but then he straightens up. "Yeah. Fine. Why?"

I look over at Layla—a tall redhead. She's a ballet dancer in the Los Angeles Ballet, and though I don't know her well, she's always been quiet and shy with me, an introverted book nerd, Zoe tells me. She and Zoe are really close, though—which I've always been grateful for. She's wearing a long, black dress, white makeup, and has fangs like Orion.

"You're pining," I murmur, my voice low.

Orion turns and scowls at me. "I am not."

I hold my hands up. "Forgive me for overstepping. It's something I've noticed as a big brother."

Orion turns back to look at Layla. "Like I said, I'm fine."

His body language and demeanor tell me he's anything but fine. However, I don't want to push his buttons. Before either of us can say anything, Malakai walks into the kitchen.

I bark a laugh. "You're kidding."

Bea grins and coos, her mouth full of cheerios as she reaches for her Uncle Kai. He's dressed in all red—dark red pants, red blazer, and white button-down. It's all pulled together with demon horns on his head.

He shrugs and sighs. "I figured it was an easy joke," he says, laying a bag on the counter. "I brought some alcohol."

I walk over and pat his shoulder before flicking one of the horns with two fingers. "A bit too on the nose."

He frowns and looks at me. "You're one to talk, *Professor,*" he grumbles.

He then proceeds to pick up his drink, which appears to be straight vodka, and takes a sip.

Interesting choice for the headmaster and head pastor of a Catholic private school.

Miles saunters over to us. "So, who's this person Layla brought with her?" he asks me quietly, looking around.

"Stop being such a scandalmonger," I mutter.

"I'm sorry, a *what*?" he asks, chuckling.

"He's over there," I say, pointing to the only non-Ravage man in the kitchen. He's tall and slim, wearing a plaid button-down and black jeans. Notably, the *only* one not in costume. He and Layla are now talking with Zoe in one corner of the kitchen.

"Are we talking about Layla's date?" Malakai asks, scooting closer to us so Orion doesn't hear. "I heard he's one of the ballet dancers in her company," he adds.

"You're both incorrigible gossips," I mutter.

"I need to put Bea to sleep," Miles says, lifting her up and out of her high chair. He gently wipes her face off and walks over to Stella, whispering something in her ear.

I see Stella blush before he walks away, and my eyes automatically search for Zoe.

She's already watching me—her eyes dangerously dark.

The remote is suddenly heavy in my pocket, and my hand twitches at my side.

Not yet.

I look away and continue talking to Malakai and Orion, sipping my water as I try not to look in Zoe's direction. Chase and Juliet help Stella set the large dining room table in the next room—complete with spooky music, jack-o'-lanterns, and Halloween-themed food. My eyes rove over the "bloody" meatballs, white chocolate covered "ghost" strawberries, and "severed finger" rolls, which are basically miniature hotdogs. There's a fog machine and ghost projections going, too, and I have to hand it to Stella. It's incredible, even if it's just for family.

Well, and the guy Layla brought.

Miles comes back down a few minutes later, and we all meander into the dining room to eat. Zoe takes a seat next to Orion, and I sit next to Chase and Juliet.

"How's it going with Zoe?" Juliet asks, sipping her wine as she moves her long, light brown hair over one shoulder. She came to the party dressed as a rooster, which must be some sort of inside joke between her and Chase. When she looks up at me, her eyes are sparkling with mischievousness.

Sighing, I run my hand through my hair. "Chase told you."

"He tells me everything," she says, her voice proud as she eyes her husband, who is clad in a full Wolverine costume. I grunt as I play with my water glass, not bothering to respond. "It seems like it might be the real deal for her," she adds. "And that must be terrifying because you're the last thing she has left. You, us—without that, she's truly alone. So the fact that she's been eyeing you all night like she might stop breathing if you're out of eyesight says everything, Liam."

I take a steadying breath as Juliet's words wash over me, causing my chest to ache and my eyes to drift up to Zoe's. She's talking to Orion, but the second my eyes land on her, it's as if she can sense it, and her eyes flick over to mine. Pursing her lips, she takes a sip from her wine glass without breaking eye contact. I watch as she swallows, her throat bobbing before her tongue runs along her lower lip briefly.

"Seems like she's not the only one," Juliet adds, chuckling. "Think of it this way. You want her. She wants you. Why cause more turmoil when you could just... have her? Don't break her heart, Liam. She seems strong, but I don't think she's as strong as she looks."

I start. "That's probably why we *shouldn't* do anything."

"No, that's exactly why you *should*. She needs your guidance, both as her only remaining family, but also as her Dom, eventually. She needs stability. She needs to relinquish control of that massive brain of hers to someone she trusts. It's pretty obvious why she chose you."

"She's had other Doms too," I mutter.

"Yes, but I can bet you a thousand dollars she doesn't look at them like they can hang the moon for her."

I grunt. "She spent fifty *thousand* dollars on lingerie today," I admit.

Juliet snickers, covering her mouth. "Oh my god. She's trying *so* hard, and you're over here all stoic and angry... it's so obvious."

"What's obvious?" I ask, gripping my fork a little too tightly.

"Your dynamic. She is *begging* for you to punish her. Now, be a good Dom and make her pay for her impertinence."

I finish my eyeballs in silence while Juliet turns to talk to Chase.

A few minutes later, after we've all had a casual dinner, Stella ushers us into one of the lounges, where she proceeds to turn the music up. I sip my water as I watch over my siblings instinctively—Chase, who is sitting on the couch with Juliet on his lap, her arm draped around his neck. Miles and Stella, the latter of whom is dragging a grumpy Miles to the middle of the room to dance. Malakai, who looks a bit tipsy, standing with a furious-looking Orion.

It doesn't take me long to find the source.

Layla is dancing with her date, whose name is Raphael, and the two of them are giving everyone a show with their sensual slow dance.

Oh boy.

Just as I walk my water over to the mantel, someone shouts, and before I realize it, Raphael is on the floor with a bloody nose.

Fuck.

Layla crouches down and looks at Raphael, glaring up at Orion, who is looking between Raphael, Layla, and his bloody knuckles.

"What the fuck?" Raphael shouts.

Chase and Juliet jump up from the couch, and Miles walks over to Raphael.

"What happened?" I ask. As the oldest, this type of thing falls on my shoulders, even though I know my other brothers can handle themselves.

Raphael spits blood onto the cream carpet, and I hear

Stella gasp. "You need to get your mutt of a brother under control," he hisses at me before glaring at Orion. His French accent is more pronounced now that he's been punched.

None of us help him up, though.

When I look at Orion, his expression is amused.

I cross my arms and look down, and it takes me a second to realize that Layla isn't offering to help him up, either. My gaze shifts to Orion again, who stands there and smirks.

"And you need to keep your hands to yourself," Orion growls, stepping closer, a vindictive spark in his eyes. "When a lady says no, she means no."

"Alright," I grumble. "You should leave before security ushers you out," I tell Raphael.

He balks. "Your whole family is fucked up; do you know that? I only came here tonight to see it for myself, and I was right." He pins his angry stare at Orion. "I will be pressing charges."

"Looking forward to it," Orion mutters, his lips twitching. "Next time I'll make sure you leave in an ambulance."

"The door is that way," I add, pointing toward the front door.

The man looks around and shakes his head. "Charles Ravage and his crazy fucking kids. My lawyer will be in touch."

Then, he turns and leaves without a word to Layla, wiping the blood streaming down his nose on his sleeve.

Layla is watching everything unfold with wide eyes.

Orion walks over to her with a confident swagger only a Ravage man could muster. He stops right in front of her, and then he cocks his head.

"You're welcome," he tells her.

And then he walks off, leaving all of us in a stunned silence.

I immediately search for Zoe to make sure she's okay, but she's nowhere to be found. After telling Miles I'll be right back, I quietly walk through the first floor, checking every room until I find her in the library. She must not have heard me enter, because her back is still to me as she inspects a book in her hand. As I walk around the leather chair, I get a clearer visual of her, and she reaches up to pull something from one of the top shelves. She holds it in front of her face, but I don't care what it is.

I'm too mesmerized by the backs of her golden thighs.

Her long, slender neck.

The tendrils of hair spilling out of her two braids.

Every hesitation—every iota of self-control—snaps in half when she turns and finds me standing there.

Like she was fucking expecting me.

"Hey," she says, setting the book down quickly and turning to face me fully.

"You okay?" I ask, gauging the situation.

"I liked how you stood up for Orion back there," she says, tilting her head slightly.

I take a step closer. And another. Until I'm a few inches from her.

"Don't change the subject," I murmur.

"I'm not. It was... hot," she says slowly. "Do you think Orion will be okay?"

I chuckle darkly. "The Ravage men can be quite possessive. Orion isn't old enough to have learned self-control. It takes practice."

Her lips quirk up. "Is that so? Are you saying you've learned?"

"I unlearned very quickly when you put on that lingerie earlier, little rebel," I nearly whisper.

Everything inside of me is throbbing, and the *need* to be inside of her is potent.

She leans forward and stands on her tiptoes, so her lips are inches from mine. "Prove it," she whispers, patting the pocket of my jacket before turning and walking away.

CHAPTER FOURTEEN
THE LIE

ZOE

Liam enters the living room a few minutes after me. He gives me a dark, glowering look before walking over to Orion, and I turn my attention to Chase and Juliet, the latter of whom asks me about college. I really like Juliet —and Stella, for that matter. They've looked out for me since the time they entered into the family, and it's been nice seeing Chase and Miles find their *people*. The drinks are flowing, the conversation is entertaining, and soon, with Raphael gone and only the "family" left, we devolve into a tipsy game of truth or dare.

Just what I need.

I'm still waiting for Liam to turn the damn vibrator on, too—and something tells me he's waiting for the perfect moment. He never does things just to do them.

There's always a reason, and he always thinks things through fully before acting.

Sitting in a circle, I notice how Layla and Orion haven't spoken since Raphael left. Malakai is slurring his words and joking around with Miles. Orion and Liam are still conversing, and Stella, Juliet, and Chase are telling Layla and me all about video cassettes and how you used to have to leave your house to rent a movie.

Gag.

Malakai clears his throat. "Okay, now it's time for truth or dare," he says, eyes twinkling. "And as the middle brother, I think it's fair to appoint the youngest person in this room to go first."

I glare at him before clearing my throat. "Fine. Truth."

Orion laughs and mutters *oh boy* under his breath.

"I'll start easy," Kai murmurs, pressing his lips together and pretending to think. "Where do you see yourself in a year?"

Damn. He could've given me something easy to answer, but instead it's the last question I currently want to think about.

I cross my arms and legs on the chair I'm sitting on, pondering how to answer such a loaded question.

I don't dare look at Liam—I can't see his face when I tell the complete truth about this, because it's been on my mind all day, and I know he's going to hate it.

"Well, until this morning, I would've told you that I could see myself in my final year of undergrad, working hard before going to law school. I probably would've been interning for a law firm in LA, and I'd have a list of my top law schools—though UCLA would've been number one." I take a deep breath. "But since I walked out of the LSAT this morning—"

"Wait, what?" Layla asks, sitting up straighter.

"You walked out?" Orion asks, looking between Liam and me.

I nod and look down at the floor. "Now, I see myself writing full-time. Taking a break from college while I work on getting my book published. I worked so hard for so long, a bit of a break sounds really great right about now."

I finally let myself look up at Liam, and he's *fuming*. Chills skitter down my spine as he cocks his head and narrows his eyes. He's still leaning back against a wall a few feet away, but I swear I can hear him grinding his teeth to keep from saying something cruel.

"That's news to me," he says, his voice eerily calm. "Why wouldn't you finish your degree since you're almost halfway done?" he asks.

"I could. But with law school out of the question, I think taking a year or two off to figure out what I want to major in is a smart move, especially considering my scholarship is for the expedited pre-law major. Once I change it, they could revoke the scholarship—"

"I'll pay for your education," Liam growls. "It's the least I can do. You never have to worry about money with me," he adds.

Everyone else stays quiet as we argue, and my cheeks heat at how ridiculous we must look.

"It's not about the money. Why would I waste *anyone's* money on something so frivolous?"

"That's interesting, considering your purchases from earlier."

My eyes widen, and I see Layla stand up. She knows *exactly* what kinds of things I bought earlier, and I can tell she's about to save my ass.

"Okay, next person," she says sweetly. "That's me, right?"

Liam doesn't look away, but everyone else seems to have moved on now that the tension is broken.

I let my eyes slide away from his. "Truth or dare?" I ask her.

"Dare," Layla replies, giving me a knowing smile.

Looking between Orion and Layla, I make a bold decision. "I dare you to kiss Kai." Layla's eyes widen as Miles huffs a knowing laugh. Arching a brow, I cross my arms. "Go on, then."

Orion is *fuming* as Layla walks over to Malakai, and she gives him a friendly peck on the lips. It's over in less than a second, but Orion looks like he's about to body check his older brother.

Miles winks at me before Layla turns to Juliet, who is the next youngest. "Truth or dare?"

"Truth, always," Juliet says, smirking at Chase.

I hardly hear Layla ask her question as Liam pushes off the wall and comes to stand next to me. My pulse begins to whoosh in my ears, and everything else sort of drops away whenever he's nearby. His hand rests on the arm of the chair I'm sitting in, and somehow, I can sense the anger radiating off him just from how the pronounced veins and how it's splayed out on the bright turquoise fabric.

Almost like he knows he's staking a claim over me.

"Are you kidding, Zoe? Dropping out of college?" he asks, his voice low enough for only me to hear.

"I know it's hard for someone in education, someone like you, to think outside the box—"

"When I told you to take the time to figure out what you wanted, I didn't think that meant dropping out of school."

My nails dig into the fabric of the chair. *God, he's so aggravating.*

"If I'd known your advice had stipulations"—I narrow my eyes as I look up at him—"maybe I wouldn't have listened to you. So, what, it's okay to follow my dreams as long as they align with your normative views on higher education? Which is, by the way, a crock of capitalist bullshit—"

"Careful, Zoe," he growls, his hand leaving the couch to brush the hair from my face. I'd taken the witch's hat off to eat earlier, and I knew my hair—despite being in braids—is a wild mess of waves. The rough pad of his fingers grazes my jaw. It's an oddly gentle action, and I try not to react to the way my skin breaks out in goose-bumps at his touch. "You're not exactly in a position to defy me right now."

I'm about to respond with something snarky when Layla saunters over to us. Liam takes a couple of steps away, smiling politely at the redhead as she comes to sit down on the arm of the chair.

"You okay?" she whispers.

"Fine," I explain, letting my eyes wander over the people in the room. I didn't hear Layla's question or Juliet's answer, but everyone is laughing so it must've been funny. Stella is tucked under Miles's arm drinking a martini. Malakai is sipping whiskey with Chase nearby. It takes me a second to realize the youngest Ravage brother is missing.

"Where's Orion?" I ask.

It's not that I'm not close to the rest of Liam's family, but Orion and Layla are much closer in age to me, so the three of us usually hang out at these kinds of events.

"No idea. He skulked off a minute ago," Layla says absent-mindedly. Sipping from her drink, a mojito, by the look of it, she turns to faces me. "So, how mad was Liam earlier?" Her eyes follow something—or someone—over my shoulder.

I turn to find Liam walking away, his dark gaze finding mine for a second before his hand pats the pocket of his jacket.

A warning.

I squeeze my thighs together subtly, my skin hot from the anticipation. I can still feel the vibrator inside of me, and I've been wet all evening from the anticipation.

"Very mad," I breathe, suddenly wanting something alcoholic. "How are you doing with Orion?" I add casually. "That was some show he put on earlier."

Layla rolls her eyes. "He takes his role as protective stepbrother very seriously."

"So are you on speaking terms again, then?" I ask.

Neither of them ever told me what happened, but one day they just… stopped talking. They're cordial in person, but that's about it.

She chews on her bottom lip. "No." Pinning me with her large, hazel eyes, she frowns. "You're changing the subject on purpose. What's going on with you two?"

I shrug. "I don't know."

"Have you…"

Yes.

I shake my head.

Orion saunters into the living room again, and his eyes immediately find us. Well, they immediately find *Layla.* Liam settles in the opposite corner of the room, and Layla stands up.

"I need another drink. Want one?"

"Sure."

As soon as Layla vacates the arm of my chair, Orion saunters over. My eyes rove over the bandage wrapped around his knuckles, and he must notice what caught my attention.

"Not my finest moment," he tells me with a lopsided smile, the artificial fangs making him look like a real vampire.

"So possessive," I say coyly, smiling, my eyes roving over to Liam, who can see us clearly, as I arch a brow. *I dare you,* I think. He stands taller and pins me with a darkened glare as I turn back to Orion. "Annoyingly, the fangs suit you," I say.

He smiles a genuine smile. "I know." He seems to relax a bit, too, and his arm comes around my shoulder in a friendly manner.

Nothing *ever* happened between Orion and me, and it never would, but Liam doesn't have to know that.

"So, no more law school," he muses.

"Um, yeah. It's probably a very rash decision, but it felt right at the time."

"You're okay though?"

I nod. "I am. Thanks for asking."

A second later, Juliet and Chase walk over to me. "Zoe, I need your input," Juliet says. Her eyes are glassy and bemused as Chase grins down at her.

"Mine? What is it?" I ask, looking at Liam, who is now close enough to hear us.

"Chase and I can't agree on something, and I figured I'd ask you, Layla, and Stella."

I smirk. "Fine."

"What age did you lose your virginity?" She gives a pointed look at her husband, and he laughs. "He says eighteen is too young, but I asked him to find one woman who lost it after eighteen," she explains.

I swallow. *Fuck.* The one secret I've kept locked up for over a year threatens to spill over.

"I was eighteen," I say quietly.

Out of my peripheral, I see Liam straighten.

"Second question," Juliet says. "Did you know the guy you slept with very well?"

Don't look at Liam. He can never know.

"Yes," I answer.

"See?" Juliet says. "I'm right. Most of us have a similar story, though now I'm curious to hear your story, Zoe—"

Orion laughs. "You didn't know? She met some guy in Catalina last year and he was the reason she joined the lifestyle."

Oh, fuck.

Fuck, fuck, fuck.

"Really?" Juliet asks.

I swallow. "Yeah."

"That's amazing," Juliet says, giggling. "But you said you knew him well, so I'm confused. If you just met him, how did you know him well..." Her mouth drops open, and Orion blows a slow breath of air out of his lips. Chase looks between all of us with a confused expression.

"Fuck," I whisper, finally looking at Liam.

If I thought he looked angry before, it's nothing compared to how he looks now. His forehead vein is protruding, and his eyes are so hardened that I hardly recognize him.

He pushes off the wall and stalks over to me. "I need a word with you."

I don't have a chance to see anyone's reaction because he's already dragging me away and down the hallway.

"Where are we g—"

A sharp tug cuts off the rest of my question, and then he's pulling us into the nearest closet.

"We have to stop meeting in closets," I joke, thinking of Catalina to try and break the tension.

When I look up at him, my body heats at the danger lurking behind his expression in the darkness. It's not one I've seen before–cold, ruthless, and determined. He presses me against the wall. He licks his lips as his hands grip my waist, and my eyes flutter closed as his leg comes between my thighs.

"I can't tell if you're asking to be punished," he growls. "Or if you truly enjoy disobeying me."

"I'm sorry," I tell him, a heavy ache bearing down on my chest as my eyes flick between his, trying to decipher his hurt expression.

He's disappointed—and that thought kills me.

"You *lied* to me that night. I asked, and you said you weren't," he growls, his quiet rage sending chills down my spine.

"I'm sorry!" I tell him, my voice breaking. I place a hand on his chest, and I realize too late that it's shaking. "I shouldn't have lied."

I snap my mouth shut, knowing that whatever I say will only make it worse. He pushes my hand away, and my hackles rise as he peers into my eyes. His anger isn't outward facing; it's not flared nostrils and panting, clenched fists or yelling. It's a quiet rumble of a feeling, almost like the earth is about to open up beneath me.

Which wouldn't be the worst thing in the world right now.

"Why *did* you lie, Zoe?"

My lips press together, but I don't answer him. I *can't*. Telling him that I wanted him for years before that or how I wanted him so badly that I didn't care about the pain—the embarrassment would kill me.

It would make me look pathetic and young and inexperienced, and I'd worked so hard to overcome that feeling.

"Fine," he breathes, sighing. "I'm not really into playing games. We will discuss this later when I'm calmer."

"Liam!"

"Count," he murmurs, his voice gravelly with ire.

I open my mouth to ask what he means, but it becomes clear when he removes the remote from the pocket of his jacket and presses a button.

A low humming settles low in my core, and it takes me a second to realize it's coming from *inside* of me— and buzzing against my clit at the same time. It's low— and on some sort of staccato rhythm. It's not enough to get me off, and he knows it.

It's just enough to *tease*.

The staccato progressively gets stronger before tapering off, buzzing every second or so, though I can't hear it at all, luckily.

"This is how you want to punish me?" I ask, my voice strained as the rhythm gets stronger again before tapering off.

"Oh, little rebel. There are so many other ways I want to punish you. This is just the start."

He turns it up a level, and it sends a flash of pleasure through me.

"Liam," I whimper, shifting my weight slightly so that the toy is pressing fully against my clit. "Oh, fuck!"

Instead of stopping, he presses his thigh harder against my core.

My eyes roll back as he turns it up again, his thigh keeping it perfectly against my aching, needy clit. My underwear is drenched, but Liam doesn't touch me other than one hand on my waist holding me still.

"Do you want this, Zoe?"

"Yes," I pant.

"Tell me what you want. I need to hear it."

"I need you. I need to come," I moan. "And I need you to take control," I finish.

"Why should I give this to you when you lied to me?" he asks, his voice almost indifferent—like he's closing himself off.

"I said I was sorry," I tell him, rolling my hips against his thigh. "I can say it as many times as I need to. I'm sorry—"

He turns the strength up on the vibrator, and I tremble. It's too much—being this close to him, the scent of licorice permeating the air, the feel of his warm thigh between my legs...

"If we're going to do this, there are things we need to establish," he growls.

"My safe word is Catalina."

He goes still. "Are you sure you want to be snarky right now?"

Adding two more levels to the vibrations, I moan as all my muscles coil, as I barrel quickly toward my climax. A low, deep noise rumbles in Liam's chest, and it's like he can sense that I'm close—like he can't help but be aroused—despite being disappointed in me.

"Come for me, little rebel. Don't make me wait any longer," he grits out, using his hand to hold my waist so he's settling me on his thigh.

His words aren't affectionate, though. Nothing about this is romantic.

It's *punishment*—demanding, quick, and ruthless.

Everything burns and tingles all at once. It's overpowering, and I'm fully gasping now as my body convulses. I'm close, but not there yet, so I circle my hips slightly, which nudges the front part *and* the part inside of me, giving me the friction that I need.

Liam realizes what I'm doing, removing his thigh, and cupping me with his hand instead. It's *really* fucking hot, and through my lashes, I watch his mouth drop open as I grind myself on his hand.

He's breathing hard, too, and his grip against me tightens, pressing the vibrator directly onto my swollen bud. My core flutters waiting to grab onto something.

"Oh fuck," I whisper. He begins to move his hand slightly to give me the traction I crave, but the feeling is too intense. "Liam, wait, it's too much—"

"It's a good thing I know your safe word, then," he growls, not relenting at all. "I don't have all night, baby girl," he murmurs. "Come. *Now.*"

It's the *baby girl* term of endearment for me; it sends me over the edge.

I throw my head back as my orgasm explodes through me. I'm glad he's holding me up with one hand, because my knees give out and my back arches as I cry out.

I reach up without thinking and grab the back of his neck, pulling his mouth to mine as my body twitches, as my hands tremble.

He kisses me back with fervor, and I vaguely register him pulling his glasses off as they clatter to the ground, and then his tongue slips between my lips as one orgasm carries over into another one.

I cry out against his lips as everything inside of me pulses, as my fingers grip the hair at the back of his head. He groans as I fuck myself against his hand, and then all of a sudden it's too much. I pull away and gasp, nearly ready to collapse, but Liam quickly turns the vibrator off.

When he does, my clit is still pulsing and buzzing—like phantom vibrations. I can hardly catch my breath, and a bead of sweat slides down my back as Liam looks down at the remote before pocketing it again.

Then, he surges forward, one hand gripping my neck as he kisses me again. His tongue pushes past my lips and everything else falls away. My whole body is warm and pliant against his, and I groan when one of his large hands comes to my hip, squeezing it once.

He pulls away at the sound, panting as he stares down at me. Without another word, he bends down and retrieves his glasses, giving me a knowing look.

"Maybe we should get back out there—"

"Did you think I was done?" he asks, his voice calm.

It's the eerie calmness that has me in a chokehold. I hear the click of the remote before the vibrations begin again—and this time it doesn't start off as soft and teasing.

It's relentlessly strong.

I choke on a gasp, and my back arches—on the brink of another quick and fast orgasm. Reaching out for him, he takes a step away—and it feels... *wrong.*

My hips rock of their own accord as he keeps his eyes on me, studying me.

"Liam."

"Don't fight it, little rebel. This is one of many."

I chew on my bottom lip as I do fight it. My body goes taut against my will, and I curl my hands into fists, pushing it away.

I'm completely powerless, but I won't give in. I can't let him win whatever this little war is. My arousal spirals closer and closer, and I'm gasping when he taps the remote two more times.

God!

"Liam, no."

"You're more than welcome to use your safe word," he murmurs, his darkened eyes sliding back and forth between mine. "You just have to use it and this stops."

Fuck.

If I'd known that Liam was capable of this kind of dominance... It's really fucking hot. And frustrating. And *intriguing.* My arousal flares to life, and I squirm, trying to get away from it. My traitorous body begins to tremble as he turns the vibrations up to the highest level. It's so intense that it's almost painful, and my back bows as my climax slams through me.

Oh god, oh god.

I grit my teeth and cry out as Liam chuckles, his hands coming to my hips to keep me from falling. Short, loud pants break free from my mouth, and I whimper as my overly sensitive clit begins to throb painfully.

"Please," I whisper, squeezing my eyes shut. "Turn it off."

He presses a button to stop it and relief washes over me. My clit is on fire, and I'm so sensitive that every breath has me twitching. I close my eyes to let the shaking subside, feeling and hearing how he takes a step away from me.

"Get yourself together. We're leaving," he says quietly. *Too* quietly.

When I open my eyes, I see that he's staring at me with a clenched jaw. I quickly smooth my hair and take a steadying breath, but he doesn't give me any warning before he's throwing the door open and stalking out.

I follow him to the kitchen where everyone is gathered around a chocolate cake that's decorated to look like a graveyard.

"Zoe's not feeling well so I'm taking her home," Liam declares.

All eyes turn toward me, and my cheeks heat. *Can they tell he just gave me two explosive orgasms in a closet?* If they can, no one says anything—and I give them all a quick wave before following Liam to the front door and out into the dark, October night.

Heavy rain begins to soak us, and though I know he's mad at me for lying, he still takes his tweed jacket off and covers me with it as we run to his Jeep. He grabs his keys from the abandoned valet stand and then he's throwing the passenger door open once we round the corner for parked cars, ushering me inside. I'm acutely aware of the vibrator still inside of me as I sit down, and I quickly remove his jacket and my cape from my shoulders.

When he climbs in and closes the door, the rain pounding on the roof of the car is deafening. It's nearly pitch black out now that the motion sensor lights have turned off, and we both sit there, breathing heavily, for at least a minute.

"I'm sorry," I say again as I buckle my seatbelt. Liam's fingers turn white from gripping the wheel so tightly. Then, he turns the engine on and pulls out onto the long driveway.

"I know you are," he growls.

The silence hangs between us as we get onto one of the two-lane roads that wind over the hills to our house. When we get to a red light, he looks over at me after stopping the car.

"Are you going to tell me the real reason you lied or am I going to have to pull it out of you?" he asks, taking the remote out of his pocket.

I don't answer—I *can't.*

A pained sound escapes my lips when he turns it on to a medium level.

"Oh fuck," I cry out, gripping the sides of the seat. "Please, Liam–"

"You're so cute when you beg," he says casually, as if he's discussing the weather.

His indifferent tone makes this whole thing *so* much worse. It's like he knows his detachment will affect me more than the forced orgasms, because it's completely new to our dynamic. He's letting his emotions get in the way and rule his decisions because this is all new to him. If I'm really going to teach him how to do this, I'm going to need to talk to him about it—but not right now.

He kicks the vibrations up a few levels, and I keen out loud. "I c-can't," I stutter, panting as my cunt grips the toy tightly, as warm arousal pools low in my belly yet again. "Please, not again."

"You know what I want," he says, driving forward. "I can do this all night if I have to. Full tank of gas, nowhere to go..."

God.

"Fine," I whimper, circling my hips. "I'll tell you."

"Go on, then." His voice is calm. Collected. Unaffected. It's like he was made to do this. "For the record, once I know *why* you made such an egregious mistake, there will be another punishment for lying to me about something so important," he grits out.

Gasping, my orgasm slams into me at his words, and though it feels incredible, it's also mixed with guilt, embarrassment, shame, and a plethora of other emotions. I'm convulsing, begging him to stop it with harsh whispers on my tongue, when he pushes the button for the vibrator to stop. I'm nearly sobbing, my breath catching in my throat with every inhale. Everything is raw—my nerves, my body, my emotions, my mind...

What if I tell him and lose him?

But what if I *don't* tell him and lose him?

"I wanted y-you," I gasp out. "I didn't want you to s-stop that night. I'd wanted you for y-years, and you were *finally* mine, finally giving me e-everything I ever wanted." I snap my mouth shut before I admit more than I'm willing to share.

Tears track down my cheeks as Liam swears and pulls over, stopping the car. I'm flooded with emotions—from the orgasm, my confession, or the events of the day. Everything is catching up with me, and before I realize it, I'm sobbing.

"Fuck, Zoe," Liam growls, unbuckling me, tugging on my arm, and pulling me onto his lap. My legs bracket his hips, and his hands come to my face.

I squeeze my eyes shut as more tears spill down my face. "I was worried if I t-told you, that you'd stop. I would've rather had the pain because if you stopped, it would've b-broken me," I confess.

"Zoe, look at me."

"No," I whisper, not wanting to see his expression. I don't know if I can handle the rejection, or worse, if I can handle him breaking off whatever this thing between us is.

His warm hand skims along my bare thigh, and I shiver in his arms. Every nerve ending is frayed, and his touch isn't helping things. Before I can react, his hand is between my legs, and I gasp when he pushes my soaking underwear to the side and pulls the vibrator out.

The absence of it only makes me cry harder. I recognize this feeling, and I know exactly what's happening. *Emotional release.* The multiple forced orgasms, the lack of limits or talking things through... we didn't exactly go about this in the healthiest way. Still, that knowledge doesn't make it any better. Everything is so tender, and his gentle caresses only enhance the feeling of shame and guilt.

"Look at me. *Please.*"

He wipes my tears away with his fingers, and one of his hands comes to my back, slipping under my blouse and resting against it, pressing my body into his. He kisses my chin, which only makes a tight squeak escape my throat.

"I'm sorry," he murmurs. "If that was too much, I'm sorry. For what it's worth, I wanted you; whether or not I was ready to admit it or not is another story. Your feelings were never one-sided."

Relief floods me, and I open my eyes, but I don't look up at him. Not yet. Not while my emotions are all over the place. I need to get a grip. I need to quell my anxiety, to tamp down the need to *be* with him, to be near him, touching him. Because that's all I can think about. His fingers twitch against my bare back, and my nerves explode again as goosebumps cover my skin.

"That night in Catalina was an unleashing for me, little rebel. You pushed me, but I crossed that line myself.

And despite telling myself that I could stay away, well... it turns out that I can't. No matter how much I try."

Each word clings to one of my wild emotions, settling my scattered mind with every syllable. It's the most potent feeling of relief, and my body sags against his fully.

Liam's voice grounds me completely, and despite feeling wrung out, I'm also comforted. His fingers caress the skin against my spine as he continues, taking my silence as a sign to keep talking.

"When I told you that day in my classroom that you were going to be the death of me, this is what I meant. You... me... it's been us against the world for four years, and I'm terrified of fucking this up and losing you."

I move and press my lips against his without thinking. He groans, one hand flying to my hair and fisting it. Except, instead of the wanton need from earlier, this feels like we're sealing some kind of silent agreement.

I pull away after a few seconds. "Thank you for telling me."

"I'm sorry," he says quickly. "That won't happen again. If you really want to do this, if you want me to be your Dom, I need to be better about reading your cues. Forgive me?"

Brows scrunched, I pull my lower lip between my teeth. Even in this aspect of his life, he's considerate.

"I forgive you."

"We should probably outline our limits before we do anything else. I didn't ask you if that was okay."

"You have my consent. We can either use my safe word, or the traffic light system. Green, yellow, red."

"Yeah, I read about that," he murmurs.

"You did?"

His hands come to my hips. "Yes. I did a lot of research, in fact." He tilts his head slightly, smirking as his eyes study me with glittering rhapsody. "But I still have a lot to learn. Maybe you should teach me," he says, his voice a low purr.

I swallow as his right hand comes up to my face, and he slowly drags his thumb across my lower lip. "You're doing just fine on your own," I offer.

"Still," he growls. "We should *both* outline our limits. Even if unofficially until we're both more settled emotionally."

He moves me off him and sets me back in the passenger seat. I'm about to protest when he starts the ignition.

"What about my other punishment?" I ask, thinking back to his earlier promise for punishing me for lying.

He lets out a low chuckle. "We'll see. I need to think about it, but I don't think we should go any further tonight. I'll be upset about the lying for a while, but I don't want to hold my forgiveness over you," he says slowly, pulling back onto the road. "That's not fair to you, and it's not fair to me. I just... feel a bit out of control, but that's on me."

"I know. I'm sorry," I whisper—all my fight vanishing.

"Fuck," he mutters, grimacing. "You lost your

virginity up against a wall with no foreplay. And if I could do it over, I'd spend the entire night making sure you'd never want to leave my bed again."

"Maybe you'll get the chance to make it up to me," I offer.

"Or maybe you'll get the chance to make it up to *me*," he retorts.

I'm quiet the rest of the drive home, and as Liam pulls into his driveway, he shuts the engine off and sighs.

"I had some CDs for you. I forgot them at the castle."

"What are CDs?" I ask, turning to face him with heavy eyes. Just as his mouth drops open, I laugh. "Kidding."

"Zoe..." He looks away as his arms rest on the steering wheel. My heart stutters, and for a second I think he's going to reject me again. "Come on. Let's go inside and get you to bed."

"But—"

"Let me take care of you. Show me what you like when it comes to aftercare."

Oh.

I smile as he reaches over and unlocks my door.

CHAPTER FIFTEEN

THE RUIN

Liam

Once we're inside the house, I close and lock the door. When I turn around, Zoe is watching me as she leans back against the entryway table. I walk up next to her, my eyes boring into her as I drop my keys into the bowl with a loud clang. Captain nuzzles up against her legs, and she absentmindedly pets the top of his head. It's domestic and it almost heals the hole in my heart, but thinking about her in this capacity is dangerous.

"Upstairs?" I ask, my voice hoarse.

Her pupils blow out as she nods once, turning and walking down the hallway ahead of me.

"Stay," I tell Captain gently, brushing his spine with my hand. "I'm not sharing her tonight, buddy."

He lies down in front of the door and starts to purr.

I follow Zoe upstairs, and every second is frenetically charged.

I know she can feel it, too.

She walks past her room, going straight to my closed door and pushing it open.

Good girl.

I turn and close the door with a soft click, and it's as if that soft click is a thousand decibels loud, because there's suddenly a roaring in my ears as I turn to face Zoe.

Her chest is rising and falling quickly—her lipstick is slightly smeared, and there's mascara on her cheeks from crying earlier. There's no way she wants more.

She pounces, jumping into my arms and pressing her soft lips against mine.

Fuck.

I groan, my hands moving quickly to support her legs which she has wrapped around my hips. I walk us to my bed, tongue pushing past her lips as her hands grab my hair. Growling, I set her down on the bed and pull away.

"Greedy girl," I purr, looking down at her. "I brought you up here for aftercare."

She smiles. "I don't want aftercare yet."

I sigh, running a hand over my face. "What are you doing to me?" I whisper, my voice pained.

"I know what I *want* to do to you," she answers, her voice a breathy pant.

"You make me fucking mindless, Zoe."

"Good. I want you mindless. But *inside* of me," she adds.

I cock my head and ignore her snarky response, assessing her. She seems better now that we talked—almost relieved. More like herself. Guilt wracks me when I think of how her cheeks were wet with tears, because I'd nearly broken her with my anger. If we were really going to do this, we had to do it the right way.

"What happened earlier was—"

"Please, Liam," she murmurs, kicking her shoes off and scooting back on the bed. "I don't want to talk about that right now. I want to be your good girl," she murmurs, opening her legs slightly.

Her fingers move to her skirt, lifting it inch by inch as she spreads her legs until I'm breathing heavily. I glimpse a peek of white lace as she lets her knees fall apart—

Fuck, she makes it really hard to think straight.

I walk forward, placing my hands on her knees and bringing them together.

"Not before we have a little chat," I tell her, delighting in the way her cheeks flush at my command. "Sit."

She grumbles as she sits up, her lips pulled into an adorable pout. I remove my jacket and place it over the back of a nearby armchair, and then I walk over to the bed where Zoe is watching me with something akin to reverence.

"You don't want to?" she asks.

I chuckle. "Oh, I want to. Trust me. But we need to establish a baseline. Confirm limits, safe words—"

"I told you. Green is keep going, yellow is—"

"Zoe," I say sternly.

She tilts her head as her eyes skim over my face, then to my chest, and finally... to my straining cock pressing against my pants.

"Let me touch you," she begs. "Please."

"Fuck, you're good at this," I say, sighing as I run my hand down my face.

I consider letting her touch me before we talk, but then I remember her pained expression earlier when I held her face, and I reluctantly hold myself back.

"I need to know what you expect from me—from this. I'm brand new to this... lifestyle."

"Can't we talk after?" she asks, reaching for me.

With every fiber of thin resistance still holding my self-control together, I push her hand away.

"Look at me," I growl. Her smile disappears as she faces me fully. "I don't want to push your limits. I never want to see you cry like that again unless it's from pleasure. I didn't enjoy watching that. So, yes. We need to talk before we go any further."

She gives me a small smile. "Fine."

"Lay it on me," I tell her, rubbing my jaw.

"Okay..." she says slowly. "To be honest, I think it comes naturally to you. That night in Catalina was..." She bites her lower lip. "We can use the traffic light system. Green means keep going, yellow means pause and/or evaluate, and red means stop the scene."

My brows furrow. "Scene?"

She sits up straighter. "We have to decide if it'll be 'scenes' or if you want me as your sub 24/7."

Fuck me.

"As amazing as that sounds, I think we'll both need breaks from this dynamic, no?"

She nods enthusiastically. "I agree."

"Okay, so only in the bedroom, so to speak. What about limits? Do you have any?"

"I have a couple. Things that involve pee or other types of bodily waste..." she says, grimacing.

I'd looked at a few lists of limits, but I must've missed that.

"Got it. What else?" I ask, rocking back on my heels.

She looks down as if she's shy, so I walk over to the bed and sit down next to her—but not too close. She's supposed to be the experienced one, so I start speaking gently.

"I need you to be open with me, little rebel. This will only work if we're communicating. I'm not going to make you sign your soul away, but I need to know these things since I'm so new."

She looks up and gives me a soft smile. "I know that. You're doing great," she says gently. "It's annoying how natural this comes to you."

"Don't change the subject," I tell her, leaning back.

"I was merely making an observation."

"Tell me, then."

She smirks. "I'm not a fan of any sort of water play. Aside from what I told you, my other hard limits are asphyxiation and breath play."

"Choking?" I ask, trying to keep my voice nonchalant.

She nods. "Anything having to do with water, or breathing..." She looks away.

Fuck. Because of her parents.

"Of course."

"That's it," she says. "I enjoy being tied up, restrained, and rope play. Handcuffs. Blindfolds. Any sort of restraint," she adds. I nod, taking in all of this information.

"Good to know," I murmur, urging my hands to stay put on the bed. "And what about exclusivity? Are we *hanging out*?" I ask, my tone slightly too biting to be casual.

Zoe looks over at me. "That's entirely up to you."

I let out a long, slow breath. "As long as we're doing this together, we're exclusive. Understood?"

"Yes."

"So, are we done, then?" I ask.

She shrugs. "What are your limits?"

"Same as yours, I think."

"And what do you enjoy?"

The corner of my lips curve into a smile. "Making you come. Forcing orgasms out of you. Watching you come undone before my eyes and on my tongue," I add, thinking back to the night in Catalina as I stand up.

"That's it? You don't want me to cage your cock, or fist your ass—"

She stops talking immediately as I drop down to my knees and push her legs apart.

Fucking brat.

"Yes, that's it," I murmur. "I get off watching you get

off," I tell her, running my hands up her calves. "And controlling how many orgasms you have. I find my pleasure when and only when you're completely and utterly spent from what I've done to you." Gripping the flesh of her inner thighs, my cock twitches when she lets out a breathy gasp. "Once I'm satisfied, I'll fuck you until you come again. Maybe twice or three times, until you can't move. Is that understood?" She nods, panting as my thumb grazes the white lace of her panties.

"Can I ask one more question?" she breathes, and I grin at the way she feels the need to ask me. I nod once. "What do you want me to call you? Daddy?"

I grunt, hooking my thumb underneath the delicate white lace. "You enjoy pushing my buttons, don't you?" She lifts her chin slightly, eyes twinkling with mirth. "You can call me Liam," I growl, and then I roughly twist the fabric and quickly pull on them until they tear away from her.

"Hey!" she cries out. "Those were expensive."

But I can't look away from her exposed cunt. It's glistening, and pink, and *so fucking perfect.* Dark, trimmed curls frame the prettiest fucking clit, still swollen and red from earlier.

However, that's not what has me hardly breathing.

A small, cursive tattoo sits on her upper thigh at the junction of her pubic bone. I didn't notice it earlier.

LR

I don't move. I can't.

She must notice my hesitation because she chuckles. "Oh. I forgot to tell you. I had that done after Catalina."

I lift my eyes to hers, scowling. "What does it mean?" I ask, my voice hoarse.

"Originally I got it for my nickname. Little Rebel. But... it's not a coincidence that they're also your initials."

LR

Liam Ravage.

Fuuuuck.

I suck in a sharp breath and move up so that I'm hovering above her. I'd planned on feasting on her pussy, but after seeing that... I need to claim her in the only way I know how.

"What do I say to start a scene?" I ask, kissing her neck.

She groans, and I push her further back on the bed so that I'm on top of her.

"You don't need to say anything. Just... start."

"Fuck, Zoe," I rasp. "You're going to ruin me, aren't you?"

"Maybe you should get a taste of your own medicine, Liam," she whispers into my ear. "You know, since you ruined me that night in Catalina."

I know I should hate that I was her first, but I don't.

Not even a little bit.

I growl, sitting up. "Take your clothes off."

She crawls up to her knees and slowly unbuttons her shirt, and the feral beast waiting to sink into her is a lot more impatient than me, because before I know it, I'm swiping at her shirt and tearing it down the front.

Buttons go flying, and her eyes widen slightly before she lies down and removes her skirt and holster.

"If I haven't told you before, you should know that your little body drives me crazy. Those high-waisted jeans, the garters, the fishnets... and when you were wearing that old band tee a few weeks ago..."

She smiles as her hands come to her breasts, and she begins to massage them. "Tit for tat, Liam. You're always out back chopping wood and making me wish you'd throw me over your shoulder and have your way with me."

I chuckle as I remove my shirt, and then I step off the bed to remove my pants. "You might regret saying that," I tell her, my voice low. "Because I'm about to show you exactly what I would've done that night if I'd known you were a virgin."

She cracks a smile. "If you knew, you would've stopped."

I drop my boxers, and her eyes widen. "Do you realize why it was so irresponsible of me to fuck you against a wall with no foreplay?" I growl, stroking my cock from shaft to head.

"Your tattoos," she breathes.

I sigh. "The first time you see my cock up close and that's all you can pay attention to?" I ask, smiling.

Her eyes glaze over. "Trust me, Liam. It's the size of an anaconda and quite hard to miss." I climb on the bed and knock her knees apart as I chuckle. "I like them," she says, her voice soft. She's referring to the stars low on both hips, which are a product of emo music and too much tequila. "They remind me of—"

"Shh," I whisper, not wanting to talk about my tattoos right now. Licking my thumb, I reach down and gently brush it over her clit. She hisses.

"Hmm. I suspected you might be quite sensitive," I tell her, bringing my hand to her mouth and pressing two fingers inside of her soft lips. "Suck."

She moans as she sucks, her warm tongue swirling around my fingers before she pops me out.

A shiver wracks my body when I think of my cock inside of her mouth, between her teeth, down her throat...

"Very good," I murmur, trailing my fingers down to her opening. "I learned a long time ago how to prepare a woman properly," I add, slowly inserting one finger.

Zoe arches her back and inhales. *Fuck, she's tight.* I add my second finger, trying to stretch her properly while fighting against the impatient part of me that wants to take her again.

"The first time I fucked someone, I was fifteen." Her eyes go wide, and I laugh as I curl my fingers inside of her. The muscles in her stomach quiver as she grips me, and she sighs contentedly as I continue speaking. "Yes, I was young. I had no idea what I was doing, and let's say I was the only one who came."

"Learned a thing or two in your old age?" she asks, smirking.

I let my thumb swipe over her too-sensitive clit. "Careful, baby girl."

She groans and her body twitches, and I focus on my two fingers as they prep her as much as I can.

"I soon learned that while spontaneous sex was fun, it never seemed to do anything for the other party," I say, using her wetness to slick up a third finger. "So, I learned how to change that," I growl, inserting a third finger and using it to swirl around her opening. My other two fingers find the soft, spongy part against her inner walls. Her legs start to shake, and I laugh. She's so fucking responsive.

"You certainly know what you're doing," she gasps, trembling.

"It got to a point where I enjoyed bringing the other person to a climax, so I kept learning," I murmur.

"Yes you did. Fuck, Liam, I'm—"

I let my thumb graze her clit, and she bows off the bed, her pert nipples peaked and taut.

Fuck yes.

"It was fun," I admit. "But nothing compares to watching you fall apart underneath me, little rebel."

"Oh, fuck," she whimpers. I use my other hand to spread her legs a little wider, slowing my tempo with my three fingers. When I make a scissoring motion inside of her with two of them, her mouth drops open, and she screams.

"That's it," I grit out. "Do you feel that? Has anyone ever made you come like this before?" I ask, brushing my fingers against her slick channel, knowing if I keep going, she's going to shatter beneath me.

"No," she groans, arching her back as her eyes roll back in her head. "No one except you."

I look down to see my initials sitting prettily on the flushed skin of her hip, and I nearly pull my fingers out so I can sink my cock in.

"Tell me when you're about to come," I tell her, feeling her cunt beginning to grip me and I slowly pump my hand into her.

"Liam," she says, her voice hoarse.

"You're so wet and needy for me, little rebel," I say, brushing a light kiss against one of her taut nipples.

"Fuck, I'm close." I pull my fingers out and she glares up at me. "Wh–what—"

I bring my fingers to my cock, stroking it and using the copious amount of precum and her arousal to lube myself up before I crawl between her legs.

"Birth control?" I ask, a piece of hair flopping down in front of my eyes.

"I have an IUD," she says quickly, angling her hips up so that her hot center brushes against the head of my cock.

Fuck.

"And I'm regularly tested. You?"

"Well, considering I haven't fucked anyone since my last birthday..."

She goes still, light brown eyes widening. "Really?" she asks, her voice a whisper.

"Is it so surprising?" I ask.

She nods, her face softening. "It is. I thought that you—"

"I'm no saint, Zoe. Please don't place me on a pedestal. I just... couldn't ever bring myself to erase you from that part of me."

"Fuck," she whispers. "I need you inside of me right now."

I smirk. "Have you already forgotten who's in charge here?"

"Please, Liam."

"That's it," I purr, sliding my cock up and down her slit to make sure I'm fully lubed for her. "Breathe for me, baby girl."

CHAPTER SIXTEEN

THE UNRAVELING

ZOE

Liam shifts his hips forward an inch, and my mouth drops open as he pushes inside of me the tiniest bit. It burns—he's *by far* the biggest guy I've ever slept with. I'm still amazed that I didn't bleed that night in Catalina. I'd checked—and chalked it up to being mindlessly aroused and inebriated. But this? While I'm nearly sober? It hurts. Taking a steadying breath, his piercing blue-grey eyes, which are darker than I've ever seen them, dart between mine.

"Okay?" he asks, his voice a shaky whisper.

"Give me a second," I tell him, panting as I lock my ankles around his waist.

Liam looks almost proud as he watches me take another breath. One of his hands comes to my left nipple, and he twists it the tiniest bit. It's enough to elicit a moan from me, though, and as my whole body sparks with pleasure from his touch, he pushes in another inch.

"Fuck," he says. "I can't believe you let me take your virginity," he growls, obviously still a little angry about it. "I should've... done so many other things. If I could change that night..."

I reach up and press my hand against his mouth. "Stop talking and fuck me, Liam. I'm ready."

At my defiance, he pushes all the way in—causing me to cry out. A sharp, shooting pain erupts inside of me, and I remove my hand and pant loudly as he goes still above me.

"Zoe."

"I'm fine. I'll say yellow or red if I'm not."

Still, it fucking hurts, and the pain isn't abating. He's massive. As thick as a can of soda. I'm not used to it, and I still can't wrap my mind around how it didn't hurt anywhere near this much when I had a hymen.

"No, you're not. Do you trust me?" he asks, brows furrowed.

I nod, pressing my lips together so that he doesn't hear me whimper in pain.

Without another word, he reaches between us and drags my left leg over his right shoulder. Instantly, the pain nearly dissipates, leaving only the feeling of being *full* of him behind.

"How did you—"

He places his free hand over my mouth, just like I'd done before. "Because I taught myself to read cues, and because I know which position can help you accommodate me."

His thoughtfulness stuns me, and as he removes his hand from my mouth, my arousal sparks to life again as he slowly, *slowly*, pulls out. And then even slower, he pushes inside of me. It still stings, but barely. Shifting, his cock presses against the front of my pelvis, and—

Oh.

"Fuck," I say, my voice a breathy wheeze.

"Better?" he asks, giving me a cocky grin.

"Yes," I whisper, dragging my nails down his back. He shudders on top of me, his shoulders straining as he holds himself up above me. "Sorry, I like to scratch," I add.

"Don't apologize, baby girl. If I'm not marked up with your own personal version of graffiti by the time I'm done, then I haven't done my job well enough."

I huff a laugh as he slides in a bit deeper, and I rock my hips to meet his thrusts, making every thrust a little easier, with less resistance.

"Fuck," he rasps, placing a kiss on my lips. It's surprisingly respectful, almost sweet in the way he pulls away an inch as his tongue licks the area below my ear. "If I'd remembered how fucking good your cunt feels wrapped around my cock, I never would've walked away. You're like an addiction; so sweet, so wrong, but you feel so fucking good," he says, arms trembling as one hand comes up to my ass, squeezing my flesh tightly. He lets out a low rumble, and it gives me goosebumps because everything about this is possessive and divine.

It's such a Liam thing to do: kiss me sweetly before whispering filthy nothings in my ear.

He pulls out and then slams back in, as if he's trying to prove a point.

"Yes, Liam," I warble, my voice breaking at the sudden intrusion, the aching feeling of him hitting my cervix, and the electric feel of my pussy gripping onto him as my nerve endings go haywire. He continues driving into me with steady, hard, long thrusts, pushing me into the bed and moving me up with each one. I reach up once I get to his headboard, using it to hold myself still as he pounds into me and lifting my hips to meet his thrusts.

There's no more pain now.

"Yes, yes, yes," I chant. "Harder."

"This is what you wanted?" he asks, his voice hoarse. "You've been dying for my cock again, haven't you?"

I moan and throw my head back, my nails digging into his flesh as my pussy contracts around him once. Whatever angle he's utilizing is pressing the head of his cock right up against my G-spot, and I don't care that I might be drawing blood. I don't care that I'm going to be sore tomorrow. I need to come, and I need him to do it.

"Yes," I rasp, squeezing my eyes shut.

"You were searching for this feeling when you fucked all the other guys, weren't you?"

"Yes!" I cry out, pressing my chest into his as his thumb comes to my sensitive clit.

He purrs as his large hand comes to the leg over his

shoulder. Squeezing my flesh, he pistons in and out of me until I'm gasping for air.

"And little did you know, I was right here all along." My eyes fly open at his words, and my cunt grips and flutters around his cock with every snap of his hips. In one quick movement, he moves my leg around his waist, and the *full* feeling intensifies. "Lift," he says, large hands gripping my hips. I do as he says, and then he leans back slightly, holding me still as he tilts my pelvis up ever so slightly.

"Oh, fuck, please."

Every thrust sends me spiraling closer to my climax. I've lost count of how many times I've come tonight, and Liam watches me with a darkened expression, his hands holding me like I'm the most precious thing in the world.

"Keep talking, Zoe. I need to hear you say it," he growls, squeezing my hips so tight that I think I might bruise.

"I want this," I tell him, surprised by my honesty. "No, I need this."

"What do you need from me?" he asks, beads of sweat clinging to his hairline. "Tell me."

"I need you. Not just like this, but all the time," I say, my voice a strained rush. "You take such good care of me, and—*fuck*—I'm so close, Liam."

When my eyes find his, I see his dominant expression falter for a second, but then he grips my hips harder. His eyes are nearly black, and his hair is disheveled, a few pieces falling over his forehead. His arms and chest are shiny, with sweat, I realize, but he's giving me no indication that he's tired or that this is hard. His hands are holding my hips tight and steady, and his eyes flick down to where we're joined. Something about seeing those star tattoos on his lower hips... it's so fucking hot.

"Fuuuuck, Zoe," he murmurs, his voice breaking slightly on the last syllable of my name. And then he begins to mutter expletives under his breath—like a prayer. I'm not sure he knows he's talking out loud, but his eyes squeeze closed, and his mouth drops open when I roll my hips in tandem with his thrusts.

This. This is what I wanted.

I wanted to tease him so relentlessly that he broke completely, unraveling before my eyes.

He's always in such control, but this? As his muscles strain, as he makes noises I've only ever dreamed of, as his muscles pull and contract as he pounds into me, with his messy hair and his incoherent muttering...

This is my favorite version of him.

I use my nails and drag them over his corded forearms as all my muscles pull taut inside of me. Liam's eyes snap open, and he holds me still, growling as he glares down at me.

"Is there something else that you want, little rebel?" he grits out. "How about I decide what you get, when you get it," he adds, nails digging into my flesh to keep me from moving.

A thrill goes through me, and I huff a laugh. "God, you're already too good at this."

With furrowed brows, he clenches his jaw as he slows his movements. "You want to disobey me that badly, do you?" I make a whining sound, but I don't respond. He chuckles, letting go of my hips and pulling out. "You asked for it."

He flips me over onto my stomach, and I yelp as he drags my ass backward and pushes my legs apart. White-hot heat flares through me when he lines his cock up with my core, pushing into me in one long stretch.

His hands come to my ass, smoothly running his calloused fingers over my sensitive skin, and I shiver at his touch.

"You want to be my submissive? Fucking act like it. You asked me to be your Dom, Zoe. And I know you like to be a brat. I know you like to bluff, the lingerie earlier is a fine example," he growls as my cunt begins to feather around his cock. I'm *so* close. "And yet you fight back every step of the way. Why is that?" he growls.

I'm nearly sobbing now, fisting the duvet as he drives into me with so much force that I'm worried he's going to fuck me off the bed.

"Because," I sputter, moaning. "I do it all because I expect to lose. I *want* to lose. Don't you understand? I want you to punish me, Liam."

His thrusts falter, and for a second I think he's going to stop.

No, please. I'm so fucking close.

His hand comes down on my ass so hard, spanking me and throwing me right into a strong, intense orgasm. It slams through me so quickly that I don't convulse; I just go still, mouth open in a silent scream as wave after wave slams through me. I cry out as he spanks me again.

"Fuck yes," he mutters. "How badly do you want my cum, Zoe?"

I'm unable to speak. My eyes roll into the back of my head as his cock thickens and curves inside of me. It stretches me wider, and his hand comes down on the other ass cheek, sending me straight into yet another orgasm.

"Such a good girl," he purrs, pulling me onto his cock. "I'm going to come." He seizes behind me and lets out a low, primal groan as he stops moving.

The hot spike of his cum shoots into me. I close my eyes and gently circle my hips. He doesn't stop me, instead, he lets out another satisfied noise as he pulses into me. He's breathing heavily, and each exhale has puffs of air skittering across my spine, making me shiver.

Sagging slightly, my body soon falls onto the mattress. He pulls out at the same time before lying down next to me.

"Well, fuck," he murmurs.

Looking over at him with heavy eyes, I smile. "I'd give that an A+."

His resounding laugh sends a smattering of butterflies to fly through my abdomen, and before I know it, he's cleaning me up with a warm washcloth and ushering me into the en suite to pee.

Like I said... *so* considerate.

When I'm finished, I walk into his bedroom on shaky legs. He's wearing a pair of boxer briefs, and he's sitting on one side of the bed with his back against the headboard. Opening the duvet, he pats the navy blue sheets.

"Come here." I climb in, completely naked, and he covers me with the duvet. "Now is the part where you tell me what you need from me again," he murmurs, brushing my hair out of my face.

Emotion claws up my throat as I consider his words, and what he's offering. I'm raw and exposed, completely and utterly spent, lying naked in his bed. In a word... it's overwhelming.

"Maybe some water, a snack, and a cuddle?"

He chuckles, hopping out of bed. "Now *that* I can do. Be right back, baby girl."

After he leaves the room, the *baby girl* term of endearment makes me smile, and my eyes grow heavier as I sink into his mattress. At some point, Captain Sushi nuzzles my arm, chirping in a way that sounds almost like he's confused about why I'm in Liam's bed. Letting out a loud sigh, he settles in the bed next to me, his heavy head resting on my hip.

The last thing I remember is being lulled to sleep by his deep purring.

CHAPTER SEVENTEEN
THE LESSON

LIAM

I widen my stance and cross my arms, scowling at the sign above the dining room table.

Die, Cry, Hate

She must've had it custom made, because it matches my **_Live, Love, Laugh_** sign perfectly—same size, same colors, same font.

Little rebel.

The corners of my mouth tilt up when I consider the possibilities.

It's been three days since the Halloween party, and since that night, I've hardly seen Zoe. When I got back upstairs with her snacks and water, she was asleep. I curled around her and shortly fell asleep too, but she was gone the next morning, with only a text as proof that the night before had even happened.

ZOE

> helping layla w something. then headed
> to library 2 study. stop worrying, im fine

I'd spent the weekend catching up on grading poems, and then I'd gone out with all four of my brothers on Monday night before Chase and Juliet head back up north. There was a lot of tequila involved, and I'd eventually caved and told them everything. When I got back after taking a taxi, Zoe was sound asleep in her bed.

And this morning, she was gone, having left me yet another text. This one was far more enticing.

ZOE

> early study sesh. see u in class,
> professor ravage

After drinking my double espresso, I'd gone into the dining room to grab the poems I'd graded, only to notice the new sign. Pulling my phone out, I open our message chain.

> Bold choice.

Three dots almost immediately appear. *Studying, my ass.*

ZOE

> I thought it was funny

> Hm. It appears you're still trying to get my attention, baby girl.

The Dominant tone and nickname are new for me, but with her, it's easy to push back. It comes naturally, and it seems to make her happy when I do it. After the class when I found out my kink score, I'd gone on a deep dive of resources for Dominants. Truthfully, it didn't surprise me as much as I thought it would. Unlike Chase, I'm not about the technicalities and contracts. I know what Zoe's limits are, but because I focus on pleasure, I can read her like a book—especially because I went way too fucking far the other night in the car.

As long as we communicate, I'll be happy to explore this with her.

She texts back a minute later as I'm climbing into my Jeep.

> ZOE
> and?

Chuckling, I decide to text her when I get to campus.

Once I park and walk onto campus, I stop by my office to drop my things off before heading to class a few minutes early. When I get there, a few people are loitering near the back, and they stop talking once they see me. Taking a seat at my desk, I pull my phone out and shoot a quick text to Orion, asking him for ideas on how to... manage Zoe.

He responds a minute later as a few more people trickle in.

ORION

The best way to drive a brat crazy is to ignore her.

I stare at the phone for a beat. Not a terrible idea, and I know it'll drive her to the brink of insanity. Besides, I like the idea of making her squirm while I teach the class.

I'll give it a try. She's exhausting.

ORION

No, she's making you work for it. There's a difference.

Swallowing, the hairs on the back of my neck stand up, and in my peripheral, I see someone enter the class— a woman, dark hair, black clothes. Despite not looking directly at her, I can tell it's Zoe, because I swear I can smell her violet-scented shampoo from here. Busying myself with the papers, I keep my eyes down as I sort them alphabetically.

I can still feel her eyes on me.

I'm not going to cave that easily, little rebel.

At exactly 10:15, I stand up and walk to the white-board, writing *CRAFT* in all caps. When I turn around, I let my eyes skim over Zoe for half a second. She's sitting in the front row, wearing a long, black silk skirt, white converse, and—

One of my old Jimmy Eat World shirts.

Fuck.

She really wants to push my buttons today, doesn't she?

I don't make eye contact, instead focusing my attention on the back wall as I lecture.

"Now that we're more than halfway through the semester," I say slowly, crossing my arms and keeping my eyes focused on the other side of the room. "It's time to delve into our writing craft. While we do study the famous poets in this class and try to pull apart their relationship with nature, for your final exam, there will also be a focus on crafting a poem. So for the first part of class, I want you to find one of the poems that resonated with you the most during this course."

"Once you find it, I want you to analyze the techniques these poets used to evoke emotions, weave narratives, and portray the environment. Analyze their use of language, rhythm, and metaphor. How do they create a symphony of words that resonates with the spirit of nature? In about forty minutes, you're going to let this inspire the crafting of your own poem. Not just any poem, though. I'd like for you to really concentrate on making your peers feel something. We'll share during a peer review session first thing on Thursday, so don't worry if you don't finish today. Any questions?"

Out of the corner of my eye, I see Zoe raise her hand.

Schooling my features into neutrality, I let my eyes slide to hers, and *fuck* this was a bad idea. She's watching me with a tiny smirk, eyes twinkling with mischief.

Such a fucking tease.

"Yes, Ms. Arma?" I ask, my voice a little too gruff.

"Are we partnering up for this assignment?" she asks, her voice slightly too sweet to be genuine.

"No," I say sternly. "But feel free to talk amongst yourselves if needed."

I'm about to turn around when she raises her hand again, chin high and eyes boring into mine.

"Yes?" I nearly growl.

"I think it might be beneficial to pair up, so that we're not working alone for the duration of class. And, that way we can bounce ideas off our partner."

My jaw rolls as I heave a heavy sigh, irritation trickling through me. "If I wanted you to get paired up, I would've specified that."

I turn around quickly as a few people murmur, sitting down at my desk and willing my eyes to stay down on the papers I was in the middle of grading.

I manage to make it a few minutes, and when I chance a look up, I see people working quietly—Zoe included.

The next twenty minutes go quickly as I finish up my work, and at 11:00, I instruct everyone to begin on the crafting portion of the assignment. I let myself look at Zoe, and our eyes meet for a fraction of a second before I look off into the distance, my face composed and giving nothing away.

At 11:45, I dismiss everyone, and the flurry of movement is distracting and loud enough for me to slowly walk over to where Zoe is sitting, legs crossed, as she packs her computer up.

"May I have a word with you?" I murmur.

She looks up at me with wide eyes, and I watch as her throat bobs. "Okay. Your office?"

Giving her a single, tight nod, I walk to my desk and gather my things. I don't bother waiting for her; she knows where my office is. And if she doesn't, she'll figure it out. Once I unlock my door, I leave the door open and take a seat behind my desk. I turn my computer on for the first time in weeks. My typewriter and legal pads get much more use, and I can check my email on my phone.

But it gives me an excuse not to look up when she walks in.

In my peripheral vision, I watch her start to sit down, but I snap my eyes up to hers.

"Close the door."

I swear I see her visibly shiver as her lips quirk to one side, and she turns around and closes the door before walking over to my desk.

I have every intention of asking her about the sign—possibly making her squirm a bit. In fact, I'd been planning what I was going to do and say when we were alone, so I could convey, again, that I want to partake in this dynamic with her.

But what I don't expect is for her to walk around to my side of the desk and drop to her knees.

My body goes taut, and I lose the ability to speak when she leans back and places her palms on her thighs. As she straightens her spine, the smirk she'd been wearing earlier drops off her face, and instead it's replaced with an open, focused look, and—*fuck*.

I like it.

No. I *love* it.

Her eyes are downcast, and she's staying almost

impossibly still. It hits me then that *this* is what she's done with other men as their submissive. Did they delight in her long neck, too? Her shiny, wavy hair that's the exact shade of dark chocolate? Her petite body and heart-shaped face? Because right now, I'm not sure I've ever seen anything more beautiful. A wave of possession washes over me when I think of this being something she's done with others, and I make it my personal mission to ensure I erase every single one of them from her memories.

I don't know what to say in this situation. I don't have any experience with this, so I go with what feels right in the moment.

"I only have fifteen minutes before my next class," I say slowly.

Her eyes are still on the floor, but I see her lips twitch slightly. Still, she doesn't look up or answer me. In my research, I vaguely recall that some want permission to look up and to speak, so I wager a guess and try to keep the wince out of my voice when I speak next.

"You can look up and speak, Zoe." Immediately, she lifts her head slightly, and her eyes find mine. "Is that what you want? For me to give you permission?"

"It's up to you, I guess," she replies casually.

"It feels odd to give you permission."

"It's normally a sign of respect for the Dom. But if you don't enjoy it, we don't have to do it." Her candidness is refreshing, and I realize that she's eons more knowledgeable about all of this than me, and that I'll probably have a lot of questions and hesitations over the course of whatever this is. "Would you like my opinion?" she asks.

"Go on," I tell her, leaning back.

"I enjoy power play. But I also know the difference between the fantasy of being someone's property, and the real world. Out in the classroom? I'll talk back until I'm blue in the face. And if I want to be punished, I may do it on my knees, too. But at the end of the day, I enjoy submitting. I trust you. If at any time you're uncomfortable, use our safe words."

"Good to know," I drawl, taking in the way she's sitting so prettily before me. My cock has been straining since the moment she walked into the office, but watching her chest slowly rise and fall, seeing how the collar of my shirt drapes perfectly over her collarbone... "Like I said, I only have..." I check my computer. "Twelve minutes."

A devious gleam enters her eyes, and she tilts her head slightly. Her eyes flick to my desk, and a shudder works through me when she reaches for my gold, engraved pen—reaching behind her head and pinning her hair up with it. Explosive currents race through me at the sight of that pen holding her hair up for what she's about to do.

It's innocent and so fucking dirty all at the same time.

"I only need five."

She is going to kill me.

As if on cue, my cock twitches in my dress pants, and Zoe pulls her lower lip between her teeth.

"May I?" she asks, scooting closer.

Fuck.

I don't answer her, because truthfully, I've never been a huge fan of receiving pleasure. It feels selfish, and I get way more turned on by giving pleasure. It's become a sort of game over the years... learning all the tells a woman makes when she's about to come. Learning their unique sensitive spots, learning about their anatomy, and utilizing that knowledge to make them come again and again. Whenever they want to reciprocate, I enjoy fucking—*who doesn't?*—but I can count the number of blowjobs I've gotten on one hand.

Zoe must notice my hesitation because her expression softens. She runs her hands up my thighs, and my body jerks at the contact.

She huffs a laugh. "Tell me what you like, Liam. Let me serve you."

"I don't know what I like. I'm so used to... giving," I tell her honestly.

"You don't have any selfish needs? Not one?" she asks, pouting when I shake my head. "Let me," she purrs.

"Zoe."

"Let me suck your cock, Liam." Her eyes widen slightly when she realizes her mistake. "*Please.*"

"I'm not going to stop you, baby girl," I murmur. "Lock the door."

Giving me a tiny grin, she stands up and walks to the door, turning the lock. Then she comes over to me and kneels, smiling at me while her little hands get to work on my belt. The jangling sound is loud in the large office, and my hand automatically comes to her arm as she works my fly open.

"You have five minutes," I tell her, and her eyes flash with the challenge.

"Yes, Liam," she says, her voice a breathy whisper.

Fuck, I like the way my name sounds when she says it like that.

She frees my cock, and I relish in the way her mouth drops open slightly. When she scoots closer, I let out a long sigh, letting my hand come to the back of her neck.

She doesn't waste any time.

I hiss as her warm mouth envelopes the head of my erection, tongue swirling around once to clean up the precum. *Holy shit.* My hips buck of their own accord when she takes me almost fully into the back of her throat, and I have to actively fight the possession that rolls through me when I think of all the practice she must've had to be this good.

It doesn't matter.

She's mine now.

Mine forever.

The thought jolts through me as I watch her through hooded eyes. Her head bobs along my shaft, and her slender neck moves up and down smoothly. She's using both of her hands, and when she begins to twist them, my mouth drops open. Whatever she's doing brought me halfway to coming in her pretty, little mouth.

"Fuck, Zoe," I murmur. Pleasure claws down my spine and shoots straight to my balls.

She hums, and the vibration in her throat sends an

electric current through me, and I start to pant. Moving her mouth up and down, she tightens her grip slightly, slowing down her tempo. *Fuck, she's good.* Automatically, I start to thrust into her mouth and my hand flattens against the back of her head to keep her in place. It occurs to me that we haven't discussed a non-verbal safe word, so I don't force her to take more of me than she can, though the idea of her gagging nearly sends me over the edge.

"That's it, Zoe. Fuck, you're good at this," I tell her, and she hums again.

Another question was, 'Do you enjoy being praised in bed?' and again, I answered with a five.

Her answer after taking the kink quiz comes back to me, and I loosen my hold on the back of her neck, instead running my fingers over her cheek.

"Yes, baby girl. Look at you on your knees for me," I purr.

She audibly groans this time, and when she looks at me through her lashes, I nearly explode down the back of her throat.

"Fuck. I'm never going to forget how you look with your mouth full of my cock," I tell her. "So. Fucking. Good," I grunt, clenching my teeth.

She moans again, and this time she starts to slow down.

"Don't you dare stop, little rebel." With wide eyes, she continues, and throbbing currents of pleasure tighten in my balls. I can't help but thrust up into her mouth now, chasing my climax as her teeth scrape my cock. It's *fucking* incredible, and I let out a low groan as my cock curves up and toward my body. "Zoe, I'm going to come," I hiss, hips bouncing erratically now.

She doesn't heed my warning. Instead, she reaches down and squeezes my balls, and I see spots as my orgasm crashes through me. My cock pulses and erupts down the back of her throat at the same time as my mouth drops open and a heady groan fills the room. She swallows every couple of seconds, which only enhances the suction.

It feels as if my soul is leaving my fucking body.

A full minute later, I'm still panting as my cock twitches, and she releases me with a soft pop. Licking her lips, I watch her with hooded eyes as she stands and straightens her skirt. My heart is still hammering in my chest, and I'm genuinely speechless. She grabs her purse and walks to the door—luckily, my desk hides my still-hard cock, otherwise I'd make more of an effort to tuck myself away.

"Have a great class, professor," she says, unlocking the door and walking out—with my pen still holding up her hair.

It takes me a full three minutes of staring at the ceiling to recuperate, and after I tuck myself away and buckle my belt, my legs are still shaky. Running a hand through my hair, I take a couple of steadying breaths before making my way to my next class.

On time, I think, smiling when I think of how no one had ever gotten me off that fast.

And how I couldn't fucking wait to do it again.

CHAPTER EIGHTEEN
THE HOUSE

ZOE

I look down at my phone before glancing up at the group of people sitting in the large booth on the back wall. Orion is on the end, talking to an older woman. They're laughing, but it looks platonic. Next to him are two women who appear to be deep in conversation. And then a younger guy I think I recognize from one of my classes at Crestwood University. There are a few other people chatting, and it's nothing like I thought it would be.

Smiling, I walk up to where Orion is seated. "Hi," I say, my voice barely a whisper.

Orion turns and looks at me, a crooked smirk on his face. "Well, well, well. Look what the cat dragged in."

I laugh, instantly at ease. "Scoot over."

He does, and then he introduces me to the people in the

booth. *There are eight of us total, and as my eyes flick over each and every face, I relax.*

I'd been so worried that being here—being a part of this kind of thing—would mean I'd be hanging around people in leather or wearing collars. Instead, most of them look like an average person. If I didn't know I was at a munch, I'd never guess any of these people wanted something different in bed. And that fact alone allows me to relax instantly.

No one talks about BDSM or kink right away, so I'm one beer in when Kandie, the woman next to Orion, leans over and begins to talk to me.

"So, what brings you here, Zoe?" Her face is open and friendly, and despite Orion promising me that I didn't have to say anything about my sexual preferences, something about her makes me want to say something.

I shrug. "I'm just curious." I see Orion raise his brows as he takes a sip of his water, so I continue. "I've been reading up on BDSM, and I think I want to know more."

She grins. "You're in the right place. I'd be happy to mentor you and help you become better informed if you'd like?"

"Me too," Carla, another one of the women chimes in.

"Me three," Orion says, smiling. "You are family, after all," he drawls.

Everyone else agrees, murmuring their willingness to help, and it's...

I swallow the emotion clawing up my throat. "Thank you," I say slowly, realizing they're all waiting for me to speak. "I know I'm young, but I think... this is something I'd like to explore further."

"You can ask us anything," Kandie says gently, placing her hand on top of mine. "Once you come to one of these, as long as you're not a dickhead, you're in for life."

I give her a watery smile before clearing my throat. "How do I find out what I like?" I ask. It's the one thing that's been eating at me ever since—

Since Catalina.

"There are quizzes online," Orion offers. "I can text you the links. Once you have a baseline, you can do more research. There are videos, seminars, articles... the information is out there. And if you come to the weekly slosh, we can answer any questions you may have."

I give him an appreciative smile. "Okay. So... where do I start?"

————

Thinking back to my first munch and now this one, where we're all playing a very inappropriate game of Cards Against Humanity in a public place, makes me teary-eyed. These are my people; the same people I've spent every week with for the last year. And while I don't plan on going anywhere, it's still crazy to think that it's been a year. As I say goodbye to everyone, including Orion, who doesn't mention Liam at all, I find myself wandering down the main street of Crestwood with a sappy grin on my face.

It's past seven, and most of the shops are closed, but I still peruse the windows anyway. I've come to appreciate Crestwood as my home. When I get to a small house on the edge of the main street, I stop and wrap my arms around myself. It's light green with white trim, and there are hedges along the perimeter. The porch light is on, and I almost walk up and knock, but I turn around and walk away instead.

What would I say, anyway? *Excuse me, I'm sorry to disturb you, but my father grew up in this house. He's dead now, though, and I miss him.*

Huffing a laugh, I walk past the coffee shop, and my eyes catch on a sign tacked to the door.

Elevate your writing prowess alongside acclaimed authors! Craving real-time, expert evaluations for your work?

Embark on a transformative 30-day workshop in the heart of London, meticulously designed to immerse you in a writing experience like never before.

This exclusive opportunity is tailored for unpublished talents seeking to hone their craft.
Inquire now but be forewarned: invitations will be extended only to those meeting our discerning criteria.

With limited spaces available, our selection process is rigorous.

Dare to join the ranks of the chosen few?

I type the website into my browser, and immediately

I'm pulled in. The workshop takes place in a 18th century townhouse in central London, and as my eyes take in each author who's run the workshop in the past, excitement lances through me.

Holy shit.

They've gotten some major people in the industry— famous writers, agents, and even publishers.

I keep scrolling for more information.

It's a scholarship, and the award is based on talent. *Great.* No big deal. It's thirty days *in London...* a place I've always wanted to go ever since Stella told me about her experience growing up there. The next session takes place over my Christmas break—in seven weeks. Applications close tomorrow...

Before I know it, I'm sitting on a bench underneath a streetlight and filling out the application. It asks for a writing sample, so I copy and paste my favorite part of my book, hoping it's good enough to be selected.

I hit *submit* before I can second guess myself.

The worst thing that could happen is I don't get in.

I'm standing up when my phone chimes.

OVERLORD DADDY

Why have you been standing in front of Perky Roasters for an hour?

Laughing out loud, I text him back.

u tracking my location is a bit ott

OVERLORD DADDY

And what is 'ott' for us old folks?

over the top *eye roll emoji*

OVERLORD DADDY

You didn't answer my question.

im lying in a ditch, nbd

OVERLORD DADDY

Ha ha. I'll come pick you up.

My stomach flutters with butterflies. I can't deny that I enjoy how protective he is of me.

i thought u had to work late

OVERLORD DADDY

Despite how scintillating the task of grading papers is, I'd much rather spend my night with you.

Something dangerous and low swoops inside of my stomach, and I can't help but smile at his response. It's been an extremely busy week for both of us, and I haven't been alone with him since the blowjob in his office. We've texted of course, but we were like two ships passing in the night. I'd barely had time to eat, a fact that I'm sure would piss Liam off.

The fifteen minutes in his office earlier this week took the edge off, but I was still using all of my fancy toys every night to calm my racing, aroused mind.

ok, ill stay here

OVERLORD DADDY
Be there in twenty.

While I wait on the bench, I pull up my notes app and begin typing out the next chapter for *Between All Realms.* I'd chosen the title earlier this week during my American History class, and I was nearly finished with the first draft. My classwork has been slacking a bit, but I promise myself that I'll refocus once I'm done writing. I'm so engrossed in the story that I don't notice Liam's Jeep until it pulls up right in front of me.

I save my draft and gather my purse before walking to the passenger side of the car, but Liam opens his door instead and climbs out.

"What are you—"

He pulls a garment bag from the car and then locks it, walking over to me. But it's not the garment bag that has my attention.

It's his suit.

It's a dark blue, three-piece suit, and he's paired it with a purple tie, a dark brown belt, and dark brown shoes. His hair, which is normally mussed up, is slicked back slightly with product. As he rubs his scruff with his hand, he cocks his head and smiles.

"Fancy something to eat?"

I open and close my mouth as the pieces come together. It's Friday night, Liam is here in a suit, and he presumably has something for me to wear—either that or he expects me to wear my wide-leg jeans and black, cropped sweater (with holes) to a fancy dinner.

"Are you taking me on a date?" I ask, grinning.

He smiles—a *real* smile—and shrugs. "I am."

"Why?" I ask, my voice barely a whisper.

He takes a step closer, and his dress shoes click against the concrete sidewalk. One hand is holding the black bag, and the other is resting in the pocket of his trousers.

"Are you opposed to the idea of me trying to wine and dine my submissive?"

Well, fuck.

Pressing my lips together, I give him no indication that his words have an effect on me.

"Am I? Your submissive?"

He nods once. "If you'll have me."

I nod, and Liam takes another step closer. *God, he's so fucking good at this.*

"I need to hear you say it, Zoe."

"I'll be your submissive," I say quickly.

But I also want to be your girlfriend.

The thought rushes through my mind so quickly that I shake my head. I suck in a breath of air when he steps closer and lifts my chin with his finger.

"We can talk about what else this is after tonight, little rebel."

"How did you..."

"Because I can see it written all over your face. This isn't some one-sided dynamic, Zoe. I want this. With you. So, as your Dom and maybe something else, too, let me take you to dinner before I fuck your brains out later."

My knees shake a bit as his words wash through me. Heat rushes down to my core, spreading like a wildfire between my legs until my clit is pulsing.

"Okay," I whisper.

"Have you eaten dinner?" he asks, letting go of my chin and taking a step back.

My lips twitch. "No."

His jaw hardens slightly before he sighs. "I figured. Come on. You can change when we get there," he says, walking away toward the end of the street, the garment bag in tow.

"Where are we going? There aren't any restaurants that way," I tell him, jogging to keep up with him.

"We're not going to a restaurant," he says with a lopsided smile. "I hope you're hungry."

I squint as I study the storefronts that lead to the end of the street. They're all dark, and there's no indication that Liam is going into any of them. I follow him for another minute, confusion whirling through me. Just as I open my mouth to ask where we could possibly be going, seeing as we're at the end of the main street, he stops.

Directly in front of the house my dad grew up in.

Liam looks at me, and the shock must be evident on my face, because he rocks back on his heels, drapes the bag over his arm, and looks over at the small, single-story bungalow with me.

"Your grandparents passed this house onto your dad when they died," he says slowly. "He was in the process

of renovating and putting it up on the market when..."
He pauses and waves his hand in the air. "Anyway, it
went to auction because despite having a very rigorous
trust and guardianship set up for you, it seems he forgot
about the house. The bidder wanted half a million, so I
offered a million in cash. After the payment went
through, the auction house handed me the keys and the
deed. I had every intention of finishing his renovations
and putting it up on the market, but I could never bring
myself to do it."

I don't realize I'm crying until the taste of salt hits my
lips. "Why did you buy his childhood home?"

Liam looks over at me, his eyes heavy and sad.
"Because I wasn't ready to say goodbye," he says quietly,
his voice breaking on the last word. "Fuck," he hisses,
sniffing. "I had every intention of making this night
romantic, and now we're both crying."

I fling myself into his arms, and he catches me even
though he's carrying the garment bag. His arms come
around my waist and squeeze me, our bodies pressing
against each other as I process everything he told me.
He's warm, and this... it's too much. It's a very small part
of my dad, but it's more than I had before, and probably
more than I'll ever get again.

"Thank you," I whisper.

He runs a hand down my back before reaching into
his pocket to retrieve a key. And on the keyring is a small
magic eight ball. He pulls away and hands it to me.

"The lock is a bit finicky. I'd only ever visited a couple
of times before I bought it, so I don't know a lot about it.

But I do know which room was his, and that the back-yard is full of buried treasure."

I laugh, and take the key from him, walking to the front door and inserting it into the lock. Once the door is open, I'm overcome with nostalgia. I'd never been here—my grandparents both moved back to Portugal before they passed away when I was a young kid. But somehow, it smells like my dad. The same earthy scent, the type of wood...

I walk around the small house. There are walls that are half painted, and the kitchen doesn't have any appliances, but it's clean and cozy.

"The food should be here soon," Liam says, walking up to me and handing me the garment bag. "The bathroom is down the hall. Take as much time as you need."

I don't know what to say, so I take the bag and walk down the hall without another word. After I close the door of a small bathroom, I hang the bag on the towel rail and unzip it with shaky hands. Inside the bag is a beige lingerie set—a soft, lace bra and a matching thong —and a stunning green velvet dress with thin straps and a square neckline.

Grinning, I quickly step out of my clothes and freshen up before pulling the lingerie on. It fits perfectly, and I arch a brow at the *Agent Provocateur* label.

Seems I'm not the only one with good taste.

I slip the dress over my head and pull my hair out of my scrunchie, making sure I give it some body. At the bottom of the bag is a tan shoebox, and my mouth drops open when I see that they're black Christian Louboutin heels.

How did he know?

Slipping them on, I exit the bathroom and stop walking when I see Liam sitting at a makeshift table. It's covered in a white tablecloth, and there are several purple candles in crystal holders scattered around. He's turned down the lights, and despite being a house in the middle of a renovation, it's the most romantic thing anyone's ever done for me.

Some kind of unfamiliar emotion clogs my throat, and I stop walking for a second to clear my thoughts.

He skipped his work for me.

He brought me here instead of a restaurant because he knew how much it would mean to me.

He spent time picking out not only a beautiful dress, but shoes from my favorite designer. And the lingerie? It's gorgeous.

I tamp the emotion down as my eyes flick over the plates and silverware, and I can smell the food wafting in from the kitchen. I quietly walk forward, and when he notices me, his expression softens as he stands up. I swallow and look around, my hands clasped together in front of me.

I'm nervous—and I'm not sure why.

Should I be acting like his sub? Or should I be acting like someone who lost her father? Or... should I be acting like someone who is slowly realizing she has feelings for her father's best friend?

"The dress is beautiful," I say, smiling. "And the

shoes..." I stop to show them off, biting my lower lip to keep from grinning like a maniac.

"Stella helped me," he admits. "However, I did find that lingerie shop all by myself. Every single item in there is horrifically overpriced," he adds.

I laugh as I walk over to him, reaching out for his purple tie and straightening it. "But you enjoy the results," I murmur, looking up at him.

He smirks as his hands come to my hair, and he runs his fingers through it. "Oh, I'm very much looking forward to seeing you in the things I picked out."

Even in heels, I have to stand on my tip toes and pull his head down to me in order to kiss him. When our lips meet, he inhales sharply as his hands roam from my scalp down to my waist, pulling me tight against his body. I groan as his tongue finds mine, and sparks of electricity scatter down my spine as his hands grip my hips firmly.

He pulls away with a heavy breath. "Fuck. If we keep going, I'll want to eat you for dinner instead of the five-course meal I've ordered."

I huff a laugh as I lick my lips. "I don't see an issue with that."

He takes another step away and gives me a smug smile. "We're eating food first."

Tilting my head, my lips twist to the side as I walk around to my chair. "Is that an order from my Dom?"

Something darkens in his expression as he walks over to me and pulls my chair out. "Do I need to answer that?"

That's a yes, then.

I straighten my spine and sit down primly as he pushes my chair in for me before walking into the kitchen. I want to ask him what kind of food he's serving, but the submissive in me stays quiet. A minute later, he comes out with two small bowls of soup.

"I called in some favors," he says slowly, setting my bowl down with a soup spoon. "Chase knows the owner of The Black Rose."

"The fancy place on the other end of the town?" I ask, looking down at the dark red soup.

Liam nods. "The chef prepared five courses for us and cursed me out when I asked for takeaway boxes." I smile and look down at the soup. It smells divine. "The first course is beetroot soup with horseradish cream. Don't ask me what else is in it because I'll butcher it."

I smile as I take the first bite, and my mouth fills with saliva. "Oh my god. It's like an orgasm for my mouth," I say without thinking. Liam is watching me eat with an unreadable expression, and as I pat my mouth and set my spoon down, I swallow and clear my throat. "What?"

He shakes his head as his expression softens. *Fuck,* something about watching *him* watch *me* is so sexy. Because for most people, his expression is serious.

But for me?

He looks at me differently than anyone else.

His lips twitch. "I like watching you eat. You know... since you're really bad at it when I'm not around."

I snort and cover my mouth. "I *do* eat. I just... forget sometimes."

"Keep going," he says, his voice rough and laced with dominance.

We finish our soup in near silence, and as he brings in the next four courses—aged beef, grilled scallops in a half shell, a winter mushroom and squash salad, and finally, fig leaf ice cream with flakes of edible flowers on top.

It's completely over the top, but I can't help but smile the entire way through. As I lean back and watch Liam clear the plates, my stomach erupts in butterflies again. He slowly walks into the living room, and my heart skips a beat. He's too handsome for his own good, and I can't believe I get to be *with* him.

"Shall we?" he asks, offering his arm.

"Where are we going?" I stand up and walk over to him.

"For a walk."

Liam offers me his coat when we get outside, and he doesn't say anything as we walk along the quiet main street. The pub and Orion's new bar are busy, but other than that, we have downtown Crestwood to ourselves. I know Miles spent a lot of time commissioning the city council to get the city to look as nice as it does, and as we walk underneath old-fashioned lamps and string lights, I secretly thank him for making it so cozy.

When we arrive at The Grand hotel, Liam gestures for me to go inside.

"Here?" I ask, eyes widening. "Rooms here are like two-thousand dollars a night."

He takes a step forward and pulls me into him by my

waist. I let out a tiny gasp as his other hand comes to my cheek.

"Here's what we're going to do," he purrs, holding me close as a couple walks out the revolving door of the hotel. Kissing the top of my head affectionately, we both smile at them as they walk away. When they're out of earshot, Liam brings his lips to my ear, sending a shiver down my spine. "You're going to walk into the hotel with me, and once I pay, we're going to go up to our suite," he adds. "Every snarky comment will be tallied up, so choose your words wisely."

Holy. *Fuck.*

I'm having a hard time believing that Liam has never done this before me.

"Okay," I concede as a thrill goes through me. "Daddy," I add, trying to hide my smile.

Little does he know, I've been waiting for him to punish me for weeks.

Liam stiffens, and his lips tug down into a frown. "One," he says sternly.

Goosebumps run down my arm at his warning. He turns and ushers us through the revolving doors.

I take a deep breath, gearing up to show him how much I want to make him work for it.

CHAPTER NINETEEN
THE DOMINANT

Zoe

The lobby of the hotel is small, but they've spared no expense decorating it. Thick, luxurious rugs line the old, polished hardwood floors, and the furniture is modern and bright. Fresh flowers sit undisturbed on every surface, held in glass vases that look like books. Massive, gilded frames on every wall house what could very well be real renaissance paintings. A large crystal chandelier hangs overhead, and once I'm done gawking at the opulence, I jog to keep up with Liam.

"Hello, Barbara," he says, his voice low yet familiar.

"Mr. Ravage!" She beams, flashing white teeth as she flips her long blonde hair over her shoulder. "Would you like your usual room?" she asks, and my mouth drops open.

It hits me then. His *usual* room. He comes here a lot,

then? I know he said he hasn't slept with anyone else since Catalina, but what else would he be doing in a hotel room regularly?

I don't normally consider myself a jealous person, but I can't ignore the lancing pain that cuts through me when I consider that perhaps Liam wasn't telling the truth. Or that I'm not the first woman he brought here.

"Yes, please," he says politely.

I look between Barbara and the other receptionist to see if their expressions will give anything away, but she clicks on her computer for a second before looking at me.

"And your guest's name?"

I clear my throat. "Zoe Arma."

Barbara nods. "And one night like usual?" she asks Liam.

My stomach fills with dread and I suddenly feel so duped. Why would Liam stay single or not sleep around? He's a warm-blooded male who got unlucky when he became my guardian. Of course he'd need a place to screw random women. Even if he has been celibate since Catalina, there's no doubt in my mind that this is where he disappeared to all those nights when I was younger.

The thought of him hiding that part of himself from me... it hurts.

"Oh, I think we'll only need a couple of hours. Like *usual*," I grit out.

Keeping my eyes on Barbara, I notice when she stops typing and coughs once. Liam sidles up to my side, and I don't look at him as he bends down.

"Two."

He thinks we're just playing a game—that I'm being a brat, so he'll punish me.

But all I want to do is cry.

Barbara gives us a large smile and hands us two cards.

Liam removes one of them and holds it up. "We only need one key but thank you."

Before she can take it back, I snatch it out of his hand and give him my most charming smile.

"You never know, Daddy. It's good to keep our options open."

Liam's jaw rolls, but he doesn't say anything as his eyes bore into mine. Out of the corner of my eye, I see Barbara and the other receptionist exchange a look.

He quickly turns to Barbara. "Have a good night."

Grabbing my hand, he drags me away from the reception desk.

"Three and four," he growls under his breath, walking too quickly for me to keep up in my heels.

I'm jogging to keep the pace so I don't fall flat on my face, and both of our shoes click against the old wood floors.

Pressing the *up* button on the elevator, he turns to face me. And *fuck*, his expression is full of ire. Despite his tense body language, his eyes are almost twinkling— almost like he's enjoying this.

When the elevator dings, and the gold doors slide open, he ushers for me to walk in before him with a darkened expression. I step inside before he does. The ride up to the ninth floor is slow and tense, but my veins are singing with something uncomfortable and slimy. I don't enjoy feeling jealous, but all I can think about is how Liam has possibly been here with other women–especially after such a romantic night. No one has ever done anything that kind for me, and it hurt more to think that I was going to be another one of his conquests.

Surely, it was all a misunderstanding, right? They knew him from something else, something innocuous. But as the doors slide open and he walks out ahead of me, I can't help but think of all the nights he came home late.

As we stop in front of the door labeled *Presidential Suite*, I roll my eyes when he indicates that I walk in first. As if his money could ever impress me. I didn't grow up rich like him, but I knew he had a lot of money. I wasn't a fan of corporate greed, so it never appealed to me. And this hotel? With this suite? It feels... *different*. His house —*our* house—is large, but it's not flashy like this.

I'm still stewing as Liam closes the door behind us, and after he locks it, he walks over to me and gently takes my chin in his hand.

"Don't think I didn't see that eye roll," he mutters. "That's five."

I'm about to respond when he drops my chin and walks toward the bedroom. Well, I guess we're getting straight down to business. It's not unlike the other experiences I've had with Doms, but I suppose I thought it would be different with him. As I enter the bedroom, he gestures to the black box waiting for me.

"Please put that on. I'll be waiting in the other room."

He turns and walks out, leaving me feeling bereft and cold. Once the bedroom door clicks shut, I walk over to the box and peer down at the label. *Bordelle*. More lingerie, then. I run my finger along the box, wondering what could possibly be waiting for me. *Bordelle* specializes in bondage-style lingerie. Maybe he thinks he can recycle the same hotel room he's used for other women while testing out this dynamic with me?

My thoughts rapidly fire back and forth between wanting to be mad and wanting to find an explanation. As a sub, I'm no stranger to communication, and I know I should very well go out there and ask him why he brought me here. But a small part of me *wants* to do this with him, even if I'm not the first woman he's brought back here. There's a bigger part of me that wants to see what he has planned for tonight–as he's obviously put a lot of thought into it.

I'm confused, and my mind isn't in the right place. It's like all of my insecurities about us are coming to a head now that we're *actually* doing this.

Making my mind up, I step out of the velvet dress and lingerie from earlier, kicking my shoes off in the process. Maybe it's the brat in me, or maybe I want to one up him a little. Either way, I'm practically smiling when I grab the white robe hanging on the back of the door.

A minute later, I enter the living room. Liam is standing by the window that overlooks downtown Crestwood, and as his gaze turns guarded and dark, I almost wish I hadn't put the robe on.

"Interesting choice of apparel," he says calmly. "Are you sure you want to defy me before you know what your punishment will be?"

I shrug. "I figured it would all be coming off me anyway," I say slowly, swallowing as his eyes flash.

"I see. Care to tell me what's bothering you?"

Fuck. How did he know?

"Nothing," I lie, and the words taste like ash in my mouth. I don't enjoy lying—especially to him. But my hang-up is not a rational one, and I don't want him to think I'm the jealous type. "Why do you think something is bothering me?"

"Despite your tendency to be a brat, I noticed your change in demeanor as soon as we checked in. So, you can tell me what's bothering you, or I can stop the scene."

I visibly shiver at his words. He truly has no idea how good he is at this, but I suppose it makes sense. Oldest brother of five fucked up kids. Always the caretaker. Always making decisions. Always reading people and seeing more than he lets on. Discovering his Dominance is only another facet to the protective, commanding persona that Liam embodies every single day.

"I said nothing's wrong."

Liam's jaw ticks as he rubs his mouth with his hand. As he takes a step closer, my heart begins to race, and I wipe my sweaty palms on the robe. When I look up at him, all of the anger and wrath is gone from his expression, replaced only by indifference. It sends icy goosebumps to erupt along my skin. Because while I could at least predict when I'd piss him off, I couldn't predict that he'd choose to end the scene or call this whole thing off altogether.

"Take your robe off, please," he says, his voice detached and unaffected.

He never sounds like that with me—like he's talking to a stranger.

I bring my hands in front of me and waffle between telling him I'm sorry and doing what he says. When I don't move, he sighs and walks over to the couch, leaning against it.

He visibly sags, looking almost defeated and very unsure of himself, "Yellow."

"What? Yellow, as in... *yellow*?"

"Yes. I'm doing something wrong," he says slowly, running his hands over his face before looking up at me. "I'm new at this, and you haven't been yourself since we walked into the hotel. So, either I'm doing something wrong, or you're not telling me something."

My chest aches from his words, and when his soulful eyes find mine, it nearly cracks in half. I've never had a Dom safe word like he just did. I know it happens sometimes, and I know it's because I'm not communicating. Even though he's in charge here, he's still new, and I'm doing us both a disservice by not telling him what's wrong.

"No, you're doing great," I tell him, walking over to the couch and stepping between his legs. Taking his hands, I place them on my hips. "I'm sorry. Barbara said something about seeing you again, and I just thought..."

I bite my tongue. *Am I really about to admit that I'm acting this way because apparently Liam turns me into a jealous fiend?*

"What?" he asks, pulling me close so that our bodies are pressed together. "You thought what?"

I chew on my lower lip and debate whether or not to tell him, but then his hands slide to the opening of the robe, and his fingers press against my clit without any warning.

I gasp as my knees buckle.

"I don't enjoy seeing you unhappy, little rebel," he murmurs, inserting one finger into my slick core. "But I've been waiting to sink my fingers, tongue, and cock into your perfect, little cunt all night long, and my patience is wearing thin."

"God." I hiss as he inserts another finger. Pleasure spikes through me, and I know it won't take me very long at all to come. With him, it seems to come so much easier because he knows *exactly* what to do to make me lose control.

"So," he says slowly, working his hand faster. "I'll ask you again. What's bothering you?"

My eyes roll into the back of my head as he curves his fingers and presses them against my G-spot. The feeling is relentless; it's like someone is shocking me with a live wire, and my body begins to coil and tighten as his thumb brushes against my clit. The combination has me gripping his shirt as I let him bring me to orgasm quick and fast, with no pretenses.

"I just... thought... you brought... other women.

Here," I mutter, a groan escaping my lips as my climax draws unbearably close.

As his thumb circles my clit—as my cunt begins to contract—he removes his hand. My mouth drops open as my ruined orgasm claws through me. It's horrendous; there's nothing to grip, nothing to use for friction, so it quickly dissipates into nothing. The ache turns into a physical pain, and I squeeze my eyes shut.

"Look at me," Liam says softly.

My eyes snap open, and he gives me a small, satisfied smirk. "So you can listen to directions." I don't say anything. I'm still shaking from the ruined orgasm. He continues. "Barbara knows me because I often book a few hours in this room to write."

My mouth drops open. *Oh.*

"You know, when I said I hadn't fucked anyone since Catalina, I wish you would've believed me. I'm not a liar, baby girl."

His words wash over me, and I suddenly feel guilty for doubting him. For doubting *us*.

"Why do you come to this room?"

"A lot of my favorite writers have written books in this room. Even though I haven't written anything in years, coming here is inspiring. It's a change of scenery. Also, I live with this incredibly sexy woman who drives me crazy, so I needed a place to concentrate."

"I see," I say slowly.

"Is that what was bothering you? That you think this was some kind of bachelor pad where I brought women to fuck?" I nod, and he chuckles. "God, Zoe. If you only knew..." He shakes his head. "I don't know what your other Doms were like, but I hope you know that this is it for me. I'm not planning on going back to how things were. I can't exist in a universe knowing what you taste like and what you sound like when you come on my tongue and not be with you. I want to do this with *you* and you only. If you'll have me, that is."

I swallow the emotion ready to burst out, instead taking my hands and placing them on his neck.

"That's the thing. You've always had me."

His resounding smile is large, and it causes my stomach to swoop with something dangerous and completely crazy, so I ignore the feeling and smile back.

"Good girl," he praises. "Now, where were we?"

"I believe you asked me to go into the bedroom and change?" I ask, turning my expression neutral and acquiescent.

"On one condition," he says slowly. I nod to show that I'm listening, so he continues. "Use your safe word next time. There are some things I want to try tonight, and because I'm new at this, I don't want to keep second guessing myself. I need to be able to get into the mindset without worrying about breaking the scene again. Understood?"

"I can do that."

"I know you can. Now, go get changed."

Feeling much lighter than normal, I walk into the bedroom and change into the black lingerie set he's picked out. It's simple—just a black mesh bra and panties. However, they come with a matching silk blindfold and soft tie, presumably for my wrists. Smiling, I decide to take things into my own hands and show him how *good* I can be.

I pull the blindfold over my eyes and slip my wrists into the silk tie. It's not a true restraint; I can get in and out of it by myself easily. And I appreciate that Liam is starting slow. After a few minutes, there's a soft knock on the door, and I school my face into neutrality as I hear Liam open the door. I squirm slightly when I think about what he's going to see when he walks in...

Me.

Tied up with my hands behind me and blindfolded.

Kneeling.

His footsteps are heavy as he walks closer, and even though my eyes are covered, I keep my face angled down at the ground. A shudder works through me when the tips of his fingers brush along my left shoulder, and the heat radiating off his body only makes me feel hotter. I expect him to tease me a bit, but he's quiet. I shift my weight to alleviate my aching core, wondering all the while what he's thinking.

Is he displeased? Or does he enjoy seeing me on my knees?

"Please sit on the edge of the bed."

I try to gauge the tone of his voice, but without being able to see his face, it's hard to tell how he's feeling by those seven words. I stand up and he places his warm hands on my shoulders, guiding me to the edge of the bed. As he gently pushes me down so I'm sitting on the edge, I pull my legs together before he takes his hands and spreads my legs. I inhale sharply, but I don't speak.

My heart starts to beat erratically when I hear the rustle of his clothes and the warmth of his body against the inside of my thighs. His hands come to my bare hips, and in one swift motion, he tilts them up.

"What are you doing?" I whisper, my whole body shaking with anticipation.

"I told you that I was going to punish you for acting out earlier."

"But..."

"We talked, yes, but I never said I wasn't going to see that part of it through."

My skin heats as his breath fans against the mesh material of my panties.

"I want you to count, Zoe."

"Count?"

Before I can process what he could possibly mean, his teeth are dragging the mesh over my mound to the side, and then his tongue swipes from my core to my clit in one warm, flat motion. I jerk at the sudden contact, and the mesh material of my bra rubs against my hardening nipples. I squeeze my eyes shut even though they're covered, arching my back slightly as he chuckles against my skin.

"You respond so well to me. Even that first night. It's like you were made just for me."

I gasp as he slides his tongue up and down in smooth, languid motions that have me bucking my hips every time his tongue presses against my clit. Like before, he must know exactly what he's doing, because that long, slow motion has me trembling and curling my toes already.

"I wish you could see yourself," he murmurs, his finger sliding underneath the elastic band of my underwear. Slowly pulling them down, the motion of them sliding down my legs gives me goosebumps. Everything inside of me is pulsing, and I can't help but try to calm my heavy breathing. "So fucking wet," he adds. "So fucking beautiful. *Waiting* for me to give you pleasure, but most importantly, trusting that I *can*."

With that last word, he inserts two fingers, and I let out a guttural groan. I'm still aching for release because of my ruined orgasm, and the sensation of his fingers and tongue on me is nothing less than exquisite.

"Yes," I say, agreeing with him. "Please, Liam," I whimper, circling my hips as much as I can so that he takes the hint—*harder.*

Faster.

More.

"That's it," he murmurs, his breath hot against my skin. "My good girl."

My back arches at his praise, and I start to roll my hips while he pumps his fingers into me.

"Liam," I rasp, wanting to fall onto the bed. "Can I touch you?"

"Yes," he whispers.

The wrist tie is gone in an instant, and my hands are in his hair as I lean back.

"Fuck yes," I cry out, throwing my head back and gripping his hair and pulling him closer.

"Take what you need from me, baby girl," he mutters, before he swipes his tongue against my sensitive bud. "Give me everything. I want you to squeeze my fingers, and I want to hear you scream my name." With his free hand, he hikes one of my legs over his shoulder, giving him better access to me, and I realize that my legs are shaking. "Don't forget to count."

"I'm close," I tell him.

"Take off your blindfold."

With one hand, I shove it over my forehead and nearly gasp at what I see.

When I look down, I see him watching me, and the intensity of his gaze has me shattering around his fingers with his tongue flat against my clit. My hips undulate as I clench my teeth and whimper, body convulsing as my orgasm slams through me, hard and fast. Liam doesn't relent–instead, he doubles down and works his tongue faster, curving his fingers slightly as one orgasm immediately rolls into a second one. I'm gasping for air and despite wanting to squeeze my eyes shut, I love the look of Liam kneeling between my legs more.

"One, two," I say, shaking.

Liam pulls back and I nearly gasp at the sight. His pupils are blown almost black in color, and his lips are shining with... *me.* Giving me a lascivious smile, he kneels and looks up at me, hands on his hips.

I can see where his cock is straining against his pants, and despite coming twice, I want more in the form of him inside of me.

"You're going to give me three more," he growls, and before I have a chance to argue, his mouth is on my cunt.

I jump at the contact, but he goes soft and slow, flicking his tongue in small, teasing strokes against my sensitive nub.

"You taste so fucking good on my tongue," he says, using one finger to push into my opening. "Take off your bra and lie down."

I reach behind me and unclasp my bra before letting myself fall fully onto the bed, using my one leg to push against his shoulder. I'm about to ask if he wants me to scoot back when he lifts the other leg over his other shoulder. One warm hand comes to my ass and squeezes. The feeling is... *fuck.*

I can hear how wet I am every time he pushes his finger into me, and the way he's groaning—the sound almost too low to hear—makes me seem like the most decadent thing he's ever tasted. No one has ever treated me like this. Like I'm the main course and he can't wait to devour me. I roll my hips against his mouth, and he chuckles as my hands fly to his hair.

"Yes, Liam," I gasp.

"Come on, baby girl. Give me two more, and then you can have my cock for the last one."

Fuck.

"So fucking perfect," he mutters against my clit, his tongue feathering lightly and working me into a frenzy. He inserts a second finger into me, and as I open my mouth to cry out, he adds a third. "So tight. Need to stretch you and get you ready to take my cock," he adds, his voice low and reverent.

"Yes, please, please, please."

"You can do it, little rebel. Come on my tongue. Such a good listener. Do you see what happens to good girls who listen?"

His praise sends warmth through me, and everything pulls taut as his lips seal over my clit and sucks.

I explode with a scream. "Oh god, fuck yes, just like that, I'm coming, I'm—"

My orgasm intensifies, and my eyes roll back as he continues pumping into me without any relief. My mind goes blank, and my hips jump with every swipe of his tongue. Every muscle in my body aches from the constant push and pull, and as he continues his attention on my clit with his tongue, there's nothing I can do but endure it. It's almost... painful... and I try and push him away with my hands.

"Please, please, stop, I can't."

He laughs against my core. "You did perfectly, Zoe. But I'm not done, remember? I didn't hear you count."

"Three, three, please, I can't keep going!"

My legs are shaking on his shoulders, and everything aches. I lift my head and look at him, but he gives me a devilish smirk before diving into my sensitive core.

My hands smack onto the duvet and my fingers curl around the fabric, pulling it to stop the onslaught of my nerves being on fire. It's too much, and my mouth is open in a silent scream as Liam works up to three fingers again.

"I can't. I can't come again."

"You can, and you will," he says, his voice husky. "Even if it means I have to stay here all night."

"Oh fuck, Liam," I whimper, trying to get away from his mouth, trying to give myself some sort of reprieve. Even with past lovers, it never felt this intense. My body convulses with every movement, yet he somehow gets me worked up again.

"That's it, baby girl. You're gripping my fingers so hard. I told you that you could do it."

"It's too much," I say, half-sobbing. My cheeks are wet, and I realize with a shock that I've been crying.

Liam slows his movements, and his free hand comes to my stomach. "Zoe, look at me."

I lift my head, and though he's slowed down, he still has three fingers in me. His scruff is wet, and his lips are red. The dedication in his expression has me rolling my hips against his fingers, despite telling him that another orgasm wasn't possible.

"Give me a color," he says, his voice gentle.

"Green," I tell him, sniffling. "Keep going. *Please.*"

His resounding grin is beautiful, and when his teeth graze my sore clit, it sends a smattering of pleasure clawing down my spine. I don't know if I want to escape or beg for more at this point. *Both? Neither?* My body is chasing the pleasure and my brain is begging for it all to stop. A minute later, after spreading my legs wider and running his free hand down my leg, I come apart on his tongue for the fourth time.

"Four, fuck! Four!" I scream, fully sobbing now.

My body is no longer my own, and my vision goes white as the forced orgasm sears through me. This one almost hurts. The muscles in my body are sore, and my pelvis feels like it's been split open. Still, I whimper when he removes his fingers, already missing the sensation of being full of him.

He stands up and looks down at me with a warm expression. His hair is messy from me running my fingers through it, and his tie is askew. Somehow, watching him unravel like this is hotter than anything else. He worked *so* hard to make me come. It's like he has a personal stake in my pleasure.

"Do you think you can take one more?" he asks, unzipping his dress pants and pulling out his cock.

My mouth drops open as his thumb works over the dark pink head, swirling the moisture gathered there.

"Yes," I say, because it's true.

He gathers some of the clear liquid onto two fingers, and then he leans forward and presses them into my mouth.

"Look at how worked up I am because of you," he murmurs, and I groan when the salty taste of him hits my lips. I swirl my tongue around his fingers, and his heady groan sends a flash of need through me. "That's it. Fuck, you're perfect."

I respond by popping my mouth off his fingers and scooting back. His gaze dips down between my legs, and I spread them open for him.

"Fuuuuck, Zoe. I love it when you show me what's mine, little rebel."

The possession in his words only makes me wetter, and before I can react, he grabs my ankles and flips me onto my stomach. I steady my hands and knees, feeling vulnerable to be so exposed to him. But he runs a hand over my ass and comes up right behind me, knocking my knees apart slightly. He groans again, and like before, the sound is so low that it's barely audible.

Without saying anything, the head of his cock pushes into my overused pussy, and a hiss of pain escapes my lips when he moves into me inch by inch. His hand comes to my hair, and he gently fists it and tugs me back so my spine is arched.

"Fuck, this is my favorite view," he murmurs, slowly filling and stretching me.

When he's all the way inside of me, I let out a shaky breath. "Harder," I beg.

He pulls me up so that I'm upright on my knees, and his body is pressed against my back. "Very well. Hold onto the headboard."

I reach forward until my hands are gripping the wood, and he pulls out slowly before slamming into me.

I'm glad to be holding on, because he begins to fuck me relentlessly. He's fucking into me so hard, and I'm worried he's going to break the bed. I scream as more tears slide down my cheeks, because it feels *so fucking good,* and my aching body coils and tightens. Liam runs his hands over my body, my waist, my hips, before coming around to my breasts as he drives into me. His mouth finds my shoulder, and he bites, causing my pussy to clench around him.

His resounding groan makes me do it again, and that's when his hand comes around to my jaw, gripping it tightly.

"Such a brat," he growls, his voice a low purr.

"Your brat," I tell him, whimpering as he thrusts up and into me.

I rock backward, seeking the friction that I need, before both of his hands grip my hips and hold me still.

"Yes you fucking are," he says. "Mine. Always."

The reverential way he says that has me moaning, and each snap of his hips has me careening toward my fifth climax. I roll my hips and move against him as his movements slow, his fingers that had been gripping my flesh loosening. I take that as a sign that he's letting me lead, so I ride his cock until he's groaning with each push back of my hips. The sound of my wetness and our skin slapping against each other mixes with his low vibrations and my breathy noises, and for a minute, that's all I hear. My fingers curl around the wood as my climax gets closer, and I let one of my hands drift down to my clit, using our wetness as lube to rub small circles despite being swollen and sore.

After one particularly hard thrust backward, his hands fly to my waist and hold me still.

"I'm close," he whispers.

"I want to feel you come," I tell him, moaning.

"Not before you do. You owe me a fifth orgasm."

He drags his cock out of me slowly before slamming in, and I clench my inner muscles around him again.

"Fuck, Zoe, I can't."

His movements stutter, and his hands dig into my waist as he lets out a long, slow groan. One of his hands comes between my legs, and he begins to work my clit between the two rough pads of his fingers. Between the staggered movements he's making, and the low, gravelly noises leaving his lips, I know it'll only take a couple of swipes of his fingers against my clit to make me come.

"Yes, like that," I say, my voice hoarse as my fingers dig into the wood headboard. "Fuck, Liam–"

"Not so fast," he growls, pulling out. I gasp as the empty feeling washes over me. I was *so* close. "I want to watch you."

I turn around to face him on shaky legs, and then I lower myself onto my back as he slowly strokes himself and climbs between my legs. He doesn't move; he only watches me, legs spread, as he works his cock with his hands. And his face... he looks both mesmerized and frustrated. His hair is a complete mess, falling over his forehead haphazardly. His forehead and neck are shining with the exertion of fucking me, and his shirt is mostly untucked and wrinkled. Suddenly, the urge to make him fall apart is too much to ignore. I lift my hips and silently ask for what I want.

Him.

Inside of me.

Looking almost resigned, he angles his cock down and places it against my opening. I hike my knees higher to give him better access, and out of the corner of my eye, I see his hands fist the fabric of the duvet on either side of my head.

His eyes don't leave mine as he pushes into me, and *fuck,* I never want him to leave. Liam inside of me feels like everything good in the world poured into one thing, and the way he's looking at me makes my chest ache with want. He's quiet as his body begins to shake on top of mine, and I don't need his fingers or tongue to come. I only need to see him lose control on top of me. My eyes don't leave his as he pulls out and slowly drives into me. I relish in the way he's watching me with the most intense expression I've ever seen. It's raw, and wild, and it makes everything inside of me sing. I raise my hips slightly, and I swear my heart skips a beat when his lashes flutter.

This. This is what I crave as a submissive. Sure, I enjoy the power play. But watching my Dom fall apart on top of me, like nothing in the world could pull us apart? It's like nothing else, and I've never experienced it this intensely before.

"I'm close," I tell him, feeling one of his hands come to the back of my thigh as he moves over me,

"Show me," he says, his voice barely a whisper. When his chest rumbles with a groan that he tries to hold back, I lose it, and everything inside of me snaps powerfully.

My toes curl, and I see stars as my fifth climax slams through me. I try to twist away from the sheer power of the orgasm, but he doesn't let me. He holds me still, and each wave shocks me to the point of almost passing out. My cunt greedily contracts around his cock, milking him as my body bows off the bed, and I'm not breathing. No air is entering my lungs, because I can't move...

I gasp when his cock hardens, and I hear him moan on top of me. He slows his pace, holding back slightly.

"Liam," I plead. "Please. I want to feel you come."

Liam drops his head to my neck as his teeth graze my skin, the sound of his incoherent words feathering against my skin. He leans back slightly so that he can support himself on his legs, and his hands come to my hips, gripping them in a bruising manner. I clench my core around him again, reveling in the way he twitches.

"Fuck, fuck, Zoe." My name falls from his lips in such a devoted way that I can only stare at him as he approaches his breaking point.

He continues muttering incoherently, and then his face slackens, and his mouth drops open. His hands take mine as he laces our fingers together, and it's both sweet and intense.

Watching Liam come apart is a religious experience. His thrusts turn erratic, and then he stills completely as he begins to pulse deep and hard inside of me. The warmth spreads through my core, and I can't look away as he watches me, as his eyes bore into mine. The dark blue color is intense and profound in a way that makes me want to grieve that it's over, that he's finished.

And it terrifies me.

He goes still and almost instantly collapses on top of me, save for his abdomen, which he manages to keep from crushing me completely. His arms are shaking as he kisses my neck, my collarbone, the spot underneath my ear...

His cock is still twitching inside of me.

"Fuck," he says, taking three deep breaths as he rolls onto his back and pulls me with him, slipping out of me.

I drape one leg over him as he holds me, and we both ignore his seed seeping out of me against his thigh. When I look up at him, he's smiling.

"That didn't feel very much like a punishment," I tease.

He chuckles, and the sound of it against my head on his chest makes me giddy and happy. And *tired*.

"I'll have to rectify that next time, but first I need a bit more guidance on what you like in that department. I never..." He swallows. "I never want to hurt you." Squeezing me tighter, he sighs contentedly. "That's probably a conversation for another day. Now, since you fell asleep the last time I tried to give you aftercare, let me make it up to you this time."

"Snacks?" I ask, my voice hopeful.

"Go use the restroom. When you come out, I'll clean you up and we can have all the snacks you want."

CHAPTER TWENTY
THE HARNESS

LIAM

The next few weeks pass in a blur of never-ending poetry to grade, Zoe locking herself in her room to get all of her schoolwork done, and me trying to finish up Chase's Lamborghini Miura in time to give it to him for Christmas. Most big brothers get their younger brothers wallets or ties, but no. He's getting a fucking car.

Not to mention I've started writing again, and it feels fucking incredible.

I hardly see Zoe except for in class, and the fifteen minutes between our Tuesday and Thursday afternoon classes is spent having quickies in my office or going down on her, despite her insisting that she pay it forward. Some mornings, I press her against the counter as I take her from behind, and I almost never have time for proper aftercare. On weekends, she's busy with schoolwork and writing, and I spend any free time I have helping Orion with yet another bar he opened on the edge of town.

Despite texting Zoe every day and seeing her most days, it's usually in passing. Aside from class, we haven't spent more than two hours together since the night of the hotel. Which is why I can't concentrate the Friday before finals week in mid-December—because Zoe and I have cleared our schedules and booked *two* nights at The Grand. However, before we can make our reservation, we promised Orion that we would attend the opening night of his new bar.

I nervously tidy up the kitchen as I wait for Zoe to come downstairs. My overnight bag—complete with my big surprise for Zoe—sits by the door, and I run my hands over the lapels of my wool blazer a few times between checking my phone. As I'm pocketing it, I hear her come down the stairs. I turn around and straighten as she walks into the kitchen and sets an overnight bag down by the door.

My heart stutters as she gives me a coy smile, and I can't help it when my eyes roam down to her outfit. We're both dressed casually, but I can't help the way my mouth goes dry when I let my eyes wander down to her leather high-waisted trousers, cinching her narrow waist and accentuating her round hips. On top, she's wearing a tight, long-sleeved, cropped mesh top that subtly hints at the dark red lingerie underneath—and it also matches the dark red shoes I bought her last week as a present for finishing the first draft of her book. Her lips are red, and her hair is down and wavy around her shoulders.

I open and close my mouth to tell her how fucking stunning she looks, but the words die in my throat. Splaying my hands at my sides, all I can hear is my pulse rushing in my ears, and suddenly, I wonder why the fuck I waited so long to make her mine.

"Hi," she says slowly, her heels clacking against the wood floors of the kitchen as she walks toward me.

I'm still speechless as she gets closer, and my body thrums with need when her scent invades my nostrils.

It hasn't been enough.

The quickies, the glances, the casual touches... it hasn't satiated my need for her *at all*. Because right now, all I can think of doing is texting Orion and apologizing that I'm not able to make it to the opening of his bar— that I'm too busy feasting on Zoe to do anything else but make her come all weekend long.

"Cat got your tongue?" Zoe teases, and Captain Sushi chirps as he trots over to her.

She laughs and kneels down to pet him, but that doesn't help whatever it is that I'm feeling. Nor did the piles of clean clothes, the leftovers in the fridge, or the genuine smiles she would give me whenever she saw me. Despite both of us being busy, I never felt lonely or like she wasn't on the same page as me.

It felt like I finally had someone else on my team to take the burden of worrying about everything away.

When she stands, she reaches out and pats the lapel of my jacket. I'm dressed casually too, wearing dark jeans with a black button up and a black suit jacket, and despite us not intending to match, I like that we're both in black.

"Hi," I reply belatedly. "You're beautiful."

She beams, her cheeks turning rosy as she grabs my collar with both hands, stands on her tiptoes, and places a chaste kiss on my lips.

My cock doesn't get the memo, though, because it's painfully pressing against the front of my pants.

"How long do we have to stay tonight?" she asks.

"An hour, tops. And then I have you for exactly thirty-nine hours."

She grins—her adorable dimples making me *ache* for her—and takes a step back. "You counted?"

I give her a lopsided smile. "I have plans for each and every one of those hours."

She visibly shivers and *fuck* I could do this with her all day, every day. It hits me then that despite living with her, I want *more*. We're both so busy, but I want her sleeping in *my* bed and showering with me in *my* shower. I want to wake up every morning with her wrapped around me, and I want to fall asleep every night to the sound of her steady breathing.

I am so fucked.

"I sure hope so, considering how much you're over-paying for that room."

I huff a laugh. "Let's get going, then. I don't want to waste another minute," I say, eyes piercing into hers.

Once I've loaded our bags into the car, I turn on the playlist she sent me a few weeks ago. It had been a particularly long stretch between quickies, and I was missing her. I couldn't deny the fact that her making me a playlist—which equated to her burning me a CD in elder millennial lingo—was fucking hot. She gives me a small smile as the music plays softly in the background, and as I drive down the long driveway, I let my hand wander down to her thigh.

"How are your classes?" I ask, my voice sounding brusquer than I intend it to.

"Good. I'm especially excited to be done with this one poetry class I'm taking. The professor is too hot, and I haven't learned a thing all semester."

I grin as I pull onto the road. "Hmm. Considering you've aced every assignment, according to my peers, I don't believe that's true."

"Are your classes going okay?" she asks, placing her hand on top of mine.

"Can't wait for finals week because it's usually a lot slower than normal, but I'm not excited to grade over four-hundred poems. And your book? How are edits going?"

She'd told me she'd finished the first draft last week after one of our quickies in my office. I'd been so happy for her that I'd gotten on my knees and pulled two quick orgasms out of her. We were both late to our next class, but it was more than worth it.

"Ugh. The worst. I hate every minute of it. What about you? How's your mysterious book coming along? Are you ever going to tell me anything about it?"

I stop at a light and run a hand over my face. "You can read it if you want. I'm almost done."

Zoe's quiet for a moment, and I can hear the trepidation in her voice. "That's amazing, Liam. What is it about?"

I contemplate not telling her. The analogies and metaphors I've woven through the book could be passed off as fiction, but since she knows me, she might see right through me.

"It's dark. I'm not quite sure what to classify it as. But the premise is about a boy who grew up in a castle."

This quiets her, and as the light turns green and I drive forward, she doesn't say anything for several seconds.

I continue. "A war breaks out, and the boy has to choose between saving his younger siblings or saving his father. He chooses his siblings, and deals with the repercussions of that choice for the rest of his life."

"I want to read it."

My lips twist as I squeeze her thigh. "Only if I can read yours."

She throws her head back and laughs. "I should've guessed you'd say that."

The rest of the drive is filled with light conversation, and though my body craves her, it *needs* this more—the connection. The small talk. The checking in. *This* is what I miss the most when I'm not with her.

After we park and I open her door for her, we walk into the bar. It's casual and art deco themed, and I glance over at the gleaming, refinished bar with pride. I'd spent most of last month here when I wasn't teaching, helping Orion lay new hardwood floors, refinishing the vintage bathroom, and ensuring the bar—which was beautiful but falling apart—could be revived. It involved a lot of woodwork, staining, sanding, sawing, and wood putty, but in the end, we got it working.

There's a stage set up in the back, and Orion plans to open it up to anyone who wants to perform once a week. The tables and chairs are made of dark wood, and the booths lining the back wall are made up of dark red leather. I'd also helped him hang the fan-shaped sconces and crystal chandeliers. The outcome is better than I expected, and as I take in the sultry jazz music and low lighting, I'm struck by how good Orion is at this.

"I can't believe you guys pulled this off in a month," Zoe murmurs, looking around the crowded bar and grinning.

"Well, I just helped. This is Orion's baby."

"Have I ever told you how hot it is that you're so capable of fixing things?" she asks, her honey brown eyes going a bit dark as she purrs the last two words.

My hand slides around her waist, and I squeeze her exposed abdomen once as I bend down to speak directly into her ear. "And have I ever told you how these tiny little shirts you wear drive me crazy? I never knew that an inch of skin could be so mesmerizing, baby girl."

Zoe pulls her lower lip between her teeth as one of her hands comes to my chest. "Come on. Let's go mingle. And then I want to leave."

I'm already hard as I grab her hand and lead us toward the bar. Zoe looks down in surprise.

"They know about us," I tell her, referring to my brothers.

Zoe beams proudly, and it makes my heart soar. "Good."

Much to my surprise, when we get to the bar, Orion is behind the bar with a martini shaker, brows furrowed in focus as he pulls one of the signature martini glasses from the glass cabinet he had custom made. It strikes me how much self-control he has in regard to alcohol—being around it all day, every day. As we walk up to the bar, he glances up and smiles.

"You made it," he says slyly, looking between Zoe and me.

I'd enlisted the help of Orion and Chase to plan this weekend with Zoe, and Orion knows that we won't be staying long tonight. In fact, the last two nights I'd helped him with the bar, he'd given me lessons on bondage—something I want to try with Zoe this weekend. I'd practiced with the leather restraints a few times in front of Orion, and he gave me pointers on what to be aware of. I feel prepared, but I'm also worried as fuck about accidentally hurting her.

"Of course," Zoe says sweetly. "This place is amazing."

"Do you want something to drink?" he asks, arching one brow at me. "Non-alcoholic of course, since you're underage."

Zoe pouts. "I suppose I'll just have water."

"Same for me," I tell him.

Orion winks before grabbing two crystal tumblers and filling them with water. He's soon occupied with another patron, so Zoe and I take our drinks and wander around in search of Miles and Stella, but they don't appear to be here yet. I'm getting antsy, so with a hand on the small of Zoe's back, I guide her to the only empty booth. She moves to sit down first, but I intercept her by sitting first and tugging her down onto my lap.

If we have to stay another fifty minutes, I may as well make it count.

She leans back against me as my fingers brush the hair off her shoulders. Leaning forward slightly, I kiss the tip of her ear and hear her hum with satisfaction.

"I've missed you, little rebel," I tell her, my hands coming to her waist as she moves on top of me.

"You too," she says, her voice a breathy pant.

I chuckle as my hands inch higher. Because we're in public, I can't do what I really want to do, but I can get her as worked up as possible, so that she can enjoy the rest of the evening. Besides, seeing her aroused is the best vision in the world. My index finger slowly drags down between her legs and back up, and her rapid breathing tells me she's already there. I suppose we've technically had weeks of foreplay. Just as I shift my hips to line my cock against her, I hear someone gasp from nearby.

Zoe and I both turn to find Carolina, Elias's sister, staring at us from a couple feet away.

Oh, fuck.

Fuck, fuck, fuck.

I vaguely recall forwarding the opening invite to her.

And now that I'm watching her eyes take in Zoe sitting on my lap...

I can distinctly remember her responding that she was excited to see both of us.

The woman—a formidable human rights attorney who is single and childless by choice—glares at us.

No, glares at *me*.

After Elias died, I made it a point to check in with Carolina periodically. We mostly talk about Zoe, who is her only living relative, but we get along fine. There's no bad blood between us at all. I used to wonder if Zoe would've been better off with Carolina instead of me after her parents died, but Elias was adamant about me being Zoe's guardian.

The last thing I need is for her to find out about Zoe and I like this. I hadn't really thought of how we'd broach the subject, but it would require careful planning to earn her blessing, because our relationship isn't exactly something she'll approve of right away—that's something I'm certain of.

Instead of after careful planning, we're apparently doing this now—as Carolina watches me fondling her nineteen-year-old niece.

This looks so, *so* bad, and when I open my mouth to explain, Zoe hops off my lap and rushes forward.

"Aunt Carolina! I didn't know you would be here," she says. I can hear the slight tremor in her voice.

Carolina pulls away and looks between Zoe and me, eyes narrowing. "What the hell is this?" she asks.

My blood turns cold.

Because it's not Carolina repeating those words back to me in my mind.

It's Elias.

"Maybe we should talk," I say calmly, standing and holding my hands up in a surrendering motion.

"Please tell me I did not just walk in on you feeling Elias's daughter up," she adds, her voice turning colder with every word.

I open and close my mouth. Zoe's eyes go wide, and she looks to me for guidance. And... *fuck.* The last thing I want to do is lie, but this is the exact opposite way I ever wanted her to find out. The mediator in me comes out, and I let out a heavy sigh before I take a step toward her.

She backs up, and the motion sends an icy shard of doubt through me.

"You did. And I can explain everything, but—"

Her face scrunches up and she gives me her most venomous look. "You're a monster," she hisses. "How long has this been going on? Since she was underage? I'm not opposed to involving the authorities."

"No!" Zoe shouts. "No, nothing *ever* happened until I was eighteen!"

Carolina looks at Zoe and her expression softens, but only a little. "Oh, Zoe. It's called grooming," she adds, turning and glaring at me again.

"N–no," I sputter, throwing my hands out. "I didn't *groom* her."

Carolina holds her hand out to stop me from continuing. "I don't want to hear your excuses. My brother gave you *one job* when he died. He'd be rolling around in his grave if he knew you'd come onto his daughter when she was barely legal."

Her words cut into me, slicing through every insecurity, every fear, every guilty thought I've ever had, until my insides and my emotions are completely shredded. Something low and heavy sinks to the bottom of my stomach, and when I open my mouth to ask her if I can explain again, she grabs Zoe's hand.

"Are you okay?" she asks, her voice a low murmur.

Zoe yanks her hand away. "You're being *cruel*," she says, eyes glittering with tears. "I'm an adult. And I'm in l–" She stops herself, eyes roaming to me for a second before turning back to Carolina. "If you only knew–"

"I can't do this," Carolina says, stepping away from both of us. It's then that I see the tears tracking down her cheeks. "My brother would be so disappointed."

In one swift motion, she turns and stalks out of the bar.

My whole body feels as if I've been dipped into a bucket of ice, and my eyes catch on Zoe's hands curling at her side.

"Fuck," she whispers, turning to face me. She swipes under her eyes and shrugs. "Well, that went well," she says, her voice thick as she sniffs. "Fuck it. We can talk to her next week. Let her cool down. Explain the situation." Stepping into me, her arms wrap around my waist. "I don't want it to ruin our weekend," she adds, voice soft. *Vulnerable.*

I squeeze my eyes shut as doubt rushes through me. It sits like a stone inside of me, too heavy to ignore. But as Zoe's hands squeeze me once, and I inhale the scent of violets, some of the tension dissipates.

Carolina was surprised. She'll come around.

We stand there for a few minutes as I sway us to the ambient music. Finally, Zoe pulls away.

"Let's go."

"Now?" I ask, looking around for Miles and Stella.

Zoe must notice my hesitation, because she pulls her phone out of her pocket and quickly taps a text out before a loud whooshing sound permeates the air around us.

"There. I told them we'd had an unfortunate run-in with Carolina, and that we weren't in the mood to stay." Swallowing, she takes my hand. "It's not a lie."

I'm in a daze as she leads me through the bar to the exit. I follow her out the door to the parking lot, where I grab our bags out of habit and wrap my coat around her shoulders. The walk to the hotel is quiet–but not in a comfortable way. I swear I keep seeing Zoe open and close her mouth in my peripheral, but neither of us says a word until we check in.

Unlike last time, Zoe is quiet as I talk to Barbara, and as we head up to the ninth floor, she squeezes my hand once.

Inside the room, I close and lock the door slowly, my mind still reeling from Carolina's words.

You're a monster.

My brother would be so disappointed.

I swallow and close my eyes briefly, taking a steadying breath before turning around to face Zoe.

The sight before me makes me nearly fall over.

Zoe is kneeling next to the couch, palms up, looking down at the ground.

Whatever the fuck happened with Carolina is the last thing on her mind, and seeing the way she's lined her shoes up next to the couch and folded my jacket over the back before getting into position immediately...

Fuck it.

We've already crossed the line, so why not dance on the other side?

I remember her words from earlier, too. How she almost said something that makes my heart nearly stop with shock.

I'm an adult. And I'm in l—

I know what she was going to say. Her emotions were pure and evident on her face.

And I'm in love with him.

"Look at me, please," I murmur, my hands in the pockets of my jeans. Her head snaps up, expression neutral, and I almost smile at how good she is at this. "Before we start, I want to check in. Are you okay?"

Something passes behind her eyes, but she nods once. "Yes. I've been waiting all week for this, and—"

"I didn't ask if you were excited," I say, my voice quiet and collected. "Nor if you were looking forward to this." Walking closer, I place my hand against her cheek, and she nuzzles into my touch. The motion does something to me, and I clear my throat to hide the emotion trying to claw up my throat. "I think we both know how excited we are," I add, letting my voice turn low and husky. "How long we've waited. How much we *want* this weekend. But I'd be remiss if I didn't ensure you were okay *emotionally* after everything that just happened."

She swallows and looks down. "It was... shocking. But I can compartmentalize. At the end of the day, *you* mean more to me than anything. What we have is..." Her voice breaks, and she pauses for a second. "What we have is the best thing that's ever happened to me, and I'd really like to start our weekend now, if that's okay with you."

Moving my hand down to her jaw, I lift her chin and stare down into her watery eyes. Letting my eyes scan her face for several seconds, I ensure there's no hesitation in her expression—nothing hiding behind her honey-brown eyes. However, the only thing I see on her face is adoration.

Devotion.

Submission.

Something warm cracks in my chest at the look she's giving me, and my thumb grazes her cheek fondly.

"You're so perfect, do you know that?" I murmur, my voice gentle.

"Thank you," she whispers.

My chest aches with whatever's unsaid between us, so to distract myself, I walk to my overnight bag.

"I thought we could try something new."

Unzipping the bag, I pull the small, black box out and hand it to her. I watch from a few feet away as she pulls the top of the box open, revealing the luxury bondage restraint I'd ordered for her—for *us*. I know she likes to be restrained, and after some research, I'd consulted Orion and chosen this particular piece.

It's essentially a thick, black leather harness that comes across her chest, with six loops secured behind her for her arms. As Zoe lifts it out of the box, her eyes go dark as she holds it up by one finger.

"I love it," she says, her voice strained. "Can you put it on me, please?"

It takes me a second to realize the unevenness in her voice is excitement. Smiling, I walk over to her and help her onto her feet.

"Turn around."

Once she's positioned in front of me, I take my time undressing her from behind. My fingers linger a second too long each time I touch her, and as I hook my hands underneath her mesh shirt to pull it off, she shudders beneath my touch. Once it's off, I lay it over the back of the couch before moving to the button of her trousers. When it's unclasped, I let my hands slide between the trousers and her dark red, lace panties—chuckling when she shivers again.

"Someone's sensitive," I say, my tongue flicking against her ear at the same time my cock twitches against her back.

She lets her head fall to one side, and I take the

opportunity to kiss her neck. Another shiver. I *fucking* love how responsive she is to me.

"Someone's teasing me," she retorts, and I can't help but smile.

Pulling her trousers down, she steps out of them as I take the leather harness and run my hands over the soft leather. I'd spent way too much money on it, especially considering I'd never used bondage before, but I wanted to ensure she was safe. I liked the idea of rope, and one day I wanted to test it out, but when Orion started rambling about nerve damage and avoiding arteries, I knew I needed something more foolproof.

Zoe's back rises and falls rapidly as I unclasp her bra and pull her underwear down, discarding them both. Then I undo the multiple buckles of the harness and wrap it around her from behind. The top sits like a bra; the straps go over her shoulder and come down around her breasts. It then wraps around her, forming a line down her back with the six loops for her arms. Everything's adjustable, and I feel comfortable knowing I can get her out of this quickly if needed. Once I buckle the part around her chest and adjust it so that it's tight but not uncomfortable, I take her arms and snake them both through the loops, side by side.

Her breathing hitches with every touch, and my cock is pulsing in my pants. If *this* is what really turns her on, I'll tie her up all day, every day. Seeing Zoe completely aroused like this is a massive boon to the part of me that wants to torture her with pleasure.

"Walk over to the couch," I tell her, keeping my voice

calm.

She does as I say, and I place a hand on her upper back to bend her over the top of the couch.

"I'm going to tighten the arm loops now. Please use your safe word if you need it, okay?"

She nods. "Okay."

I secure each loop individually. It's not supposed to hurt, so I know she's okay if I err on the looser side. She gasps when I do the first one, essentially locking her arm behind her back. With each buckle, she starts to squirm —rolling her hips slightly, making little, breathy sounds, moaning—and it's everything I wanted out of this weekend.

I'd planned to go slow, planned to give her a few orgasms before fucking her, but seeing her bent over the couch like this? It does something to me—*awakens* something in me.

I quickly unbuckle my belt and unzip my pants. Zoe must realize what's coming, because she groans and arches her spine, giving me easier access.

"You should see yourself right now," I mumble, pulling my hard shaft out and stroking it a few times. My thumb swipes the precum from the tip, using it as lube as I walk up behind her. "So goddamn beautiful all tied up for me," I say, one hand finding her hair as the other hand comes to my mouth. I lather my fingers up with spit before running them between her legs, and the movement causes her to start shaking. "Spread your legs for me, baby girl."

She does, and I waste no time. Shifting my hips

forward, I push into her tight cunt and we both moan at the intrusion.

"Oh god," she whimpers, and I see her fists curl against her lower back.

I push all the way in before pulling out, admiring my glistening cock, and wishing I'd tasted her before letting my impatience win.

"Fuck, you feel so good," I growl, one hand in her hair and the other one grabbing onto the harness. Her pussy is milking my cock, so wet and needy, practically sucking me into her. I groan, knowing I'm not going to last long at all. Every single thought is centered on her and watching my cock move in and out of her from behind.

"Pull it tighter," she begs me, and I can't think straight as I adjust the buckles on her wrists. Perhaps I'd been too soft, too worried about hurting her, so I tighten them by one hole. "Oh fuck, Liam, tighter, pull all of it *tighter*, please."

Her cunt begins to feather around my cock, and I'm lost in pleasure—lost in watching her come undone so soon, so easily. I want to give her all the pleasure in the world, *fill* her with it like I want to fill her with my seed. That thought has me emitting a loud moan as my hands fumble with the top buckle. She feels so fucking good —*too* good. My mouth drops open as I work the harness tighter, skipping over three holes and pulling her wrists tighter in one rough motion.

She cries out, and I close my eyes as my balls start to tighten, as my cock thickens.

Zoe screams again. "Red! Fuck, red, red, red!"

CHAPTER TWENTY-ONE
THE LETTER

LIAM

It takes me a second too long to realize that red means stop, and when I pull out and flip her around, her eyes are wide, and her face is strained with pain.

"The harness," she pants, eyes brimming with tears. "My wrists!"

"Fuck," I hiss, twisting her around again and unbuckling her as my heart pounds in my chest. My hands are shaking as I undo each buckle, and when I'm done, I remove the harness completely, wincing at the sight of the red welts left on her skin from pulling it too tightly. When she turns around and brings her hands in front of her, I can see her left wrist hanging limply while her right one cradles it. "Fuck, Zoe, I'm so sorry."

She's gulping in air as I gently take her injured wrist

and hold it up. She hisses in pain, and the only thing I can think is that this is all my fault.

"I–I can't move it," she says slowly. "I'm sorry, I thought..."

I place my hands on either side of her face. "You're sorry? Zoe, there's nothing to be sorry for. I'm the one who fucked up."

Her face falls at my words, and she begins to cry. "No, you didn't. It really hurts, though, and—"

"Let's get you dressed. I'll drive us to the emergency room."

Saying the words out loud is like I'm being doused with cold water for the second time tonight.

Emergency room.

The very last place I ever expected to be going with her this weekend.

I help her get dressed into the pajamas that she packed, and I soon follow suit, slipping black joggers and a T-shirt over my head before I'm grabbing my wallet and keys. Zoe's still cradling her injured wrist, and I use the walk to the car to text Orion.

> I know it's opening night, but I need your help.

Orion answers almost immediately, so it's likely that he's no longer behind the bar.

> ORION
>
> Of course. Anything. You guys okay?

Zoe's wrist... I'm not sure what happened, but we're headed to the emergency room at Crestwood Hospital. Would you mind please grabbing her medical records? They're in the bottom drawer of my desk, in a folder labeled "Zoe."

ORION

I'll meet you there in an hour.

After helping Zoe into the Jeep and buckling her in, she reaches for my shirt and pulls me in for a slow, sensual kiss.

"This wasn't your fault. You know that, right?" she asks, whispering the words against my lips. "Once they wrap this thing up, maybe we can resume—"

"Zoe." I sigh, closing my eyes as my lips brush against hers. "Let's get you checked out, okay?" I pull away and walk to my side of the car, and that heavy weight inside of me from earlier only intensifies.

What I don't tell her is that no matter how much she says this isn't my fault, I know better. I'm the one who bought the harness, the one who tightened it. She had to use *red*, for fuck's sake. We hadn't used *yellow*. Had she ever had to use a safe word with any of her other Doms? Did they *know* how not to hurt her?

You're a monster.

You're a monster.

You're a monster.

Carolina's words roll around in my mind during the entire ten-minute drive to the hospital—so much so, that my fingers are nearly white from gripping the steering wheel so hard. Once I park, I carefully lean over and open Zoe's door. She doesn't move, though, instead, she takes my hand with her good hand.

"This isn't your fault," she murmurs, her honey-brown eyes boring into mine. "I could feel you stewing the entire drive over here," she adds, smirking.

I don't have it in me to smile, so instead I push away from her and exit the car on my side. After helping her out, I put an arm around her shoulder, and we walk into the lobby of the hospital. Zoe checks herself in while I find us two seats, though it's pretty crowded, so it might be a long night.

When Zoe walks over to me in her flannel pajamas, I can't help but berate myself.

"I'm having Orion bring your medical records," I say slowly.

Her head rears back. "Why? I know my own medical history."

"You fell down the stairs of your house when you were two. Fractured your wrist."

Her eyes shutter. "I did?"

I nod. "Figured it would be useful for the doctor to have, in case it's the same wrist."

"That makes sense," she answers quietly.

The receptionist calls Zoe forward and hands her paperwork to fill out. I try to contain my smirk as her brows furrow, glancing down at the insurance forms. She's so adamant about doing everything herself, and yet she has no idea that I've been taking care of her in so many ways for years.

"Umm..."

I reach over for the forms, and Zoe hands them over with reddened cheeks. The thing is, I've been filling out so many of these forms for her—for us—that I have everything memorized. Her social security number. Her date and city of birth. Her medical conditions and surgery history, such as when she had to have her appendix out at sixteen, or that she's allergic to certain types of antibiotics. After I complete the insurance portion, I hand the form back to her, and she fills out the rest—luckily with her uninjured right hand.

When she finishes, she walks the paperwork to the reception desk, and it's then that I see Orion walking toward us, carrying the manila folder.

"Hey," he says quickly, looking around. "What happened?"

I stand up, trying to swallow the guilt at having asked him to abandon his bar on opening night. "The harness," I say glumly. "I got too overzealous, and I don't know what the fuck I'm doing."

"Hey," Zoe says, looking at me cautiously. Turning to Orion, she gives him a genuine smile. "It was my fault. I was in a frenzy and pushing boundaries."

Orion looks between us before glancing down at Zoe's wrist. "Happens to the best of us." Looking back at me, I notice his expression is softer. Gentler. "You shouldn't blame yourself, okay? It's really easy to have accidents in a scene."

His words should placate me, but instead I feel worse. "I'm sorry you had to leave opening night."

Orion holds a hand out. "I was more than ready to leave," he says, his voice low. "Layla showed up."

"Because I invited her," Zoe interjects, quirking her lips to the side.

"Yes, well, the last thing I need is to see some guy hanging all over her."

"Because you love her," Zoe adds boldly.

Orion huffs a laugh. "Seen Miles lately? You're worse than him when it comes to gossip."

My lips twitch. "I asked her the same thing a few weeks ago."

Zoe grins. "Well, I'm fine, so you can get back to your night," she tells Orion. "Thanks for indulging your brother's overprotective side."

Chuckling, Orion looks at me. "Hey, you know you can always call me if you need anything, right? You don't always have to play the older, stoic big brother. You're family. You're more important than any bar or party." My throat aches, and it's suddenly too bright. Before I can react, Orion pulls me into a hug. "Stop blaming yourself. Be thankful you're not here for a lost butt plug."

I bark a laugh as I pull away. "Have experience with that, little brother?"

Orion shrugs. "Let's just say, I do not recommend buying cheap toys on the internet."

I'm still smiling as he walks away, and when I turn to face Zoe, she's watching me with a small, shy smile.

Maybe it'll be okay. Maybe it's just a sprain, and we

can go home where I can take care of her. Maybe I won't hate myself forever, and we can actually move forward with whatever this is between us.

One of my hands comes to her cheek, and I let all of my feelings show on my face—every single thought, every hope for our future. Her good hand comes to rest on top of mine.

"Liam, I just wanted to say—"

"Zoe Arma?"

The receptionist calls Zoe's name, and we both turn to face the desk.

"Do you want me to come with you?" I ask her, handing her the folder in case she needs it.

Shaking her head, she smiles as she takes it from me. "I think I'll be okay by myself. I'll meet you here when I'm done, okay?"

I nod, still in a daze, and she stands on her tip toes and gives me a quick kiss before walking over to the nurse who is waiting to take her back. I watch her go, smirking when she gives me a small wave before walking through a door. Sighing, I run a hand over my face. I'm about to go find a seat again when a white envelope sitting on the floor catches my eye.

I don't breathe as I bend to pick it up, and when I turn it over, the heavy stone inside of me plunges farther down, sinking and burrowing into my guilty conscience like a boulder.

It's Elias's letter—the same one that accompanied his trust and will.

The same one I've been too much of a coward to open.

I'd found it a few years ago and thoughtlessly stuck it in her folder without a second thought. And now, as I turn the white envelope over in my hands, I make a decision I was too scared to make years ago.

Taking a seat near the back wall, I quickly tear the letter open. Another two envelopes fall out—one for Zoe and one for Carolina. I set them aside, and before I can digest my best friend's words, the familiar, sloppy handwriting makes my chest cave in on itself. Taking three deep breaths to quell the emotions clawing viciously up my chest, I glance down at the letter and begin reading.

Liam,

If you're reading this, it means I'm dead. And I'm sorry to inform you, but I've elected to donate my body to science. I never wanted to do the whole funeral thing, and if I'm gone, there's a chance Brooke is gone, too. She'll have made the same decision.

I sniff once, thinking back to how Zoe and I had learned there'd be no grave, no ashes to scatter. Instead, her parents volunteered themselves to science. Brushing the stray tears away, I keep going.

If you're reading this, you're also likely aware that Brooke and I have elected you to be Zoe's guardian. Sorry, man. Probably should've mentioned it at some point, but it was kind of a no-brainer for us. I know we don't hang out as much as we used to but know that my love and respect for you runs soul deep.

I'm not a man of many words, so I'll keep this brief. Please take care of Zoe. Protect her. Watch out for men who will hurt her. Keep her safe, no matter what. That's all I'm going to ask of you. I could tell you to buy a gun and scare them all away, but Brooke would kill me if I said that. I guess it's good that I'm already dead, right?

I know you'll watch out for her. I've never doubted that. Sorry for springing it on you. I promise we'd meant to have that conversation with you a hundred times, but we always got distracted.

I've enclosed a note for Zoe when she turns eighteen, and one for Carolina. Make sure my sister doesn't turn bitter and lonely hidden away all by herself. Though I guess the same could be said for you, you grumpy, old recluse.

Speaking of... I don't know what to say, because I know you'll be okay. Your brothers will come together and help you. Promise me that you'll let them. You can be a stubborn asshole, so don't be afraid to be vulnerable.

Live your life, too.

I love you.

Don't forget you promised me we'd go see the Vans Warped Tour one last time before we turned old and grey. Think of me in the mosh pit...

    Love,

    Elias

My hands curl around the two pieces of paper as I swipe at my cheeks and lean back in the cheap waiting room chair.

Fuck.

Standing abruptly, I grab the letters to Zoe and Carolina before walking to the bathroom. Then I close and lock the door behind me as the panic begins to send my nerves spiking. I suck in air through my nose and close my eyes, leaning my arms against the wall and hanging my head as I slowly exhale.

In for ten, out for ten...

Quickly folding the letters, I place everything in my back pocket and walk to the sink, splashing my face with ice cold water. Skin still dripping, I glance up at my reflection in the mirror, and the shame spiral worsens as Elias's words rip through every lie I told myself about Zoe, every hard truth I'd ignored.

I was responsible for her, and not only did I hurt her, but I'd gone against everything Elias would've ever wanted.

Protect her.

Watch out for men who will hurt her.

Keep her safe, no matter what.

That's all I'm going to ask of you.

No matter how much we tried to convince ourselves that what we wanted trumped all logic, I couldn't ignore the heavy doubt now settling inside of me. I was supposed to protect her, be strong for her, *keep her safe,* and yet I caved the very first time she came onto me.

I should've pushed harder, tried harder, but all I did was take her virginity against a dirty wall in the back of the restaurant.

My hands curl around the sink, and I have the urge to punch the mirror—but I don't. I take more steadying breaths as I look at my reflection with as much self-loathing as I can muster.

My brother gave you one job *when he died. He'd be rolling around in his grave if he knew you'd come onto his daughter when she was barely legal.*

And now I had Elias's letter to back his sister's statement up.

Hanging my head, I shut the water off and get myself together.

The best thing I can do—for myself and for Zoe—is stay away from her.

For good.

CHAPTER TWENTY-TWO
THE PROTECTOR

Zoe

After an hour of waiting, they finally bring me back for an X-ray, only to be told that my wrist is sprained, not fractured, like Liam was worried about. I do have to go back in a week for another X-ray to double check. The nice doctor gives me a wrist splint and tells me to manage the pain with over-the-counter painkillers. It's a best-case scenario. I won't be able to use my wrist for a week, but at least I don't need surgery. I guess it's something that's common with this type of wrist fracture.

When I walk into the waiting room, my smile drops from my face when I see Liam bent over with his hands in his hair. As if he can sense me, his head snaps up, and his eyes find mine immediately. We meet halfway, but when I wrap my arms around him, he stiffens slightly and pulls away.

"Just a sprain," I tell him. "Though I have to come back next week to confirm, as sometimes fractures don't show up the first time." His face blanches, and I can't help but laugh. He looks like I've given myself a death sentence. "It's okay. I'm in good hands. And it's not my dominant hand, so that's good."

It's as if the news doesn't placate him at all. Instead, his brows pull together slightly. "Let's get you home so that you can rest." He walks off without another word, and I quickly follow him.

"What about the hotel?"

"I'll go to the hotel and collect our things after I drop you off at home."

Cold. Unemotional. *Distant.* That's how he's acting— like he's pulling away.

I swallow the worry that begins to eat at me as he helps me into the car. His eyes linger on the wrist splint before they move to my face, devoid of any emotion. It breaks my heart to see it, and I make a mental note to talk to him about it.

All in all, the events of tonight went from bad to worse, but it doesn't mean we can't salvage something.

And it definitely doesn't mean we can't continue our night together. He may be spooked, but I'll make sure he knows that this isn't going to deter me.

When he drives out of the parking lot and toward the main road, I almost ask him if everything's okay, but he quickly turns the music on, drowning out any words that may have left my lips. *Fine.* We live together, though; it's not like he can avoid me forever.

Twenty minutes later, we're pulling up to the house. He puts the car in park, but he doesn't turn the engine off.

"You have your key?" he asks, jaw hard as he looks at me.

I nod and pat my purse. "I always do."

"Okay. I'll see you later."

Unease slithers through me. "Liam, you need to stop beating yourself up."

"I can't talk about this right now, Zoe."

"Please–" My voice cracks.

"No, I don't want to talk about it."

I start to panic, and my words come out much wobblier than I intend. "Liam, you need to listen to me—"

"Red," he murmurs, looking sad.

I stare at him, unbelieving. "What?" I whisper, my voice breaking.

"I said *red*," he grits out. "This is my boundary, and I'm using the safe word."

Shaking my head, tears begin to well in my eyes. "You can't weaponize the safe word just because you don't want to talk right now. That's not fair."

"Well, you were pushing me, and I didn't know how else to get through to you. I do not want to talk about what happened tonight. Okay?"

Hot tears stream down my face as I use my good hand to unbuckle myself. "Fine. You've made it crystal fucking clear," I add, opening the door and slamming it closed behind me before he can respond.

As I walk to the front door, I let the tears free, and I don't look back as I unlock the front door and let myself into the house. Once I close and lock it, I slide down onto the floor, clutching my wrist as sobs wrack through my body.

Is he really going to let a tiny detour like this change our entire dynamic? I mean... yeah, it's not the most ideal situation given what we were supposed to be doing all weekend, but we can still spend the night together. I stand up and swipe at my cheeks, clearing the tears away as I look around. Just then, Captain Sushi trots over to me, purring loudly as his head nuzzles against the back of my knee.

"Your dad is an idiot," I tell him gently, petting his head with my good hand.

I walk upstairs, and Captain follows me; he must sense that I need some company. Instead of wallowing, I get proactive. I carefully remove my splint and take the slowest, hardest, one-handed shower of my life. It involves a lot of squeezing bottles between my chin and my chest, but I manage to get clean by the time I'm done. After changing and putting on comfortable clothes, I wrap the wrist splint around my sore wrist before climbing into bed.

It's nearly eleven and I'm exhausted, but I don't sleep.

I can't help but worry when I check the time, realizing that Liam has been gone for nearly two hours. I pull my phone out as my heart races.

> i know you dont want 2 talk about it, but can u at least let me know if youre alive?

I stare at my phone for several moments, watching it go from *delivered* to *read*. I await his response, but nothing comes—not even three little dots.

Okay, so he's alive.

The tears threaten to spill as I sit against my headboard and pull my knees to my chest, but I refuse to cry.

Refuse to shed more tears until we can sit down and *talk*.

The *You've Got This* sign taunts me—glowing bright pink when I do not *have* anything.

A couple more hours pass, and I spend most of that time slowly editing my book at my desk with eyes that ache and sting. Captain dutifully stays at my feet, a light purr permeating the quiet room. It's late, and my body is heavy from tiredness. I'm just about to give in for the night, at nearly three in the morning, when I hear Liam's Jeep crunch the gravel out front.

I'm instantly awake. I leap out of bed; startling Captain so much that he stands with his back arched and his tail puffed as he looks around.

"Sorry, Cap," I whisper, walking out of the bedroom as he purrs and runs behind me.

Liam quietly opens the door as I step into the entryway. His eyes find mine, and he looks almost surprised to see me.

He thought I'd be asleep. That's why he waited so long to come home.

I try to cross my arms, but it's impossible with the brace, so I stand there in leggings and one of his old T-shirts. It's not a band tee; it's one of his worn, thin white T-shirts. I'd stolen it a couple of weeks ago, and as his eyes linger for a second too long on my peaked nipples, I realize that I may have a small chance to win him back over.

He may think he wants to give up on us, but I wore him down twice before. He's *happier* with me. Being with him is... indescribable.

I have to try because I'm not ready to walk away from whatever this is.

"You're still awake," he says, his voice almost hoarse. When he closes and locks the front door, I take in his disheveled appearance. His shirt now hangs loose and wrinkled. His joggers are equally wrinkled, and his hair is messy, as if he's been running his hands through it for the last four hours. He sets our overnight bags down by the door and turns to face me, and it slams into me that perhaps he wasn't alone tonight.

We never did decide to be exclusive, after all.

That inky, uncomfortable feeling from the first night of the hotel returns, and I hate it. I have to believe that he wouldn't do that.

"I was with Orion," he says, as if he can read my thoughts, and I can't help but be relieved.

"We should talk," I say quickly. "You're scared, and that's normal. If you want, we can go slow."

"Zoe, this needs to stop."

His words slam through me, sucking all the air out of

my lungs. My emotions go haywire; despair comes first, followed by pure, unadulterated anger. One hiccup, and he wants to walk away? One slight deviation from the plan, and he wants to stop everything between us like it never happened? The despair and anger mix together, mingling and forming something akin to betrayal. It lances through me when I think of what he's trying to tell me.

When I don't respond, Liam takes a step toward me, and to my surprise, Captain begins to growl.

We both go still and look down at the large cat, wondering if we misheard. Liam takes another tentative step forward, and sure enough, Captain growls again, stepping forward in front of me.

Liam's eyes are wide as they go from his cat to me, and I huff a cruel laugh.

"Guess I'm not the only one who thinks you're being a coward," I tell him, my words laced with venom.

My vision blurs as Liam's expression falls—long enough to show me that he doesn't *really* want to end things.

He just thinks he has to.

He takes a slow step forward, and Captain emits a low, steady growl. He pulls something from his pocket and sets it down on the foyer table.

"You're right. When your father died, he wrote me a letter. I haven't had the courage to open it until tonight. Until it slipped out of your files."

That's the last thing I expected him to say. "What did it say?" I ask.

Liam's jaw ticks as he looks down at the floor. "He told me to protect you and to watch out for men who hurt you," he adds, voice low. "I could've really hurt you. I *did* really hurt you. The only thing I should be doing is protecting you."

Realization slams through me. "And you think he meant this?" I ask, my voice high as I gesture between us. "That you making one small mistake was what he meant, despite how much you've given back to me? Despite always looking out for me?" A sob breaks free from my chest. "I don't know what my father would've thought about us, but quite frankly, I'm sick of trying to appease him because it *doesn't matter.* We're the ones who have our whole lives ahead of us. Don't you—" I choke out another sob. "Don't you want that? With me?"

Liam sniffs and looks away, and I swear I see him quickly wipe a tear away. "He wrote you a letter, too," he says quietly, pointing to the white envelope on the foyer table. "I'm sorry it took me so long to give it to you."

My chest cracks as I walk over to the table and take the letter. When I look at him, he's looking away.

"Liam, there's nothing in this letter that would make me change my mind about you. No matter what he says, I will always choose you."

Liam squeezes his eyes shut and backs up as I take a step closer. "I need some time, Zoe. I'm going to go stay with Orion for a couple of days."

My chest—*my heart*—cracks in half. "Really? You're just going to run away?"

Liam's anguished expression tears through my heart, straight down to my very soul. "Zoe."

"Can't you see that *this* is hurting me?" I say, hiccupping as I cry. "*Not* being with you is hurting me."

"Your wrist says otherwise," he growls, his expression a wall of self-deprecation.

He wavers for a second, looking between me and Captain before grabbing his bag and opening the door. I fight the urge to hurl the glass vase on the table at the door after he walks through and closes it. Instead, I lock it, set the alarm, and jog upstairs, gripping my dad's letter tightly in my hand. I set it down on my desk before falling into my bed.

My phone chimes with a new notification, and I sit up quickly, thinking that maybe it's Liam texting me to say he's sorry.

It takes me a second to realize it's an email. My thumb is shaking as I unlock my phone to read it.

Dear Ms. Arma,

We're delighted to tell you that you've been accepted for the 30-day writer's workshop in London on a full scholarship. We were completely riveted by your writing sample, and we hope you'll join us next week.

Below you can find more information and paperwork, but for now, all we need is your confirmation to secure your spot.

If possible, can you please let us know if you're still interested?

Looking forward to speaking soon.

Best Regards,
Anna St. Claire
InkLondon: A 30-day Immersive Program for New Writers

I hit the reply button, and my fingers move quicker than I can think.

Yes, I'm still interested. See you next week!

CHAPTER TWENTY-THREE
THE RECKONING

LIAM

I wake up in one of Orion's guest rooms, groggy and feeling like total shit. I stare out of the large window that overlooks Crestwood as I run my hand through my hair. After yawning, I lean over and check my phone, but I don't have any texts from Zoe.

Same as the last eight days.

Because it was the last week of school, I'd gone through the motions while staying at Orion's downtown loft. I saw Zoe twice in class, but she'd completely ignored me—which I guess I deserved. I had groceries delivered a couple of times, and I know Stella had been over once or twice to check on her, so I know she's at least surviving.

My phone chimes as I set it down, and I fumble with it as I check the screen.

ZOE

wrist is fine, def not broken.

My heart begins to race at her words—at seeing her name on my screen.

I really fucking miss her, but if I say that, I'll only confuse her. Still, we should probably have a conversation soon about how we're going to move forward.

That's good.

Are you home?

I quickly throw off the duvet and pull my pants on, buttoning them quickly as I stare down at the screen. Three dots appear and then disappear multiple times, and by the time I pull a shirt on and brush my teeth, she still hasn't responded.

We should talk.

Like before, three dots appear. This time, a long text comes through, and I wonder if she's been drafting it this whole time.

ZOE

im on my way 2 the airport. with all the
craziness these last 2 weeks, i forgot to
tell u—i applied for a writing workshop
and got accepted. its 30 days long, so ill
be back in time for classes in january. i
appreciate u wanting to talk, but i still
need some space. u really hurt me by
pulling away, and if i see u, i might not
want to go to london. let me know if i
need to have layla watch captain while
im gone, or if youll be going back to your
house.

Cold, potent dread works through me at her words.

30 days.

You really hurt me.

Your *house—not our house.*

Swallowing, I type out a reply.

Congratulations on the workshop. I'm
proud of you. I'll take care of Sushi…
don't worry about it. Be safe in London.

ZOE

thx

You still have my credit card, so feel free
to use it.

ZOE

i left it on the counter. ill be okay.

I chew on my lower lip and wonder how I can make
sure she at least has money for food and sightseeing
when she texts me back.

ZOE

> my phone wont work there but if u need
> to get ahold of me, u can contact
> inklondon at +44788 977219

I debate arguing with her, but I can't possibly hold her back from this.

After doing a quick internet search, I see that it's a legitimate program, so I sit back down on the bed and run my hands through my hair. The idea of spending the next thirty days alone is depressing, but I suppose I can go home now. Hopefully Captain won't maul me once I'm through the door. He's always been protective of Zoe, but I never considered he'd be protective against *me*.

I'm packing everything up when my hand brushes against Elias's letter for Carolina. Pulling it out, I sigh heavily.

I suppose I can make one pit stop before going home.

––––––––

The drive through the canyon to Malibu is picturesque and beautiful. The sky is a bright, blue color, and the hills are green from the recent rain we've gotten. It's a balmy sixty-five degrees out, so I crack the windows as I make my way up the winding side street near Zuma beach.

I've only been here a few times before, as whenever we had dinner together, she usually opted to come to us.

I park behind her car in the driveway and walk up to the large, modern house that overlooks the coast. Her letter is in my right hand, so I ring the doorbell with my left hand.

Carolina opens the door a minute later, and at first, she looks almost surprised to see me.

"Liam?"

Being almost ten years older than Elias, she was always a very competent big sister, and in that way, we always got along. We used to bond over being the oldest, over having to care for our younger siblings.

"Can we talk?" I ask her, rubbing my mouth.

She stands off to the side and gestures for me to come inside.

Once I walk into her house and she closes the door behind me, she leans against it and crosses her arms.

"I assume you're here for the same reason Zoe came and saw me last night?"

I open and close my mouth. "Zoe was here?"

Carolina rolls her eyes and walks past me. "I'll get us something to drink."

She disappears into her kitchen, and I walk around the spotless living room. I smile when I see it's mostly pictures of Zoe scattered along her bookshelf—Zoe as a baby, Zoe wearing a sweatshirt with Carolina's law firm logo as a little girl, Zoe's prom picture...

A pang goes through my chest when I think of not seeing Zoe for a month. Not hearing her low, throaty laugh. Of not smelling the sweet, powdery scent of violets, or the way she forgets to eat and turns into a hangry menace. Of not joking around with her, or watching her eyes roll whenever I inevitably say something in "elder millennial lingo."

I clear my throat as Carolina walks into the living room, holding two shot glasses and a bottle of silver tequila.

"Bit early for that," I mutter, intending to make a joke.

Carolina stares at me as she sits on one of the chairs facing the couch, and then she pours us both a shot before picking hers up.

I press my lips together and try not to smile as I pick mine up and shoot it back. I don't wince—the burn feels good.

If this is what it takes for me to get on Carolina's good side again, then so be it.

"What's that?" she asks as she wipes her mouth, pointing to the envelope still clutched in my right hand.

"A letter from Elias." Her face goes white as they dart between the envelope and my face several times. "You know, I assumed Zoe would go live with you when I found out about what happened," I say slowly, sitting down on the couch opposite her. "You have a good job, a big house, and you're family."

Carolina doesn't say anything—she listens, expression open. So I continue.

"But the day they went missing, Zoe called me in a panic. She was all alone—" My voice breaks, so I take a deep breath before continuing. "I went to go pick her up at her house and we formed a plan. We went to the police station, and we were told we couldn't file a missing person's report until it had been twenty-four hours. So, we decided not to tell you. We didn't want to worry you."

"Well, you know what happened after that. We all joined the search party, and then they found the bodies..." I swallow. "Anyway, I assumed you would get custody of Zoe. And then I was told it was me..."

"I'm glad it was you," Carolina offers, pouring us both another shot. "As much as I love Zoe, I'm not cut out to be a mom."

We pause for a minute as we each take another shot.

"Elias wrote me a letter, and inside was a letter to both you and Zoe."

Carolina's brows pinch together. "And you're giving it to me now?"

I shake my head. "No. I mean, yes. I only opened mine last weekend."

Carolina's expression softens in understanding. "After what I said to you, I'm sure it wasn't easy to read it. That's why Zoe came to see me last night."

I nod. "Maybe. I don't know. We haven't really spoken since that night."

Carolina sighs and takes the letter when I hand it to her, opening it as she leans back. Her eyes flick over her brother's words, and her hand comes to her mouth after she finishes, placing it down on the table before taking another shot. She fights against the tears, but one slips through. Brushing it off her cheek, she sniffs and shakes her head.

"I'm sorry for what I said, Liam."

My brows furrow. "You weren't wrong—"

"I *was* wrong. And I told Zoe the same thing last night. When I saw the two of you at the bar, I assumed something untoward was going on. But Zoe filled me in last night. I'd planned to come see you and apologize, but you beat me to it."

Relief washes over me as I lean forward. The tequila shots are making me dizzy and emotional, so I reach over for a third one, shooting it back with a grimace.

"She explained that nothing ever happened until she was a consenting adult. That she pursued you. And that she was in love with you."

My head snaps up at that, heart pounding. "She said that?"

Carolina smiles. "She did. And after she told me everything you've done for her... everything you continue to do for her..."

I put my face in my hands and try to tamp down the emotion clawing up my throat.

Fuck.

Zoe *loves* me.

Smart, kind, funny Zoe is in love with *me*.

It slams through me then...

The way she feels in my arms. The way her brows pinch together slightly whenever she's worried about me. The way her smile makes me feel like I'm on a roller-coaster, free falling.

"I'm in love with her, too."

I quickly take a fourth shot, and Carolina's eyes track each one of my movements.

She holds up the letter. "Elias told me to tell you not to spend your life as a recluse. That if need be, to set you up with someone who would push your boundaries. Who would challenge you."

I huff a laugh. "Zoe is very good at pushing my boundaries in every way."

Carolina laughs. "That's good."

"Fuck," I groan, drunk and sappy. "I'm an idiot."

"Yes, you are," Carolina agrees. "That girl is so head over heels for you. And while I might not understand it completely, you have my blessing. And, because I know you're wondering, I think Elias would approve, too."

The heavy, potent feeling threatening to spill out of my throat comes out sounding like a choked sob.

Hearing Carolina give us her blessing... while it's not technically Elias's blessing, it's the next best thing.

I give myself a minute to regroup, rubbing my eyes. "She's gone," I say, my voice quiet. "I fucked up."

I grab the bottle and take two more shots subsequently, not tasting it this time.

Carolina smirks as she grabs the tequila bottle and stands. "That's true. But I also think she needs this time away—to discover who she is as a writer, as a young woman, without your influence. Let her go this month, and make sure you're there for her when she gets back. That's all you can do."

I rub my chest as Carolina walks away with our shot glasses and tequila bottle, so I twist around to lie down on the couch and cover my face with my arm, feeling like an asshole.

Instead of comforting her, I pushed her away.

Instead of talking to her, I shut her down.

If I could go back in time, I'd change everything.

My whole life has consisted of fixing things, of being the most responsible person, of thinking through the consequences. But with Zoe, she taught me how to listen to what *I* want.

And what I want is a life with her.

I must fall asleep at some point because I wake up what feels like hours later, but Carolina is reading in the chair across from me.

"Have a nice nap?" she asks, lips quirking to the side.

I sit up, but the room spins. "I don't normally drink this much liquor."

Except for that night in Catalina.

"It's fine. You must've needed it." She flips the page. "I have a man friend coming over soon, so I called your brother to come pick you up."

I groan. "Which brother?"

"Miles."

Rubbing my face with my hand, I let out a heavy sigh. Being the two oldest brothers means that we're quite close, but I don't exactly need Miles—my serious CEO brother with a new baby—to see me drunk off my ass.

"Should've called Kai. He won't be so judgmental."

Carolina laughs. "Well, I had some of Zoe's old baby clothes lying around which should fit Beatrix perfectly, so it's also my selfish need to declutter."

I smirk. "Fine. Thank you."

I'm about to stand up when there's a knock at the door.

"It's open!" Carolina shouts.

Miles walks through the front door, eyes scanning the room until they land on me. His mouth twitches in an almost smile, and he closes the door and walks over to the living room, eyes twinkling.

"Well, well, well," he drawls, crossing his arms.

"Piss off," I say, though my tone is joking.

"Oh, you're certainly pissed," he replies, almost gleefully.

Wonderful.

"Hi, Carolina," Miles says politely. He bends down and kisses her on both cheeks.

"Don't forget the baby clothes," she says, pointing to the bags of stuff by the door. "Also, when you're done with them, Zoe would like them. You know, just in case."

My head swings around until my eyes land on Carolina's brown ones.

"Uhm—"

"Oh, this is excellent," Miles mutters, rubbing his hands together. "Come on, old man. Let's get you home." He turns to look at Carolina. "I'll bring Liam back tomorrow to get his car."

"I'm not a child," I retort as Miles pulls me up and steadies me.

A second later, Carolina is standing right in front of me holding Elias' letter. "Thank you. For this. And for taking such good care of my niece." Wrapping her arms around me, my shock subsides as I hug her back. "If you break her heart, I know exactly what to say to convince a jury it was an accident."

Miles barks a laugh as I pull away, smirking. "I promise not to hurt her."

Unless she begs for it.

That thought enters my mind quickly, and it surprises me how much I like the idea of it.

Of Zoe begging.

"Have fun with your friend, Carolina. Lovely to see you, as always." Miles says, eyebrows arched in a playful manner.

"Oh, he's just—it's not like that—"

I don't think I've ever seen her so flustered, and I can't help but laugh as I bend down to kiss her on the cheek.

"He would want you to be happy," I say, almost slurring the words together.

Carolina's large, brown eyes bore into mine with watery intensity. I never realized until today that Zoe's eyes are exactly the same shape, and it makes me miss her. Fuck, it makes me miss her a lot.

After Miles leads me to his car—which is a black Escalade with a driver, the pompous asshole—he turns and faces me with a scowl.

"You smell like a refinery."

"And you smell like spit up," I offer, eyes tracking down to the stain on his tie.

He laughs and leans back. "So, curious minds want to know…"

"Here we go," I groan.

"When, exactly, did you and Zoe get together?"

"Catalina for my thirty-ninth birthday. There were edibles, in my defense."

Miles laughs. "Of course there was. Well, I guess all I can say is you're welcome, then."

Realization slams through me. "What? Did you cancel on purpose?"

He chuckles. "No, but now I wish I had."

"I'm not sure I believe you," I mutter, suddenly queasy.

"I do love a good, well-thought-out meddle, but unfortunately that was all happenstance. And look... it all worked out in the end, didn't it?"

"We'll see. She might hate me forever."

"You of all people know she might need a little nudge. You remember when Stella lived with you for a week when she wasn't speaking to me, but I eventually won her back?"

"Yes, with a pair of goat socks," I blurt.

Miles laughs again. "So, what's *your* equivalent of goat socks? Just do that, and tell her you love her—"

"How do you know I love her?"

Miles tracks his green eyes over my face when I look over at him. "Because it's obvious. Love wrecks you, in the best way."

"It certainly does," I respond, closing my eyes so I don't vomit all over his car.

CHAPTER TWENTY-FOUR

THE SIGN

Zoe

One Month Later

"When all is said and done, I think this is one of the best debut fantasy romances I've ever read," Cheryl finishes, setting my printed manuscript down.

My hands are shaking when they come to my face, and I resist the urge to kick my legs and scream with joy.

"Really? Because I know we talked about that bit at the end, with Ethan and the demon. Do you think the readers are going to hate me for making it a cliffhanger?"

Cheryl, a British literary agent who is my mentor at the workshop today, leans forward. "Readers say they don't like cliffhangers, but their actions say otherwise. Besides, I've not seen a twist quite like this before. I mean, we have sweet Ethan, who becomes *possessed* by the demon, and Lily's internal conflict when they kiss..." She kisses her fingers. "It's literary butter."

I laugh as my heart swoops with excitement. "Thank you for all of your help. This workshop has been life changing."

Cheryl stands up and brushes her hands off. "I truly hope to see your book on the shelves of my local bookstore in the future, Ms. Arma. You have a real knack for words. Have a safe journey home, okay?"

I nod, and once she leaves our workshop room, I let out an excited whoop that almost sounds like a sob. While I'd finished my book last month, I spent my days in London self-editing and making the words pop. I took a red pen to my book, and between my fellow writers and the amazing line up of mentors they had for us every few days—including award-winning authors, agents, and editors—I feel *really* good about *Between All Realms.*

In fact, I would be going home with a list of agents to query, as well as resources for starting up my social media accounts, learning how to market my book to boost sales, and recommendations for how to write a three-book series.

I'm still grinning as I walk up the old stairs to my bedroom.

London was everything I'd dreamed of and more. The workshop was located in an old townhouse across the street from Hyde Park, and I had a perfect view of the Christmas decorations, the old lanterns, and the black taxis. When it snowed the first week I was here, I spent an entire afternoon making a snowman with a few other people in the workshop, and I had my first true white Christmas and New Year's. Apparently it was rare for this time of year in England. My bedroom overlooked the lake, and it was absolutely stunning— the perfect spot to hone my craft and focus on my book.

Most of my days were spent waking up early and going down to the frosty kitchen to make a piece of toast and a cup of tea.

While in England, after all.

Most days, I finished working around one and then spent a couple of hours workshopping what I'd written with the mentor assigned to me for the day. After that, I had about an hour before the sun set, and Stella had given me a list of must-see things to do in London, and I took advantage, checking every single thing off her list.

I made sure to send her lots of pictures, because I knew she missed her home country.

I went to Harrods, visited all the museums, and rode the Tube. I took a freezing cold river tour along the Thames, stared at more art of old white men than I thought possible, and ate the best Indian curry of my life on Brick Lane. Doing all of it without my phone was a task, especially since I'd grown up with access to the internet at my fingertips. But somehow, I managed.

And I missed Liam. *A lot.*

Mostly at night, when I was cuddled up under the duvet, shivering and wondering why English people relied on a piece of metal on the wall to heat a room.

But also when I used his pen that I'd stolen—which

was every day. It was silly, and insignificant, but it felt like I had a small piece of him with me.

In those moments, I would think of how his hands felt on my skin—the rough pads of his fingers caressing the delicate areas of my body.

I would think of his Dominant voice, getting myself off every night when I thought of how good he was with his fingers. Mine aren't nearly as long as his, so it always left me feeling wholly unsatisfied, and after I came, I would get *sad,* because there was a chance we could never be together like that again.

But it's not only the physical parts of him that I missed during my month away.

I would think about his soothing voice, the warmth of my cheek against his beating heart, and how cozy it felt to hug him. I would think about how he always ensured I was fed and hydrated, how he couldn't help but love when I pushed him to do something he was scared of.

Like being vulnerable with me.

I'm still mad that he chose to walk away, sure, but the experience in London has dulled my anger. Now, I'm just... *hurt.*

Because if he doesn't want to be with me when I get back...

I set the printed pages of my book down on my writing desk with a soft *thwack* once settled in my bedroom. I sit down on my bed and close my eyes, thinking of anything and everything *other* than Liam, just like every other time he crosses my mind—which is a lot.

Truth be told, if he doesn't want me anymore...

It might break me.

I look around the small, single bedroom that's home to a long bed, tiny desk, and dresser. Even though my flight to Los Angeles leaves tonight, I can't help but feel nostalgic for this place.

It was the first place I've ever felt was all my own. Liam's house was always *his*. And I lived with three other classmates in the dorms of Thatcher Prep. For the first time in my life, I have a sense of direction and purpose. I'm *excited* for the future with regards to my book, but the funny thing is, I can't wrap my mind around everything that happened with Liam.

As excited as I am about everything, there's still a massive hole in my chest. There's still such a potent longing to be held by him. I miss him, and I don't know what our future holds, but I can only hope that we can at least remain friends.

The word *friends* makes me grimace, but instead of wallowing, I decide to get a head start on packing.

It takes under an hour, and by the time I make my rounds and say goodbye to the seven other students, I'm ready to don my coat and hat to wait for my taxi to Heathrow.

As I drag my suitcase down the cobblestone road, a black SUV drives up to the sidewalk, and a window rolls down.

"Zoe Arma?" The older man opens his door and steps out.

He's tall and has silver hair. Something about him is vaguely familiar, but I can't pinpoint why. I have enough stranger danger to know not to answer him, and my expression must be one of vague alarm because he laughs and reaches for my hand. "I'm Prescott Deveraux. Estelle's father," he adds, his accent half-English, half-French.

"Oh, hi!" I say, shaking his hand.

"We met at Miles and Stella's wedding. The *real* one," he adds, and I laugh when I think about the small ceremony they had when Beatrix was younger.

"Right. I thought you looked familiar."

"Anyway, I was told to escort you to the airport."

I look between him and the black SUV. "By whom?"

"Estelle, of course." I arch a brow—that does not sound like something she would do—and he laughs again. "Fine. It was that pushy boyfriend of yours, and since you're family, there was no question."

Liam?

I shift my weight from hip to hip as he reaches out for my suitcase, taking it from me and walking it to the trunk.

"But I thought you lived in Paris?"

Prescott chuckles as he lifts the heavy suitcase; he's surprisingly strong for someone in his seventies.

"I do."

He doesn't offer any other explanation though, just opens my door for me and smiles. "After you, ma chérie."

My lips pull into a smirk as I slide into the leather seat. "Of course Liam would be overbearing from across the pond."

Prescott smiles. "The best ones always are."

Closing my door, he walks around to the other side. As we drive through London, Prescott asks me about Miles, Stella, and Beatrix. We talk about my book and my studies. I ask him about Stella's childhood in London. We both laugh when we think of Miles having to one day handle a teenager. Signs for Heathrow appear on the motorway, and as we make our way through the dusky suburbs of London, I already know I'll miss the city more than I can imagine.

"You know, my late wife was twenty years younger than me. Did you know that?"

"I didn't," I say softly, remembering how Stella told me that her mother died during childbirth. "I'm sorry you didn't have more time with her."

Prescott looks out of the window, expression peaceful yet... almost longing. "There is a saying in French, and I'm not quite sure how to properly translate it to English. *Si jeunesse savait, si vieillesse pouvait.* It means, 'if youth only knew, if age only could.'" I swallow as I digest his words. Before I can respond, he sighs. "Life is short. I wish I'd had more time with my wife. If age only could..." Sadness reverberates in his voice, and he turns to face me as we pull into my terminal. "My advice would be not to waste time on silly things, but to enjoy each other while you still can. Don't waste a *second*, Zoe."

His words cause something sharp to lance through me—because he's right.

"Thank you," I whisper, as we pull into the departure area.

"Of course. I'll be in Crestwood next month to see my granddaughter. Hopefully I'll be seeing you and that scary boyfriend of yours."

I huff a laugh as I climb out of the car. After giving Prescott a quick hug, I look at the terminal building and take a deep breath.

If youth only knew...

———

I read my dad's letter on the plane ride home—which is spent in pure, first-class luxury.

There's no question about *who* upgraded me, though I'm not entirely sure *why*.

I'd spent the last month debating about whether or not to read it while doing the workshop, but decided to hold off in case it caused my mind to veer off track. As my finger slips beneath the seal of the envelope, I pull a piece of white parchment out. My eyes sting as I take in my father's handwriting—something I haven't seen in years. And then, thirty-five thousand feet in the air, I read the last thing my father will ever write to me.

My Dearest Zoe,

If you're reading this, then the unimaginable

has happened. I'm so sorry. Just know that I hope you never have to read this letter. But if you do, I want you to know three very important things.

You are the best thing that ever happened to me. When your mom found out she was pregnant, we were both scared shitless. But we got our lives together and decided that if we were going to be parents, we'd be the best parents in the whole entire world. I don't know if we accomplished that, but we tried. Still, the day you were born... it changed my life forever. Thank you for making me a father and thank you for being the best daughter anyone could ask for.

Don't be afraid to fly. The sky is the limit. I hope you spend your days dreaming about all the things you can accomplish. And I hope you know that <u>no matter what</u>, you have my support.

Be happy. I hope you never question if I would've approved your life choices. I would have as long as they make you happy. So if it brings you joy, I am smiling down from heaven. Or up, depending on how the big guy in the sky sees the irresponsible actions of my late teens. Ask Liam about that.

Speaking of Liam, you've probably worked out by now that your mother and I chose him to be your guardian. First, he has a good job, large house, and he knows me better than anyone.

That much is obvious. But the second reason is twofold, and maybe a bit selfish of me.

He might say he's fine, that he enjoys his job, that he's happy in that house without internet (try and convince him to at least get a landline, yeah?) But I know better. He's lonely, and he's spent his entire life taking care of his brothers. You might be asking why I gave him another person to take care of, but I hope you can show him that sometimes, it's okay to have someone to share the burden of always being there for other people.

I love you, Zoe. I wish I could be there to watch you grow up, but I know you'll be okay. You're strong and resilient (you get that from your mom... I'm a huge baby).

Love,
Dad

My face is completely wet by the time I finish, and one of the flight attendants must notice, because she scampers over to where I'm sitting.

"Ms. Arma? Is everything okay?" she asks in a British accent.

I huff a laugh as I wipe my face. "I'm fine. Thank you."

She inspects my face for a second before determining that I'm telling the truth, and then she walks away.

After tucking the letter away, I lean back in my seat

and look out the window, thinking about my dad's letter the entire flight home.

By the time we land, I'm still in a bit of a daze. I couldn't sleep on the flight, instead having about five lattes, and as much free food as I could, so I'm both exhausted and strung out.

When I come down the escalator, I'm not looking for Liam, because why would he be here? I keep my head down, eager to get to the rideshare line so that I can be home. But as my eyes flick up to see where I am, it's the sign that catches my attention.

Large and white, a few people are snickering when they point it out, and I stop walking when I take it in.

Languish
Lament
Loathe

Tracking my eyes down, I see Liam holding it with a small smirk on his beautiful face.

I don't realize that I've let go of my suitcase or started running, but before I know it, he's letting the sign fall onto the ground and I'm leaping into his arms, wrapping my legs around his hips. People cheer as I place my hands on either side of his face, and I'm grinning as he kisses me back.

His large, warm hands slide underneath my T-shirt and grip the flesh at my waist. I choke out a sob, and then his tongue pushes past my lips. He lets out a low groan that only I can hear. I start crying in earnest because he's kissing me back.

Because we're going to be okay.

Because he's *here*.

Goosebumps break out along my skin, and I press myself closer to him—wanting to crawl on top of him completely. I kiss him with reckless abandon, crying and laughing as he holds me so tightly, like he never wants to let me go again.

"I'm sorry," he whispers against my lips. "I'm sorry, I'm sorry, I'm sorry," he says, peppering kisses along my jaw and cheek.

My emotions whirl and skid with each of his movements, ebbing and flowing until my brain is short-circuiting.

Finally, I pull away, my hands still on either side of his face. "I'm sorry, too. I shouldn't have pushed you."

"We can talk in the car," he says, his voice husky. "But right now, I need to keep you wrapped around my body to hide my massive hard-on from all of these strangers."

My resounding laugh has a few people smiling and cheering for us, and all I can do is wrap my arms around his neck and cling to him as I grin like a maniac, breathing in his licorice scent.

This—*he*—is home.

CHAPTER TWENTY-FIVE
THE DESPERATION

LIAM

I can't stop smiling as Zoe gushes about London, telling me all about her month there. She flails her arms excitedly when she tells me about her mentors and the advice she received from them, and her face lights up whenever she talks about her book. I'm focused on the road, of course, but I can't help but sneak quick glances at her whenever we're stopped in traffic on the 405, or when we're waiting at a light.

She's the same, but also a little bit different. She carries herself with more confidence, and she seems surer of herself and where her book is going. She has a plan for the next step—and I couldn't be any fucking prouder of her.

"Have you ever been to London? It's such an incredible city. I think you'd like it."

I chuckle as I pull off the freeway in Crestwood. "I've been before. I do enjoy a nice cold pint of lager in a pub."

"Oh, and thanks for asking Stella's poor father to drive me to the airport," she says, rolling her eyes and smirking at me. "I'm sure he had much better things to do with his day."

I laugh. "Well, he happens to owe me a favor. So, now we're even."

"I think he's a bit scared of you," she adds as I pull to a stop in downtown Crestwood. Her eyes sparkle as they bore into mine.

"You think? I guess I assumed he was used to over-bearing Ravage men."

"He was friends with your father, right?"

I nod, jaw hardening as it always does when I think of my father. "He was. Until my father fucked him over. Miles took care of it."

"I wonder why Orion still talks to his—*your*—father," she muses.

I debate telling her that he was too young to remember the neglect. Too young to remember Miles in the hospital with third degree burns. In time, he'll figure it out, but it isn't my place to come between him and our father.

As I turn onto the road that winds up to our house, I find the courage to tell her how sorry I am again.

"Listen, Zoe..."

"Stop apologizing," she admonishes, her small hand coming to my thigh. "I know you're sorry. I knew it that night. But when I got that email about London... I couldn't let myself dwell on it. And when Prescott told me you'd sent him, I knew it was your way of saying sorry."

I ruminate on her words for several seconds before responding. "That's good. Because I spent the last month really fucking miserable. Even Sushi couldn't stand to be around me."

As I look over at her, she gives me a small smile. "Just promise me two things," she starts, her voice thick with emotion. "Instead of pushing me away, *please* talk to me."

"I promise," I say too quickly.

I'll do anything.

"Good," she replies, pursing her lips with such conviction that I can't help but smile. "And the second thing... stop beating yourself up about us. I actually spoke with Carolina, you know."

My lips twitch. "I know. I spoke with her, too. And then proceeded to get rip-roaring drunk when I realized what a massive fucking mistake I made."

Zoe laughs. "You're lucky I forgive easily," she says, hand sliding a bit higher on my thigh. My nerve endings go up in flames at her touch, and I shift in my seat slightly to accommodate my growing erection.

"Did you read the letter?" I ask her, trying not to sound like I've been really fucking curious about what it said.

"I did. On the plane ride home."

"Oh?"

"You want to know what it said?" she asks, her tone teasing and light.

I consider her words for a few seconds, wondering if I should say what I've been curious about for weeks. But when I really think about it, it doesn't make sense that he would ever consider the possibility of us. I don't need to know, and I don't need his approval.

"You don't have to tell me. Whatever he said is between the two of you."

Zoe doesn't respond, and when I chance a quick look over at her, I can see that she's watching me with a shy smile.

"He wants me to be happy, and he said he'd support every decision I made—no matter what—as long as it made me happy."

I swallow as my hands curl around the steering wheel, not realizing how much I need to hear words like that.

"He also wanted me to make sure you wouldn't end up alone. He wanted you to be happy, too," she adds, her voice quieter and more serious now.

I sit with her words for a few minutes, chest burning with raw emotion as I make my way to the house.

Zoe's hand stays on my thigh, and when I finally put the car in park, I turn to face Zoe.

"I misinterpreted your father's words," I admit. "He told me to protect you, and for so long, I thought that meant from me. But it doesn't matter what he meant by those words, because no one will protect you like I will. I'm not sure what else I can say to make up for how much I fucked up that night but know that I'll do my best to make up for it every damn day of my life."

Her watery, honey-colored eyes bore into mine, and then in one quick motion, she unbuckles her seatbelt and crawls into my lap—her knees on either side of my hips. Her face is inches away from mine, and despite her hair smelling different, there's still an undertone of vanilla and something else—something that makes me roll my hips underneath her.

"One last stipulation," she says, her voice husky and low. "No using the safe word outside of the bedroom."

"I'm sorry—"

Her lips are against mine before I can finish my sentence, and the feel of her on top of me, her warm center pressing against my erection, her soft lips and tongue that drive me crazy—

"I love you," I say, caught up in the moment. She goes still and pulls away, eyes wide. I realize what I said a second too late. "I mean, I think it's obvious by now, but it's okay if you don't feel the same way—"

Her mouth collides with mine once again, and she groans as her hands come to my hair, fisting it gently.

"I love you, too," she whispers. "Please take me inside now."

I manage to get us both out of the car and through the front door with her legs still wrapped around me. Once we're inside, Captain comes trotting into the foyer, chirping excitedly.

"He missed you," I tell her, letting my lips trail down her face to her exposed collarbone as I walk her to the foyer table. "But I missed you more." She groans when I set her down next to the vase of violets before positioning myself between her legs. "I really want to fuck you on this table, but I don't want Captain to watch us."

Zoe giggles and looks over my shoulder. "Go up to my room, Sushi."

To my utter astonishment, Sushi lets out a resigned, quick purr before turning around and walking off.

"I think he's a robot," Zoe says, arms coming around my neck. As she combs her fingers through my hair, my eyes flutter closed as I smile.

"Why?"

"Because he listens like a human. It's actually quite scary how well he understands me when I talk to him."

I lower my lips to hers, gently nibbling on her lower lip as my hands come up underneath her shirt.

"I didn't realize the two of you had conversations," I mutter, moving my lips down to her jaw and flicking my tongue against her skin.

"Only sometimes," she breathes, panting as I undo her bra in one quick motion. Her eyes catch on the flowers next to her, and she gasps. "Violets."

My chin dips slightly. I've never been a big romance guy, but violets always have and always will remind me of her.

"You remember?" I ask carefully.

"I remember. They're beautiful."

"They remind me of you. Orion told me violets represent loyalty and protection."

She huffs a laugh. "Of course you'd find a way to be overbearing with your gifts."

"Of course. Take off your shirt," I whisper, helping her pull it over her head.

Once it's off, I let it fall to the floor as she shimmies out of her bra—a hot pink, lacy thing. I groan as my eyes track over the material, letting my fingers brush the soft fabric before my hands come to her bare breasts. As my thumbs caress her nipples, she arches her back and whimpers.

"Take off your pants," she says quickly, reaching out for my belt buckle.

Her fingers fumble with it, and I chuckle as I brush them away. "Impatient, are we?"

"Aren't you?" she whines, trying to reach down to my erection again. "I'm desperate," she begs.

I lower myself to my knees. "So am I." Not giving her the chance to protest, I hook my fingers underneath the waistband of her leggings and peel them off her legs, discarding them somewhere behind me. "Desperate and starving," I mutter, pulling her matching hot pink panties to the side and exposing her cunt.

I slide my tongue through her wet folds, groaning and gripping her thighs tightly. She shifts her hips slightly, angling them up as I pull her forward to get better access.

"Fuck," she whispers, hands coming to my hair. I swirl my tongue over her clit, moving my tongue quickly as one of my fingers comes to her opening. After sliding it in, I pump it in and out slowly, curling it so that the tip of my finger drags against her G-spot. "Yes—fuck—right there."

"So responsive," I growl, biting the inside of her thigh. She cries out, so I do it again—loving the way she clenches around me when I do. I'm smiling against her, thrusting my hips against nothing to get myself some kind of friction. "You're making such pretty noises for me, little rebel."

I insert a second finger and bring my mouth to her clit, focusing all of my attention on her swollen bud as my fingers twist and curl inside of her, scissoring them with every other thrust into her. I'm well aware of the effects of the maneuver, and after several more seconds, she begins to circle her hips underneath me.

"Harder," she says, her voice disappearing into a soft groan.

"I want to hear you beg," I tell her.

"God, I'm so close—"

"That doesn't sound like begging to me," I tease, looking up at her from between her legs.

"Please," she growls, teeth clenched.

I laugh in earnest, pushing her legs wider. "You can do better than that, baby girl. Come on. If you cooperate, I might be more inclined to give you exactly what you need," I add, inserting a third finger.

Her mouth drops open as her eyelashes flutter. "Please let me come, Liam," she moans, hands fisting in my hair as I flick my tongue against her swollen bud.

Laying my tongue flat against her, I let her roll into my mouth, taking her pleasure from me—taking everything she needs from my mouth and fingers. Using my hair to hold on, her rhythm gets jerky, and I swear to fucking god, her cunt squeezes me so hard that she nearly pops my fingers out.

Screaming, she rocks her hips against my mouth and tongue, sliding her hips up and down over my fingers. I groan when she contracts around me, imagining how she'd be milking my cock like this very soon.

"Yes, yes, yes!" she cries out, throwing her head back as she comes.

I don't take my eyes off her, looking up between her legs.

Keeping one finger inside of her, I slowly thrust it into her to drag her orgasm on for as long as I can, and with every swipe of my fingertip against her G-spot, she quivers. She's *so* fucking sensitive, and I love every second of watching her unravel like this.

Without giving her a chance to protest, I throw her left leg over my shoulder and angle her hips higher.

"Give me one more," I command.

"Wait—no—I can't."

"Give. Me. One. More," I grit out.

"Liam—" She gasps when my tongue hits her clit again, rocking her hips and pushing against my head as if she's trying to get away from me.

"You're so cute when you squirm like that," I mutter, using my free hand to hold her hips down so that she can't move away from me.

"Oh god," she whines as I insert a second finger again. "It's too much..."

I don't give her a chance to argue any further, lapping up her juices with enthusiasm, curling my fingers just so, moving them in and out of her with enough force to make the table creak.

In this moment, I'm glad I've been chopping so much wood lately and working my arm muscles so vigorously.

"Liam—"

Zoe's voice cracks as her cunt begins to feather around my fingers, and when I look up, I see her eyes roll into the back of her head.

The sounds she's making are so fucking hot—a mix of moaning, crying, and whimpering. I don't slow down this time—don't give her a chance to recover before inserting the third finger and making her scream my name ten more times.

She comes a third time, her back arching as her arousal trickles down her bare thigh. I lap it up with my tongue, using the rough pad of my thumb to gently graze over her, giving her numerous aftershocks. When I remove her leg from my shoulder and lean back on my heels, she's watching me with mascara-stained cheeks and blotchy, red skin.

For a second, the panic that I went too far eclipses everything, and my brows furrow as I run a hand along her thigh.

"Give me a color," I ask gently.

She smirks. "Green."

I smile as I stand, but before I can help her up, she scoots off the table and lowers herself to her knees.

"You don't have to—"

"It's been a month, and I want it to last longer than two minutes, okay?" she snarks.

I huff a laugh and reach a hand to the back of my neck, letting my arm hang there as she undoes my belt buckle and pulls the zipper down. My cock springs free when she pulls my boxers down, and I let out a low growl when her tongue flicks against the tip, now dripping with precum.

"Still a brat, I see," I tell her, my voice affectionate as I run my hands through her dark hair. She looks up at me as she opens her mouth, and if I could immortalize one image, it would be this—Zoe, on her knees, with her mouth full of my cock. I move my hips forward so she takes me into her mouth fully, but she beats me to it—taking me all the way to the back of her throat. I hiss with pleasure. "So eager for my cock," I mutter.

She brings her hands to my shaft, fisting it as she works her mouth around the head, and my whole body convulses as she pulls me deep inside of her mouth again, gagging this time.

I expect her to stop, but she—*quite literally*—sucks the soul out of me with each suck, each swallow of her throat, each slide of her hands. I start to mutter incoherent words as I watch her, tears tracking down her cheeks as she works me closer.

"Oh fuck, Zoe. You're such a good girl. I'm close..." I curl my hand around her hair, pulling her mouth onto my cock and thrusting into her throat. "Tap my thigh three times if it's too much," I rasp, unable to stop moving, chasing my climax like it's the next hit of the most potent drug on the market.

I continue fucking her mouth, and a few seconds later, a hard and fast orgasm slams into me. My cock hardens inside of her, and as my knees buckle, I groan. She swallows with each jet of hot cum that slides down her throat, and the sensation of her mouth squeezing around my shaft causes me to buck my hips erratically.

It extends my orgasm, causing my whole body to tense. When she's done, she audibly swallows and stands up, wiping her mouth with the back of her hand.

I grab her arm, pulling her into my body as I kiss her —wanting to savor the evidence of her dedication. She groans when my tongue swirls against the taste of my own cum, and I swear, the sound of her being aroused has me at half-mast again.

"I need to be inside of you," I whisper against her mouth.

"Then do it," she retorts, her inflection sassy.

I growl as I lift her up, walking her backward until her body is pressed against the front door. She's fully naked, and I'm still dressed, but I enjoy how erotic it feels to be the only one clothed. I press her against the smooth wood, enjoying how she's watching me with arousal written all over her expression. That look alone has me hard again.

Lining my cock up with her weeping core, I push into her in one smooth motion.

Fuck, she's always so tight.

Really fucking tight.

"Yes," Zoe whimpers, rolling her hips. "More, please."

I smile as I kiss her, my lips more punishing than gentle, as I pull out and snap my hips forward roughly.

"Oh fuck," she whimpers.

I continue the movements—slowly pulling out before shifting my hips in and up, fucking her into the door, making it groan with the exertion. One of Zoe's hands comes to the back of my neck, squeezing. I groan as the sensation skitters down my spine and straight to my cock, causing me to fuck her harder.

"More," she says, voice hoarse.

"Such a greedy girl," I mutter, leaning down to nibble on the flesh at the base of her neck. "I fucking love it. But do you know what I love more?"

Zoe cries out when I bite down on her flesh, her cunt ripples around my cock, and my eyes roll into the back of my head.

She feels so fucking good.

Well, fuck.

I'm not going to last long now.

"What?" she asks, her voice breaking on the word as I pound into her.

"When you beg."

She rolls her hips then, taking me *all* the way in, moving on top of my cock as she clasps her arms around my neck to give herself something to hold on to.

"Please fuck me harder. I promise you won't break me."

I wince at her choice of words, thinking about her

wrist, but Zoe takes her hands and places them on either side of my face.

"Please," she whispers.

"You asked for it," I growl, placing one of my hands against the door as I move my hips back and snap them forward with such force that Zoe moves up the door a few inches.

"Yes," she moans.

My balls draw up as my cock thickens, and she must feel it because her head drops back against the door and her eyes flutter closed.

"Look at me," I tell her, rolling my hips into her with reckless abandon.

Her eyes pop open as her pussy clenches around me, milking me with each wave of her climax. A low, heady groan leaves her throat, but her eyes don't leave mine. Her expression is almost unsure as she rides out her orgasm, shaking in my arms as her cunt continues to squeeze me. My free hand comes to one of her breasts, and as I cup it, her pussy squeezes me—hard.

So.

Fucking.

Responsive.

My orgasm tears through me aggressively, and I stop moving as pleasure claws up my spine, hot jets of cum spilling into her so quickly that the hand against the door curls into a fist, and my breathing turns ragged. I look down and watch as my cock throbs inside of her, feeling the resistance of her tight opening as my cock continues to pump her full of my seed.

Okay, so that's my second favorite sight.

When I look up at Zoe, I realize she's looking down at where we're joined also, and when her eyes slowly find mine, she physically sags against me.

I hug her close to me, letting my breathing return as I run my fingers along the sides of her body. When my cock slips out of her, I lower her to the ground, not letting go.

"Come on," I say, running my hand through her hair. "Let me clean you up, and then we can cuddle in bed with snacks and some water."

"Are you even real?" she asks, eyes hooded with exhaustion.

I chuckle. "Are you?"

She smiles dreamily. "You know what sounds really good? Some of your chicken."

I laugh. "You're in luck. Come on, let's go take a shower, and then we'll come downstairs and eat some chicken."

Zoe's eyes flick between mine as one of her hands comes to my cheek. "You're perfect. I love you."

I bend down and kiss the top of her forehead. "I love you, too."

CHAPTER TWENTY-SIX

THE CONCERT

ZOE

Ten Months Later

The crowd goes wild when Blink-182 walks onto the stage. I scream and jump, throat raw, as Travis Barker begins to drum the melody for "I Miss You." Tom DeLonge looks out into the large crowd before the first guitar chord cuts through the noise.

Liam's arms wrap around my stomach as he tugs me against him, and then we both let the song wash over us completely. It's strange to hear it live—to hear it from the actual band instead of a cover band. The songs hit harder, and I swallow the lump in my throat as the lyrics cause my chest to ache.

"Your dad would've loved this," Liam says, chuckling behind me—though I can hear the way his voice catches slightly, giving his emotions away. "So many kids here who weren't even born when we first heard this song."

I bark a laugh as a stray tear falls down my cheek. "It's not our fault that you're old."

Liam's chest rumbles with laughter behind me, and I close my eyes as the band plays the rest of the song.

I think about my dad when he was younger, being at one of their concerts with Liam. I can't help but smile that, despite my dad being gone, there's a small chance that he's looking down (or up, according to him) and smiling while he watches us.

What would he say if he knew Liam and I were engaged and getting married in December? Would he grumble and eventually accept it?

I have to think he would.

The band finishes their set, which is a good thing because Liam is limping as we walk to the grassy hill behind the venue.

"You okay?" I ask as I lace my fingers through his.

"I can't stand for two hours anymore," he mutters, smirking as I giggle.

"I can buy you some orthopedic shoes for your wedding gift," I offer, cocking my head and letting go of his hand as I walk backward.

He leaps forward and I squeal as we tumble onto the soft grass near our blanket. The venue is located outside of Las Vegas, and it's warm for October. The sun is low on the horizon, and it'll be dark soon, but the sun on my skin is amazing.

"Very funny," he mutters, giving my lips a quick peck before helping me sit up between his legs.

"Who's on next?" I ask, thinking about the amazing lineup of my favorite bands.

"Not sure, don't care," he mumbles, kissing the top of my head. "I'm just here among the youths so I can feel my hot fiancée up."

I smile as I lean against his chest—and the hard evidence of his delight. "Hmm, I see. Are you ever going to stop telling everyone that I'm your fiancée?" I ask, thinking back to him telling both the man checking our phone for tickets, the bathroom attendant, *and* the security guard that he was here with his *fiancée*. It would be annoying if it weren't so adorable, especially coming from him.

Turns out Liam Ravage is a giant cinnamon roll.

"No, never. Not until I get to call you my wife."

His words send shivers down my spine, and when his right hand comes to rest on my bare thigh—despite not being alone—I scoot down slightly so it's resting right at the hem of my cut-off shorts.

"I know what you're doing, little rebel," he growls into my ear as his other hand moves my hair away from my face. "Are you trying to tempt me in front of all of these innocent people?"

"I would never," I tease, raising my leg slightly so his fingers catch on the edge of my shorts.

My breathing hitches as they curl around the hem, lightly caressing my skin. Even now, almost a year into our relationship, I still can't breathe when he touches me.

I am a woman consumed, and all I want to consume is *him.*

"I never took you for an exhibitionist," he says, murmuring into my ear.

"I've been *so* preoccupied with wedding stuff," I tell him honestly, and his hand leaves my thigh to play with my hair. It feels *so good* to be cradled by him like this—to have him running his large hands through my hair. Humming out loud, I close my eyes. This might be the first time I've felt this relaxed in weeks. "Remind me never to release a book the month before we get married again."

Liam's low, rumbling laughter behind me relaxes me further. "No one told you to release a book the month before you get married, baby girl. But you can do it. I know you can."

I smile when I think about how supportive he's been of my writing. After spending six months querying agents, no one took a bite of *Between All Realms.* So, I decided to take things into my own hands, and I started marketing it on TikTok. When I got enough hype to justify it, I decided that traditional publishing wasn't for me. I had it professionally edited and bought the most gorgeous cover from a highly sought-after cover artist, and now I'm self-publishing it next month.

The number of preorders for a debut author makes me want to cry every single day in the best way, and I know my choice of staying in school was the right one.

Studying and trying to publish a book—all while planning a wedding—is a lot. I'm taking fewer classes this semester, and I want to be sure I finish my English degree. The wonderful thing about giving up my law school dream is that I can go slowly, and I won't have to graduate next semester like I originally thought.

I think Lena, my academic advisor, nearly died of shock when I told her I wanted to *slow down* earlier this year.

"How many preorders have you gotten today?" Liam asks.

Dashboard Confessional starts to play next, but we're far enough away to be able to talk loudly and still hear each other. Plus, as I crane my neck to look up at Liam, I can tell from his closed eyes that he needs to rest for a little bit.

"I haven't checked. I've been too busy at the festival with my fiancé."

He chuckles, and I twist around and push him down to a lying down position, curling my body around him. My head rests on his chest, and he begins to trace patterns along my exposed back with the arm underneath me.

"See? You do it, too."

I smile and close my eyes, enjoying the warm earth below us, and the tendrils of warmth from the setting sun, all while listening to my favorite music.

"The last time I checked, I had over eight hundred preorders."

Liam stiffens. "Seriously?"

I lift my head to look at him. "Yeah, why?"

He grabs my face with his free hand and crushes his lips against mine for a quick kiss. "That's fucking incredible. I'm so proud of you."

My heart soars at his words, and I laugh as my left hand comes to his face. The orange sun reflects beautifully against the ruby stone of my engagement ring.

"Are you nervous?" he asks, holding me tight against his chest.

"Terrified," I admit. "Two of the most important things in my life happening in succession..." I swallow and close my eyes, afraid to put a voice to my deepest fears.

"But...?" Liam asks, his low voice gentle and soothing, like always.

It takes me a few seconds to answer. I've never been one to withhold how I'm really feeling, but for some reason, the book release followed closely by our wedding has me so scared that it's all going to disappear at any minute. Not only is life with Liam incredible and dreamy, but the writing has gone really well, too. I've started writing book two, and I hope to be done by the end of the year. I've surpassed three preorder goals, and I spend my weekends thinking about marrying the man of my dreams. It's so good —*too* good.

And sometimes, it doesn't seem real.

It's a fairytale of my own making.

"I guess I'm worried it's all too good to be true. You, my book, our life..." I take a steadying breath. "It's everything I've ever wanted, right at my fingertips, and I worry it's all going to disappear one day."

Liam makes a sound of acknowledgement but doesn't answer right away. Instead, he holds me close as the anxiety works through me.

"I don't know if this helps, but when I think about the future and how good it sounds, I let myself enjoy it. I can't predict the future—you and I both know that anything can happen at any time, but I *do* believe that you and I have gone through the worst hell imaginable. Literally people's worst nightmares. I think the human soul can recover from a lot of different traumas, but the death of a loved one is something we never recover from."

My throat clogs with emotion from his words, and my fingers curl around his vintage All American Rejects shirt.

"You're right," I say, my voice thick with unshed tears.

He maneuvers us so that we're facing each other, and then his hands come to either side of my face.

"It's you and me against the world, baby girl. Never forget that. No matter what happens, you'll have me."

Another one of my worst fears unlocks inside of my brain, and I can't help it when a tear rolls down the side of my face.

"I mean, realistically, you'll die before me because you're so much older than me."

I don't mean for it to come out so bluntly. Liam's eyes

flash with amusement before he laughs, his head thrown back and a large smile on his gorgeous face.

I wipe my tears away as I laugh with him.

"Well, I promise to haunt your sexy ass for eternity then."

"Promise?" I ask, my voice breaking.

"Zoe, there's no reality—in this life or the next—where I won't want to spend my days right next to you. You. Are. It. For. Me. Haven't you ever wondered why I never dated around? Never married anyone? Chase was nearly ten years younger and proposing, and then Miles got together with Stella... I thought something was wrong with me. But I think the universe was making me wait for you."

A sob cleaves through my chest, and as I reach out for his face, a clap of thunder startles me out of my romantic trance.

Instinctively, I sit up, eyes wide as I frantically look around.

The previously orange sky is now a dark, cloudy grey, and a second later, large raindrops fall from the sky.

"Liam—"

Another clap of loud thunder makes me jump up, and my heart races as people scatter. I reach down for my purse, assuming we'll want to take cover somewhere, but Liam comes to stand next to me.

The rain is so loud, and the band continues performing. A few people start to laugh and dance around, and though my heart is galloping a mile a minute inside of my chest, I can't help but smile when I see them.

"Take my hand. Let's wait the storm out and enjoy it."

I reach out for his hand, and then I look up and close my eyes, letting the rain fall against my face. Before I know it, I'm half-laughing, half-sobbing. Another crack of thunder so loud it has the ground vibrating underneath me turns it into full sobs.

Not terrified sobs, though; it's almost cathartic.

Before I know it, we're both soaked through, and the rain doesn't relent.

This is how my parents died, I think, saying it out loud in my mind. *It's okay to miss them, but I don't have to be scared of storms anymore.*

Liam pulls me into his firm body, arms wrapped tightly around me. "They would be so fucking proud of you," he says against my forehead.

I squeeze my eyes shut as his words wash over me. He's always been so good at deciphering my emotions—always knows exactly what I need. My hands grip the fabric of his shirt as another thunder clap sounds over us, and I let myself feel it. I let myself cry and get anxious and get *angry* that my parents are gone, and I allow myself to feel *so fucking excited* about the future. I let all the emotions roll over me, and to my surprise, the grief hurts but doesn't cripple me like it used to.

The gaping wound has turned into a tolerable, hollow ache.

"I love you," Liam rasps, and I pull away to see that he's crying, too. "Always and forever, baby girl."

Giving him a watery smile, I bring my hand to his wet face. "I love you too. Always and forever."

He tugs me into his body as we wait out the rest of the storm—not caring that we're soaking wet. Not caring that the thunder is loud and scary. Not letting it bother us.

Because when I'm in his arms like this? Nothing else matters, and I know I'm safe.

I know I'm home.

EPILOGUE
THE BILLBOARD

LIAM

Three Years Later

I sip my beer as I watch her from across the cocktail bar, cock already growing hard from the outfit she chose to tease me with tonight. It's a simple, form-fitting black dress with a large slit and thin straps. It hugs every single one of her curves in a way that makes me want to gouge out the eyeballs of any man who deigns to lay his eyes on my wife. Even from this far away, I can tell she's not wearing a bra–and knowing how naughty she loves to be, she's probably not wearing underwear, either.

My fucking brat.

She laughs at something the bartender says, and it's then that I know she knows I'm watching her. Tucking her short hair behind her ears, she leans in close on her elbows, one eyebrow arched as the bartender laughs at her response. My nostrils flare, but I don't react.

Being jealous of my wife flirting with another man is not the role we agreed upon tonight, so I take another large sip of beer to distract myself. However, my eyes don't leave her—not when she stirs her dirty martini, and certainly not when she opens her mouth and delicately places an olive between her red lips.

I smile as I look down at my empty beer.

Such a fucking tease.

Checking my watch, I can see that it's ten after eight. I promised to give her fifteen minutes to compose herself, but the thought of waiting another five minutes before I can be near her is excruciating. Pushing back from the other side of the bar, I slowly walk to where she's sitting, legs crossed, one heel of her patent leather Louboutin's tapping against the steel rod of the bar.

She catches my eye, feigning surprise as her face lights up.

"Professor Ravage? Fancy seeing you here tonight," she says, her voice a sultry purr.

I cock my head and lean against the bar, propping myself up on one elbow. "Surely you're too young to be drinking."

She laughs, and I can't help but smile. Even when we're pretending, her laugh is infectious.

"I'll have you know that I'm twenty-three now."

I hum as I let my eyes rake over her unabashedly. "Yes, you do seem to have grown up, Ms. Arma."

Her cheeks flush at the use of her maiden name, and

as her darkened eyes rove up to meet mine, she gives me a shy smile.

"Do you live in New York?" she asks, eyes flitting around the bar quickly.

I nod. "I do. I got a tenured position at NYU teaching creative writing at Tisch. You?"

"I'm actually a published author of six books."

I smirk as I get the bartender's attention. "That's incredible. We should celebrate. Let me buy you a drink."

Zoe grins. "I'd love that."

The bartender walks over to us, and I lean over the bar to place my order.

"Sparkling water for both of us, and an extra dirty martini for my former student," I tell him.

The bartender looks between us for a minute before nodding once. When I let my gaze wander down to Zoe, she's watching me with a hooded expression.

"No alcohol for you?" she asks innocently.

I shake my head. "I have a one drink rule whenever I bring someone back to my room."

Zoe's mouth twitches, but to her credit, she doesn't laugh. "That's very presumptuous of you, Professor Ravage."

As my eyes bore into hers, I delight in seeing the way her chest becomes flushed—in the way she's taking rapid, shallow breaths. If her pupils weren't so dark, I'd know she was aroused by the tint of her olive skin.

I lean down to murmur in her ear. "It's hard not to be presumptuous when you're wearing a dress like that. Plus, I like to be in control, and that requires a certain amount of... mental clarity," I add, letting my voice get low and growly just the way I know she likes it.

"Why the water?" she asks, her voice breathless.

"To keep you hydrated."

"Sounds very controlling," she retorts. "I don't remember you being this controlling as a professor."

I chuckle. "Yes, well, I don't tend to fuck former students."

She smirks. "You're so confident you can have me, then?"

I step closer so that she has no choice but to crane her neck up to look at me. "Oh, I have no doubt in my mind." The bartender sets our waters down. "Drink up, Ms. Arma."

Zoe quickly drinks the entire glass before setting it down. "I don't know if I need that second drink. Something tells me I'll need some of that... *mental clarity*," she adds, giving me a look that makes my cock twitch in my pants.

I place some money on the bar, smiling and holding my hand out. "Shall we?"

Zoe places her hand in mine, and once I wrap my fingers around hers, I pull her off the barstool and through the bar.

"Do you have a coat?" I ask once we get to the door.

She shakes her head shyly—all a part of the game.

I shrug my suit jacket off and place it around her shoulders. It's not winter yet in the city, but if last year is any indication, it's way too cold to be walking around with bare shoulders.

"Come on. I'm staying a few blocks away."

I don't let go of her hand as we walk down the park side of 5th avenue. The cacophony of taxi horns, cyclists, and tourists lining up to take pictures is a familiar one now, but I continue our little game as we walk.

"Do you live in the city now?" I ask.

Zoe nods. "I do. I've been here for about eighteen months."

I hum in response. "Interesting how we both seem to have ended up on the opposite side of the country. Do you like it here?"

"I love it," she gushes, and I know she's not playing around now. "It feels like I always should've been living here–and it's the first place that feels like it's all mine. Plus, being a writer in the city is such a novelty."

I chuckle. "It certainly is."

"Did you ever publish your book?" she asks.

I nod. "I did. Two, actually, since you took my class."

"Wow. Congratulations."

A minute later, I pull her across the street to the black and gold entrance of The Plaza.

"Wow, they must pay you well at your new job," she murmurs, looking around as if we don't come here a few times a year.

Once we're through the front door, we walk hand in hand toward the private elevator. Once inside, I use my card to take us up to the Royal Suite. Zoe whistles when we step inside, taking in the large suite. Before I'd met her at the bar, I'd taken great care to hide her things, so it would feel as authentic as possible.

As she turns around and looks at me, her cheeks are flushed. "This is incredible."

I smile as I gesture for her to walk through the suite, giving her a quick tour. She *ooh's* and *ahh's* when we get to the bathroom, her long, red nail trailing down the gold accents.

"Would you like a drink?" I offer, and the furrow between her brows nearly makes me laugh.

So impatient.

"No, thank you," she says quickly. Walking over to me, her heels clack against the tile of the bathroom. Laying her hands on my chest, she looks up at me hopefully. "I'm already very hydrated," she adds, eyes flashing as she arches one brow in challenge.

"Good girl," I mutter, doing my best not to react to her in the way a husband would. "Why don't you go wait for me in the master bedroom?"

"How would you like me?"

Fuck...

"Kneeling and naked, palms up. Leave your shoes on."

"Naked? Really? So we're going to get right down to business then?"

I cock my head at her. "Tell me, Ms. Arma, since you were always such a good student," I purr. "What did you think I had planned tonight?"

Zoe's breathing turns erratic as she stares at me boldly. "I don't know. How often do you bring former students to your fancy suite and ask them to serve you?" she asks, crossing her arms.

Ah, so I get my defiant, little wife tonight.

Fine.

"You're the only one. I seem to have a provocation for bratty brunettes who like to torture me by wearing *fuck me* heels."

She inhales sharply, and I can tell the control over my emotions is affecting her—which, from past experience, means she really needs me to double down now more than ever.

"I'm not going to ask twice," I tell her.

I see the second she concedes—the way her expression goes from resistant to compliant. With a small huff, she walks out of the bathroom, and I watch her go, listening to the way her heels click with each step—and faltering when she notices exactly what kind of surprise is waiting for her on the bed.

After three torturous, long minutes, I walk out of the bathroom, across the suite, to the master bedroom. My hands are casually in my pockets, and I smile when I see Zoe kneeling—naked—by the side of the bed.

I take in the spike of her heels against the soft skin of her ass and hips, fingers curling with anticipation.

"Do you like your present, Ms. Arma?" I ask, walking over to the leather restraint and picking it up with one finger.

"I do, Professor Ravage."

Letting my eyes peruse her body, I take in her soft, voluminous breasts—her soft stomach, her hips, and the gorgeous stretch marks spanning her lower abdomen and thighs.

She looks like the most beautiful warrior I've ever seen.

"That's good. For a long time, I refused to try bondage," I tell her, though she knows the truth. "But tonight, I think I can manage it. Is bondage something you enjoy?"

Zoe quickly exhales, and I have to try not to laugh at her obvious excitement. "Yes. I love it."

"Stand up and bend over the bed, please."

She does as I say, teetering slightly as she walks to the bed and lays across it, ass up.

I walk up behind her, enjoying the way her skin pebbles when I brush against her. Even now, almost four years later, her response to me is beautiful. I lean over her small frame and pull her up slightly, placing the leather straps around her breasts before buckling it around her ribs. And then, with a tiny bit of trepidation, I buckle her arms behind her back.

"Since you're so new at this," I mutter, fingers working the soft leather through the silver buckles, "you should know that red means stop, yellow means pause and/or slow down, and green means keep going. I will be checking in for the duration of our scene. Is that understood?"

Zoe nods, her cheek against the soft duvet.

"I need to hear you say it, baby girl."

My nickname for her slips out, but it doesn't seem to deter her.

"I understand," she says, her voice hoarse.

"Good."

I finish securing the restraint, but I don't move her. Instead, I gently push her legs apart, so that I have a clear view of her bare cunt.

"I can never get enough of you," I mutter, running a hand over her ass.

"You've never had me," she grinds out, still pretending.

"Mmm. You're right. But I imagined it every single time I saw you sitting in my class."

"What did you imagine?" she chokes out as I let my index finger trail over her wet center.

"You, legs spread just like this, over my desk in the classroom."

"It's a shame we never got the opportunity," she mumbles, groaning when I insert one finger.

Just that noise and the feel of her pussy sucking me into her has my control nearly shattering around me.

"We'll have to make up for lost time," I murmur, taking my other hand and running my fingers through her shortened hair. Using the hand that was inside of her, I unzip my pants and free my cock. "I'm not normally this impatient, but I've been waiting years to be inside of you," I grit out, sliding my cock inside of her without warning.

She lets out a tiny gasp as I slip easily between her legs.

"You are perfect," I growl, fingers tightening in her hair.

"So are you."

I look down and watch as her hands curl into fists. "Tell me what you need."

"I want—the restraint—" she mutters, questioning herself.

"Tell me," I repeat. "Use your words, Ms. Arma." Slowly pulling out, I don't thrust all the way in. Instead, I stop moving completely.

"I'd like the restraints a bit tighter."

Grinding my jaw, I reach down and try to will my hands not to shake as I relive one of the worst nights of my life.

"Fine. One hole at a time."

"That's what she said," Zoe whispers.

I laugh. "Very funny. Take a deep breath."

She does, and I tighten the strap around her ribs. Her cunt flutters around me when she realizes how tight it is, and I groan as I begin working on the arm loops—tightening them by one hole.

When I'm finishing, my cock is throbbing—not because I've been fucking her, but because with each tightened restraint, her core clenched tightly around my cock. I still need the friction to come, but feeling her pulse around me like that has me a hell of a lot closer to coming now.

"How's that?" I ask.

"Tighter," Zoe begs.

Clenching my teeth together, I tighten everything again by one hole. And again, her greedy, little cunt loves every second of it.

"How about now?" I ask, my voice husky.

"It's perfect," she says. "Fuck, Liam, I'm already close."

I groan when she uses my name, because I know it means she's frenzied and frantic, not thinking straight, not pretending anymore. She's dropped the facade, instead resorting to our normal dynamic. And truth be told, when she's out of her mind like this, it's my favorite. Because I know what to watch for.

Because I know how to take care of her.

"You're close?" I ask, dragging my cock out before slamming into her. I grip her restraints for purchase, using them to pull myself into her dripping pussy.

"Yes," she breathes. "Keep pulling—harder—"

I reach down to the bed and grab the thing I've been aching for—the thing I discovered is my one weakness when I started really exploring my kinks years ago.

The gag strap is made of leather, and the actual ball is made of black silicone. I fasten it around her head, smiling when she opens her mouth for it.

"Since you can't talk, just tap my hand three times if you need me to stop," I murmur, maneuvering my hand inside of hers as my other hand presses down on her back to hold her down on the bed.

She moans, unable to speak, and *fuck...* the sight of my gorgeous wife, gagged and bound on the bed for me...

I hold my orgasm back, hissing and stalling a few times until she's shuddering around me, until her pussy is squeezing me so relentlessly that I can't help but fall over the edge with her. I explode inside of her, hips stuttering, seeing stars. When I'm finished, I quickly release the gag and it tumbles onto the bed. I do the same with the restraint, eyes scanning her to check for injuries when I'm done.

"I'm fine," she says, her voice sleepy. "I promise."

"Are you sure?" I ask, running my hands over her skin.

"Yes, Liam. I'm fine. Come cuddle me now."

Lying down next to her, I pull her body into mine, wrapping one leg around her so that she can't move. She laughs, knowing how possessive I get after a scene like that.

"I didn't last long," I tell her. "You teased me for too long."

"You're not the only one. You got me to agree to go back to the hotel room before the second drink. Touché."

Chuckling, I move her hair away from the back of her neck and nuzzle my face against her scalp.

"Is it horrible that I kind of want to go to sleep now?" she asks, yawning.

"Why would it be horrible? I got to fuck and gag my wife. I'm a happy man."

"I know, but we have the whole night, and Carolina is—"

"Hey, let's take the pressure off ourselves, okay? We need sleep as much as we need sex."

"Fine. Maybe some morning sex, then?"

"Oh, most definitely. But first, go use the restroom. I'll get us some water and food."

Zoe sits up and gazes down at me. "My aftercare knight in shining armor," she teases.

Rolling my eyes, I swat her ass as she giggles and runs to the bathroom. I climb out of bed, grumbling, before setting up our snack station. Fortunately, I had room service stop by with all kinds of food that I can reheat in the kitchen, so I go about making us a full meal. I know she hasn't eaten since lunch and is likely beyond starving. Zoe joins me a minute later wearing a white robe that matches mine, and then we take our feast to the couch.

"Oh my god, breakfast burritos!" She moans, taking a massive bite of her burrito.

I laugh as I watch her eat, as I realize that as wonderful as being her Dom is, I love being her husband and caring for her just as much.

"I figured you'd want something hearty."

"It's perfect."

We eat in comfortable silence, and when she finishes, she sets her plate down and looks over at me.

"That was fun. We should do it more often."

I place my plate next to hers and pat my thigh. "Come here." She quickly comes and sits in my lap, wrapping her arms around my neck. "I had fun," I tell her, kissing her neck. I learned a long time ago that Zoe needs words of affirmation and non-sexual physical contact after a scene, so I pull her closer so that she's fully on top of me. "You were so good, baby girl. From the bar to the role playing... I fucking loved it."

She hums with delight as I stroke her bare thigh with my hand. "You were, too. Thanks for making one of my biggest fantasies come true."

"It wasn't hard," I tease. "You were always such a good student, little rebel."

She grins as she looks me in the eye. "I'm so tired. No one told me twenty-three would turn me into an old lady."

I huff a laugh. "Now you're rubbing salt in the wound," I say, leaning forward and nibbling her ear. "Let's get some rest, okay? We have a big day tomorrow."

Zoe's face is bright with excitement as her hands come to her face. "I still can't believe it's happening."

"I can. Because you're an amazing writer. Come on, let's go get ready for bed."

"It's ten o'clock," she whines. "We have the suite at The Plaza. And my very hot husband just gagged and bound me beyond my wildest dreams."

"And?" I ask, hand roving higher up her thigh.

"One more?"

"Zoe—"

"Come on. Just a quickie," she says, rolling her hips over my erection.

I groan as I spread her legs across my lap slightly. "Fine. One more. But this forty-four year old dad is tired."

She laughs as I flip her onto the couch. "You're a DILF if I ever saw one."

I smile as I reach down and undo the belt of her robe, opening it and staring at her body. The soft skin. The feminine curves. Just knowing she carried, birthed, and fed our son...

"Fine," I say, sighing dramatically. "One more for my

greedy girl." She giggles as I dive between her legs, squealing when I *very* gently bite down on her clit. "But only if you say please."

"Please!" she yells, bucking her hips. "God, please," she whimpers.

That's more like it.

————

Zoe

Liam doesn't let my hand go the entire mile walk to our condo in Lenox Hill. I'm still grinning from the three orgasms he pulled out of me the minute I woke up, and he truly lived up to his word of making sure I enjoyed our time away. As Liam carries our overnight bag over his shoulder, he looks down at me and smiles.

My stomach explodes with butterflies—*still.*

When we reach the awning of our building, Liam tugs me into him for one last hug before we're inundated with parenting duties.

"I had a great time with you," he says, hands on either side of my face.

"I did, too," I say, smirking. "I mean, I *am* a lot of fun."

His eyes flash like they always do when I snark back. "Cheeky. Come on. I bet there's someone bouncing off the walls to see you."

We walk into the lobby and greet Herald, the door man, before taking the elevator up to the penthouse. I tried—and failed—to convince Liam to buy a smaller condo when we started looking at places to buy in the city, but he insisted that Bronte would need space as he got older. So, of course that meant the best of the best, *because he's a Ravage and his son* would *need the best of the best.*

I still roll my eyes whenever I think about how insistent he was about getting such an elaborate place to live. At the time, I was hardly able to contribute to our finances, so I didn't quite have a say. But now that I'm a millionaire... maybe I can convince him to downsize.

As we walk down the carpeted hallway to our door, I hear the latch click open, and out runs a tiny toddler with dark, curly hair.

"Mama!" Bronte squeals, still slightly unsteady on his feet at thirteen months old. He hobbles over to me as I crouch down and open my arms for him, squeezing my eyes shut when he runs into them.

"Hi, sweetheart," I coo, cradling his small body to me. "I missed you so much," I whisper, my voice catching on the last word.

"Dada!" he cries out, running from my arms to Liam's.

I smile at them for a second before standing and turning to face Carolina.

"Thank you so much for watching him," I tell her, giving her a hug.

"It's really not a problem," she argues, waving me away.

I study her for a few beats. When Liam got the job at NYU, I was newly pregnant with Bronte and Carolina insisted on following us east to help us. She started another highly successful law firm in the city, and she lives a few blocks away on Madison Avenue. Despite her many flings, she opts to stay single and childless—and she absolutely spoils Bronte because of it whenever she can.

"Well, we had a relaxing night," I say, looking over at Liam, who is holding Bronte as the latter plays with his face like play dough.

"Good. You deserve it. You know I've been telling you to take a night away since he was three months old—"

I laugh. "I know, but he's still nursing, so it's not as easy. Speaking of..." I trail off, my hands coming to my breasts automatically. "I need to feed him before my boobs explode."

The four of us head inside, and Liam and Carolina talk for a few minutes before she says goodbye, leaving me to sit on the sofa with my son.

I look down at him as he dozes, and he grabs my finger and falls asleep as soon as he's had his fill.

Liam quietly comes to sit next to me. "I could use a nap," he says, rubbing his face.

I laugh. "Me too."

When we decided to have a baby, I wasn't sure how I felt about being a mother. The thought of Bronte losing me like I lost my parents was almost too much to bear. But then I thought about Liam, and how he deserved to have a child or two—and how he deserved to have them before he got too old. It was just a fact of life having a husband twenty years older than me. So while I never envisioned becoming a mother at twenty-two, it was the best decision I ever made.

"We should get ready," Liam murmurs, closing his eyes as he leans against the couch.

"Yeah. In a minute," I murmur, looking down at Bronte.

Bronte—whose name means thunder.

Naming my child after the thing that scares me the most might seem contradictory, but for me, it was the perfect way to let go of that fear and move on completely.

Of course, Liam agreed to it very quickly because of his love of literature.

After letting Bronte and Liam snooze for a few minutes, I carry Bronte to his nursery to let him nap while I get ready.

An hour later, the three of us are on the Q train headed to Times Square. Bronte is strapped to Liam's chest, and my dashing husband gets more than a few admiring glances from other women.

I scowl at each and every one of them, and Liam can't help but notice what I'm doing.

Once we get off the train, the three of us walk to the infamous, flashing billboards. My palms are sweaty as we get closer, and I can't help but continue checking my watch.

"Five minutes," Liam says, stopping when we get to the middle of the square. Bronte kicks and squeals against Liam's chest, facing outward and grabbing for each person that passes us. "You okay?" he asks, coming to stand next to me.

I wipe my hands on my jeans, realizing that they're shaking. "Yeah, I'm fine."

Walking a few feet away, I turn around and continue pacing, trying to quell my racing heart, repeating that for a couple of minutes.

"One minute," he says, looking up at the billboards. "Which one will it be on?"

Panic flashes through me. "Oh god. I don't know! I didn't ask my agent."

"Wait," Liam mutters, eyes glittering as he points to one of the boards over my shoulder. "Look, there you are!" he yells.

I spin around and instantly start crying when I see the large billboard displaying my newest release, *The Storm Princess*.

And underneath... *Now a #1 New York Times Bestseller!*

"Holy shit!" I sob, hands flying to my face as the cover of my book flashes across not one, not two, but *three* billboards.

When *Between All Realms* released, it completely flopped. I had a good number of preorders, but it didn't sell well. I never ended up finishing book two, instead trying my hand at YA Fantasy.

Liam likes to take credit for starting my *Percy Jackson* obsession, which ultimately led me down the YA path.

I self-published *The Ice Princess* six months after *Between All Realms* released, and it exploded. I ended up signing with an agent, who sold it to a big-five publisher, and they signed me on to write six more books in the series.

Every single book has hit the New York Times list.

And *The Storm Princess* hit number one last month.

I'm the youngest millionaire signed with my publisher, and I do enjoy rubbing it in Liam's face that *technically,* my salary is higher than his.

"I'm so fucking proud of you," Liam says.

"Prow, mama!" Bronte cries out, his high-pitched voice making me cry higher. "Love mama!"

Liam steps closer, pulling me into a hug. Bronte kicks and giggles, loving the fact that we're all squeezed together.

"I love you too, Bronte," I tell him, kissing him despite my cheeks being wet with tears. "And I love you," I tell Liam, standing on my tip toes to kiss my husband.

We watch the billboard for a few minutes—even after it changes.

And as another advertisement slips over the three billboards, I take Liam's hand.

"Who's hungry?" Liam asks.

"Hungy! Hungy!" Bronte says, looking up at his dad.

I smirk as I finish wiping my tears away. "I could eat."

Liam squeezes my hand as we make our way to the Q train, and I can't help but be so fucking grateful for him. For Bronte. For our life in Crestwood, and now New York. I miss California, but we visit enough for me to be okay about putting down roots here on the east coast. It took weeks of convincing Liam to take the tenured NYU position—he was worried about leaving his brothers.

But after weeks of talking about the food and the culture, I finally convinced him. And for the first time, he did something for *himself*.

"Excuse me? Are you Zoe Ravage?"

A little girl no older than thirteen is standing next to me as we wait for our train, and she's holding a copy of *The Storm Princess*.

"I am," I say slowly.

Holy shit. She's reading *my* book.

The girl starts to cry—warbling about how she's scared of storms and how my book helped her overcome her fear.

I have to actively work to keep from crying as I sign her book and watch her walk away, skipping over to her parents who wave at me gratefully.

"That'll never get old," I say, my voice breaking.

Liam hugs my shoulders as we walk to our train. "That's because you're amazing."

"'Mazing, mama!" Bronte chimes in.

Liam looks at me and grins, and as the train doors open, he tugs me inside after him.

————

Thank you so much for reading Ward Willing! Are you ready for Orion's story? Preorder Step Brute here:

mybook.to/StepBrute

If you want to sign up for Ravaged Castle release news

and updates, as well as receive excerpts and teasers before anyone else, be sure that you're subscribed to my mailing list. It's the best place to follow me!

www.authoramandarichardson.com/newsletter

(Psst... you also get a free student/teacher novella as a thank you for joining!)

ACKNOWLEDGMENTS

Thank YOU reader for picking up a copy of Ward Willing. Each book in this series has given me such a different writing experience. Liam and Zoe imprinted on my soul in a way I didn't expect. I think it has to do with the fact that I wrote it slowly over the course of five months. I *really* got to know them and their quirks, fears, and sort of *lived* inside their head for months on end. I dreaded finishing this book because I didn't want to say goodbye. And I still don't.

Also, a lot of this book is so personal. I lost my mom in 2020, and though I haven't talked about it much, in a way it felt as though the rug had been ripped out from under me—just like it had for Zoe and Liam. Grief is strange and unpredictable. If you've lost someone you love, I'm so sorry for your loss. It's the fucking worst feeling in the world, and I'm sending you a big virtual hug.

There are a lot of people I have to thank for making this book a possibility.

First and foremost (always) is my husband, MVP #1. My life would be in shambles without you. Out of all of my male characters, Liam is most like you. No one else could tolerate my bratty ass like you, and thank you for always feeding me. ILY.

For my boys. I love you both so much.

Brittni... where would I be without our plotting sessions? THANK YOU for the pot brownie idea, lol. Your input is always invaluable and so much of these books are because you seem to know exactly how my brain works.

To Tori Ellis for the flawless editing. I promise I took most of Liam's growls out.

To Erica, Brittni, and Macie, thank you for the fabulous alpha reading. Thanks for always being willing to reread a scene after I change it. I'm sorry I'm such a chaotic delulu mess.

To Lo and Kerrie, thank you for the sensitivity reads. I've learned so much from both of you and I'll be forever grateful that you're both on my team.

To Jess, Jasmine, and Lacie, thank you for being the best beta readers a girl could ask for.

To Shelbe, for helping with so much of the back end stuff, especially with this book. I'm so glad I've brought you onto my team!

And Sam! I love our coffee meet-ups. Thank you for all of your help with TikTok.

Emma, your covers are always flawless! This one especially captures "Liam" so well.

To Rafa, thank you for always somehow having the perfect photos for the Ravage men.

Michele, thank you for always being so quick and

thorough with your proofreads! I'm so glad we connected last year.

To all of my author friends... I know some of you are reading this and I just want to say that I love you all. I hope we can all continue inspiring each other.

ABOUT THE AUTHOR

Amanda Richardson writes from her chaotic dining room table in Yorkshire, England, often distracted by her husband and two adorable sons. When she's not writing contemporary and dark, twisted romance, she enjoys coffee (a little too much) and collecting house plants like they're going out of style.

You can visit my website here:
www.authoramandarichardson.com

ALSO BY AMANDA RICHARDSON

For a complete and updated list of my currently published books, you can visit my website here:

www.authoramandarichardson.com/books

Printed in Great Britain
by Amazon

38234411R00270